DISTANT MEMORY

His forehead creased with the puzzled frown she knew so well. "I think I've seen you before . . . in a dream. But you *know* me? You know who I am? What I'm doing here?"

His helplessness, his vulnerability was so complete it hurt, bringing tears momentarily to her eyes. "Yes, Ma'khleen. I know you *very* well."

" 'Ma'khleen'?" He tasted the name. "They call me 'Macklin' here."

"I know. I've been hunting for you a long time."

"I . . . I thought I was going crazy! I didn't know who I was! I just knew . . . just knew I didn't belong here!"

"What *do* you remember?"

"I remember . . . a city, with blue light everywhere. People, lots of people and . . . and people who didn't look like me. Like *us*. The sky . . . the sky was very different. Beautiful, spectacularly beautiful, but very different. Different stars. A different sun. I guess this isn't making much sense. It's kind of hard to explain."

"You're doing fine. That's Shanidar you're remembering. That's *home*."

"Home?"

"We're not from Earth . . ."

FRONTIER EARTH

BRUCE BOXLEITNER

ACE BOOKS, NEW YORK

FRONTIER EARTH

An Ace Book / published by arrangement with
the author

PRINTING HISTORY
Ace hardcover edition / November 1999
Ace mass-market edition / January 2001

All rights reserved.
Copyright © 1999 by Bruce Boxleitner.
Cover art by Cliff Miller.
This book, or parts thereof, may not be reproduced
in any form without permission.
For information address: The Berkley Publishing Group,
a division of Penguin Putnam Inc.,
375 Hudson Street, New York, New York 10014.

The Penguin Putnam Inc. World Wide Web site address is
http://www.penguinputnam.com

Check out the Ace Science Fiction & Fantasy newsletter
and much more on the Internet at Club PPI!

ISBN: 0-441-00794-5

ACE®
Ace Books are published
by The Berkley Publishing Group,
a division of Penguin Putnam Inc.,
375 Hudson Street, New York, New York 10014.
ACE and the "A" design are trademarks
belonging to Penguin Putnam Inc.

PRINTED IN THE UNITED STATES OF AMERICA

10 9 8 7 6 5 4 3 2 1

To Melissa,
my guiding light.

I would like to thank Bill Keith and Ed Gorman for their invaluable help with the manuscript, Larry Segriff and Marty Greenberg of Tekno Books, my editor at Ace Books, Ginjer Buchanan, Matt Bialer of the William Morris Agency, and my manager and friend Alan Iezman.

FRONTIER EARTH

PROLOGUE

HIS NAME WAS NA-A-CHA, AND HE WAS A *DIYI* OF THE APACHE.

Na-a-cha did not think of himself as Apache, of course. It was the Zuni who had given them that name, a word meaning, with good reason, *enemy*. The Chiricahua Apache called themselves simply *N'de*, The People. What others, even the *Indaa*, wanted to call them did not matter. For centuries, The People had stood alone, save for the Powers.

And that was as it should be.

As the night fell across the desert, Na-a-cha stood on the rock outcropping above the purple-shadowed, broken land far below, swinging the *tzi-ditindi* in great, moaning arcs about his head. As the sounding wood circled on the end of its long tether, its fluttering cry mimicked the wind . . . and the cries of the spirit-powers beyond, calling to them, summoning them. He was already *diyi*—a healer—but he wanted more.

He'd been called by his Powers to be a lightning shaman. He needed a ceremony from them, and their blessing. Na-a-cha was waiting for a sign.

He could sense the powers gathering . . . an auspicious night. A night of omens. *"Gun-ju-le, chil-lit, si-chi-zi, gun-ju-le, inzayu, ijanale,"* he chanted softly, coiling the sounding board's tether. "Be good, oh Night. Twilight, be good. Do not let me die. . . ."

In the east, the Moon hung low above the Chiricahua Mountains in glorious, full-silvered spectacle. *Klego-na-ay* was the Apache's name for the full moon, and to them its shining face signified Killer-of-Enemies, the son of the Sun. Na-a-cha reached into the buckskin pouch containing *hoddentin*, the yellow pollen of the tule cattail, and blew a pinch toward the rising Moon. "*Gun-ju-le, Klego-na-ay, gun-ju-le.* . . ."

A blaze of light split the darkening sky, and two stars fell from the east. Na-a-cha's heart quickened. He had been expecting some demonstration of the Powers but nothing so spectacular as this. One star, blazing red and yellow, fell toward the south . . . close by the *Indaa* place the white eyes called Tombstone. The other passed so low above the *N'de diyi* that, for an instant, twilight became brightest day and he felt the heat of its passing.

Thunder rolled for a long time across the desert, echoing off the eastern mountains.

Na-a-cha's heart hammered within his breast. He had been chosen! His Powers had chosen him, delivering this sign! The second star had touched the earth, so close that he could still see its glow upon the desert floor! Perhaps . . . perhaps this meant his acceptance as a lightning shaman.

He tried to listen to the inner voice of his Power.

I have sent you this gift, Na-a-cha, the Power whispered in his mind. *Go. See what I have given you this night.* . . .

A gift, a sign from Killer-of-Enemies . . . the Apache Moon.

Na-a-cha of the *N'de* hurried down the hillside to see what it might be. . . .

ONE

Long before the Apache, before even the cliff dwellers, there were nomads upon this land. The N'de called them the Lightning People and prayed to them as they gathered the chipped-stone points they'd left behind. Some of the beliefs of those vanished nomads had been passed down to those who'd come later. For instance, there was Wind. . . .

The sudden, whining wind that stirs the surface, that howls down from the mountains, that blinds all creatures, snake and lizard and man alike, with searing sand . . . the nomads of thousands of years ago called Wind "The Cries of the Dead."

For them, Wind was the sound of their dead crying out from the other side.

The night desert. Ten miles north of Tombstone, Arizona. October 22, 1881. . . .

✦ 1 ✦

WHERE AM I? WHO AM I?

The twin thoughts filled the lone man's aching head, as the moaning wind filled his ears and soul. Staggering across the desert, head slick with blood and spinning dizzily, he could barely stand.

Wind-gusted sand lashed at him, burning his skin, caking his mouth. Overhead, the night sky was clear, star-glittered, and bright with the swollen moon.

That moon . . . what was it about that moon? Full and ice-silver, it followed him, haunted him with inwardly echoing fragments of vanished memories. There was something about that moon, that cold, silver-white demon's-eye dispassionately watching his staggering trek through the desert here below . . . something . . . *something*. . . .

The wind was no help. Ghostly shapes of sand gritted into his eyes and nose and mouth and scoured his skin. His clothes—blue work shirt, Levi's, fake leather shoes comically out of place in the desert—all were saturated with sand.

And then there was the *sound* of the wind, centuries of sand-blasted misery and death in a rising screech from which there was no escape.

He stopped, turned, and stared back the way he'd come. The pod that had delivered him to this place lay upended in the desert, partly obscured by the blowing sand. The lone man did not know what the pod was or what he'd been doing inside.

The pod, at least, had offered shelter from sand and wind, but with the sight of the moon, the man knew that he had to get away from the pod, that *they* would be here soon, hunting him.

He didn't know who *they* were, any more than he knew his own name. . . .

He had to keep moving . . . had to get away. . . .

With his next step, pain and concussion and loss of blood took their inevitable toll, and he collapsed, toppling face-down into the sand. . . .

✦ **2** ✦

NA-A-CHA SCOWLED AS HE LOOKED AT THE STILL FORM on the ground before him. What kind of trick was this?

Indaa . . . a white eyes? He'd come expecting a sign from his Power.

Or . . . was this the sign his Power had been leading him to? Na-a-cha was not sure.

Falling stars could point the way to an enemy, he knew. Was this white eyes an enemy? Na-a-cha had never seen him before . . . had certainly never seen anything like the silver-polished egg lying in the sand nearby, and from which this white eyes had apparently crawled.

The vision required thought and understanding.

The two stars had fallen from the direction of the Moon, from Killer-of-Enemies. According to the old stories, when the world was divided up between the brothers Child-of-the-Water and Killer-of-Enemies, the former had taken the things reserved for the N'de—the forested mountain, the bow, the food that grew wild—while the latter had taken the things reserved to the white eyes—the lands rich with minerals like gold and silver, the gun, the tame foods that needed to be sown and harvested. Killer-of-Enemies had always been associated with the white eyes and, like the white eyes, could never be completely trusted.

Perhaps this was a trick.

Or a test.

The man groaned, his eyes fluttering. It looked as though he'd hit the back of his head. Had he been injured falling out of the sky?

Na-a-cha had no problem with people living in the sky. The Lightning People lived there, loosing the beautifully crafted stone points and blades that could be found in the arroyos and washes, sometimes, after a heavy rain. Never in any of the stories he knew was there any mention of people riding the clouds in a great, silver egg. Perhaps that was part of the new ceremony his Powers were showing him.

Carefully, Na-a-cha touched the gash behind the man's

left ear . . . then snapped his hand away as a tiny spark crackled against his fingertips.

The shock had been a small one, scarcely felt . . . but the spark had looked like a minute flash of lightning. It seemed to confirm that this *Indaa* was one of the Lightning People. A second cautious probing failed to release another spark, as though the agency that had created it were now dead.

Nothing in any of the stories Na-a-cha knew could have prepared him for this. The Lightning People were white eyes? It seemed inconceivable. Or . . . might there be two kinds of Lightning People, as there were *indee* and *indaa* here below?

Na-a-cha struggled to put what he was seeing into terms he could make sense of. He wanted to understand, to be open to what his Power wanted him to see.

Carefully, he rolled the man onto his back. There was something around his neck, a thong of something like rawhide but more pliant. Na-a-cha opened the buttons on the man's shirt.

The thong was attached to a cloth bag or pouch . . . a bag that weighed heavily in Na-a-cha's palm. Opening the pouch, he was not surprised to see a number of gold coins inside. The white eyes were crazy for gold. It seemed fitting that one would carry gold as the N'de carried a medicine pouch. . . .

And then Na-a-cha saw what was on the man's chest, low on his breastbone, and he dropped the pouch, his eyes widened, and he very nearly ran away. What *was* this creature, born of lightning, fallen from the sky . . . ?

Clearly, this was no ordinary man. The Lightning People, for all their power, were still just men; this one, though . . . he might be *ga he,* a mountain spirit. Or even *kan,* one of the gods of the sky.

And yet he was injured, perhaps dying. And clearly, he'd been delivered to Na-a-cha for healing.

Thoughtful, Na-a-cha buttoned up the man's shirt, leaving the gold and . . . and what he'd seen there, in the man's chest, untouched. The man, whatever he was, carried powerful medicine. He would need powerful medicine to be healed.

Na-a-cha pulled some *hoddentin* from his pouch and sprinkled a pinch on the man's forehead, then in a cross on his chest. The wind defeated his efforts, catching the pollen and blowing it away. He tried again, placing some in the man's mouth, but the proper words of healing would not come.

The man is a white eyes, Na-a-cha's inner voice, his Power, told him. *He needs the white eyes' medicine.*

Aa. Yes. That made sense. But how to get him to the white eyes?

There might be a way. . . .

◈ 3 ◈

MOVEMENT . . . AND INTENSE DISCOMFORT IN HEAD AND STOMach and chest. He was being carried, head down, with a curious rocking motion that intensified the pain in his head and left him feeling queasy.

After a long time, he felt rough hands pulling at him, felt himself sliding, then falling, collapsing in a heap on the ground.

He might have lost consciousness then. He wasn't sure. When he opened his eyes again, however, he saw a man's face, a wrinkled, hawkish face beneath a white bandanna, peering down into his.

"Who . . . ?"

"You stay," the man said. He had a green stone of some sort, tied on the end of a leather thong hanging about his neck. It swung before the wounded man's blurred vision like a pendulum. "Wait here. No move. Soon, your people come."

Then the hawk-faced man was gone.

Or . . . had the man been there at all? Was he beginning to hallucinate?

He couldn't stay here. He had to . . . go . . . go *somewhere*.

Where?

He had the feeling, deep-seated and urgent, that he wasn't so much going somewhere as he was fleeing . . . *something*.

Who? Or . . . what?

Have to get away. Have to get to . . . have to get to . . .

Somehow, he pulled himself into a sitting position. The wind was still keening across the moon-shadowed desert . . . but the man with the bandanna and the green stone was gone.

✦ 4 ✦

They hungered, but the prey was gone.

It was full dark now, with a wind that moaned on the night as the desert bled away the heat of the day into an open sky clotted with stars. Two Kra'agh approached the fallen pod, wary of traps, wary of lurking ambush. It would be perversion of Chahh kkit, the Blood Law, for the Hunters to become the hunted.

N'gah'regh Kah—a rough translation might have meant Deathstalker—touched the slick, still-warm metal and plastic of the pod with one questing feeding-hand. It had not been here long. "The natives of this world do not have the technology to build this," it said. "And it is not Kra'agh. This is a craft from the Associative."

It sensed Gra'vad G'drax—Painspinner—moving on the

other side of the object, felt its flicker of satisfaction as it found a hidden pressure switch. "I have it," the other said. "The hatch."

Deathstalker dropped to all fours and moved around to where Painspinner was examining the opened hatch. "An escape pod," it said, turning one wide-pupiled eye to Deathstalker as it came closer. "From the Monitor ship."

"We will hunt. And kill."

"Droo'kah! Droo'keh!" In the principal veh-language of the Kra'agh, the expression blended greeting with agreement and promise. "Good hunting! Good eating!"

Deathstalker turned, scanning the sandy floor of the desert for lingering heat traces but seeing none. In this desert, the daytime heat would mask the heat trail of any prey.

"We must pattern some of the local higher life-forms in order to blend in," Painspinner said, sensing Deathstalker's thoughts. "It may take time. I suggest that we separate. Two hunting sweeps double the chances of finding bloodtaste."

Deathstalker closed one feeding-hand in agreement. "Kkre!" it said, an exclamation of agreement and understanding that meant, literally, "Death-grasp."

It stepped closer to the open pod, questing. Something of the escaped Monitor-creature still clung to the interior of the pod. Deathstalker could taste lingering hints of . . . of fear. Of pain. The creature was injured, it thought. Yes! A salty coppertaste of blood still hung in the tiny compartment. Leaning in further, Deathstalker examined the thin-padded seat with its tangle of unbuckled harnesses. One feeder-hand snaked out, touched something wet on the chair's headrest, drew back with a slick of dark liquid. Excitement pounding in its hearts, it showed it to the other Kra'agh.

"Blood!" Painspinner exclaimed. "We have a blood-trail!"

Deathstalker carefully cleaned its finger with its sucking tongue, savoring bloodsalts, the irontaste of heme, proteins, and the delicate seasoning of fear.

"We will follow its blood," it said, as the wind sighed and moaned above them.

✦ 5 ✦

HE TOUCHED THE GASH ON HIS HEAD, AND IT CAME AWAY WET with blood.

He wondered if he was imagining it all.

By this time, two hours later, he had imagined so many things.

He'd seen light . . . the light of the moon, impossibly huge and close, seen it shift and blur . . . becoming stars, endless stars, a vast and tangled forest of stars crowding Heaven, and, set among them all like a gemstone on black, diamond-encrusted velvet, the tiny, fragile blue and white marble of the Earth.

He'd seen the Earth blur . . . melting, opening now into clouds and sky and barren mountains and desert landscape.

And hanging in the sky above, the great, silver demoneye of the moon. There was something, something desperately important, that he needed to remember. Something more important than who he was, than what he was doing here in this place of death and moon-gilt bones.

If I could just remember . . . just remember. . . .

He was hearing voices now, voices thin and ragged astride the keening wind.

"Let go. Let go, and let your body remember. If you stop to think, you are already dead."

The language was not English, but he understood.

He understood many languages, he realized. English. Nihongo. Français. D'thalat. In none of them was a clue to who he was, or why he was here.

"You must relax your mind for your body to remember." The language was Gtai. The speaker . . . he couldn't remember. *"The memory of the act is in your muscles, not your conscious mind. Let go . . . and remember!"*

He couldn't remember.

And then the moon was vast and close enough to touch, its pocked and battered ancient face hanging against the sky only a few twelve-cubes of *irans* distant, its light blasting through the canopy as he heard the woman's scream, shrill in his ear. *"Ma'khleen!"*

The scream snapped him awake with a scream of his own. He was sprawled full-length on the ground, sand caking his face and hair, gritty on his swollen tongue.

Holding himself up on trembling arms, he looked around for the woman whose voice he'd heard.

There was nothing . . . nothing but the night, the moaning wind . . . and the silver moon above.

He'd imagined it . . . dreamed it . . .

He'd imagined so much, so many impossible things.

So he was probably imagining that sharp, clanking jingle, too. . . .

Rising unsteadily from the sand, he turned around, his angular, haunted face tense with hope. He brushed lank, dark hair from his eyes.

A kind of enclosed boxlike wagon drawn by four large, leather-harnessed animals.

The name of the thing came to him, as unbidden as the apparition. *Stagecoach.*

But it was just another hallucination, he was sure of it, the desert playing more tricks on him.

But the sounds . . .

Snorts and whinnies and slamming hooves, the grind of

iron-covered wheels as they bit into sand over and over again . . .

Horses. The animals were *horses.*

He saw the tracks now, the tracks of previous horse-drawn coaches worn into hard ground. Somehow, a good many *irans* back, he thought, the hawk-faced man of his dreams must have picked him up and carried him here, leaving him beside the road. *Soon, your people come. . . .*

He waved an arm. He felt a jolt of newborn strength that was almost intoxicating. He waved both arms, standing in the path of the oncoming coach. He didn't care anymore if it was a hallucination or not. He would just assume it was real.

It was a big red Concord, and a fancy one at that, the paint so shiny it had to have been rubbed down with pumice, an expensive extra.

How do I know that? He shook his head, trying to clear it. Tatters of desert-crazed dreams filled his mind yet, evaporating like morning mist.

He smelled horse now as the coach drew upon him, smelled horse and heard shouted human exclamations from inside the coach itself.

And then there was quick, cold blackness as he felt himself pitch forward. He tried putting his arms out to break his fall, but the blackness was coming up too quickly and too surely.

The driver was just putting on the brake and shouting at his animals to stop when the desert man lost consciousness completely once again. . . .

✦ 6 ✦

DEATHSTALKER STOPPED, ITS POWERFULLY MUSCLED BODY RIP-pling forward on all fours, scent-tongues flicking air, tast-

ing sand, tasting . . . yes! The prey had passed this way, and recently. Very recently.

Rising, arm-legs and feeder arms extended, angular head weaving in the moonlight, it barked out the ancient bloodcry, the geh-*speech that was speech before there were words, an instinctive shrilling that proclaimed, "The prey is here. I have found bloodtrail!"*

Somewhere in the night, its partner bayed acknowledgment. "I come. Droo'kah! Droo'keh!"

Deathstalker quested farther. The prey had been following a path through the desert, stumbling . . . crawling . . . and then it had fallen . . . here. Bloodtaste soaked the sand, promise of a crippling wound.

But there were other scents on air and sand . . . sharp scents, unfamiliar scents, the tastes of an alien world. . . .

❖ 7 ❖

SENSORY DATA—THE SMELLS OF PERFUME, CIGAR SMOKE, whiskey, axle oil, sweat. The sounds of thoroughbraces groaning beneath heavy weight, the rise and fall of hooves, the lurching rock-and-sway of movement, a distant mutter of human voices.

Catalog data . . . input.

Perfume. A volatile distillate worn by females to emit or enhance an agreeable body odor.

Cigar smoke. Airborne particulate residue of the combustion of the dried leaves of certain plants, inhaled for the addictive effects of nicotine and as a mark of social status.

Axle oil. A lubricant employed on the moving parts of certain primitive, wheeled conveyances.

Whiskey. Distilled grain alcohol, consumed for a variety of addictive effects.

Sweat. A biological exudate of water and certain chemical salts, part of the excretory system, released through pores in the human skin as a regulatory response to heat, and as a result of extreme systemic stress or fear. . . .

His eyes snapped open and he started.

"Whoa, easy there, feller," a man's voice said nearby.

He was sitting on a cushioned seat. A pretty woman in a body covering of a yarn-dyed fabric that some deep-down part of him recognized as *gingham* was sitting next to him. She was daubing something on his head, which burned and stabbed and pounded with pain. Perfume—lilacs. It was her perfume he smelled.

Across from them sat two others, a small, round man in a three-piece checked suit and a dour, pale man in funereal black with a silver-knobbed cane, a celluloid collar, and a string bow tie. Even in the moonlit shadows of the jouncy stagecoach, the second man's eyes were bright with amusement and with something more, something almost like malice. He looked at the round man and said, "Almost worth it to get your head kicked in, havin' a pretty lady like her workin' on you."

The other snorted agreement.

"And I know a lady who'd be happy to kick your head in, too," the pretty woman said, her hands still working nimbly on the throbbing gash behind and above his left ear.

The dour man smiled. "My name's John Holliday, mister. What's yours?"

The woman's ministrations had helped . . . a lot. She'd washed the scalp wound and given him water to drink. He felt stronger, but Holliday's question revived a panicky undercurrent of emotion, and again he felt the cold blackness clawing at his thoughts. *Who am I? I don't remember? I have to remember! I can't . . . I can't . . .*

Again, in his mind, he heard a woman scream. *"Ma'khleen!"*

"Ma . . . khleen. . . ." The name rasped across his swollen tongue.

"Wassat?" the man in the checked suit said, leaning closer, his brow furrowed. " 'Maclean'? I knew a Maclean, once't."

"Ma'khleen," he repeated, coming down hard on the first syllable, before the click of the glottal stop.

"Sounded like Macklin," the woman said.

"Is that your name, feller?" Holliday said. "Macklin?"

Macklin nodded. It felt . . . almost right. If only he could remember. . . .

"You got a first name to put in front of that?" Holliday said.

"Maybe he don't want to tell you," the woman said. "Maybe it's none of your business!"

Holliday winked at the other man. "Guess I been told, huh?"

"Guess you have," the man smirked.

"What I want t'know," Holliday went on, "is what the sam hill you're doin' out in the middle of the desert at night! Was you lost?"

"Lost." That seemed to fit. "Yes. I'm . . . lost."

"Doc Holliday," the woman snapped, "can't you see the poor man is hurt? Why don't you just leave off with the questions until he's had a chance to pull himself together?"

"Wh-where . . . where are we going?" Macklin said. He'd almost asked who he was, but something deep inside resisted the temptation to reveal too much to these people. His memory loss could be perceived as weakness. Could make him a target.

But a target for who?

"Tombstone," Holliday said. "You been there before?"

"Tombstone?" The name meant nothing as a place but

conjured the image of a graveyard, of cold monuments and bones in the earth.

"Yup. The drummer here's going to make himself some money sellin' dry goods and the like to the haberdashers."

Drummer. The word had something to do with selling wares, he thought, with travel from place to place selling . . . things. . . .

How did he know?

"And me," Holliday continued, "I'm gonna get me some rest." He coughed . . . then coughed again, a long, wracking explosion that left him paler than he'd been before. He brought a white handkerchief to his mouth, and when he put it away again, Macklin saw spots of blood.

"Some rest," the woman scoffed. "There's no rest for people like you, Holliday. Not this side of Boot Hill. Maybe our town'll get lucky and you and the Earps'll fight the Clantons and the McLaurys and you'll all kill each other off, and good riddance!"

Holliday grinned at Macklin, and the pale face looked eerily like a skull with a handlebar mustache. "Seems like a lot of people are wishin' for that these days. I guess we ain't what you'd call real popular anymore."

The drummer had a real good laugh over that one, and Macklin wondered what the joke was.

◆ **8** ◆

"THE TRAIL IS STRONG . . . TO HERE." DEATHSTALKER GESTURED with a feeding arm, claws unfolding, glistening in moonlight. "The prey was carried here on a living creature. It then was placed here . . . lay bleeding, then got up and moved . . . to here."

"It fell again," Painspinner said, closing its clawed foothand in agreement. "Others—other humans—stepped here, lifting it."

"The tracks. A primitive conveyance, drawn by living creatures."

"They carried the prey away in the vehicle."

Deathstalker vented a long, soft hiss of puzzlement. "But which way? These curved, bow-shaped tracks point both ways. Which way was the vehicle traveling?"

"We should split up again," Painspinner said. "The prey must not get too far ahead of the hunt. We must not lose bloodtrail."

"Kkre." Deathstalker pulled a small device from its harness, slick and cool black plastic that spoke softly to him in patterns of heat on its oddly curved surface. "There are native habitations in this direction, within a few eights of y'ghrezh. The prey could be sheltering with them."

"Check it. I shall follow the trail in the other direction. Good hunting!"

"Droo'kah! Droo'keh!"

⋄ 9 ⋄

BY THE TIME THE STAGECOACH RATTLED PAST THE OUTLYING settlements north of Tombstone, the woman had filled Macklin in on the practical realities of life in the bustling metropolis.

Her name was Sarah Nevers, and she'd been one of the first women, one of the first *decent* women anyway, to move to Tombstone after the bustling, scrappy little mining camp had gotten started four years before. She'd come here from Springfield, Illinois, with her husband Curtis, an agent for the Wells Fargo Company. She was a widow now, she explained. Her husband had been killed—"murdered in the street," as she put it—two years ago. She'd opened up her home to boarders and made her living now that way, supplemented with a small widow's pension from Wells Fargo.

"There are two outlaw gangs in Tombstone, so far as

I'm concerned,'' she told Macklin, as the bored drummer and a grimly amused Holliday listened. ''The God-fearing people of the town are caught squarely in the middle. On the one side are the Cowboys. That's what they call their gang, anyway. It's the Clantons and the McLaurys, along with a bunch of other riffraff, operating off the Clanton Ranch, south of town. They're cattle rustlers and worse. They're known to slip across the Mexican border and raid cattle and horses, then come back up here to sell their loot off. They're also not too particular about whose beeves end up with their herds on this side of the border, either . . . and everybody's pretty sure that they were behind all of the stagecoach robberies around here lately. They *own* the county sheriff, a nasty, bribe-taking politician named Johnny Behan.'' She'd finished washing the cut on Macklin's head, and there wasn't anything else she could do for it. Using some water from the driver's canteen, she wet down a fresh silk handkerchief and pressed it against the cut behind Macklin's ear. ''Okay . . . you just hold that now,'' she told him. ''The bleeding seems to have stopped, but you keep some pressure on it. When we get to town, we'll see that you get to a doctor. Now, where was I?''

''You were telling me about the Clantons and the McLaurys,'' Macklin told her.

''So I was. But on the other side is the Earp brothers. They're supposed to be lawmen, but I swear they're just as bad.''

''C'mon, now, Sarah,'' Holliday said with a chuckle. ''Where's your Christian charity? You don't mean that!''

''Don't I, now?'' She gave Holliday a hard look. ''Well, James—he's the oldest—he's okay, I guess. Ain't never heard nothin' bad about him, leastwise. Then there's Virgil. He's the town marshal, and he's also deputy federal marshal for southern Arizona Territory. He can be a mean one, and he has the *look* of a killer. Don't know that much about his past, but he's always on the outs with the town sheriff, Behan.

"Wyatt, though. He's a real piece of work, that one. He had a reputation as a town-tamer back in Dodge City, but they say he ain't even killed a man. I don't believe that, not for a second. He's as cold and ruthless as they come, a real killer. For a while, he was deputy sheriff under Sheriff Slibell, but Slibell fired him—some say because he was shaking down the town's business people—and that made him mad, 'specially when Slibell hired Behan to replace him. Seems Wyatt wants t'be sheriff *real* bad, probably because the sheriff is in charge of collecting taxes and gets a big cut of everything he takes. He and Sheriff Behan hate each other's guts. No surprise there. Behan has the job Wyatt wants . . . and Wyatt has the girl, an *actress,* so-called . . . that he stole from Johnny Behan!

"Nowadays, he's deputy to his brother, Virgil. He also owns part of the Oriental Saloon . . . and he works girls in some of the brothels and he's a card hustler and con man to boot. Word is, back in Texas, before he came out here, he got run out of town for selling gold-painted bricks to folks, so that'll give you an idea of just how devoted he is to law and order!

"The youngest brother is Morgan. He deals faro at the Oriental . . . and sometimes gets deputized too. He's a real hothead, always gettin' into scrapes and trouble, and he follows Wyatt around like a puppy.

"And finally, there's this . . . this *gentleman* sitting across from us. He's a dentist, so they call him Doc, but he's also a gunfighter and a gambler. He's the best friend the Earps have in this town and the worst killer of all, if the truth be known. God alone knows how many towns he's been run out of for killing some poor soul or other. You notice how he's coughin' all the time? He's s'posed to be dyin' of consumption and most people wish he'd hurry up and do it. In fact, most people in Tombstone wish they'd all hurry it up, have one big gunfight and have both gangs kill each other off.''

She sat back and looked out the window, at the lights spreading out on the flat, sandy land. She detested *all* gunfighters, the Earps and the Clantons both, with a passion that could leave her breathless.

"It's not quite as bad a picture as she paints, Macklin," Holliday said. "She didn't tell you about the Citizens' League, for instance."

"The Earps just put *that* together as a front for their own politicking," she replied. *"Politics!"* She sneered the word, as though it tasted bad.

"Why do you stay?"

"What?" She turned, looking at the man beside her.

"It's clear you don't approve of the way things are run here," Macklin said. "I was just wondering why you stayed."

"Because this is my home, Mr. Macklin," she said firmly. "My husband and I were building something, building something *good* here. In time, Tombstone is going to be a good place to live, to work, to raise a family. Curtis died making a place for me and our future out here, and I'm not about to let a bunch of ruffians like Holliday and his lot run me back to Illinois like a whipped dog!"

"That sounds like a good reason," Macklin said. He smiled, and Sarah's heart warmed at the sight. "The best reason there could be!"

"Civilization is coming to the West, Mr. Macklin. The gunfighters and cowboys don't believe it and don't want it to happen, but it's going to happen, like it or not. The reason I'm on this stage . . . up on top is the grandfather's clock that belonged to my father, back in Springfield. I had my sister ship it to me, and that's why I went up to Benson today to pick it up at the train station. It's . . . it's a symbol, don't you see? A symbol of civilization and culture and the good things in life that honest, God-fearing, decent folks are bringing into these parts.'' She fixed Holliday with a savage glare. ''And we're *not* going to be driven out!''

The stage was clattering now through the streets of Tombstone, a gaudy, cheerfully bright place of lit-up saloon fronts and tinkling pianos, of barking dogs and shouting, laughing men and occasional gunshots. They pulled up next to the stage depot on Allen Street. The drummer opened the door and hopped out, followed by Holliday. Holliday doffed his black, flat-crowned hat and offered Sarah his hand, but she coldly ignored it. ''Now, we should see about getting you to a doctor, Mr. Macklin,'' she said, turning to help Macklin as he gingerly followed her off the coach.

''I'll take care of him, Mrs. Nevers,'' Holliday told her. ''You've got that clock contraption up there t'see to. I'll walk him over to Doc Shea's.''

The offer surprised her. ''That's very decent of you.''

Holliday coughed. ''I ain't the villain you take me t'be, Mrs. Nevers,'' he said, a trace of bitterness sharpening the words. ''Y'know, it don't set easy on a man, knowing he ain't gonna live much longer. And he likes knowin' that others think kindly of him in the meantime.''

For a moment, Sarah considered apologizing for her hard words . . . but then she decided that, like as not, Holliday was making fun of her or, worse, just trying to gain her sympathy with that rasping, wet cough of his. Best to leave things pleasantly hostile.

''Mr. Macklin,'' she said, reaching into her handbag for a folded piece of notepaper and a fountain pen. She wasn't about to be outdone by the likes of Doc Holliday in the good deeds department. ''You'll be needing a place to stay." Awkwardly, she scribbled out an address on the paper, then handed it to Macklin. "That's my boardinghouse. I have a couple of vacant rooms, and you're welcome to stay there until you get your feet under you."

"Why . . . thank you, Mrs. Nevers!" That boyish smile tugged at her again as he accepted the paper. "Thank you very much!"

She didn't want him to get the wrong idea, however. "It's eight dollars a week," she told him. "That includes room and breakfast. If you're hard up for cash just now, I can carry you for a couple of weeks, I suppose, until you get settled. . . ."

"Why, that's awfully good of you," Holliday said, grinning. He nudged Macklin with an elbow. "I think she *likes* you, boy! You must bring out her mothering instincts."

"*Mister* Holliday!" The man was insufferable.

Laughing, Holliday took the confused-looking Macklin by the elbow and steered him away from the stage. Sarah turned and began giving directions for the unloading of her grandfather clock and its delivery to her home.

She did like Macklin, though.

TWO

❖ 1 ❖

DOC HOLLIDAY HAD WALKED MACKLIN UP TO DR. MILO SHEA'S
office, which was on the ground floor of his Cape Cod–
style house on Fulton Street, four blocks north of the Allen
Street strip called Whiskey Row. The place, Holliday had
explained with a laugh and a cough, was a considerable
improvement over several other doctors in town whose of-
fices were in tents. Shea, Holliday opined, must be pretty
good, because he was making enough money to be able to
afford a place like that.

The medical office was a large room with a wood-and-
leather operating chair, three cabinets crammed with dusty
bottles of medicines and fearsome-looking instruments, and
a large color lithograph of the human body next to Shea's
medical diploma.

"So how'd it happen?" the doctor said, wrapping the
roller bandage around Macklin's head.

"I don't remember."

"Drunk? Thrown from your horse?"

Macklin shrugged. "Maybe." Somehow, those options
didn't feel right.

"Looks more like someone whacked you from behind.

Whatever they used on you, they sure done a good job.''

"I don't remember much. Barely my name is all, and I'm not real sure about that.'' He fought down the dark terror inside. ''Doctor, I don't remember *anything*!''

The doctor shrugged. ''That happens sometimes with a hit on the head like this. Amnesia is the medical term. You remember anything at all?''

Macklin closed his eyes, trying to picture . . . something. ''I remember waking up out in the desert,'' he said. ''The wind was blowing. There was a . . . a man there, helping me. Rough, wrinkled face. Dark eyes. Kind of dark, swarthy skin. He had a white cloth wrapped around his head and a piece of green stone hanging around his neck.''

Shea's eyes widened. ''Ha! Sounds like you met an Injun!'' Reaching up with one hand, he lightly touched the top of Macklin's head.

''What are you doing?''

''Well, you still got your scalp, so I'd have t'say you was hallucinatin'. It happens, after a knock like you had.''

''It was awfully real. I also . . . I remember a woman screaming. . . .''

''Out in the desert?'' Shea laughed. ''Son, if I had t'guess, I'd say you was dreamin'. You ever been scared by Injuns, mebee? You remember ever meetin' any?''

''I don't remember anything.''

''Yeah, so you said.'' He frowned. ''That green stone sounds like malachite. Apache medicine men carry it, show it off, the way I show off my medical school diploma on that wall over there. Their badge of office, you might say. But I can't imagine you meetin' up with Apaches and still bein' alive t'tell about it!'' He laughed, a harsh cackle. ''Course, mebee what you don't remember is getting whacked over the head by some Apaches, robbed, and left fer dead in the desert. That might explain—'' He broke off suddenly, frowning.

"What's the matter?"

· "I was just thinkin', I should probably ask you."

"Ask what?"

"You got money?"

"Money?"

"Yeah, money," he said, tying off the bandage. "You must remember what *that* is," he added sarcastically.

"I suppose I do."

"Why don't we settle that right now? Here, you stand up for a minute. Check your pockets," Dr. Shea said, leaning closer. He was a portly man with cheeks and a nose he apparently dipped in rotgut whiskey several times a day. They were so red, they looked chafed. He wore a dirty white shirt beneath a stained tan vest and a pair of black trousers shiny with age. Every time he breathed out, his whiskey breath threatened to peel off a layer or two of wallpaper.

"Back off," Macklin said. "Please!" The doctor's breath was making him feel sick. His head was pounding, and strange images kept straying through his mind, phantoms he could not pin down.

"A doc deserves to get paid like anybody else," Dr. Shea said, his voice rising to something just short of a whine. "So I'd appreciate it if you'd check in your pockets."

There won't be any money in my pockets, Macklin thought. Shea's theory about him being attacked and robbed explained a great deal . . . but if he didn't have any money left . . .

He turned out the pockets of his Levi's. Nothing. Shea's eyes narrowed. "Now see here, mister. This here ain't a charity ward—"

"Wait. Maybe—"

He'd become aware of something heavy, hanging by a cord about his neck. He'd been aware of it in the desert, too, as it had chaffed and dragged at him . . . but he'd been too worn down and hurting to be curious about what it was. Reaching into the top of his shirt, he pulled out a leather sack attached to a thong looped around his neck so it dangled over his chest.

"Whatcha got there?" the doc wanted to know.

There was a string cinch that closed the top of the small tan leather sack. Macklin opened the sack and spilled the contents onto the Shea's table. A double handful of gold coins jangled across the surface of the table, looking freshly minted and shiny on the scratched wooden surface.

"What the hell?" the doc said. He reached out and snapped up one of the double eagles—a twenty-dollar gold piece—before Macklin could stop him.

Macklin watched as the doc peered at the coin, turning it over in his hand and then giving it a careful bite. After a moment, the doc looked at the other coins scattered on the table.

"Just who the hell are you, anyway?" he asked.

Macklin shrugged and started scooping the coins back into the little leather sack. "Well," he said, "at least you know I can pay you. How much?"

Shea darted out a finger and scooted two more coins back to his side of the table, then scooped them up. He glanced at Macklin, watching for a reaction, and then his eyes followed the other coins as Macklin put them away.

"Well," he said, sighing a booze-thick cloud. "I guess we can get on with the full examination now. How's your head feel?"

"It hurts. Kind of throbbing. And I feel a little dizzy."

"Got just th' thing." Walking to a cabinet, he opened

the glass panel with a key, pulled out a bottle, and poured some into a small glass. He handed the glass to Macklin. "Drink this."

"What is it?"

"Laudanum. Fix you right up."

The name meant nothing to Macklin. He downed the liquid in one swallow. It had a slightly bitter taste.

"Good. Now, why don't you take your shirt off and sit in that chair?"

Macklin reached up to his top shirt button, then dropped his hand again.

"Just as soon leave my shirt on."

"Then how'm I gonna use my stethoscope to hear your heart?"

Macklin thought a moment. No . . . he *really* didn't want to take it off.

But why? Dr. Shea meant him no harm, he thought, except perhaps to overcharge him. And he was right, how could he give Macklin an exam if he kept his shirt on?

"All right," Macklin said. "Guess it won't hurt to take it off."

"I'll get my stethoscope," Dr. Shea said, turning and walking over to a small table that was covered with two stethoscopes and several other, smaller instruments.

Macklin started unbuttoning his shirt. He was idly looking at the color lithograph of the human body on the wall in front of him.

Something like fear, a deep and queasy unease, caught at his throat and sent shivers down his spine. No. He wasn't going to do it. He had to get out of this place, had to get away. It felt to him as though the walls of Shea's office were closing in on him. He started buttoning the shirt up tight again.

Dr. Shea was just turning around. "What the hell're you doing?"

"I've got to get moving," Macklin said, sliding out of the fancy medical chair.

"I was just gettin' ready to examine you," Shea said, waggling his stethoscope at him like a hungry, black snake.

Macklin really was in a hurry now. So many questions, the main ones being just who was he and what was going on?

"Keep the money, Doc," Macklin said. "Thanks for your help."

Macklin was already on his way out the door.

◆ 2 ◆

TOMBSTONE, COCHISE COUNTY, ARIZONA TERRITORY.

The town was raw and new, as bright and eager as a young prostitute early on a Saturday night, a place of gaudy lights and tinkling saloon music. Lying on desert hills between the San Pedro Valley and the Dragoon Mountains, the nighttime town resembled one of those fabled crooked cities out in California one heard so much about.

Back in '77, a man named Ed Schieffelin had come up into these hills, determined to find pay dirt in the San Pedro Hills, a wasteland occupied by snakes, tarantulas, and Chiricahua Apaches. "All you'll find out there is your tombstone!" a scornful acquaintance—the legendary scout Al Sieber—had told him.

The laugh was on Sieber now. Schieffelin had struck silver, and the town was born soon after, as eastern investors crazed for another major silver strike, like the fabled Comstock Lode of the '60s up in Nevada, poured into the region. In 1879, Tombstone had boasted a population of one thousand. Two years later, there were perhaps ten thousand people in the whole county, most of them miners, laborers, merchants, cowboys, and ranch hands . . . though, as in all silver towns, there was a fair percentage of gamblers, whores, gunmen, and lawmen with what one might charitably call "questionable pasts."

Some of those elements had clashed recently. Tombstone was in the middle of a power struggle, with the Clanton-McLaury Cowboy gang and Sheriff Behan on one side, and the Earps and Doc Holliday on the other. Things had gotten so bad for a while, with stage robberies and a bad fire along Allen Street the previous June that had left Behan and the Earps pointing fingers at one another, that the territorial governor had threatened to declare martial law.

It was a rich, violent, and proud town, boasting of big, new money and the rich and ornate buildings that were the mark of a western boomtown. The Grand Hotel on Allen Street—part of the notorious "Whiskey Row." The Oriental, where the infamous Wyatt Earp held court. Some of the fanciest buildings were on Sixth Street, where most of the town's brothels were clustered. There were mine shafts beneath all of the streets . . . and one mine, the Goodenough, actually had surface workings right in the middle of the street, at the corner of Toughnut and Fifth.

The people who lived in the town had a grim joke: Tombstone had a man for breakfast every morning . . . which meant someone had been killed the night before and been planted in the ground.

It was a rough place for rough men . . . and a dangerous one for a man who didn't belong there.

◆ 3 ◆

THE TOWN BEDAZZLED MACKLIN AND SCARED HIM, TOO. SO much noise, light, sex, rage, jubilation, despair, laughter, and violence all right out in the open. Men puked on the sidewalks, whores did up men right in the mouths of alleyways, and there was a fistfight every half block or so. The cool air smelled of horseshit, tobacco, perfume, whiskey, beer, female musk, and the day's heat from the surrounding desert.

The strange thing was, while all this fuss should have cheered him—he was once again with people, alive and back in what passed for civilization in this part of this world—a melancholy had gripped Macklin, a melancholy that carried with it fear and sorrow.

The fear he understood. He was alone, injured, didn't know who he was . . . and that was enough to scare anyone. The sorrow, though, he didn't understand. When he stepped out into the dirt street in front of Shea's house and looked up at the moon riding high and lonely in the night sky, he was gripped with an empty, desolate longing impossible to put into words, impossible to understand.

What is it about that moon . . . ?

He desperately needed to think, to find someplace where he could collect his thoughts and try to figure out what had happened to him. It wasn't just the fear of something terrible having happened to him that had him reeling. There was something else, a dread, a nameless horror centered on *something* that he had to remember. . . .

So, what did people do to pull together scattered thoughts, to remember their troubles . . . or to forget them?

He found himself thinking of getting a drink . . . though he wasn't sure whether he meant water, or something else.

He walked a few more blocks, a hayseed gaping at all the false fronts, walking wide of any fistfights, shaking his head and pushing on when a girl asked him if he had the money for a good time.

He wanted a nice, quiet saloon, but this was Tombstone and there was no such thing. Not with a mining boom going on, there wasn't.

He finally turned into a place called The Alhambra.

He was about halfway through the bat wings when somebody shouted ''Duck!'' He responded instantly, crouching down just in time to miss a flying whiskey glass that smashed against the door frame behind him.

Those who paid attention—those who weren't spending time with a roulette wheel, a dance girl, a poker game, or a fistfight—laughed at the tall stranger as he finished his walk inside. No explanation or apology, of course. This was Tombstone.

He walked over to the bar. Behind it hung a pair of the biggest moose antlers he'd ever seen. To the right of the antlers was a long painting of a larger-than-life-sized naked woman. He stared first at one, then at the other for quite a spell, trying to remember if he'd ever *seen* moose antlers before . . . or a naked woman, for that matter. He knew what the antlers were but didn't know *how* he knew. As for the painting, he was sure he had seen a naked woman somewhere, sometime.

But he couldn't remember who it might have been.

A woman's scream. ''Ma'khleen!''

He looked into the face of the nude woman for a long time, trying to remember.

Who was the woman he'd seen in some of those hazy memories, the woman who'd screamed his name?

''What'll it be?'' a bartender asked. He sported a fancy mustache that was nearly as wide as the moose antlers on the wall.

Macklin had kept a couple of gold dollars loose in his pocket, to avoid another scene like the one in Shea's office. What to order? Looking down the bar, he saw a man with a schooner of beer.

''What he's having. Please.''

The bartender took the dollar and returned a moment later with the beer and some silver change.

The beer tasted awful. Warm. Rancid. He forced himself to drink, though. He was badly dehydrated after his trek through the desert, and something told him he could use the sugars and proteins in the tepid stuff as well.

He swallowed as much as he could stomach, then decided to give it a rest. He turned around, elbows on the bar, and watched the festivities. There were card tables on one side of the saloon, a keno game, roulette wheel, squirrel cage, and blackjack table down the other. In back, on a raised platform, was a three-piece band: banjo, violin, and piano. The music was terrible but at least it was loud. Directly in front of the platform was a dance floor big enough for maybe ten couples. It was crowded. The men pressed close enough to rub their chests against the breasts of the dance girls. The dance girls winced at the weight of the hicks upon their shoes. With women in short supply, some of the men danced with each other.

The serious drinking was done at the bar, in small groups of three or four. Macklin found himself listening carefully, trying to pick up something, anything, that might jog his tattered memories into something like coherence.

Nothing he heard seemed to have a bearing on his problem. There had been some Indian raids sixty miles to the west, it seemed, so there was a lot of talk about that, and a bank had gone bust in the Territorial capital, leaving a couple of once-wealthy miners near-broke. There was man-patter about girls and fistfights and desperadoes, jokes about sex and dying and horses, all shouted above the band and the din of the gamblers.

Macklin gave his beer another try. It was funny, the way his mind had read the word so clearly when he'd seen someone else drinking the stuff: *beer*. But when he tasted it, he hated it. And it couldn't have been just his beer that was ruined. Nobody else was objecting to theirs.

Plus, his headache was back, a dull, aching throb, and he was feeling muzzy in the head. He was starting to wonder about the stuff Shea had given him. Laudanum? What was it? All the noise was hobbling him. He needed sleep. He had to find someplace. At least he knew he had money.

He showed the bartender the address Sarah Nevers had written out for him, and was told how to get there ... southwest part of town, on Toughnut.

Macklin picked up his change and left the saloon. Nobody paid any attention.

He was glad to be in the cool, clean night air again. Getting his bearings, he started walking south.

He'd gone no more than half a block when he heard footsteps coming up fast behind him on the board sidewalk. Just as he turned to see what was going on, he felt cold metal jab into his back.

"There's an alley right up here, friend," a male voice said. "Turn in there or I'll put a hole in you."

The man smelled of the dead day's heat and sweat and beer and tobacco.

Macklin walked to the alley, turned in, stopped after taking six, seven steps.

"Keep moving," the man said, nudging the gun into Macklin's back again.

There was something lonely about the alley, the way the moonlight played on the back stoops of several businesses, tomcats lurking on the steps and piles of trash and empty packing crates.

"The gold," the man said. "And fast."

"I don't have any gold."

"Don't gimme that, greenhorn. I want the gold!"

He dug in his pockets, pulled out his change, and held

his palm out. "I guess I was wrong. I've got·two gold dollars and a few—"

"The *sack* is what I want," the man said.

Now, how the hell had he known about the sack of gold? Macklin hadn't pulled it out in the saloon.

But that didn't matter. No way Macklin could give him that gold. It was all he had, and with no memory at all, and no idea what kind of skills he might have or where the gold had come from, Macklin knew he had no hope of replacing it. Without money, he'd be as good as dead.

"I said the sack," the man repeated. "Or I'm gonna put two bullets right through your skull."

Macklin's heart was pounding. He found his attention focused on the man's throat, where a rapid pulse was throbbing just beneath the skin like a nervous tic.

Let go. Let go, and let your body remember. If you stop to think, you are already dead.

The words were there, unbidden, in his mind. He felt himself relax, felt himself slide his left hand forward and up as he stepped to the left, his hand closing on the man's gun hand, thumb bearing down and in hard, felt his right hand *exploding* upward into the point of the man's chin, heel-first.

The man's head snapped back as the revolver slipped from nerveless fingers. Macklin snatched the gun clear, just as he became aware of another man in the alley, ten feet away, a man already holding a revolver of his own at eye level as he drew a bead on the bridge of Macklin's nose.

The first man collapsed to the dirt like a sack of wheat. For a terrible second, Macklin and the second man faced one another, guns pointed at one another. An exchange of shots, and death, was *that* close. . . .

Then a shadow moved at the gunman's back. "This is some welcome to Tombstone," a familiar male voice said, followed by a hacking cough. "Man just arrives here and already somebody's sticking him up. Now, mister, you hand me that six-shooter of yours, and right now."

The gunman, a chunky, straw-haired man, raised his weapon. Doc Holliday, gun drawn, stepped from the shadows at his back and plucked it from his hand.

"You turned into a Christer or somethin', Holliday?" the man asked plaintively. "I gotta make a livin', don't I?"

"Get outta here, Jess," Holliday said, holstering his own gun and holding up the one he'd taken. "Gather up your pal there and go rob somebody else. You just happened to pick on a friend of mine is all."

"Can we have our guns back?"

"I'll think about it." Then he grinned.

Jess scowled. "You sonofabitch," he said. Leaving his friend cold in the alley, he turned and walked away, back to the noise and the girls and the hooch.

Macklin thought a moment, then stooped and unbuckled the unconscious man's gun belt. Holstering the weapon, he buckled it on, letting it hang low and comfortable on his right hip, cinching the leather drawstring tight on his thigh.

"You got mighty fast hands there, Macklin," Holliday observed. "Don't think I ever seen a man take a gun right out of another man's hand that way. You know how to use it?"

I don't remember. Macklin shrugged.

"You seem to know how to wear your rig, too. I'd be interested in knowin' how well you can handle a gun."

"I sure owe you one," Macklin said as they walked back to the street. He wanted to change the subject. Holliday's pointed queries were making him nervous.

"You don't owe me anything, Macklin. But you owe yourself some sleep. You're lookin' mighty ragged."

He shook his head, trying to clear it, but the movement

brought the pain back, as bad as ever. "I'm still tryin' to figure out how Jess and that other guy knew I had a sack of gold twenty-dollar pieces."

"The hell you say!" Doc Holliday, the spare, intense man in the singular black suit, coughed and laughed at the same time. "That explains it, then. Doc Shea sicced them on you."

"Doc Shea?"

"Sure, anytime he sees a stranger with anything valuable on him, he tells Jess and Ted, and those two varmints go after them. They split the take three ways."

"He's supposed to *heal* people," Macklin said, knowing how naive he probably sounded.

"Well, he actually does a pretty good job of that," Doc Holliday said. "At least when he's sober. Which, I admit, isn't all that often."

"Well, why'd you send me to him, then?"

"I didn't exactly know you had a sackful of gold on you, did I? He's honest enough, otherwise. Where you headed?"

"Sarah Nevers's place. You know, the woman on the stagecoach?"

"That's good. There's a lot of hell-raising in the hotels. You'll want a nice, quiet place and a good night's sleep. Then . . . I tell you what. I want you to come and see me tomorrow morning at the Oriental Bar. Which is right over there." He pointed to a saloon on the corner. "Let's say around noon. I'm inclined to sleep in most mornings."

"Any particular reason you want to see me?" Macklin said, unable to keep the suspicion out of his voice. He was feeling . . . tired. And maybe a little sick now, too, though Macklin couldn't tell if that was from his head wound or the physical letdown of nearly being shot in that alley.

Maybe it was just the effects of that damned, rancid-tasting beer. Or that potion of Shea's.

Holliday clapped him on the arm. "Got a job for you. But we'll talk about it in the morning. Right now, I'm late for a poker game."

THREE

✧ 1 ✧

MACKLIN WASN'T FEELING WELL. BY THE TIME HE'D WALKED the four blocks to Sarah Nevers's house, he felt fever-hot, light-headed, and his skin was icy with oily sweat.

Walking was getting to be a problem, and so was focusing. Even with the occasional streetlamp, he seemed to be heading into a long, dark tunnel. Only the moonlight, falling upon the faces of the houses he passed, lent the scene reality, and he wished now he could escape the cold gaze of that hovering, haunting moon. There were windows and fences and dirt walks up to front doors and brick chimneys atop slant roofs. Reality. Then why did everything shimmer, as if in a fever-bred dream?

The town receded, the noise, the light, the desperate humanity. He fought against the sense of unreality that threatened to overwhelm him. . . .

He was real. His name was Macklin. He'd been injured, somehow, and he was not feeling at his best was all. Nothing more serious than that. Nothing . . .

Sarah Nevers's house was good-sized, a two-story white frame affair with a nice front porch. A swing hung in one corner and a bicycle was parked in another.

He saw all this as he approached the porch. Images: warm milk, warm blanket, sleep. Sarah Nevers, he could tell she'd liked him.

He looked up at the front of the place looming over him, at the cloud-streaked full moon looking down coldly, accusingly upon him, at the stars that seemed somehow sentient—almost as if they were speaking to him—and then the inverted V of the roof.

There were four steps awaiting him. He had no trouble with the first, a bit of trouble with the second, and when he raised his leg to touch the third step, he went over backward, his arms cartwheeling to keep him on his feet.

He cracked the back of his head hard against the dirt path that led to the house.

He was unconscious instantly.

✦ 2 ✦

SARAH NEVERS KEPT A BOOK BY ONE DR. BENJAMIN RUSH IN her bookcase downstairs. From what she'd heard, he was perhaps the most widely read doctor in the entire country. Until she'd read his book, she hadn't known, for instance, that Negroes were black because of a strain of leprosy; or that bloodletting could cure just about any disease you cared to name, except for madness, which was frequently caused by tobacco. Thank God for Dr. Rush's little tome on health. It was so sensible and practical.

Sarah was thinking of Dr. Rush as she began to remove Macklin's clothes. A light sleeper, she'd heard him collapse on the front steps. Then she had to awaken two of her boarders, who helped carry him up to a vacant room on the second floor. She was there now, working by the light of a whale-oil lamp that she had recently had refitted so that she could burn kerosene, which was cheaper. The light flickered on the new wallpaper and the clean doilies on the small mahogany table by the window. She took a well-deserved pride in her well-run boardinghouse. . . .

Lightly, she touched the man's clean-shaven cheek, then touched his sweat-slicked forehead, right below the bandages wrapped around his head. He was hot, a fever. She let her hand linger a moment longer than necessary, then snatched it away, angry with herself.

She did not want to have impure thoughts. She'd felt a deep attraction to him immediately, there was no denying that. She'd been two years without a man, since the sudden death of her husband. Sometimes, she had dreams of a man touching her and then being inside her, the way Curtis used to touch her and be inside her. She ached for that kind of love now . . . at least until the shame overcame her and she remembered that as a member of the Women's Purity League—aimed at driving the Earps and the Clantons and all the other so-called shooters out of Tombstone—she could never be hypocritical enough to commit such a sin. . . .

She pulled his shoes off first, dropping them one by one beside the big four-poster bed. Then his gun belt, which she regarded with distaste as she hung it over the back of a chair by the bed. He hadn't been wearing that when they'd found him in the desert, had he? She wondered where he'd 'gotten it, and why. If he was another gun-fighter . . .

Next she unbuttoned his denims and slid them off his legs. Primly, she averted her eyes as she pulled up the sheet, covering his nakedness. As she reached for his shirt, she noticed a leather thong pulled tight across his throat, and she freed that first to ease his breathing, slipping the thong over his head and pulling out a small and heavy leather bag. She couldn't resist a peek inside. Her eyes widened at . . .

three hundred ... maybe three hundred fifty dollars in brand-new, shiny gold coins, eagles and double eagles. That was a lot of money for a man to be carrying around on him.

"Just who are you, stranger?" she asked the unconscious form. Carefully, she tied up the leather pouch again, then tucked it away inside one of the pockets of Macklin's denims, which she then folded and laid carefully on a chair near the bed.

She started unbuttoning his shirt, pulling it open ... and then she stopped, eyes widening.

"What in the name of Heaven ... ?"

It was small, whatever it was, not much bigger than one of those dollars Macklin had in his pouch, but it was black and very smooth and it looked like it was actually embedded in his skin, somehow, low in his chest, just about at the lower tip of his breastbone.

It was so black that at first she thought that it was a hole, going straight through into his chest, but when she nerved herself to look closer, she could see that it was a solid plug of ... what *was* it made of, anyway? Not metal. Not wood. Strangest of all, it seemed to her she could see down into it a little ways, which made her think it might be some kind of dark, smoky-colored glass. And there, deep, deep inside that ... *thing,* she could see lights, glowing, overlapping rectangles of light that flickered on and off in no particular pattern that Sarah could see. Some were red, some blue, some green, some white. They were so deep inside that she had to look real close to be sure she was seeing them at all.

She became very aware of his man's smell and of how warm it made her feel, and she pulled back sharply, ashamed. Carefully then, afraid of hurting him, she touched the dark surface. It felt like glass, cool and slick ... but it was softer, somehow, as though it would bend or flex in a very unglasslike way if she pressed harder.

What was it? Never once in his book of sound, sensible medical advice did Dr. Rush even mention such a thing. Could this be something that only Easterners had? Or foreigners? Maybe Macklin was French or Turkish or Hindu or something outlandish like that, and this was something they did to themselves, like the tattoos and nose rings worn by the savages of the South Seas.

What, she wondered, would Dr. Rush recommend? She touched Macklin's head again and it came to her: phrenology, a way to tell all about a man's brain-power and personal inclinations simply by feeling the bumps on his head. There were charts in the book that showed exactly where the bumps would be, and what each meant.

All Sarah's impure thoughts were gone now. Her excitement was purely intellectual.

She must be careful with his head and avoid the spot behind his left ear where he was injured. Using her fingers very gently, fingertips only, she moved them silken and softly across the horizon of his skull.

Her own brow furrowed with concentration. It was hard to tell exactly *what* she was feeling. She couldn't really feel any bumps, no big ones, anyway, but there was something there, about halfway back, a ridge or the edge of something like a plate or shell just under his skin and hair. And behind that edge, which seemed to go from ear to ear right across the top of his head, there was a smooth *slickness* that reminded her of the feel of the thing in his chest.

The back half of his head, what she could feel through the bandages, anyway, felt completely smooth, no bumps at all. It was . . . it was *unnatural*.

She pulled her fingers away from Macklin's head.

Absolutely smooth. But that was impossible. Everybody

had bumps on the backs of their heads. Even Negroes and Indians and Catholics.

But not Macklin.

She put her head close to his face. His breathing was light and ragged but steady. He'd be fine here alone for the time it would take her to dash downstairs and bring the book back up here.

She wanted to know what Dr. Rush made of grown white men who didn't have natural bumps on their heads.

And who had smooth, round, black things made of glass that wasn't glass, with lights and shapes moving inside, buried in the center of their chests. . . .

✧ 3 ✧

SOMEHOW, MACKLIN KNEW IT WAS A DREAM.

He didn't know how he knew, except maybe for the fact that he was seeing some damned strange things, but he wasn't feeling afraid at all.

In fact, it was a lot like being home. . . .

It wasn't the crystalline cities bathed in blue light so much . . . nor the long, low houses with the enormous windows and the strangely shaped trees and gardens on their terraced roofs that made him feel he was home, though they certainly were familiar in a way nothing else had been since he'd arrived here.

No, it was the sky that pulled him, a deep and green-hued sky where a strange, colorfully banded world with dazzling, ice-bright rings hung low on one horizon, while not one but two suns—larger than the sun of this world, but gentler, cooler, redder—set together, the one almost touching the other, on the opposite horizon. They set slowly in a blaze of flame illuminating green clouds streaked with orange-gold and silver, and as the sky darkened, the stars came out, multitudes of them, thick-crowded against the lacy twist of pale green and red nebulae, despite the flood of colored light from the ringed giant planet in the east.

It was a world that never knew total darkness, not with the ringed giant in the sky, not with a dozen moons ranging in size from tiny to huge, not with those clotted glories of stars hanging so close overhead it seemed possible to reach up and grab them by great, glowing handfuls.

Home. . . .

He wished he knew where it was, and how he could get back there.

Slowly he became aware of the people around him . . . of men and women like himself, in soft robes and glowing garments of radiant light, and of the others, of people not like him in the least, but who exchanged friendly greetings with him as he walked past, in singsong Gtai or the clacking harshness of D'thalat. Tall and spindly legged garts; short, quick, large-eyed m'lazh; lumbering jads with legs and tentacles like massive tree trunks, he saw them all and recognized them. His friends. His mentors. His comradesat-arms among the Monitors of the Associative.

Home. . . .

And she was there as well. The woman who'd screamed and called his name. She was small, a cuddly armful with black hair and spectacular blue, blue eyes. He lay back in the bed and watched as she touched the clasp at her throat and her garment fell away, and she stood before him as naked as the woman in the painting, more so, without that shallow patina of pretended lust.

She climbed into bed, kneeling above him, and he reached up and touched her implant, a black disk of plastic embedded in her pale skin between and beneath her high, firm, coral-tipped breasts.

"I hate what they did to you." The voice was his own,

but coming from far, far away. "To this goddess-lovely body of yours. . . ."

She smiled down at him. "It's just for the mission, silly," she said, and she lightly stroked his chest. "We won't even be able to see where they were, afterward. And we certainly can't risk visiting Earth without AI backup and a full cultural database."

He glanced down and saw his own implant, gleaming in the room's soft lights.

"Darh sha, voorl enanh," he replied, grinning. The phrase was Gtai and meant, roughly, "The Old Ones are shocked and will never approve." The closest English equivalent would be something along the lines of "Heaven forbid." He added, in English, "That would be downright barbaric."

She giggled, an entrancing sound. "As barbaric as where we're going!" She touched her implant. "And they aren't so bad, really. At least, they won't get in our way."

"Are you sure they're off? I'd hate to think they were Earthwatching us."

"I don't think artificial intelligences care what humans do," she replied. "They have their own ideas about what's . . . exciting. . . ."

Reaching for her then, he pulled her down on top of him. They kissed, and he lost himself in her, in the feel of her, in the wonderful, long-lost memory of her. . . .

What is her name? *The thought nagged him.* I wish I could remember. . . .

And then it was . . . later, and the moon shone a dazzling, silvery white through the cockpit, and the two of them were doing . . . something . . . something, he couldn't remember what . . . except that they *were here,* they *were attacking . . . they* were moving in for the kill. . . .

"Maybe we can outrun them!" she called.

"It's too late!" he shouted, and the panic was a black cloud gnawing at his mind. *"The base is gone! They must already be on Earth...."*

"Target, bearing one-seven-one by plus-five-three! They've got a lock...!"

"Hang on! We might be able to lose them!"

"Range seven-five-one-one, closing!"

Stars wheeled past the cockpit, which plunged into an eerie, instrument-lit darkness as the moon fell astern. Ahead, Earth hung against a star-glittered sky, a blue-and-white marble, a gemstone, impossibly fragile and alone....

"Ma'khleen," she said. *"If the Monitor base is gone, if they have a fleet moving toward Earth...!*

"The primitives won't have a chance," he replied, grim as death. *"But maybe we can—"*

The explosion tore at them, hammering the ship. Air whistled into space, shrill and deadly. Ahead, the Earth rapidly expanded, filling the forward sky.

And then the second explosion took them, a thunderclap shattering creation. Clouds streaked past as they fell toward a wildly spinning world.

"Eject!" Macklin shouted. *"Eject! Eject!"*

"Ma'khleen!" she shrieked....

❖ 4 ❖

MACKLIN CAME WIDE AWAKE, HEART HAMMERING, SWEAT drenching his face, his chest, his bed, his breath coming in ragged, deep, gasping pants. *"Eject...!"*

He was alone.

He was alone in a dark room, where unfamiliar furnishings and wallpaper and pictures on the walls were just visible by the shaft of white moonlight spilling through the window. He was naked, sitting upright in a four-poster bed, with a chamber pot on the floor next to him. His clothes were neatly folded on a chair nearby, and his gun belt hung over the back. His pouch with the money was gone . . . but when he reached out and touched his clothes, he felt the reassuring lump of the gold tucked away inside, out of sight.

Sarah. Sarah must have found him, brought him here, put him to bed.

And the dream . . .

He sat for a moment on the side of the bed, working to control his breathing. It was just a dream . . . though an uncommonly strange one. As he tried to recapture those bizarre images, he could feel them fading away, one by one. Where had he been? What had he been doing? He remembered her, the woman who'd called his name. . . .

And the implant. He remembered the implant. That had been the strangest part of all, seeing that thing in her chest and another in his own. He shivered. The cool night air was like ice on his sweat-soaked skin.

The implant. Made him glad it was all just a—

He looked down at himself and saw the black disk set deep in his skin, riding comfortably in his sternum.

"God help me," he said, softly. "Who am I? *What* am I?"

And what was the nameless dread that still haunted him?

He wasn't sure he was ready for an answer.

✧ 5 ✧

"THE WAY I HEERD IT, HOLLIDAY HISSELF WAS IN ON THE Benson stage robbery." The speaker was Harry Fulbright. He'd been a miner until a cave-in turned him into a man with a crushed right arm that flapped like a broken wing. "Holliday hisself was the one who shot the stage driver dead!"

"Dammit, Fulbright," said a bald man named Squires.

"Use your head! Who is it who's been spreading that rumor all over town, huh? It's Ike Clanton, that's who! Doesn't that tell ya something?"

The breakfast consisted of hung beef, bread, potatoes, eggs, pancakes, and sweet Vermont syrup. Macklin had been sitting at the long table in Sarah Nevers's dining room for fifteen minutes now, ever since she'd called for him to wash up and have something to eat. He was surprised at how much better he felt this morning, despite the nightmare. He was hungry, too, and had been attacking the stack of food on his plate while listening with one ear to the spirited debate. The others were discussing the robbery of the Benson Stage—the very same stage that had picked him up last night, in fact—seven months earlier.

"Well, I heard that Wyatt Earp offered Ike Clanton six thousand dollars if'n he would kill the other people in on the holdup," said a man named McGreevy. "Why would he do that unless he wanted them silenced?"

"The story *I* heard," Squires retorted, "was that Earp just offered the money if Clanton would turn the others in! And who was it who told the story? Ike Clanton, that's who! Hardly an unbiased observer!"

"Squires, it's plain as day that the whole thing was political anyway," Fulbright said. "You know how much Wyatt wants t'be sheriff! He figured t'give Clanton the six-grand reward for those fugitives and get the glory for the capture. And the people of Tombstone would elect him sheriff by acclamation!"

"Some people say Wyatt Earp was in on the Benson robbery hisself," McGreevy said darkly. "That he planned it!"

"Bushwah!" old Mr. Sullivan, at the head of the table, snapped. "Everybody knows it's the Clantons and that there Cowboy gang that's behind every robbery in these here parts! I say the Earps is honest men!"

"You would, Yank!" McGreevy said, and the others laughed. Tom Sullivan had been a Yankee in the War and lived now in a town where most people's sympathies had been with the South. "You just like the Earps 'cause they're Yankees, too!"

"Well, I'm from Illinois just like the Earps," Sarah Nevers said, arriving at the table with another plate piled high with flapjacks, "but that doesn't make me love them! C'mon, boys, eat hearty. There's plenty more."

"Thankee, ma'am, thankee," Sullivan said, spearing two more flapjacks off the stack. "Don't mind if I do!"

"If you want t'look fer dirty lawmen," Squires said reasonably, "have a gander at Johnny Behan! Who was it got arrested by the Earps for robbing the Bisbee Stage, just last month? Frank Stilwell and Pete Spence, that's who, and both of 'em Johnny Behan's deputies! And Clanton Cowboys too, if the stories I heard are true."

"Just because his deputies was caught robbing the stage," Fullbright said, "doesn't mean John Behan was involved."

"Sure, Behan didn't need to rob that stage," Sullivan said. "He's rich enough skimming taxes and getting payoffs from the Clantons!"

"How about you, Mr. Macklin?" Fullbright asked. "What do you think about the goings-on in this here little town of ours?"

Macklin smiled around a mouthful of flapjack. "I really couldn't say, Mr. Fulbright. I just got in last night and haven't had much of a chance to form an opinion." He glanced at Sarah, who was watching him from the doorway leading to the kitchen. "I *have* had some good advice in the matter, though."

Sarah dimpled at that, then vanished back into the kitchen.

"How'd the Earps get to be lawmen in this town anyway?" McGreevy wanted to know. He darted a poisonous glance at Sullivan. "We don't need no Yankees runnin' things in this town!"

"Mayor Clum appointed Virgil town marshal when Ben Sippy left town," Fulbright said, "and Virgil turned around and appointed his brothers and Doc Holliday as deputies. That was when . . . last June?"

"And the town's been in a state ever since," Sarah declared, returning from the kitchen and taking her seat at the table. "I swear, it's like being the bone that's getting worried by two stray dogs."

"Well, things're gonna come to a head pretty soon, now," Fullbright said. "It's a power struggle, sure enough, and one side or the other's gonna have to come out on top. Question is, which one's it gonna be?"

"I just wish they'd all kill each other and leave the rest of us in peace," Sarah said.

Macklin ate, listened, and watched, fascinated.

◆ **6** ◆

SARAH NEVERS JUST SAT THERE AND WATCHED, FASCINATED, as he finished his third breakfast plate there in the dining room. The others had already left, and it was just the two of them.

"You've got an appetite," she said.

Macklin looked up and smiled at her. "Guess I do."

"Would you like more? There are still some flapjacks out in the kitchen."

"No, thanks, ma'am. This is about it for me."

He started eating again. She kept watching him, wondering if he felt her eyes on him.

"You're really feeling better this morning?"

"Yes, ma'am, I really am." He shook his head. "Don't

know what hit me last night. I think it might've been whatever the doc gave me for the pain. But I'm a hundred percent better today.''

"I'm awfully glad to hear it. She paused, catching her lower lip between her teeth. ''I'd like to ask you something, Mr. Macklin, and I hope you won't take offense.''

He paused, the fork bearing a large slice of syrupy flapjack halfway to his mouth. ''I can't think of anything that you could say that would make me take offense, Mrs. Nevers.''

She felt uncomfortable. ''I, uh, I had to take your clothes off last night, getting you into bed and all.'' He didn't seem embarrassed by her statement, but she flushed, remembering.

''Yes, ma'am.''

She hesitated. ''There's something—odd—on your chest.'' She touched herself, just below her breasts. ''Right here.''

''Yes, ma'am, there is.''

''Do you know what it is?''

He put his fork down finally and faced her. ''No, ma'am, I don't.''

''I mean, you ain't from around here, are you?''

His eyes widened a bit, then narrowed again, as though something had bit him. ''I don't really remember, Mrs. Nevers. But no, I don't think I am.''

''I was wondering if you were a foreigner. You speak real good English, not like the foreigners I've met. But, well, I never seen anything like that . . . that thing. Is it something they wear in Europe, maybe? Or Russia?''

''I'm sorry, but I can't help you there.''

''I looked it up in Dr. Rush's book and I couldn't find no reference to anything like that.''

''Dr. Rush?''

''Oh, he's just about the greatest medical authority ever.

Knows everything there is to know about medicine, I guess. Gives lectures all over the country." She sighed. "I always wanted to be a doctor, you know . . . when I was little. Before I knew that women didn't do things like that."

"They don't?" He looked genuinely puzzled. "Why not?"

"Well, I mean . . . they can be nurses, of course. And I have heard there are some woman doctors now. But it's not, well, *ladylike*."

"I would think," Macklin said quietly, "that someone like you could do anything you put your mind to."

"Well, I thank you for those kind words, Mr. Macklin, but that attitude is hardly realistic now, is it? According to Dr. Rush, men *are* naturally more intelligent than women."

He smiled again. "You've got a lot of faith in that man."

"Yes, I do. He knows everything there is to know about medicine."

"It might be you have too much faith in him." He reached up and touched his chest, where that *thing* was. "You know, I'd appreciate it if you wouldn't mention it to anybody."

"You really don't have no idea what it is?"

He shook his head. His smile had left him. "No, I don't. Wish I did."

"Don't it scare you?"

"Yes, Mrs. Nevers, it does."

"What're you gonna do about it? I mean . . . it's not *natural!*"

"Right now, nothing. Right now I've got to go see Mr. Holliday."

"Oh, shoot," she said. "Shoot shoot *shoot!*"

"What?"

"You're a good man, Mr. Macklin. I can sense that!

Don't let that Holliday and his crowd draw you into any-thing!''

"He saved my life last night, ma'am." He told her what had happened, about how two men had tried to rob him, and how Holliday had showed up just in time.

She sighed. "You ever think he himself was behind it?"

"Ma'am?"

"Doc Holliday himself. Maybe he was the one who sicced those villains on you, just so you'd feel beholden."

"You don't like Holliday much, do you?"

"I sure don't. I don't like *any* of them!"

"You make it sound pretty . . . personal."

She hesitated, wondering how much to say. Finally, "It *is* personal, Mr. Macklin. My husband was killed by a gun-man two years ago." She reached to her throat and pulled out the small, gold locket she kept there always. Clicking it open, she showed the tiny photograph within to Macklin.

"That's Curtis," she told him. "He worked for Wells Fargo, first as a driver, then as an agent, and I suppose you could say that danger was a part of his business. But he was simply standing in a saloon one afternoon, having a drink with friends, when two so-called *shootists* got into a gunfight in the street outside. They missed each other . . . but a stray bullet caught Curtis in the belly and lodged in his spine. He died the next day. Doc Shea said if he'd lived he would've been paralyzed from the waist down. I guess that was meant to make me feel better." She snapped the locket closed and dropped it back safely beneath her blouse. "Anyway, that's why I don't like gunfighters, and why, yes, it is most decidedly personal!"

"I'm . . . sorry, Mrs. Nevers."

"Not for you to be sorry about," she said. "But you asked. Anyway, you just be careful, Mr. Macklin. Very careful. They use people all the time, and the Clanton side is just as bad as the Earps.'' She cocked her head to one side. ''It's not like you need to get a job, or anything.''

He looked puzzled, then grinned. ''You mean the money.''

''I couldn't help but see it.'' She looked alarmed. ''I didn't touch any of it!''

''Of course not. I trust you.''

''But that's an awful lot of money for a man to be carrying around.''

''Is it?''

''Yes, it is. No wonder those men attacked you last night! And . . . and you don't know where you got it?''

''I'm afraid not. But at least you know I can pay you for the room.''

''I'm not worried about *that,* Mr. Macklin. But I am concerned for you. We've got to find out if you have relatives anywhere around. Friends. A wife and family, maybe. . . .'' She hesitated a moment, looking at him. ''You know, Mr. Macklin, you must think me a dreadful busybody.''

''Not at all.''

''Well . . . this is going to seem kind of personal, and all, but . . . you're clean shaven.''

He rubbed his face with one big hand, a little ruefully. ''I've noticed most men here wear mustaches,'' he said. ''You think I'm breaking the law?''

''Of course not. But, well, you arrived here last night, with nothing on you but your clothes and that poke of gold coins.'' She pointedly didn't mention the gun belt and holster he was now wearing. ''And you were clean shaven, after who knows how long wandering around in the desert.''

''Yes . . .''

''No duffle. No shaving kit. No brush. No straight razor. And here you are this morning at breakfast, clean shaven, not even a shadow. Curtis, my husband, would shave first thing in the morning, and by supper time his face would be covered with stubble again. I'm just wondering, Mr. Macklin . . . I'm wondering why it is you don't seem to need to shave.''

Macklin looked startled, as if he'd been stuck with a pin. ''Mrs. Nevers . . . I honestly don't know. I wish I did.'' He rose, suddenly. ''I've got to go.''

She sat there for a long time after the front door banged behind him, wondering about this man whom fate had delivered to her door.

FOUR

✧ 1 ✧

IT WAITED IN THE SHADOWS, ITSELF A SHADOW HINTING AT something darker. Ll'graaz, it thought, hungering. The trap closes.

It sensed the delicious blind terror of the big quadrupeds in their compartments on the far side of the structure, heard the bangs and thumps as they kicked the wooden sides of their enclosures, their snorts and snickering calls. The quadrupeds, it thought, would make excellent prey, much like the fleet-footed, rich-blooded kroth *of home. They were intelligent and powerfully muscled, bred for strength and endurance in a hard run. Excellent, challenging prey indeed.*

But pleasure would have to wait. Deathstalker was more interested in the bipeds dwelling on this world, and in the trap it had set for one.

A tickling squirm nagged at the back of its sinuous neck. Absently, it reached up with one night-black slasher claw and flicked the offending dlik *out from beneath ruffled, thickly layered scales. The parasite clicked as it dropped to the wooden boards of the building's floor, then, scrabbling wildly, vanished into a crevice.*

Silent, Deathstalker waited.

It sensed movement outside, sensed warm blood and strong emotion. One of the bipeds had just discovered the bloodgift Deathstalker had left in the enclosure outside. It rose on powerful chase-legs, freeing leg-hands and trah'neh, its deadly slasher claws.

The prey was coming near. . . .

Sunlight fell in bright, dusty shafts through the cracks and gaps in the walls of the barn, making the shadows that much deeper. Max Carter struggled those last few steps as he carried the foal inside and gently laid him on a bed of straw, arranging him so some of the light fell across the savage wounds on the animal's hind legs. George and Molly kicked and thumped inside their stalls, and one of them gave a shrill whinny. They were sure worked up; they probably smelled Sonny's blood. Maybe he shouldn't have brought the foal in here . . . but he'd wanted to get him out of the hot sun.

Max pulled up a milking stool and squatted on it, studying those wounds. The little animal's breaths were coming in short, ragged gasps, as his eye rolled wildly in his head. Pain and terror had damned near killed Sonny already, and he'd lost a fair amount of blood, too.

Christ!

Max had found the foal like this in the corral just outside moments ago, with Gertie, his mother, panicked out of her mind, snorting and rearing and carrying on like he'd never seen the normally placid bay act before. Jesus, what the hell had happened? Those slashed wounds on Sonny's hind legs . . . the last time he'd seen wounds like that, it had been, what? Eighteen years ago, on the arm of a Yankee artilleryman at Brandy Station. The guy'd tried to block a slash by one of J.E.B. Stuart's boys with his forearm, a no-good way to stop a saber stroke. That gash had been like these, opening the flesh clean and neat, slicing through tendons and deep into the bone. Both of the animal's hind legs were hamstrung *and* broken. Damn, damn, *damn!*

Something pale wiggled against the short red hairs of the foal's neck, just above the shoulder. Max smoothed the hairs back, then leaned closer, eyes widening. "What the blue hell . . .?"

He knew ticks, of course. You couldn't work a ranch and *not* know them, ugly little bloodsuckers that could torment an animal almost as bad as screwflies. But *that* was no tick . . . more like a hard-shelled earthworm with legs, way too many legs, and pinchers biting so deeply into the foal's neck they were drawing blood. Some kind of damned centipede, maybe? Shoot, they scurried around in rotten wood and some of them stung, but they didn't bother the animals. Besides, it didn't really look like a centipede either. He poked at the creature with a finger, trying to dislodge its grip. He was wearing work gloves and figured that if it *was* some kind of poisonous critter, he was protected.

At his touch, the creature whipped around like a back-broken snake, loosing its hold on the foal's neck and sinking those half-inch pinchers right through the tough cloth of his gloves with a bite like the sting of a fire ant. "Jesus *Christ!*" Max bellowed, and he snapped his hand so hard he flicked the bizarre little creature off into the shadows at the back of the barn.

He pulled off the glove and sucked on his finger, which showed two tiny blood-pricks just behind the knuckle and the promise of swelling. What the hell *was* that thing?

Replacing his glove, muttering, he returned to his examination of the injured foal. Funny-looking bugs would have to wait. There was nothing for it but to put poor Sonny down. He just wished he knew what the hell had happened out there. He'd never seen the bite of a coyote or any other varmint this clean and neat, and besides, no varmint could've got close to Sonny with his mother right there. Didn't seem likely that Sonny could've done this to himself on the corral's slats, either. Max knew damned well there weren't any protruding nail heads or anything else in that corral that could catch and tear an animal, because he'd built the enclosure himself, board by board, and he was careful about such things. Barbed wire? Max didn't have any on the place. The more Max looked at the wound, the more he was convinced that someone, some person had done this deliberately.

The foal was shuddering with pain and shock. He had to be put down now, put out of his suffering. If Max ever caught the filthy, crazy son-of-a-bitch who'd done this . . .

Rising from the stool, he drew his Colt and thumbed back the hammer.

It stirred with a hiss of scales like dried leaves in the wind, moving forward on silent struts of its chase-legs, neck unfolding, then snaking down to avoid a low rafter. It had watched from the shadows, fascinated, as the biped had carried the injured quadruped into the building and examined its wounds. Deathstalker could taste a wild tumble of emotions from the creature, anger and worry and fear and an intense curiosity and the prick of pain from the dlik and . . . and something else, something soft and tender and utterly alien mingled with all of the more familiar tastes. Suddenly, unexpectedly, the biped stooped and placed its mouth against the quadruped's head, as though to taste it. "Goodbye, Sonny," the biped said. Deathstalker captured the words, though it could not understand them, any more than it understood the cloying sweetness of the strange emotion now rising above the more familiar tang of fear and concern.

The device in the biped's hand, coldly metallic, obviously manufactured, was clearly a weapon of some kind. Death-stalker could taste something of its purpose in the biped's churning mind. It would have to move quickly, before the creature could use it.

One of the big quadrupeds in its enclosure nearby shrieked terror....

Damn, those horses were going to hurt themselves! Max hesitated, not sure whether to shoot the foal here, or take it back outside where the blood and noise wouldn't scare old Lucy and George to death.

A smell pricked at his nose, a sweet-sour unpleasant smell, like rotten eggs and corpses left too long on the battlefield....

And then he heard a sibilant whisper at his back despite the commotion from the stalls and felt a cold prickle that rose the hair on the back of his neck, a feeling that something was watching him with icy malevolence....

Max whirled, stumbling back, looking up into golden, snake-pupiled eyes, into teeth and twitching mouth parts, into claws and scales and an indescribable horror of a body that, like the jumbled parts of a nightmare, refused to come together into anything orderly or recognizable or *sane*.

He screamed. He screamed harder and louder than he had ever screamed before, a throat-tearing wail of utter terror and despair ripped from the deepest core of his being, as his mind whirled and tattered. The gun, forgotten, dropped from nervelessly twitching fingers. He screamed again as arms thicker than his own thighs snaked out of the shadows and things like clawed fingers closed around him, lifting him from the barn's floor more easily than he had lifted the foal. He stared into a nightmare of teeth and cold golden eyes and other ... *things* he could never put words to. Something like twisted branches unfolded from the sides of the horror's gaping mouth; something like fingers uncurled, and one slender arm brandished a thing like a slender, gold and silver railway spike.

His last scream cracked and broke, his breath gone, his mind tearing, as the horror drew him closer in its embrace. . . .

Deathstalker hesitated for a triple heartbeat, savoring the sharp, salt-blood tang of the creature's shrieking, howling terror at close hand. The Kra'agh hungered, hungered for the consummation . . . but it was a professional and it needed other things now than bloodtaste. Holding the creature firmly, bracing its wildly lashing head in three of its feeder-hands, Deathstalker carefully positioned the pattern-reader between and above the creature's bulging optical organs, then skillfully drove it home, punching through thin bone and deep into spongy tissue with a satisfying crunch.

The creature convulsed, its shrieking silenced, its arms and legs jerking in Deathstalker's grip. The Kra'agh brought its head closer, as though listening to the trill of electronic pulses feeding now from the prey's spasming neuromuscular system.

Chahh duk! Bloodtaste! The creature was intelligent, after a fashion . . . as the crude products of its technology seemed to suggest. Intelligent . . . adaptable . . . highly suggestible . . . It called itself . . . man, max, people, human, rancher, guy, feller . . . correction. "Max" was its name, a personal identifier. The thing's thoughts were so jumbled, almost chaotically disordered. It was going to be hard to sort through them all.

It took a long time to pattern the human, downloading its thoughts, its language, its social customs into the soul-catcher worn on the Kra'agh's throat, and all the time the creature gibbered and whimpered, writhing and twisting against Deathstalker's grip. These humans didn't seem to know how to give up once the fight was clearly useless. A positive survival trait that, one that would make them excellent prey for feeding or for sport.

At last, the patterning was done, the human's thoughts stored for later reference, its bodily shape and appearance stored for gah-projection. At last, luxuriously, warmly, the Kra'agh could feed, and it did so with the lingering daintiness of pure, almost orgasmic pleasure. When it was done, it ate the small quadruped as well, though it didn't have the same sharp awareness of what was happening to it that the human had.

In the nearby stalls, the quadrupeds . . . no, horses. *They were called* horses *. . . the horses screamed. . . .*

◆ **2** ◆

MAYBE, MACKLIN TOLD HIMSELF WITH GRIM ACCEPTANCE, *I'm just going crazy.*

The new day had done little to restore his memory or to let him find his place in this world. He was feeling worlds better now, with a good night's sleep and a full meal in his belly, but he was still lost, confused, hurt, and he had a thing he couldn't explain in the middle of his chest and odd voices in his mind and half-memories of the *strangest* damned dreams. Maybe . . . maybe the desert had fried his brain yesterday. Hell, maybe he was still lying out there in the sand, and all of this was hallucination as the sun sucked away the last of his life. Maybe . . .

Maybe it didn't pay to think too much about it. He tried to focus on what he saw and felt. Just accept it. Don't analyze it. Focus on sensory impressions. The feel of hard dirt beneath his boots. The smell and sound of horses tethered outside a dry goods store.

In the sunlight, Tombstone looked impressive. The scattering of brick buildings gave the town an air of permanence you didn't find in most boomtowns. The clink and clatter of wagon traffic filled the air with a real sense of prosperity. He passed the *Epitaph* office, samples of the newspaper in the window; the mining exchange; the Dressmaker Bourland's. At the post office, he turned right onto Allen Street and an entire block of saloons and gambling houses, the town's infamous Whiskey Row, on his way to his meeting with Doc Holliday.

He felt eyes on him. Eyes that marked him as stranger, as outcast. He didn't belong here. Maybe it was the bandage wrapped around his head, but he couldn't help but feel that it was the thing in his chest. Even though it was covered by his shirt, it was a reminder—he *definitely* didn't belong here. The eyes of passing strangers told him that, too. Even kindly older women seemed quietly startled by him when he passed, the way animals are startled when they sense some ominous and unknown creature coming into their territory. They would stand in his wake, looking back at him as he hurried along.

There was no place for him on this world. . . .

This world? The thought twisted in his grasp, but he couldn't let go. What other worlds were there? Damn, if only he could remember.

He remembered pieces of the dream he'd had last night. He remembered a kind of a street beneath a glorious sky, a street filled with people and . . . and *things* he couldn't really remember now, save as blurs of impossibilities. How come he'd felt so at home *there,* so out of place *here?*

It didn't make sense. *None* of it made sense! What worlds were there other than the one he was standing on?

The tinny, mechanical sounds of a player piano hung above the street, lending a cheering air to the scene. You could hear the piano everywhere on Allen Street. He found he could cling to the sound, could let it fill his thoughts . . . and keep the others at bay.

The Oriental was where the Earps hung out. As Macklin passed through the bat wing doors, he saw an orderly, sleek gambling house and saloon. Down the left side of the long, narrow room was a well-polished mahogany bar with a large mirror stretched behind the ranks of bottles and mostly clean glasses. A massive, square stove sat toward the back of the place, near where the gambling devices— the squirrel cage and roulette wheel—were set up, along with the table where keno and poker were played.

A variety of people occupied the tables or bellied up to the bar—dusty miners, slick if slightly shabby cardsharps, drummers, and bored travelers waiting for the next train or stage to come along. There were a few women, too, some scarcely more than girls, women who worked hard at looking like big-city sophisticates despite the unmistakable stamp of the prairies on them. Kansas or Missouri or Iowa girls who'd run away to seek the new life and the excitement of the West.

An excitement that too often meant venereal disease, illness, or death.

One of them came up to Macklin with a big smile that didn't quite mask the deadness behind her eyes. "Hello there, stranger," she said. "Don't think I've seen you in town before. Lookin' for a good time?"

"Uh . . . thanks, no," he said. "I'm looking for Doc Holliday."

The smile fell a notch or two. "Well, buy me a drink, and maybe—"

"Macklin!" Holliday waved to him from a table in the far back of the saloon. "Back here!"

"Excuse me," he told the disappointed girl.

Holliday sat with two men, positioned far enough back

that they weren't obvious, but where they could watch the people coming into the saloon. Both of Holliday's friends looked like prosperous businessmen, in dark suits, crisp white shirts, and string ties, and they were watching him carefully, with a coldness in their expressions that put Macklin on his guard.

Holliday had mentioned a job. Macklin knew the pouch of gold coins wasn't going to last forever, that he was going to *need* a job if he was going to survive here. From Holliday's expression, though, Macklin had the feeling that it wasn't going to be something safe and comfortable.

"Mr. Macklin," Holliday said as he approached the table, "I'd like you to meet my friends. Virgil Earp . . . and his brother Wyatt. They're the law in this town."

"So I've heard."

"Virg, Wyatt, this here's the feller I was telling you about."

Wyatt was giving Macklin a particularly scrutinizing look. "I believe we've met before," he said quietly.

"We have?" Macklin's heart was hammering hard now. Was it possible he'd finally met someone who knew who he was? "I'm afraid I don't remember, Mr. Earp."

Neither Virgil and Wyatt looked like the demons Sarah had described. They were expensively dressed. Their hair was neatly trimmed and so were their full, drooping mustaches. If there was anything unsettling about them, it was the feeling that they looked out at the world through eyes that just naturally considered all other creatures inferior. It wasn't arrogance so much, Macklin decided, as a well-earned self-confidence, as though the Earps had survived any number of trials that would have destroyed mere mortals.

And not only survived—they had prospered, cleaning up some very tough towns, if the stories Macklin had heard that morning at Sarah's breakfast table were true. Of course, some of the stories suggested that their prosperity had more to do with the cuts they took from the liquor sold and the prostitutes hired in the town. Law and order, apparently, were relative terms here.

It took only the space of a second or two for Macklin to take their measure. He wasn't sure *how* he knew these things about the Earps. It was as though the various comments he'd heard—from Sarah, from snatches of conversation at the bar last night, from the men at the boardinghouse that morning—were all being assembled for him into a larger, clearer picture.

"Like I was tellin' you, the boy got his head whacked last night, out in the desert," Holliday explained. "Doc Shea told me he don't remember a thing."

Wyatt's eyes narrowed. "You look a little like a man I . . . met professionally once. In Dodge City, four, maybe five years ago. You look a bit thinner now, and you shaved your mustache. Johnny Waco, wasn't it?"

The name meant nothing to Macklin. "Did we . . . work together, Mr. Earp?"

The comment elicited a grim smile, half glimpsed beneath Earp's bushy mustache, and a chuckle. "I buffaloed you! Bent the barrel of my revolver around your thick skull and hauled you off to jail! You had a name for yourself, but I cut you down a peg." Wyatt's eyes measured him, watching for a response. Macklin became aware that both men had their hands near the weapons holstered on their hips. The tension in the air was palpable; it felt like everyone in the bar was watching the tableau, waiting.

He became aware especially of another man at a nearby table who looked so much like the two Earps in front of him that he almost had to be a brother, sitting with one hand inside his coat pocket. . . .

"I honestly don't remember it, Mr. Earp."

"That's convenient, mister," Virgil said, leaning back and allowing his coat to fall open, revealing a gold star with the words TOWN MARSHAL.

"I see you're carrying," Wyatt said.

Macklin wasn't sure what he meant.

"Your gun," Virgil added. "You should be aware that we have a gun law in Tombstone. You're supposed to check your weapons when you come into town."

"Ah! Sorry," Macklin said. "I didn't know—"

Virgil raised a hand. "Don't sweat it, son. Just so you know. We run a peaceful town here. We don't allow hur-rahing or gunplay. You can check your piece most places of business—your hotel. A saloon. Frank over there, behind the bar, will take it for you. You just pick it up when you want to ride out."

"I'll do that," Macklin said. "Thanks." He was thinking that he'd heard a number of gunshots the night before, when he'd come in on the stage. For a town with a strict gun law, there'd been a *lot* of shooting going on.

He started to turn away from the table, but Wyatt stopped him. "Not just yet, Mister . . . Macklin. I'd like to see something."

"Yes?"

"If you *are* Johnny Waco, you're pretty good with a gun. Doc, here, says you handled a gun last night like you were born to it . . . and considering the source, that's pretty high praise. Just how fast are you?"

"I don't know," Macklin said. He was getting tired of that refrain. "I don't remember."

"Why don't we just find out?" Carefully, Wyatt un-holstered his pistol, popped the cylinder, and dropped five cartridges into his palm, then he reholstered the empty weapon. Macklin, prodded by a wink and a nod from Holliday, did the same.

"You know, Mr. Macklin, "Wyatt said, standing beside the table. "Being a gunfighter is a lot more than being fast on the draw. If you are Johnny Waco—"

In midsentence, without so much as a twitch of warning, Wyatt's hand was dropping to the holstered pistol and dragging it clear of leather with lightning speed . . .

. . . and at the same instant, Macklin's hand was on his own gun, whipping it free of its holster with a crisp snap of gunmetal on leather . . . and then Macklin was staring down the barrel at the other man's startled, wide-eyed expression as he relaxed—ever so slightly—the killing pressure he'd just begun to exert on the trigger. . . .

For a long, trembling moment, the two stood there, a tableau graven in sweat-soaked flesh, dusty cloth, and gleaming metal. Wyatt had barely cleared leather, the muzzle of his revolver still pointed uselessly at the polished wood floor. Macklin stood erect, arm extended, his gun centered unwaveringly on the other man's head. The casino was eerily quiet, as everyone watched in breath-holding silence.

Ever so slowly, Wyatt Earp relaxed, almost muscle by muscle, and slid his gun back into its holster.

Doc Holliday shattered the silence with a harsh laugh that slipped into savage coughing. "Our dream just came true," he said at last, as a disgruntled-looking Wyatt sat down once more. Doc waved Macklin to an empty chair.

Macklin put his gun away and walked over. The men at the bar looked decidedly disappointed. There was nothing like a little bloodshed to make a morning memorable. Especially when it wasn't your own.

"That," Holliday said, "is something I never expected to see in all my born days! You just drew down on Wyatt

Earp, my friend, and that, as anyone in this territory'll tell you, takes some doing!''

"That would seem to establish your identity beyond doubt," Virgil said easily.

"Told you," Holliday said. "Told you I thought he looked a little like Waco, and the draw proves it! Whatever the dime-novels say, there aren't many men that fast with a gun!''

"I don't know," Wyatt said, thoughtful. "Waco didn't outdraw me last time we met."

"So? He's been practicing!''

"Wyatt isn't known so much for speed," Virgil said, "as for accuracy. But still and all, beating him is an accomplishment, mister.''

Macklin had the distinct impression that he'd just passed an important test. The air was noticeably less tense now, as the two Earps relaxed, and the other patrons of the Oriental Saloon turned away to their own interrupted drinks, games, and conversations.

"I have to be honest with you gentlemen," Macklin told them. "I don't know why I'm fast with a gun. And I don't think my name is Waco.''

Wyatt shrugged. "You're fast like Waco, faster even. And Waco has a name. No one's heard of 'Macklin.' ''

"Why is that important?''

"You've been hearing a little about the feud that's on, between us and the Clanton gang," Holliday said.

"No, I've been hearing a *lot*.''

"The Clanton Cowboys include quite a few names. Curly Bill Brocius. Johnny Ringo. Billy Claiborne. We don't exactly know how many are in that gang. The number changes, almost week to week. But we figure that Ike Clanton has six or eight he can count on all the time, and maybe another fifteen or twenty who ride with him once in a while.

They tend to hang out at the Clanton spread.

"Now we have our supporters in town, of course," Holliday went on. "The mayor, John Clum, also happens to be the editor of the *Tombstone Epitaph*. He's probably our biggest supporter . . . but he shoots words, not bullets. We have some friends who've worked with us here—Bat Masterson, you might have heard that name. Buckskin Frank Leslie. Luke Short."

"Unfortunately," Virgil said, "most of our friends are gone right now. They come and go, just like the Clanton people. But with Masterson, Short, and Leslie all out of town, we're just a bit outnumbered."

Macklin understood. "You're looking for allies."

"We're looking for a good man with a gun," Wyatt said. "Someone who might make the Clantons think twice about jumping us."

"You know," Virgil said thoughtfully, "it occurs to me that Johnny Waco, here, would be even more useful right now if he could ride out to the Clanton spread, talk to some of them, maybe get a feel for how strong they are right now."

"There's an idea!" Holliday said, snapping his fingers. "How about it, Johnny?"

The name was an uncomfortable fit. "I don't know. . . ."

"Listen, it's perfect!" Wyatt said, with all the oily smoothness of a professional con man. "You're new here in Tombstone. The Clantons don't know you from beans! Now they've got a big spread down south, toward the Sonora line . . . maybe twelve miles out of town. If you were to ride down there and ask for work, maybe talk to some of the hands, you could find out who's there right now, maybe even a little of what they're planning."

"After that," Virgil said, "you just hang around town. We'll let you know if we need your help. I can deputize you if it looks like we have to face down the Clantons.''

"It sounds dangerous.''

"Maybe,'' Holliday said. He winked. "But it pays well.''

"How well?''

"One thousand dollars,'' Virgil said, "to scout out the Clanton ranch, then make yourself available for . . . let's say, two weeks. How's that sound?''

It sounded good. Sarah was right. He didn't need the money. Not yet, anyway. But more than the money, he needed to insert himself into the life of this town. By associating with the town's law enforcement personnel, he would establish a kind of legitimacy for himself that he wouldn't be able to achieve on his own.

He was tempted. . . .

He was also aware of Sarah's hatred of the Earps, of *all* gunfighters. He liked Sarah and didn't want to lose her friendship or her respect by throwing in with people she thought were scoundrels or worse.

Shoot, if he took up with the Earps, she might not even want to have anything more to do with him.

Which might be just as well, come to think of it. She made him nervous with her questions . . . and she'd seen the thing in his chest. It might be a good idea not to let her get too close.

Not until he had some idea about who he really was and why he'd found himself out there in the desert.

"The money sounds right,'' he said. "I really ought to think about it, though.''

Holliday giggled, the noise squeaky and somehow ominous. "Wish they'd make me an offer like that, mister.'' He started coughing, pulling out his handkerchief and holding it to his mouth.

Macklin considered the offer as the others watched him

carefully. Getting involved in violence held no appeal for him. He wasn't quite sure how he'd managed to outdraw Earp just now. He'd seen Wyatt reaching for his gun and the rest had just . . . *happened*. As if by reflex. But where the hell had he developed reflexes like that?

But what if he couldn't move that fast next time? What if it wasn't just one man he faced, but a whole gang? A fast draw didn't help when you were outnumbered two or three or four to one. That was a great way to get yourself killed.

"So how about it?" Virgil said. "You in with us, Macklin?"

"I guess I am."

"Well, then," Virgil said, smiling for the first time. He reached across the table, offering his hand. "Welcome to Tombstone, Johnny Waco!"

"You boys want anything?" It was the girl who'd stopped him on the way in.

"No thanks, Linda Lou," Wyatt said, his eyes glittering. "Maybe later."

"Sure thing."

Macklin spent the next hour with Holliday and the Earps. As they talked, though, his mind raised a new and unsettling possibility, one that hadn't occurred to him before.

He *was* fast. Suppose he *was* a professional gunfighter? How else could he have come by his skill with a revolver?

And with that thought came another. Sarah thought he was a good man . . . but what if he found out that he wasn't a good man at all? What if he found out that he was a thief, say, or even a killer?

FIVE

THE CLANTON RANCH WAS A FAIR-SIZED COMMUNITY IN ITS own right. There was a big house and several barns, a number of bunkhouses for the hands and cowboys who rode the range and managed the cattle, and sheds and store-houses enough to serve a small town. There was even a small telegraph office, not far from the cookhouse, that let the Clantons keep in touch with the goings-on in Tomb-stone, and anywhere else they cared to know about.

In fact, the Clanton ranch was one of the biggest and richest in Cochise County. It had been the pride and joy of old Newman Hayes Clanton, before he'd been gunned down that August in an ambush on the Mexican border. Other ranchers in the region whispered, though, that the Clantons were a little quick with their branding irons and weren't all that particular about finding the owners of any strays that happened to wander onto their grazing lands.

The younger two of the three Clanton boys, Ike and nineteen-year-old Billy, weren't all that keen on being ranchers, though, and left most of the details to their older brother, Phineas. They thought of themselves as *cowboys*, but they didn't care so much for the idea of backbreaking work and long hours on the range. Their favorite pastime was hurrahing Tombstone and Charleston and some of the other communities in the area . . . riding in drunk, getting drunker, and raising holy hell with gunfire, shouts, and laughter.

At any given time there were a number of men on the ranch who had the reputation of being hell-raisers or worse. Curly Bill Brocius could usually be found hanging out on the Clanton spread, along with Johnny Ringo and quite a few others with decidedly checkered pasts. Their most lucrative pastime was the forays south across the border into Sonora, where they raided Mexican ranches of cattle and horses and brought them north for sale. Sometimes, it seemed like there was a war going on back and forth across the Sonoran border.

Of course, some thought that the ambush hadn't been staged by the Mexicans. There was a war, of sorts, on *this* side of the border, too.

At the moment, most of the hands and cowboys at the ranch were gathered around the corral near the cookhouse, cheering and yelling as Ike Clanton took on a half-broke horse.

The job of breaking wild, never-ridden horses was one common to all cowboys in the West, from Montana to the Mexican border. The horse was the one essential of ranch life and cattle driving—working cowboys needed six to eight mounts apiece, at least, just to handle the grueling work of round-up and driving—and every outfit kept large strings of horses ready for use.

The Clanton ranch was no exception. Cow ponies were pulled in from among the four-year-old mustangs living wild on the range; though a yearly roundup of wild horses was usually held in the spring, the Clantons had brought in a number of scrawny animals during the past couple of weeks to build up the strings. A professional bronco buster, who traveled the circuit of area ranches breaking ponies at five dollars a head, had already been through to start the process, but the real work of breaking the animals' spirits and teaching them to obey their human masters was up to the ranch hands.

Ike Clanton, boots planted in the soft earth of the corral, pulled hard on the reins as the animal before him reared and bucked, trying to throw the unfamiliar weight of the saddle on its back. Earlier, he'd lassoed the animal with a lariat, then snubbed it close to a hitching post to saddle and bridle it. Now he had it cross-hobbled, ropes tying its fore-feet and one hind leg, which limited most of its motions to straight up and down, and in tight, lurching circles around the corral, as Clanton pulled it down. The animal gave a particularly hard lunge back, dragging Clanton forward a step, and the cowboys watching from the corral fence cheered.

God damn it, he would *show* this animal who was boss!

If Ike Clanton didn't care for the drudgery of ranch work and herding, he liked the excitement of busting broncs, and he definitely liked being the center of attention. All three Clanton boys, Ike, Phineas, and young Billy, had been raised to enjoy the rough and tumble of ranch life. Their father had had them breaking cow ponies when they were just squirts, a means, he held, of building character, self-reliance, and self-respect.

Ike enjoyed proving that he was the boss, even when he was proving it to an animal. Tired out by the hobble, the horse was standing still now, eyes wide and rolling, nostrils flaring as it snorted and heaved. Slowly, Ike walked his way up the reins, keeping the pressure on. The animal seemed to have lost most of its fear of people, but it still didn't like that weight on its back.

The thing about busting broncs was that it was a great way of proving your worth to two-legged animals as well as the four-legged variety. A cowboy who couldn't handle a horse was a pretty poor specimen, and a man's reputation and worth were pegged to his ability to show a horse he was master. People were like horses, too, in one respect. They had to be *shown* who was boss. And he had quite a crowd this afternoon—his brother Billy, both of the McLaurys, Billy Claiborne, Jake Thurston, Pony Deal, Wes Fuller, and three or four others. Yeah, he'd show 'em.

With the animal breathing heavily and tossing its head, Ike tugged the rope ends that freed the hobbles. Reaching up, he grabbed the horse's left ear, then gave a vicious twist, launching himself into the saddle at the same time. The sharp pain in the horse's ear distracted it just long enough for Clanton to seat himself . . . and then the ride was on!

"Ha! You got 'im now, Ike!" Jake Thurston yelled from his perch atop a fence rail.

"Ride 'im good, boss!" the half-breed, Pony Deal, added with a shrill laugh.

Boss. That felt good. *Damned* good. The horse gave a sharp turn, spinning left. Clanton hauled back on the reins, dragging it around the other way. For a tense moment, the battle of wills between man and beast raged. He had a quirt, a short whip, ready in his right hand, but he didn't use it . . . yet.

Yeah, breaking a horse made Ike look *good*, and just now, it was important that Ike look his best. The horse gave a hard buck, and Ike brought his quirt down sharply on the animal's flank. Each time it bucked, he struck it with the quirt, stinging it, teaching it the one key lesson for the day: *Obey!*

"Ike!" That was Frank McLaury. "Don't lay into him so hard, fer crissakes!"

The interruption made Ike mad and he jabbed his spurs into the animal's sides. It bucked again, hard, and he slashed it again with the whip, eliciting a shrill, terrified whinny. He would show 'em. By God, he'd show 'em *all*.

"Jesus, Ike," Frank called again. "You're gonna kill the poor brute!"

Ike turned his head to make a sharp reply, digging in his spurs once more, and in that moment the horse beneath him gave a powerful lunge and buck, sending Ike flying . . .

. . . except that something went seriously wrong.

Like most cowboys on the southern ranges at the time, Ike was wearing Mexican spurs with bells, long rowels, and a long, curved cinch hook. The hook was slipped beneath the cinch strap while riding to keep the rider from being thrown . . . but as Ike cleared the saddle, his right hook locked with the saddle's cinch ring. He went flying and hit the ground, hard . . . but his right boot was still entangled with spur and cinch ring. The horse, suddenly free of the terrifying, hurtful weight on its back, leaped forward into a run, and Ike was dragged along beside, the animal's rear hooves pounding close beside his body.

He was in immediate danger of being kicked to death. Frank McLaury, reacting instantly, leaped to the back of a saddled horse inside the corral, spurred it to a run, and galloped up alongside. Leaning way over, he grabbed the cheek strap on Ike's horse and slid from his own saddle, unbuckling the cinches.

With a thud, Ike's saddle fell from the running horse, freeing Ike.

The next thing he knew, Ike was lying flat on his back

in the dust, ears ringing, blinking up at the sky through a cold, wet haze. He was wet, damn it! How had that happened?

Frank's face appeared above an empty bucket. "You okay, Ike? You got clipped a good 'un!" Dimly, Ike was aware of the others—Pony Deal and Wes Fuller and Jake Thurston—all leaning over him.

"Ike?" his younger brother Billy put in. "You hurt?"

"I'll kill him!" He tried to sit up, but the world was still spinning, the ground tilting dangerously beneath him. "I'll *murder* him!"

"Whoa, there, Ike. You were pushing him too hard, and your spur got tangled. It's not the horse's fault."

"I mean *you*, dammit!" Ike snarled. Rubbing his jaw, Ike sat up in the puddle of mud left when Frank had dumped a bucket of water on him. "You distracted me, damn you! Broke my concentration!"

"You're lucky that's *all* you broke," Jake Thurston said, and the others laughed.

"You damn near got your fool head kicked in, Ike," Billy added.

Slowly, Ike got to his feet. Frank tried to help him, but he shoved the other man away. "Leave me alone!"

"Simmer down, Ike!" Frank's brother, Tom McLaury, said. "Frank just saved your life, in case you didn't know it!"

The other men were quieting now, as they saw Ike get back to his feet. This wasn't so good, Ike thought. Not so good at all.

"Just leave me alone," Ike said, pushing past Frank and the others. He stooped and retrieved his hat. "I gotta clear my head."

His shoulder was sore where he'd landed on it and been dragged, but fortunately there'd been no serious damage.

Tom was right. Frank had saved his life. He had a blurred memory of Frank thundering in close to loose those cinches, just before the world had gone black for a moment. But it griped him like hell to have to admit it.

He leaned back against the corral fence. The rest kept their distance from him, as Wes Fuller started to move in on the bronc for another try.

Right now, things were at kind of a delicate balance inside the Cowboys. For a couple of years, the Clantons had pretty much run things to suit themselves, on the ranch, in Tombstone, and with the gang. Everyone had deferred to Old Man Clanton, and the Clanton spread had become a refuge for desperadoes, rustlers, and young toughs of every stripe.

Last August, though, Ike's pa had waylaid a smugglers' pack train across the Mexican border, coming back with a rich haul of horses, liquor, cattle, and silver bullion. Ten days later, those smugglers—or their pals—had set an ambush of their own. Newman Hayes Clanton and five other Cowboys had been killed.

And now the struggle was on to see who would lead the gang.

Of course, Ike had assumed it would be *him*. While Phineas was the oldest of the Clanton brothers, he was more interested in ranching than the gang's business. Ike had always been the one to take charge when Pa wasn't around, and he was the rightful new leader, the real heir. He *liked* being in charge, liked having his word being law on every acre from the Mexican border almost all the way in to Tombstone.

But more and more, lately, the other members of the Clanton Cowboys had been deferring to Curly Bill Brocius. Curly Bill was a favorite of just about everybody, big, bluff, good-natured with a booming laugh you could hear all the way out on the back forty. He was outgoing, jovial, and everyone liked him. Some folks in town had started calling the Clanton gang the Curly Bill gang, and that just plain set Ike's teeth on edge.

Curly Bill had been at the center of the incident that had first sparked trouble with the Earps. It had been back a year or so ago, when Curly Bill and Ike and a bunch of the boys had gone in to hurrah the town of Tombstone. They'd been pretty drunk and letting off a lot of steam, firing their pistols and just generally raising hell.

The town marshal had been a no-nonsense sort named Fred White. He and a deputized Wyatt Earp had moved in on the Cowboys, ordering them to give up their guns.

Well, White, the idiot, had grabbed Curly Bill's pistol by the barrel and tried to pull it away from him. The gun had gone off and White had taken a ball through his belly. Wyatt had stepped in with his drawn revolver and clipped Curly Bill across the side of the head with the barrel, laying him out cold.

There'd been a trial, of course, and Curly Bill Brocius had been acquitted. Hell, even White had admitted, just before he died, that the shooting had been accidental. But, damn it, Wyatt had had no cause to pistol whip Curly Bill that way. It made a man look bad, and it had started a feud between the Earps and the Clantons that had lasted to this day.

All of that had been before Pa had been bushwacked. Before Ike and Curly Bill had started sparring with one another, without really coming out and saying so, over who was going to lead the gang.

Now, Curly Bill was off on business up in Benson, arranging for the sale of a few hundred head of rustled cattle, and wasn't expected back until next week sometime. It seemed to Ike that now was the best shot he was going to get to prove once and for all that *he* was the boss here, and not Curly Bill.

He'd been trying to break that bronc to kind of drive home the point for the others about who was boss, who was the *man* around this ranch, but getting thrown like that—and tangled in his own gear—was a no-good way of going about it.

But . . . hell. Breaking mustangs wasn't the way to lead this bunch. He needed something else, something really spectacular, to make sure the rest of the gang knew he was the leader.

He'd been thinking a lot lately about what he could do to really drive home his claim. Something better than just acting tough with the other guys. Something that would make an honest-to-God *name* for him, clear from here to Tucson.

That something, as he saw it, was getting rid of the Earps once and for all.

At the moment, the Cowboys pretty much had things their own way outside of town. Hell, with County Sheriff John Behan in their pocket, they pretty much had all of Cochise County nailed down good and tight.

Tombstone, though, which was run by Town Marshal Virgil Earp, was squarely under the thumb of the Earps . . . and their pal Doc Holliday. They had the support of the so-called "Citizens' Law and Order League," that bunch of sissy-pants shopkeepers and schoolmarms and town dandies who claimed to represent *decent* folks in the area.

Everybody knew that sooner or later there was going to be a blowout between the two factions—Behan and the Clanton Cowboys against the Earps and their Law and Order League.

Wouldn't it be one rip-staver of a frolic if the Earps went

down for good and all, with Ike Clanton at the head of the boys?

Yeah. Sweet victory . . . and poor old Curly Bill wouldn't have a leg left to stand on. It would be the *Clanton* gang, the *Clanton Cowboys* from here on out.

And then he'd show 'em all just how this county could be wrung dry.

First, though, there were some fences that needed mending right here. Turning, rubbing his head, he walked toward the others. They were cheering and laughing as the horse, bucking furiously again, tossed Wes head over heals into the dirt, but they grew quiet again when Ike drew near. He could feel their eyes on him, feel the question in their minds.

"Frank?"

"Yeah?" Frank McLaury eyed him warily, like he might eye a rattlesnake, not sure whether it was going to slither off or strike.

"Look, I was outta line. I shouldn't have gone off half-cocked like that. Thanks for what you did." He offered his hand.

Frank looked startled, then grinned. He shook Ike's hand. "Any time, Ike."

Somehow, Ike managed to keep the smile frozen on his face and not say what he *really* thought. It was Frank's fault that he'd been thrown, but Ike knew better than to make an issue of it just now. The McLaurys were neighboring ranchers and an important part of the Clanton gang. He needed their support against Curly Bill.

He'd just put the word out later, behind Frank's back, and everybody would know the way things were. He *wouldn't* have been thrown if he hadn't been distracted.

Turning, he walked back into the center of the corral, where Wes was dusting himself off. "That-un's a widowmaker!'' Wes said, shaking his head and retrieving his hat. ''I don't think he can be broke!''

''Bullshit,'' Clanton said. He found his quirt, lying in the dust, and slapped it once against his gloved palm. ''We'll just see who's boss!'' He advanced toward the horse, which watched him nervously.

''Ike! What the hell you doin'?'' Tom McLaury called out.

''Gettin' back on!'' Ike replied. ''We're gonna see who's boss . . . or this horse is *dead*, and I don't really care which!''

And Ike reached for the horse's ear, blood in his eyes. . . .

✧ 2 ✧

DEATHSTALKER FELT PLEASANTLY SLUGGISH. THE MEAL IT HAD *consumed, the man and the foal, would take some time to digest, and in the meantime the Kra'agh was vulnerable. It had found a hiding place for itself on a rocky overlook in the hills just above the human town, a place to hunker down out of sight in the harsh, daylight hours, to think, to plan.*

Smoke stained the sky to the north, behind the silently waiting Kra'agh. A quick search of the habitation next to the barn had uncovered three more humans, an adult and two smaller beings that were presumably the rancher's mate and young. Deathstalker had killed them all and set the habitation ablaze. It would have been pleasant—and prudent—if it could have saved the other creatures for a later meal, but it couldn't take the chance of having the Kra'agh presence on this world discovered too soon.

Besides, there were lots *more of the creatures. Hunting on this primitive, isolated world would be very good. . . .*

Deathstalker spent a long time watching the activity in the town. Tombstone, *the human Max Carter had called* the place, in his mind. The vehicle trackway Deathstalker had been following ran past the ridge where the Kra'agh was hiding and down the hill, straight into that primitive collection of ramshackle huts, tents, and awkward-looking buildings. The Monitor survivor, it thought, was there. Among the humans.

It wondered what form the Monitor had taken. Sometimes, according to other Kra'agh scouts, vlotls or ganits disguised themselves as inhabitants of this planet, and voorls were enough like humans to pass for them, at least in the dark and with appropriate masks and clothing. Likeliest, though, this Monitor was itself a human, descendant of one of the humans taken by the Associative generations ago, tamed, civilized, and trained in Monitor ways. It would have an artificially intelligent implant to help it with the local language and culture, and possibly advanced weapons, as well.

The Kra'agh would have to move cautiously. If the Monitor survivor warned the humans . . . or worse, if it somehow managed to warn other Monitors offworld, then Kra'agh plans for this planet would be delayed, perhaps indefinitely.

The Monitor would have to die.

Deathstalker examined again the artifacts it had taken from the habitation. Human weapons were almost laughably primitive, but they should be deadly enough, at close range. The metal construct the human had thought of as a pistol or revolver or Navy Colt carried six metal slugs in a revolving set of chambers designed to propel the slugs, one at a time, out the hollow guide tube by the explosive expansion of gas generated in a chemical detonation within a brass tube or cartridge. With so short a guide tube, it would be effective, Deathstalker reasoned, at ranges of only a few draz. The larger weapon, the Winchester, operated *on the same principle but was much longer and employed more powerful cartridges. It would be accurate at longer ranges ... out to perhaps a few eights of* draz *or more.*

Deathstalker was confident that it could use local weapons, if need be, to kill the Monitor without arousing the suspicions of the natives. But to get close enough to use them, it would need to blend in with the locals.

A shimmer appeared in the air around the crouching Hunter, a thickening of the air as Deathstalker focused its mind on the ni-shav *foci within its harness. All that the human Max Carter had been, its form, its thoughts, its memories, its basic biochemistry had been patterned and stored within Deathstalker's soulcatcher.*

Eons before, in the boundless, predator-haunted forests and mountains of the Kra'agh homeworld, the Hunters had developed the purely mental power of projecting the image of what they wanted the prey to see. Born of a subtle blend of empathic and telepathic skills, the ni-shav *ability allowed a Kra'agh to seem to take the shape and texture of a boulder, say, or a* ghanigh *shrub, in a kind of telepathic camouflage designed to mask the Hunter's presence until the prey was within easy striking range.*

Technology had enhanced and extended the power of ni-shav, *and* gah-*projection. Fed by data downloaded from the soulcatcher, computer nexuses within Deathstalker's harness could project the* gah, *or image of a patterned creature or artifact. The camouflage would be less than completely effective at close range or in bright sunlight, but it would serve well enough at night or in the shadows.*

Minutes passed as the soulcatcher's feed continued to thicken and twist the air about the Kra'agh with subtle energies. The hulking mass of the Kra'agh Hunter appeared to dwindle, to fold in upon itself. Snakelike neck and flat, triangular head reformed into the clumsy ovoid of a human skull, covered over by pasty, scaleless flesh like pink clay. In a few moments more, Max Carter stood on the ridgetop, staring down at the town.

SIX

✦ 1 ✦

VIRGIL EARP HAD NEVER SEEN ANYTHING LIKE IT.

The ranch and the barn both had burned to the ground, leaving little left at all but smoldering black stumps and ashes. The stink of the fire still hung above the Carter homestead like a bad memory, thick and suffocating.

Sheriff Johnny Behan stood nearby, hands on his hips, surveying the scene of burned-out desolation. One of Behan's deputies, a kid named Perkins, was rooting around in the rubble of what once had been the Carter house.

"What I don't see, Marshal," Behan was saying, "is how one fire could've jumped from the barn to the house, or vice-versa, and gotten 'em both. Hasn't been windy, and they're set a fair piece apart from each other."

Virgil didn't answer.

He didn't like Behan. None of the Earps did. John Behan was a venal, weak, mean little son-of-a-bitch who never should've been appointed county sheriff. The job brought with it the job of collecting taxes throughout the county, with ten percent going into the sheriff's pocket, a position that was worth a cool forty thousand a year, easy. Not satisfied with that, Behan was up to his neck with the Clanton–

Curly Bill gang. Just a couple of weeks earlier, the Bisbee
Stage had been robbed, and two of the gunmen had been
identified as Frank Stilwell and Pete Spence, both pals of
the Clantons . . . and Stilwell was one of Behan's deputies.
The Earps had brought both men in, and everyone knew
that Behan and the Clantons were mixed up in the affair.
There wasn't any way of proving it, though.

Things were coming to a head, right enough, with Behan
and his Clanton buddies running the county, and the Earps
maintaining the peace inside Tombstone. So far. . . .

What Virgil couldn't figure, though, was why Behan had
called him out here. Perkins had ridden into town half an
hour ago, out of breath and bug-eyed, claiming the Carter
stead had burned to the ground, and Sheriff Johnny wanted
the law, the town law, out there right away. Max Carter's
place was outside the Tombstone city limits—clearly in Behan's jurisdiction, but it was close enough that you could
argue there was some overlap. Virgil—despite Morgan's
and Wyatt's protests, and Wyatt's warning to "watch that
buzzard and don't turn your back to him"—had ridden out
to the Carter place with Perkins to see what was going on.

"You have any ideas, Sheriff?" Virgil asked finally.

"Yeah," the man said. He licked his lips. "Apaches.
Gotta be. I figure they rode down outta the Dragoon Mountains. Probably caught Max and his family sleeping. They
would've killed Max. Probably took Emma and the kids
with 'em and torched the place on the way out."

"That doesn't seem too likely, does it?"

"Why not? It's happened before."

"To start with, there haven't been any problems with the
Indians lately. Not with the Apaches. Not with any of the
others. We'd have heard something."

"But—"

"Besides . . . see those?" He pointed at a pair of charcoaled lumps still smoking beneath the tumbledown wrack of what had once been the barn's roof.

"Yeah . . ."

"Horses. And . . ." He pointed again, this time indicating a corral twenty yards from the barn. A single mare was pacing and fretting inside, her eyes rolling wildly, her nostrils flaring. The animal was terrified, clearly, but still very much alive. And still here.

"If Apaches had raided this place," Virgil said, "don't you think they'd have taken the horses before setting the place on fire?"

"Well . . . mebee they was drunk. Or crazy."

"Sheriff," Virgil said patiently. "Why did you call me out here?"

"If we got Injun trouble, Earp, you *Federales* have to be brought in. You're Deputy Marshal for the southern Arizona Territory, and that makes this sort of thing *your* job. We may need to notify the Army, out t' Fort Huachuca."

"John! Johnny!" Perkins screamed. He dropped the blackened piece of timber he'd been lifting and stumbled back a few feet, his face white. Then he turned suddenly and vomited noisily into the ash.

Virgil and Behan joined him a moment later and stared at what he'd found.

There wasn't a lot left. It looked like it might have been a woman—you could still see her breasts and one black arm was still clutching a smaller figure that had died beside her. Both bodies were charred black; the stink was indescribable.

Despite the cooked flesh, it was possible to make out one horror farther. Both the woman and the little girl had had their throats slashed so deeply that the heads of both of them had nearly been torn off. It was hard to tell, but it looked like their bellies had been slashed open, too. Their jaws gaped wide open, teeth shockingly white against charred muscle; rather than having passed out from smoke, the way most fire victims did, it looked like both of them had died in agony.

"Oh, Jesus *Christ* . . ." Behan said, before himself turning and vomiting.

Virgil pulled a handkerchief out of his frock coat pocket and pressed it against his nose and mouth. His eyes were watering. His stomach twisted in painful knots, but he fought back the gorge and managed to walk away, his cold dignity intact.

No. An Apache war party would have taken the horses. They would have taken the woman and the little girl, too, for some sport up in their mountain hideaway before they finally finished them off. Or maybe the kids would've just been taken and raised as part of the tribe. No, this filthy business wasn't the work of Indians.

But if not Indians, who?

Virgil was tempted to blame Behan himself . . . or maybe his Clanton pals . . . but that didn't make sense. Behan didn't want the Earps poking around in his territory, out in the county, and he sure as hell didn't want the governor calling in troops.

Besides, much as he hated the bastards, Virgil didn't think that even someone as mean as Ike Clanton could've been guilty of this. And from the way Behan and Perkins were retching back there, well . . . Virgil was pretty sure that *that* wasn't an act.

He started poking around, searching the ground between the wreckage of the house and the barn. Yeah. *There* was something. . . .

Virgil knelt to study a patch on the ground. There were

ashes scattered all about from the fire, an inch thick and still pretty hot, but here was a patch of mud next to the watering trough that hadn't been covered over.

And sure enough, something had stepped here, leaving a couple of good, clear prints. The question was, what the hell kind of varmint made tracks like *that?*

Virgil Earp had considerable experience with tracking and knew the look of tracks for every varmint in the region, two-legged and four. This one, though, just plain had him stumped. It looked something like the letter "H," with two toes sticking out ahead and two sticking out behind, with a kind of oval shape in the middle, forming the crossbar. If you looked real close, at the oval in the middle, you got the impression that whatever had pressed its weight down in the mud had had rough, wrinkled skin . . . maybe even scales, though it was hard to tell.

Some lizards had tracks a little like this thing—some birds, too. And lizards had scales. But dammit, this thing was eighteen inches long. Carefully, he pressed his thumb down in the mud nearby, taking a guess at how much pressure the thing had exerted on the ground when it had stood here. Yeah . . . the varmint that made these had been bigger than most men . . . maybe half the weight of a fair-sized horse, three hundred fifty, maybe four hundred pounds, easy. Maybe more.

Lizards and birds did *not* leave eighteen-inch tracks, and they did not weigh four hundred pounds. This just didn't make sense.

Gently, he touched his forefinger to the bottom of the print, then brought some of the ash-mud to his face, sniffing cautiously. There was something there, something odd. He could smell wood fire, all right, but there was another odor, too, lingering in the wet ash. Something musky and dark and sweetish. Something a little like rotten meat, the sick-sweet stink of dead bodies in the sun . . . though maybe that was just the lingering smell of dead horses and . . . other things, cooked by the fire.

What the devil was it?

He sensed movement behind him and spun sharply, coming to his feet, his hand hovering near the .45 holstered at his hip. Behan was there, looking sick, and not even aware that he'd just come close to being shot.

"You . . . found something?" Behan asked. He wiped his mouth with the back of his hand. He was death-white and looked ready to start upchucking again, any moment.

"Nothing that makes any sense, Sheriff." Virgil allowed himself to relax and surveyed the burned-out ruins. "It wasn't Indians. It wasn't white men. What's left?"

"Greasers?"

"Mexicans might have tried a cross-border raid," Virgil agreed, "especially if they were upset about your pals, the Clantons, rustling cattle down their way." He couldn't resist throwing in that one, small dig. "But I think the same arguments still hold. Mexican marauders would've taken the horses . . . and probably the woman, too."

"Maybe the woman and kids were already dead."

"Maybe. I hope for their sake they were."

"Maybe Max Carter did it. Killed his whole family and burned the place down to cover it."

"Maybe." Virgil doubted that even more than he doubted the idea of Mexican bandits. He *knew* Max Carter—a good, steady citizen. A member of the Law and Order League. A family man. A devoted father. A good rancher. Steady and dependable. He'd come west from Virginia to stake a claim in the silver rush. He hadn't gotten rich, but he'd pocketed enough when he'd sold his claim to let him buy this spread and a few horses.

No, it hadn't been Max. Virgil wouldn't accept that for a minute.

"I think," he said slowly, "we just have to put this one down to death by misadventure. The barn caught fire, sparks landed on the house, and the whole shebang went up. The place burned so fast that they couldn't get out in time."

"You really believe that, Earp?"

No, Virgil thought. *No, dammit, I don't.*

But he didn't give Behan any answer.

He couldn't.

⋄ 2 ⋄

Deathstalker sensed Painspinner's approach long before the other Kra'agh reached the top of the ridge. It heard the faint slither and hiss of armored flesh, a clatter of stones, smelled the familiar sweetness of mingled Kra'agh skin secretions, blood, and decaying flesh. It could even sense the cold slickness of the other Hunter's thoughts.

At the time, Deathstalker was a rock. Lying on the ridge, its ni-shav *talent focused on the grainy, rough cragginess of a granite boulder, the Kra'agh mimicked perfectly the surrounding geology of that wind-blown ridge crest. It had caught some more food that way . . . a small, furred leaf-eater with long ears and powerful hind legs that had wandered too close to the innocuous gray boulder and been snatched up by a lightning strike by one of the Kra'agh's feeder-hands.*

Deathstalker had tasted the small being's terror and pain as it had probed the thing's warm body cavity with its sucking tongue, feeding slowly to savor the ebb of a fluttering, struggling life. When the shrill squeaks had ceased, Deathstalker swallowed the carcass.

Tasty.

This world would provide a staggering diversity of tastes, of textures, of hot, pleasantly gibbering terror and iron-tasting blood for a long time to come.

"Cha-kahrr!" a voice said nearby, in the veh-*tongue.* "Cha-kehrr!" *It was both greeting and boast. "I have hunted. I have eaten."*

"Cha-kahrr! Cha-kehrr!" Deathstalker agreed. Within the image of the rock, one of its eyes swiveled to study its companion.

Painspinner wore the image of a recent kill. It appeared to be a human male, wearing the crude leather and home-spun garments these beings affected for no reason that Deathstalker could understand, with stringy black growths on the face above the slit of an omnivore-toothed mouth and a broad-brimmed covering on the head. It carried a weapon—a Winchester like the one Deathstalker had ac-quired.

There were notches carved into the weapon's wooden stock. Deathstalker found that interesting. Ages ago, Kra'agh Hunters had marked their kills in that way on the arm bones of victims worn as trophies. Was there such a thing as Hunters among these food-animal humans? Tro-vakis *running with the* kroth.

A human analogy would have spoken of wolves among the sheep.

"I'm Henry Attwater," Painspinner said, adopting the slow, clumsy, and high-pitched chirps and squeaks and blunt-edged syllables the humans used for speech. "You may call me Hank."

"Howdy . . . Hank," Deathstalker said, searching the memory stores that once had belonged to the human, Car-ter. He let the ni-shav *illusion fade, let the boulder-shape blur and melt and reshape itself into the image of the hu-man recently devoured. "Max Carter's the name."*

Communicating in . . . the language was called En-glish . . . communicating in English was ponderously slow, but Kra'agh Hunters were perfectionists, adopting as many of the habits and peculiarities of their prey as they could in order to successfully blend in with the herd, to let them move in close and strike without warning.

It was also a means of displaying, trophylike, the souls of those devoured.

"What's that smell?" the image of Hank Attwater asked, still in English.

"The human village," Deathstalker replied, but he spoke again in the veh-tongue. English lacked the proper emphasis of tastes and smells, making it a cold and ill-suited language for the full range of Kra'agh expression. "The scents are rich."

"Appetizing. I can taste . . . blood. And fear."

"And other things. Reproductive urges. Anger. Strong emotions of every kind. The richness, the flavor of life it-self." It had been sampling the tastes rising on the breeze from the town below for a long time now, identifying, cataloging them in its mind. It estimated that there were eight eights of eights of eights of the creatures down there, each with its own, individual smell.

Deathstalker wanted to sample them all.

But . . . as the humans said, business first.

"The Monitor that eluded us in the desert has almost certainly hidden itself in that collection of dwellings," Deathstalker told its partner.

"Have you scented it?"

"I am not certain. There are many, many eights of eights of separate scentlines. Sometimes, I think I might have tasted the one we seek. But we will need to get closer to be sure, to separate it from the others."

"I want its blood."

"As do I."

"It will be risky, entering that habitation area. Especially in full light."

"Agreed." Deathstalker thought about the problem a moment. "We should probably restrict our movements to nighttime unless absolutely necessary and remain out of sight as much as possible. It should be safe enough, however, so long as they don't see us close-up and in full light. The humans will not notice us if they are not expecting us."

"The human I patterned has no concept of other worlds, of other species than its own. I find that . . . astonishing."

"Genuine primitives. They believe themselves alone in the universe . . . alone or under the care and supervision of a deity they believe cares for them." Deathstalker had tasted the idea of "God" in the terrified mind of the human he'd devoured.

"When we secure this place as a game preserve," Painspinner said, "we will teach them to worship new deities."

"For as long as their species survives to serve us, at any rate. If they serve us well, we might even permit a few to survive, as breeding stock. I believe these creatures will be excellent as a long-term source of both food and sport, once they're broken."

"All of that is for the future. We must find the Monitor and kill it before it can warn the Associative of our activities here."

Deathstalker glanced up at the local sun. "Do we dare enter the town now? Or should we wait for darkness?"

"As you say, fellow Hunter, we should be safe enough if we keep to the shadows. The longer we wait, the greater the risk that our prey escapes."

"Agreed. I suggest, however, that but one of us should enter the village at a time."

"Agreed. And I should be the first."

"Why?"

"Hank Attwater," Painspinner said, chirping again in the painfully limited English of the humans, "has him some friends in that town. Powerful friends."

"Indeed? Humans who will help us find our prey?"

"Yes."

"What are these friends called?"

"Clantons," Attwater said, and his thin lips sketched the shadow of a cold, human smile. "Hank Attwater is a member of a tribe of humans called 'Clantons,' and they control virtually everything that goes on in that town.

"With their help, it shouldn't take us long to find the Monitor at all!"

⋄ **3** ⋄

MACKLIN DECIDED THAT IF HE WAS GOING TO MAKE IT ALL the way out to the Clanton ranch, he was going to need a horse. The trouble was that he wasn't quite sure how to go about getting one . . . or how he was going to control the animal once he did.

Well, if he could draw a gun through some mysterious agency outside his control, perhaps it made sense that he already knew how to ride as well and just didn't know it consciously. Riding was certainly a basic survival skill in Tombstone. Transport throughout the region seemed pretty much limited to travel on foot, by horse-drawn wagon or coach, or on horseback. Macklin couldn't recall ever having ridden one of the beasts, but he needed to get to the Clanton ranch, and Doc Holliday had told him he could probably pick up a nag on the cheap at a place in town called the O.K. Corral.

The corral was a fair-sized complex of fenced-in spaces, sheds, and a small barn, tucked in behind the photography gallery and rooms-to-let of one Camillus Fly between Allen

Street and Fremont. Folks who rode into town and planned to stay awhile could stable their horses there, and the Wells Fargo office kept fresh teams there for their stage.

And as Holliday had suggested, people who wanted to buy or sell horses often did it through the stable and the corral. A kid named Jimmy was working there, watering the animals and grooming them out, and when Macklin approached him, his freckled face split in a big grin and he said that the Widow Thompson had a chestnut mare up for sale . . . twelve years old, but in really good shape. He grabbed the animal's muzzle and made it bare an alarming smile as proof; Macklin didn't know what it was he was supposed to see in that display of teeth, but the asking price was twenty dollars, and he paid it on the spot, using one of the double eagles from his cache.

"Ol' Molly, here, ain't as young as she used t'be, mister," Jimmy told him, gentling the animal by stroking its long nose, "and she ain't fast, but she's steady and she'll get ya where you wanna go."

"That's all I really need," Macklin told him. "Transportation." He ran his hand through his lank hair, looking ruefully at the animal. He'd taken the bandage off his head that morning. The wound seemed to have closed up pretty well . . . and he didn't like the way the wrappings had made him stand out in a crowd.

"Where you headed, anyways?"

Macklin saw no harm in telling him. "Thought I'd ride out to the Clanton ranch," he said easily. "Heard they might have work out there."

"Wouldn't know nothin' 'bout that, mister," the boy said, his eyes suddenly shuttered. "But . . . you watch yourself, okay? That's a pretty tough crowd. Specially now, since ol' man Clanton kicked off last summer. They *say* they's cowboys, but most folks around these parts know different. Uh . . . you gonna need tack?''

"Tack?"

That was when Macklin found out he also needed to buy a saddle and bridle. Twenty-five dollars more, and he had a worn leather saddle, harness, and reins. Jimmy had to show him how to throw the saddle across a blanket over the animal's back, connect the straps, and cinch the girth. "Ol' Molly here'll puff herself up on you, if y'ain't careful," he said. Demonstrating, he leaned into the animal and slapped her side, hard, then drew the girth tight as she expelled a noisy breath. It looked like it ought to hurt the animal, but Molly didn't seem to mind.

Jimmy led the animal by its bridle out of the stable and into the harsh morning light. Thanking the boy, Macklin started to climb aboard as he'd seen other men do it in the town, putting the toe of his boot in one of the stirrups and hauling himself up with a hand on the saddle's pommel. It was a *long* way up, but he managed to swing his leg over the animal's back and settle into the saddle with a comfortable creak of leather.

"Jeez, mister!" Jimmy exclaimed, still holding the animal's bridle. "Don't you know *anythin'* 'bout ridin'?"

He looked down at the kid. Being mounted gave a man a whole new perspective on the world. "I beg your pardon?"

"Y' mounts from the *near* side! *Never* from the off side! What are ya, an *Injun*?"

Macklin filed this piece of enigmatic information for later use. He wasn't sure why one side of the horse was called "near" and the other "off," but evidently it was a breach of local etiquette to clamber aboard the animal from its right side. "Does that mean I get down on the right?" He was pleased with making the connection. Why else would it be called the "off side"?

Jimmy looked at him as though he were the biggest idiot ever born, and released the bridle. "Mister . . . you pullin' my leg? This here's some kinda joke, ain't it?"

But Macklin couldn't answer that right away. With a sure hand on her bridle gone, Molly had taken it into her head to wander toward the water trough nearby with heavy clop-clops of her hooves, taking her hapless rider with her. There didn't appear to be any way to guide the animal, and the mysterious agency that had guided his hand in a quick draw didn't surface to help him out. He suspected that the reins, two long strips of leather, one coming back from each side of the horse's head, had something to do with the process, but he didn't know what. He held one in each hand, battling a rising sense of utter bafflement as Molly dropped her head at the trough and began noisily drinking. He had the feeling that he was getting in *way* over his head.

Money proved to be the door to a solution, however. He offered Jimmy another twenty dollars to teach him what he needed to know. The kid's eyes had bugged wide open at that, and his jaw had dropped in a way that suggested that twenty dollars was more than he earned in a year mucking out the stables.

It took nearly an hour, most of it in practice, but at the end of that time, Macklin could walk Molly about, making her go pretty much in whatever direction Macklin wanted. He knew how to get her started with a sharp cluck of the tongue and a touch of his boots to her sides, and how to stop her with an even tug at the reins and a gentle "whoa!" He knew how to turn her with a flick of the appropriate rein across her neck, and he knew to let her have her head when they came to an obstacle in the path so that she could see it and step across. He could even get her to break into a trot, though Jimmy warned him not to overdo it. Horses got hot and tired just like people did, and pushing them too far would kill them.

"I appreciate the help, son," Macklin said. He felt a bit more comfortable now, though Jimmy's repeated warnings, that a horse had a mind of its own and he had to show her who was boss, had him a little nervous yet.

"Hey, mister?"

"Yeah?

"You're the guy everyone's been talkin' 'bout, ain't you?"

"I don't know. Depends on what they're saying, I guess."

"I ain't seen you around here before, and you sure don't know much 'bout horses or ridin'. You're the guy what lost his memory, ain't you?"

"I'm afraid so." Macklin had been learning, though, that the story of his memory loss covered a multitude of sins.

"That's crazy. I mean . . . you even fergot how t'ride?"

"I guess so. I don't remember."

Jimmy chuckled at that. "Well, Molly's a smart horse, and she shouldn't give you any trouble. You just remember to watch out for them Clantons!"

"I'll do that." Macklin reached into a pocket, extracted another ten-dollar piece, then flipped it, shining in the sun, to Jimmy. "Look . . . can I count on you to kind of keep quiet about this?" he asked. "It could be embarrassing."

The real problem was that if the tough cowboys and ranch hands and miners and other rough-and-tumble sorts who called Tombstone home found out that the man with no memory hadn't even remembered which side of a horse to mount on, "Johnny Waco" would become far too much the town's center of attention. That sort of attention could be dangerous in a place like this.

"You bet, mister!" Jimmy said, snapping the spinning coin from the air. "Mum's the word! It'll be our secret!"

"Good. I might want to talk to you later. There's lots of things I don't remember, you know? Things you could help me with."

"You bet!" The kid's eyes glowed with the prospect of more gold coins. "You can find me right here, most times. Jes' ask fer Jimmy!"

"That I will, Jimmy. Thanks."

He laid the reins on the side of Molly's neck and gave a gentle tap with his boots. The gentle mare started walking. Jimmy raced ahead and opened the gate, and Macklin walked the horse out onto Fremont Street.

"You jes' remember what I said about the Clantons!"

"I will, Jimmy. I'll remember."

SEVEN

✦ 1 ✦

IT TOOK MACKLIN LONGER THAN HE'D EXPECTED TO REACH the Clanton ranch, almost three hours, and the sun was blazing down from a clear-blue sky, beating at his head and neck by the time Molly ambled up to a corral and stable not far from the ranch cookhouse. Several cowboys were there, lounging about against the fence rails in the shade of the stable.

"Hey, lookit the shorthorn!" one called out. The others laughed.

"Whatcha want out this way, mister?" one of the men said around a piece of straw stuck between grinning lips.

Carefully, Macklin stood in his stirrups and swung his right leg over Molly's rump, dismounting on the proper side. He had to steady himself on the saddle when his boots hit the ground. He felt light-headed, a little weak in the knees . . . and good *Lord* but how his backside was hurting! It was all he could do to loop the reins around a hitching post and walk over to the fence.

He'd never dreamed that riding could hurt that much.

"This the Clanton ranch?" he asked tightly. He had to clench his jaw to keep from wincing.

"Who is it wantin' t'know, tenderfoot?"

"Looks t'me," one of the other cowboys said, grinning, "like it's more'n his *feet* that are tender!"

"Name's Johnny Waco. I heard maybe there was work to be had out here."

That elicited guffaws and chuckles from the hands. One of the men, a tough-looking kid in chaps and a leather vest, walked over to Macklin. "What makes you think we'd hire a greenhorn like you?"

"Ha! You tell him, Billy!" someone shouted.

Macklin was tired, he was sore, and he wasn't in any mood to put up with nonsense. "If you're not hiring," he said, "fine. But I didn't come all the way out here to get insulted."

"Hey, Billy!" a swarthy-skinned man with squinty eyes and a bright red vest called out. "He could take a job bustin' broncs!"

"Yeah! We've been needin' someone t'tame Lightnin'!" That brought on another gale of laughter.

"Whaddaya say, mister?" Billy said, grinning. "You want a job bustin' broncos? We can fix you right up!"

Macklin allowed himself a small smile. He wasn't quite sure what a "bronco" was, or why it needed to be busted, but he could tell by the cowboys' grins and elbow nudges that he was being set up. "That doesn't quite sound like what I had in mind," he said. "But listen. I was told I should talk to Ike Clanton. Is he the guy in charge here?"

"Anything you got to say to Ike," the kid said, eyes narrowing, "you can say to me."

"And . . . who are you?"

"Claiborne's the name. Billy Claiborne."

"You ought t' watch yourself with him," one of the hands shouted. "Billy there claims he's gonna be the next

Billy the Kid!'' He said it in such a way that Macklin assumed he was supposed to know that name. He didn't, but it did tell him that Billy Claiborne was someone to watch out for.

"Well, Mr. Claiborne,'' Macklin said. ''I've been hearing that the Clantons are looking for trouble with the Earps, in town. Sounded like they could use some help.''

"What, against the *Earps*?'' Claiborne turned the name into a sneer. ''Anytime we need help against the likes of *them* . . .''

"Sounds like you have everything well in hand, then,'' Macklin said. ''But you see, I don't have any reason to like the Earps myself.'' He reached up and rubbed the side of his head, pretending to remember. ''One of them laid the barrel of his pistol up alongside my head a couple years back, in Dodge. Hurt like hell.''

Claiborne laughed. ''Buffaloed ya, huh? Yup. That'd be Wyatt. He likes clubbing guys with his pistol, he does.''

"I've been looking to get even for a long time.''

Claiborne appeared to consider this, but then shook his head. ''Look, stranger. We got no need for grub-line riders here. 'Specially if'n we don't know 'em.''

"Yeah, mister,'' the swarthy man said. ''You wanna work for us, you gotta have, whatchacallit, refurnces!''

Claiborne folded his arms across his chest. ''Mister, you'd be best off just turnin' around and headin' back the way you came.''

"I'd like to see Ike, if I could.''

"Mister Clanton ain't here, stranger. He went on into town a couple of hours ago. Maybe you can catch him there.''

Damn. If Claiborne was telling the truth, he and Clanton had crossed paths somewhere out in the desert between here and Tombstone. Well, that was hardly surprising. The desert was a big place.

Macklin glanced at the other hands, who were watching the conversation with considerable interest. He didn't see any way to press the matter. He shrugged. "Okay. Mind if I water my horse first, though?"

Claiborne jerked a thumb at a trough near the cookhouse. "Help yourself."

"Thanks."

Untying Molly, he led the horse at a slow walk past the corral and over to the trough. There, he let her drink and scooped up a double handful of water for himself as well, before splashing more over his head and neck. The skin on his forehead and neck was painful to the touch. He was going to have a hell of a sunburn before this was over.

"You really should wear a hat, mister."

He looked up and found himself staring at a man a little older than Macklin . . . in his late twenties, perhaps, or early thirties. He looked pleasant enough and seemed to lack the aggressive, even hostile attitude of the others.

"Beg pardon?"

"A hat." The man glanced at the ranch hands. "That's how *they* knew you were a greenhorn, y'know. Nobody but a greenhorn would go out riding in the middle of the day without a hat t'keep the sun off. Even in October, the sun can get to you out there. And boots, too. *No* one goes out ridin' without good boots."

"That," he said, "sounds like the best advice I've heard all day. Who're you?"

"Name's Finn."

"I'm Johnny Waco. Pleased to meet you."

Finn shrugged. "Likewise. Hey, I heard you asking about Ike."

"Yep. I heard he's a good man to know in these parts."

Finn made a face and looked away. "Depends."

"On what?"

"On whose side you're on. On whether or not Ike likes you. On whether or not you're a part of the gang."

"The gang?"

" 'The Cowboys,' they call themselves. They get away with murder in these parts, y'know, and they've got the county sheriff in their hip pockets. They pretty much run things in this county. If it weren't for the Earps . . ." He let the thought trail off.

"Who all's in the gang, anyway?"

"Oh, bunch of guys. Tough guys, too. Curly Bill Brocius, he's the leader, really, only he ain't around right now." Finn had been reticent at first, but once he started talking, it was like he couldn't stop. "Ike's kinda taken over for him, in his absence, like. Johnny Ringo. I guess he's about the most famous. The most *dangerous*. And there's the McLaurys, Tom and Frank. Frank, he's got a reputation, y'know? A dead shot. And there's Billy Clanton. Hank Attwater. Wes Fuller. And Billy Claiborne—you met him already. Those other guys there, Jake Thurston, Tom Howe. The guy with the red vest is a half-breed Apache named Pony Deal. Mebee a dozen others or so, though guys keep coming and going, y'know?"

"Billy Claiborne says they're gonna take care of the Earps. That's good. They have a plan yet?"

"Shoot. I don't think Ike would know a plan if it bit him."

"Yeah? I heard that Ike has some powerful friends in town. Like Sheriff Behan?"

Finn was about to answer when Claiborne came up behind Macklin. "You ask too many questions, Waco. And Finn, I think you got your nose in where it don't belong. Ike wouldn't like it."

Macklin saw the flash of anger in Finn's eyes, followed almost at once by a look of sheer hatred. Obviously, Finn didn't care much for Claiborne . . . and he had the feeling he didn't like Ike Clanton either.

"I'm just going," Macklin said, with a disarming smile. "Thanks for the water. He looked at Finn. "Nice talking to you, Mister . . ." He waited for the man to supply a last name.

"Clanton," the man said, surprising Macklin. "Phineas Clanton." He turned then and walked away without another word.

◆ **2** ◆

IKE CLANTON WAS FURIOUS, AND THAT ALWAYS MADE PEOPLE nervous. "Son of a bitch!" he snarled, loud enough so that everyone in Hafford's Tavern could hear. "The Earps are all cowards! Everybody knows that! Somethin' ought to be *done*!"

They'd ridden into town, he and Billy and both McLaurys, Tom and Frank, and gone in to Hafford's Tavern, a modest establishment at Allen and Fourth Streets selling both retail and wholesale liquor, run by the portly and gentlemanly Colonel R. F. Hafford. They'd checked their guns on the rack behind the bar, as the law required, and then proceeded to do some serious drinking.

"I said it before, and I say it again! The Earps are *cowards*! They'll never fight!"

They were sitting at a large, round table toward the back of the saloon, a spot that let them keep an eye on whoever might come through the swinging-leaf doors. There were a fair number of other patrons there—most of them at least moderately well-to-do . . . mining engineers and foremen, gentlemen from about town, drummers and dandies, with only a few miners, cowboys, and similar riffraff scattered about the floor. Colonel Hafford wasn't fussy, but his establishment did tend to cater to the better class of Tombstone citizens.

And of course, someone as powerful and as well-connected as Ike Clanton and his pals was always welcome.

The love of Ike Clanton's life—at least for *this* week—sat on his lap, trying to get him to calm down. Her name was Linda Lou Evans, and she was a prostitute who usually worked out of Madame LeDeau's bagnio down on Sixth Street, but sometimes she used Hafford's as a place of assignation, working the engineers and businessmen who liked to come here and spend. She also liked to hang out sometimes over at the Oriental, working as a waitress and talking up the boys. The johns over there didn't usually have as much money to spend as the men in Hafford's, but they also tended to be a bit freer with what they had.

"C'mon, Ike," she said, and she managed a giggle as she nuzzled his ear. "You don't want to talk *business* now, do ya?"

Ike scowled at her. "This is man's talk, bitch. Shut up!"

"Yes, Ike."

Ike couldn't tell whether she was serious or humoring him. He was realistic enough to know that the girls always liked to flock around when he was feeling flush. He liked spending money on women, liked buying them trinkets and doodads that made them affectionate, but he also knew that with the girls like Linda Lou, it was mostly show. *Business*.

Even so, he liked to think he had a real way with women, just like he had a way with horses. He knew they liked it when he went to bed with them, with them all squealing and kicking and clawing at his back and gasping out his name. This little wildcat, for instance. Sure, women weren't supposed to feel the same thing in bed as men did . . . but he knew *this* little slut got real hot and horny when she was with him, and it was no act.

"The Earps," he said again, "are liars, cheats, and cowards! It's gonna be up to us to run them clear out of this town!"

"I don't think anyone's listening to you, Ike," Tom McLaury said.

It was true. The other patrons in the bar almost seemed to be pointedly ignoring Ike, hunching themselves over their drinks, or murmuring together in low tones while being careful not to meet Ike's eyes.

"S'okay," Ike said. With his free hand, he reached out, grabbed his half-full glass of whiskey, and downed it, savoring the fire as it spread from throat to gut. "They got the message, I bet."

He sloshed a bit of whiskey when he clacked the glass down again on the table. His knuckles, red and a bit raw, burned at the touch, and he lifted them to his mouth. "Damn!"

"Still think you had no call beatin' on that horse that way," Frank McLaury said. "Damndest thing I ever saw, you going up and punching that horse in the face!"

Nursing his sore knuckles, Ike glared at the man. "What business is it of yours?"

"Pa always taught us to show the dumb brute who was boss," Billy Clanton said.

"That's right," Ike said. "Tell 'im, Billy."

"Ike, you weren't showing *anyone* who was boss when you went up and hit him in the head, for Christ's sake," Tom said. "You was just plain mad. I thought you was fixin' to kill that poor animal, the way you was poundin' on him. I swear, Ike, you are the *meanest* son-of-a-bitch . . ." He broke off and glanced at Linda Lou. "Uh, no offense, ma'am." Tom McLaury was the courtly one, always sensitive to a lady's feelings, even if she wasn't exactly a *lady*.

Linda Lou graciously nodded her forgiveness at the crude language.

"You're damned right I'm a mean son-of-a-bitch," Ike snarled, "and you-all'd best remember it!"

"So, what's the plan, Ike?" Billy asked. "You just gonna go around town, bad-mouthin' the Earps?"

"What we gotta do," Ike said, "is get them into a position where they *have* t'fight, or they have t'get out!"

"Ike," Frank said. "That is without a doubt the plain dumb-ass craziest idea I have ever heard. You're trying to spark a stand-up fight with the Earps?"

"Yeah," Tom added. "I think you been out in the sun too long, Ike. Those guys're *killers*. 'Specially Wyatt."

"I don't like Wyatt Earp," Linda Lou said suddenly. "When he looks at you, y'go all cold inside. He's the sort you'd call *Mister* even if you was married to him!"

"Wyatt is bad news," Frank said.

"Ha!" Ike said, grinning. "That's where you're wrong. And that's why *I'm* the boss of the gang!"

"What," Billy said. "You know somethin'?"

"Sure do." Now that he was the undisputed center of attention, Ike's anger had evaporated. He squeezed Linda a bit tighter and let his free hand slip up beneath the hem of her green dance-hall dress. She squealed a bit as he playfully squeezed the inside of her thigh, but she didn't push him away. "I know a *lot*!"

"So?" Billy said, leaning closer. "Whatcha know, Ike?"

"I got a friend up in Benson, works in the Wells Fargo office in town. Seems he knew Morgan Earp, the young one, back in Dodge City, when he was a faro dealer at the Long Branch."

"Yeah?"

"Boys, Wyatt ain't never killed anyone. *Ever!*"

"Go on!" Billy said.

"S'truth!"

"I heard he killed a feller in Dodge, when he was sheriff there," Frank said.

"Yup. Everybody's heard about that," Ike agreed. "A cowboy named George Hoyt, and a buddy of his, was hur-rahing the town, and fired a few shots into a theater there. He was riding away, too, out over the bridge at the end of town, when Wyatt came out and opened fire. Of course, what y'never hear is that Bat Masterson and a bunch of the good citizens of the town was *all* shootin' at George. George was knocked off his horse, got his arm cut off, and died the next day. Wyatt claimed he was the one that got the feller, but it coulda been anyone.

"Point is, Wyatt has a rep as a shootist, but he ain't never faced anyone straight up in an honest fight."

"Hard to believe."

"It's true! Like I say, I heard the whole story myself from a buddy up in Benson. And Wyatt's brothers ain't no better. Virgil, he's pretty steady, I guess. But Morgan's just a hotheaded loudmouth."

"I dunno, Ike," Tom said. "It's like Linda Lou here says. You look into Wyatt's eyes, it's like looking into the eyes of Death hisself. Cold, y'know? Wound up tight. And no mercy. I don't think I'd care to face the man, m'self. Not in a stand-up fight.,"

"You yellow, Tom?"

"Hell, no! You take that back!"

"All right, all right. Don't get yourself riled. I'm just sayin' the Earps' reputation is just a little bigger than life, y'know?"

"So how does that help us?" Frank wanted to know. "Moving against the Earps still won't be easy, no matter what you say. They've got a lot of support in this town."

"Well, we got the sheriff!" Ike replied. He pulled his

hand out from under Linda Lou's skirt, then turned his attention to her tempting décolletage. She had small, round breasts that just fit in a man's cupped hand, as he proceeded to try to demonstrate.

Linda Lou squealed and slapped his hand away. "Ike! Be*have* yourself! Not *here!* Not in *front* of everybody!"

"Ha!" Ike gave a nasty snort of a laugh. "Don't give me that, bitch! You know you love it!"

Tom looked embarrassed. "Ike, if the lady says—"

"Lady? *Lady?*" He groped her hard, eliciting a small squeak that might have been pain as she struggled in his lap, trying to pull away. *"This* little soiled dove?" The expression was a common one among cattlemen, but that didn't make it any kinder.

"For God's sake, Ike, knock it off!" Frank snapped. "Tell us what you have in mind for the Earps!"

"Yeah, well," Ike said, grinning, as he extracted his hand. "I figure if we spread it around town that they're cowards, they're gonna *have* t'make a move, y'know? Either fight or get out. If they get out, our problem's solved."

"And if they don't?" Billy wanted to know.

"If they don't, we can back 'em into a corner. Like, where they try to push us around. Maybe challenge us. And that's when we sic Sheriff Johnny on 'em."

"I dunno," Frank said, shaking his head. He tossed back a glass of whiskey and slapped the empty glass on the table. "I just dunno. Sounds crazy-dangerous to me."

"Look, even if the Earps ain't never killed no one," Billy Clanton said, "what about Holliday?"

"Yeah," Tom said. "Doc Holliday's a killer, and no mistake. And, uh, he don't exactly have good feelings about us."

Frank nodded. "He's in with the Earps, tight as a tick on a dog's ear."

"Doc Holliday don't scare *me*," Ike said with a smirk. "He knows that with the Earps gone, he's a dead man in this town. Everybody knows he's been on both sides of the law. Ain't no one in town'll mourn *him*."

" 'Specially Big Nose Kate Elder," Billy said.

The others guffawed. Kate Elder had been Doc Holliday's mistress—though she always insisted that people call her *Mrs.* John Holliday. Holliday had treated her pretty bad, beating her up on several occasions. Holliday had been out of town at the time of the Benson Stage holdup the previous March, and word had gotten around—spread largely by the Clantons—that he'd been one of the holdup men. Johnny Behan had sat down with Kate Elder, talked to her nice, and bought her a few gins . . . enough to get her roaring drunk and to sign a paper implicating Holliday in the robbery.

That would've been a real coup, getting Holliday arrested for the Benson holdup. Unfortunately, Virgil Earp had arrested Kate and locked her up, keeping her away from the bottle long enough to have a serious, private talk with her. No one knew just what he'd told her, but she'd turned up at Doc's trial and taken back her statement. With no other witnesses in the matter, Holliday had been acquitted.

But Holliday had no love for the Clantons . . . and Kate Elder had no love for *him*.

"Yeah, Holliday knows he ain't no good without the Earps to back him," Billy mused. "But we're gonna have to watch our backs with that one."

"What about Johnny Waco?" Linda Lou said.

"Who?" Ike said, eyes narrowing.

"Johnny Waco. He's some kind of great-shakes shootist, just joined in with the Earps."

"Johnny Waco," Billy said, thoughtful. "The name's familiar."

"He's a shootist out of West Texas," Frank said. "Heard he killed a fella up in Dodge. Wait! You sayin' this Waco is a friend of the Earps?"

"I think he's Doc Holliday's friend," Linda Lou told them. She sounded almost pathetically eager to please. "I saw them all together the other day, over at the Oriental."

"Yeah?" Ike said. "Tell us what you saw."

"Well, this guy comes into the Oriental, where I was workin', see? He's good lookin', and he looks a little lost, y'know?"

"What do you mean, 'lost'?" Ike wanted to know.

"Oh, I don't know. It was like he wasn't all together, or something. He didn't have a hat, which was funny. And he had a bandage on his head, like he'd been hurt. And his eyes looked, I don't know. Sort of dazed, or lost, like. Sort of like he didn't really know where he was. Anyway, I went up and asked him to buy me a drink." Ike's brows came together and his frown turned to something just this side of a snarl. "It's o*kay,* baby!" she told Ike. "It was just business, y'know?"

"Go on, woman."

"Okay. So anyway, Doc Holliday calls him over to where he was sitting with Virgil and Wyatt. Morgan was there too, back at the faro table, dealing. I didn't hear what they were talking about, but they all seemed pretty friendly.

"Then Wyatt and this stranger faced off, right there at the table. Just playing, y'know? I saw 'em both empty their guns first, take the bullets out. And they drew on each other."

"Yeah? So what?"

"The stranger outdrew Wyatt. Had his gun out smooth as a baby's behind, before Wyatt could even clear leather."

"Now that's somethin'," Tom said, impressed.

"Shoot, Tom," Ike said, tugging at his Imperial. "Y'sound

like a damned dime novel!'' The others chuckled at that.
The fast draw might have been impressive in the stories
told in cheap fiction, but in real life it rarely happened. Ike,
himself, had no taste for trying to outdraw another man,
face-to-face. A shot in the back from a dark alley was just
as effective, and a hell of a lot safer.

Even so, Ike was worried. A man that good with han-
dling a gun must have a rep. He would be a shootist, no
mistake, and a good one.

"So then what happened?" Billy prompted.

"Well, next thing you know, this stranger's joining them
at the table, and they're all laughing and having a good
time. Wyatt, especially, seemed impressed with this guy. I
walked over to see if they wanted anything, and they just
kind of waved me off, but I got close enough to hear them
call the guy 'Johnny Waco.' And Wyatt said something
about tangling with him once, back in Dodge, but it was
all smiles and if-you-please there at the table. I think they
were talking about giving the guy a job, hiring him to do
something. I don't know what.''

"That don't sound so good, Ike,'' Billy said. "If this
Waco's a shooter and he's thrown in with the Earps . . .''

"Don't mean a thing,'' Ike said. "They got Johnny
Waco? We got Johnny Behan. I'll match our Johnny to
theirs any day of the week!''

"You really think we can sic the law on the Earps?''
Tom asked.

"Sure thing. They already think they own this town, real
cock-o'-the-walks. All we gotta do is provoke 'em a bit,
get 'em to go across the line. Make a threat. Try to push
us around. We know they ain't got the guts to actually start
shootin', so we get 'em into a fight where we can get Behan
to come and arrest 'em. And, y'know? Jail ain't necessarily
a safe place. All kinds of things could happen to 'em once

they're locked up. They might get shot tryin' to escape. Or they might just get so God-feared depressed about their sorry lot that they up an' hang theirselves, right there in the jail.''

"What about Johnny Waco?"

"Shoot. We'll deal with Waco. In fact, I'd kinda like to have a little talk with the gentleman, see just what it is he knows. We might find out from him just what the Earps are planning.''

"And if he doesn't want to help us?'' Billy asked. "If he's really in with the Earps?''

EIGHT

✦ 1 ✦

SARAH NEVERS HAD NO IDEA WHO THE WOMAN WAS.

Sarah had spent the morning washing clothes, and the afternoon straightening up after her boarders, dusting the downstairs, and worrying about Macklin. She was never quite sure whether it was the void of widowhood that had left her in need of a man to shower with attention and affection, or whether she simply felt the need of someone to mother, but the lonely Macklin appealed to her. She wanted to help him.

The woman, however, bothered her.

She had appeared across the street three different times. She did the same thing each time. Stood next to the oak on the other side of the dusty street and stared at Sarah's house.

It was unnerving. Sarah wondered who the woman was and what she wanted. Instinctively, she sensed that the woman had something to do with Macklin. None of her other boarders, she thought, would prompt such scrutiny.

The third time Sarah saw her, she was half-ready to go across the street and confront her, to ask her if she could help her in some way. Ask her if she had some good reason for standing there and gawking at Sarah's house. She tended to be direct in her speech and in her manner, and if the stranger *was* linked with Macklin somehow, she wanted to know.

Then, while Sarah peeked at her out through the chintz curtains in the front room, the strange woman made the first move and took care of the whole problem by squaring her shoulders, walking across the street, and hauling on the bellpull at Sarah's front door.

Curiosity mingling with apprehension, Sarah went to the door. "Yes?"

"I'm sorry to bother you, but I wondered if this was where a Mr. Macklin was staying?"

The woman was attractive, high forehead, classical nose, wide, brooding mouth. She wore a white blouse with long, puffed sleeves, a modest gray skirt with a frilled bustle and a duster, and a lace-trimmed, broad-brimmed hat that set off her face nicely . . . but no makeup that Sarah could detect. Sarah realized—my God, she was acting like a young girl—that she was jealous of this woman. What right had she to come here and ask questions about Macklin?

"And you'd be who?" Sarah demanded.

The woman smiled. She had a beautiful smile. "I suppose this does seem kind of suspicious, doesn't it?"

"A little. I don't talk about my guests or their business."

"Then he *is* staying here."

Sarah frowned. She'd not meant to let even that much slip.

"I have to know what your business is with Mr. Macklin."

"You saw me standing across the street this morning, I'll bet."

"Yes, as a matter of fact, I did," Sarah said.

"Well, I'm not usually this bold. But I'm . . . I'm his sister." For all her poise, the woman wasn't a good liar. Her cheeks reddened as she spoke, and for just a flickering moment, she looked away. "I was told that Mr. Macklin can't remember who he is, and I was told he might be staying here."

Sarah sighed. "If that darned doctor ever kept his mouth shut, it'd be a red-letter day in this town."

"My name is Doris Macklin, by the way." She put forth a slender hand, but Sarah pointedly did not accept. She was pretty sure she knew what kind of woman this Doris was, even if she didn't dress like one.

"Pleased to meet you, Miss Macklin. Sarah Nevers. I'm afraid Mr. Macklin isn't in right now."

"Oh, that's too bad. Any idea when he'll be back?"

Sarah wondered what to say. On the one hand, she certainly didn't want to encourage this . . . this *person* to come hanging around her respectable lodgings. On the other, she knew how desperately Macklin needed to find out something about his past. If this woman had the key . . .

"I'm . . . not sure," she told the woman. "I suppose you could try this evening. Is there someplace he could reach you?"

Sarah knew exactly what the mysterious woman would say. "Afraid not, Mrs. Nevers. I'll be kind of flitting around town all afternoon. I'll just stop back later. I really appreciate your help, by the way."

Sarah nodded. The Macklin woman turned and walked back to the street, then headed back toward town, skirting a noisy baseball game in the middle of the street.

Something about Doris Macklin alarmed Sarah. She wasn't exactly sinister . . . but she certainly wasn't telling the truth. Sister? Sarah didn't believe it, not for a moment. But if she wasn't kin . . . why would she want to see Macklin? Did Doris really know who Macklin was and what he was doing here in Tombstone?

Sarah wondered where Macklin was. Did this woman who called herself his sister represent a threat? She closed her eyes and thought of the strange, gentle man who didn't need to shave, who had that strange . . . *thing* pressed into the flesh of his chest and didn't seem to know how it had gotten there.

He was so vulnerable. She wanted to see him again, to touch him. Hold him.

Protect him.

◆ **2** ◆

JOHNNY BEHAN WAS NOT A HAPPY MAN.

Normally when he relaxed in his office, he'd rock back in his stiff-backed chair, prop his boots up on the corner of his desk, and maybe take a drag from a cigar. But not today. Not after what he'd seen that morning out at the Carter ranch. He sat stiff and straight in his chair, hands clasped together on the desk before him right beside the empty glass and bottle, squeezing so tight the knuckles were white. He didn't think he was ever going to be able to relax again. The sight . . . the *smell* of those charred bodies was going to give him nightmares for the rest of his life.

Damned, murdering, raping Apaches. It had to be them. *Had* to be. White men, civilized men, just didn't *do* things like that.

Sheriff Behan was not ready for Indian trouble in Cochise County.

He wished there was some way to dump this on the Earps. Damn it, Virgil Earp was the deputy U.S. Marshal for all of southern Arizona Territory, as well as town marshal, but in the end, when they'd been riding back to town from the Carter spread, the big man had just shrugged and said, "This is in *your* backyard, Behan. I don't see how we can help you."

Behan kept wondering if this was some sort of a setup by the Earps, some way to make him look bad . . . and just before the next round of elections was due. He knew Wyatt was going to be running against him again for the job of county sheriff, and he was going to be doing it on a law-and-order platform, claiming the Clantons were getting away with their desperado ways under Sheriff Behan's protection. Maybe . . . maybe the Earps had staged an Indian raid at the Carter ranch, with the idea that if Behan didn't do anything about it, he'd look weak.

He closed his eyes and again he saw those bodies, their throats slit like they were hogs, their bellies sliced open by something at least as big as a Bowie knife, their bodies burned to unrecognizable horror. A woman and a little girl.

God, he hated the Earps . . . but even *they* weren't capable of that kind of atrocity. It *had* to be the Apaches, no matter what Virgil said.

Shaken as he was, Behan still turned the problem around in his mind, looking for a way to hand this particular hot potato back to the Earps. If he could just make it clear to the citizens of the county that the massacre at the Carter ranch was the Earps' responsibility, that they weren't tending to their responsibilities the way they ought. . . .

He just didn't see how he could manage it, though.

Wyatt . . . he was Behan's big problem. Running for county sheriff and promising to clean up the whole county if he were elected, and of course that meant Ike Clanton and the rest of Curly Bill's Cowboys. Hell, there was a better than even chance that if Wyatt got to be sheriff, Behan himself would be hauled up on charges of covering for the Cowboy gang and maybe for getting payoffs from them, too. He knew he couldn't trust the Cowboys to keep their mouths shut about *that,* not if they were facing serious jail time themselves.

And there was more to it than that. There was also Josephine Marcus.

Oh, God, Josie . . . Josie . . . how could you do *this to me?*

Josephine Sarah Marcus—her friends all called her Sadie—had been an actress . . . and maybe a few other things, when Behan had met her backstage after a performance up in Prescott the year before. They'd fallen in love, and he'd brought her down to Tombstone, promised to marry her, and even set up housekeeping with her, though he'd tried to keep that part discreet. There'd been a bit of scandal anyway, of course—there was always talk and gossip in a place like Tombstone—but the couple had made the best of it. Sadie was just eighteen and the most beautiful creature John Behan had ever seen.

Only trouble was, Sadie had a taste for bright lights, excitement . . . and exciting men. She hadn't been in Tombstone for more than a few weeks when she met someone else . . . charming, dignified, and a bigger spender than Behan.

That someone else was Wyatt Earp.

Behan ground his teeth slowly at the memory, at the humiliation. It wasn't right. Earp was a married man—or, at least, that was what Mattie Earp claimed. She lived with him and washed his shirts and raised holy hell when Wyatt was seen in public with Josephine.

Damn it all, there had to be a way to get rid of the Earps, once and for all. Especially that son-of-a-bitch Wyatt.

Behan's office was on the second floor of a building on Allen Street, above the Golden Eagle Brewery. He shared the floor with none other than Virgil Earp, whose office was right across the hall outside. The door at the top of the long outside steps coming up from the street faced west, and when it was open in the late afternoon to catch the breeze, like now, the sunlight streamed into the darkened hallway, leaving a bright, hot rectangular patch on the floorboards. As he sat there, stewing about the Earps and Josephine and murderous Apaches, he heard the heavy creak of the wooden steps outside, and a moment later, a shadow filled the lighted rectangle on the floor.

The shadow . . . good God, what *was* that? Behan's heart gave a sickening lurch in his chest. The shadow on the floor was twisted and bulky and sprouting snakes and the whole thing seemed to *writhe* somehow, like a nest of snakes. . . .

Then the shadow's owner moved into the doorway, silhouetted against the sunlight. "Sheriff . . . Behan?"

The voice was familiar but a little stiff. Behan shaded his eyes, trying to make out the face. The silhouette looked . . . odd. Almost misshapen, though not as bad as that shadow.

Then the man walked the rest of the way into the office gloom, and Behan blinked. Sure, he knew this guy. Hank Attwater, one of Clanton's and Curly Bill's boys. That funny-looking shadow . . . Behan blinked, then looked down at the empty whiskey bottle. He'd been hitting the stuff pretty heavily lately. Maybe it was time to stop.

"Hey . . ." His voice cracked, and he tried again. "Hi, Hank. What's up?"

Hank Attwater stood across the desk from Behan, looking down at him with eyes at once familiar and curiously flat. "Sheriff," that voice grated again, "I was wondering if you knew anything about . . . a stranger in town."

Behan squinted up at Attwater. "A stranger? Hank, you've gotta be joking. You know how many drifters, cowboys, and God knows what-all else we have in Tombstone?"

"This . . . person might have been injured. It is important that we find . . . him."

"Injured, you say? Well, you talked to Doc Shea?"

Hank seemed to digest this information. "This Doc . . . is a medical technician?"

"He's a doctor. That's what 'Doc' usually means, you know . . . unless it's Doc Holliday, and he's a dentist, so-called." Behan cocked his head to one side. "You okay, Hank?"

"I am . . . well."

"You're acting damned peculiar."

"I will go speak with Doc Shea," Hank said, nodding slowly. "I will see if he has information about an injured stranger in town."

"You . . . you just do that, Hank."

And Hank Attwater was gone. No good-byes, no see-ya-laters, nothing. Just . . . gone, out the door with an ominous creak of the floorboards. Outside, Behan heard the shrill yapping of a dog, the startled whinny of a horse.

Behan sat there in his chair, trying to sort out his jumbled impressions. He'd never seen Hank Attwater act so strangely before. Hell, he hadn't seen *anyone* act that strangely before. And there was something more. . . .

There was something about that lingering smell hanging in the office after Attwater had left . . . something familiar, something unpleasant. It was almost . . .

Behan shuddered as he pinned down the thought. It was almost like what he'd smelled at the Carter ranch that morning . . . a kind of sickly-sweet smell, like rotten meat, and . . . and something else he just couldn't put his finger on. He'd caught a whiff of it when Virgil had shown him that peculiar track or whatever it was, and it hadn't just been the stink of roasted flesh.

His hands were shaking as he opened a cabinet at the

back of his office and pulled out a fresh bottle of whiskey. Right now, Sheriff John Behan didn't need just a drink. He intended to start himself off on a serious drunk, something that would numb the brain and stop the nightmare terrors he felt chasing one another around and around in there and maybe let him forget what he'd seen and smelled out at the Carter ranch.

God, if *only* he could forget. . . .

◆ **3** ◆

MACKLIN RODE BACK INTO TOMBSTONE LATE IN THE AFTERnoon, left his horse with Jimmy at the O.K. Corral, and hobbled his way through the streets of Tombstone. He was sore. His backside felt numb, like someone had whacked him there repeatedly with a club, but working its way up between the crack of his buttocks there was a burning pain that felt like a white-hot wire.

How in the Twelve Worlds could people stand to endure the torture of riding day after day and not seem to notice the pain at all?

The thought brought him up short, and he came to a sudden stop—so sudden that a man in a bright plaid jacket and pants plowed into him from behind, jarring him hard enough to send a fresh stab of pain up his backside.

"S'cuse me, mister," the man said, pushing past Macklin. He gave Macklin a once-over glance that seemed to say *Watch what you're doing,* but it lingered long enough on the revolver riding in the holster on Macklin's right hip to seem to give rise to a few second thoughts.

Twelve Worlds? Where had *that* thought come from?

Macklin tried to recapture the thread, elusive, slippery, and fragmentary at best. *How in the Twelve Worlds . . . ?*

The phrase felt . . . right, and very, very important, but he didn't know where it had come from or what it meant.

He kept on walking.

His eventual destination, of course, was the boarding-house, but he stopped off first at Sam Peabody's Haber-dashery. Boots and a hat. Boots and a hat. The people at the Clanton ranch had thought it pretty funny that he'd gone out there without a hat and had been riding without boots. Sam's was a store crowded with items ranging from shirts and Levi's to boots, hats, and even saddles. It took him a while to find what he needed, since he discovered that he knew neither his boot size nor his hat size, but he emerged at last wearing a pair of what the proprietor had called "the finest mule-ear boots," and a light, cool, broad-brimmed, flat-crowned hat made of tightly woven straw, something the proprietor had called a "flat."

Mule-ear boots? He knew what a "mule" was—a kind of animal used like a horse—though he wasn't sure how he knew that, or if he'd ever seen one. He wondered how big a mule's ear was, though, to make such heavy boots.

As he resumed his painful stroll down the street, he noticed passersby on the street giving him odd glances, and a few smiles, hastily hidden behind hands raised to lips.

What, he wondered, was so damned funny?

◆ **4** ◆

IT TOOK SOMETIME FOR PAINSPINNER TO FIND THE PLACE *where the human medical technician, Doc Shea, lived and worked. Some pieces of information that the human Hank Attwater had carried in its brain, the Kra'agh had found, were relatively easy to access . . . information such as the name of Sheriff Behan and where he could be found. But either Attwater hadn't known where Doc Shea could be found, or he never thought about it much. Painspinner had to risk asking a number of humans in the streets, and it* had taken it quite a long time to find someone willing to give a coherent answer.

The humans all seemed to act somewhat skittish in Painspinner's presence, and he had to assume that they were sensitive to some aspect of its presence—its scent, most likely . . . though it was possible that they were detecting flaws in the gah-projection field about its body.

It didn't matter. Humans were food, not very intelligent, and they seemed either to ignore or even to dismiss as impossible or irrelevant things they sensed but could not understand.

The Kra'agh, it thought, would be able to use that odd and decidedly contrasurvival trait to their advantage, once they began moving to this planet en masse.

One human, finally, had replied to the Hunter's demand for directions to the medical-human known as Doc Shea. "Just follow your nose, mister, then hang a right." The man's face had given a peculiar wrinkle. "You think the doc can fix that body odor problem?" Then Painspinner had detected a flush of fear. "Uh . . . nothin' personal, you understand!"

"Follow your nose?" "Hang a right?" The terms were bewildering, but the accompanying gestures of the creature's upper appendages suggested the general direction to be followed.

These creatures did appear sensitive to smell, though from what it could sense of their thoughts, most were vaguely disturbed by it, without really understanding what the problem was. The Hunter doubted that the human sense of smell was anywhere near as keen as that of a Kra'agh. Likely, they simply detected . . . difference and reacted in primitive fear.

Some creatures native to this world had keener senses than the humans, however. The large quadrupeds called *horses shied and started every time the Hunter passed close, rolling their eyes and stamping nervously; he could sense their fear. And there were others. . . .*

A four-legged creature, a carnivore to judge by its teeth, seemed to get Painspinner's scent and went into a frenzy, lunging about and making shrill, high-pitched yapping sounds or else making long, low, throaty growls while the fur bunched up in coarse bristles down its spine.

Painspinner ignored the creature at first. He wasn't entirely sure what relationship it had with humans. The Kra'agh had noticed a number of similar creatures wandering loose on the streets, though none had come as close as this one. Its yappings, though, were attracting attention, both from other four-legged carnivores and from humans passing in the street. Swiftly, Painspinner ducked into a side alley, a narrow street cloaked with deep shadows as the evening advanced.

The creature—Attwater's memories seemed to associate the word "dog" with a variety of four-legged animals similar to this one—followed the Kra'agh, still yapping.

As soon as Painspinner was sure that no humans could see, it whirled, reached down with one feeder arm, grasped the animal by its throat, and jerked it into the air. A yap transformed itself into a half-strangled whine as Painspinner tasted the terror in the creature's feral mind . . . and then it brought one leg-arm high, baring the Hunter's slasher claw, and swiftly slit the creature open from thrashing tail to rib cage. Internal organs spilled out onto the ground, steaming; the animal gave an even shriller yelp of exquisite agony, and Painspinner clamped the tentacular fingers of a second feeder arm around its muzzle, clamping the mouth shut to keep the sound down to a desperate whine.

The animal struggled in the Hunter's grasp; Painspinner

held it close, drinking sweet pain and terror from its mind as it died.

When, at last, Painspinner slashed the animal's throat to spill the last of its hot blood in the dirt and released the muzzle, the Hunter found that the force of its grip had crushed both the upper and lower jaws, shattering the large, predator fangs.

Painspinner considered eating the carcass but elected instead to toss it aside. It had eaten earlier in the day, and though Kra'agh metabolisms ran high and fast, demanding huge amounts of food, the Hunter wasn't ready yet to feed again.

When it was hungry once more, it wouldn't want to eat a semi-intelligent creature like this one. Humans were much more appetizing . . . their thoughts and terrors tastier, their death struggles more interesting, their kleh-*essence more appealing as they died slowly in a Hunter's embrace.*

But at least the . . . dog? Yes, dog. At least the dog was silent now.

NINE

❖ 1 ❖

WHEN MACKLIN STAGGERED IN THE FRONT DOOR, SARAH WAS there to meet him. "Good *gracious,* Mr. Macklin," she said. "What is that?"

"That" was his new hat, which Sarah was staring at with an expression mingling horror and amusement.

"It's . . . a hat?" he said, unsure of how he was supposed to reply.

"It's a *lady's* hat," Sarah said. "Where did you get that?"

"At a haberdashery," he replied. "Sam Peabody's."

"And did Sam sell it to you?"

"I don't know the gentleman's name. He had a mustache. . . ."

"Most men do, but I'll bet it was Sam. He always gets a good chuckle out of pulling the legs of tenderfeet." She took the offending piece of headgear from him. "Tell you what. Tomorrow, we'll go shopping. Adolph Cohen's, I think, at Fifth and Allen, and maybe the American Clothing Store. We'll find you some better clothes than those. And a proper hat. A *man's* hat."

"Would . . . would you like to have that one?" He felt clumsy saying the words.

Sarah smiled warmly. "Why . . . a present! Thank you, Mr. Macklin! I'm not sure it's entirely *proper* to accept a gift from a man I hardly know, but . . . I'm delighted!" She placed the flat on her head, cocking the brim at a jaunty angle. "And it fits perfectly, too! Thank you very much!"

He took another few steps into the parlor, wincing. "And if it's all the same to you, Mrs. Nevers, if that shopping trip you mentioned involves a lot of walking, I think I'll give it a pass."

"Trouble, Mr. Macklin?" She seemed concerned.

"I rode out to the Clanton ranch today," he told her. "On a horse. I don't think I've ever been on a horse before, and I find . . ." He stopped and rubbed himself. "Damn, it hurts!"

"Twenty-some miles, and you've never ridden before? I should think you *would* hurt!" Solicitously, she took his arm and led him toward the stairs. "You come along, now. I'll draw you a hot bath, and while you're soaking, I'll fix you some dinner. And after that, I've got a salve you can put . . . you can put on yourself." She blushed as she said it.

"Is this something prescribed by Dr. Rush?"

"It's an old family remedy," she told him. "It'll take the pain out and help loosen up your muscles. If you don't use it, I promise you it will hurt a *lot* worse tomorrow."

"Thank you," he told her. "I can't thank you enough." He thought about the salve and wondered how he could reach back behind himself to apply it. Right now, he was feeling so stiff and sore from his shoulders clear down to his toes that he didn't think he could bend that much. "About that salve, Mrs. Nevers. Do you think I could impose on you to put it on for me? I'm not sure I—" He stopped in midsentence. Sarah was staring at him, mouth open, eyes wide. "What?"

"*Mister* Macklin!" she said. "What kind of a girl do you think I am?"

Macklin blinked. She looked like she was about to strike him. "Is there a problem?"

"You *don't* ask a lady to . . . to put salve on . . . on . . ." She stopped, flustered, flailing about for words. "On your *behind*!" she finished, at last.

Macklin shook his head, baffled. She'd mentioned undressing him the other night. He knew—again, without knowing how he knew—that certain modesty taboos prevailed that considered exposing certain parts of the body in public to be wrong, but he wasn't aware of a problem with two adults in private.

But as he thought about it, other pieces of information seemed to click into place for him, isolated bits of data arising out of nowhere and falling together to create a whole. Sarah Nevers wasn't married . . . and she especially wasn't married to *him*. Those modesty taboos seemed to be especially strong between men and women, and most especially between men and women who weren't married to one another. The only exceptions were women who, in this time and place, were not considered to be proper ladies.

And Sarah Nevers was most emphatically not one of *that* type of women.

In other words, he'd likely just insulted her as she'd never been insulted in her life.

"Sarah . . . Mrs. Nevers . . ." It was his turn to stammer, and then turn red. "I'm sorry. I didn't know. I mean—"

She sighed, then took his arm again, leading him up the stairs. "It's all right, Mr. Macklin," she said. "I've heard lots worse. And if you have the grace and good manners to blush, you can't be all bad!"

Some blissful hours later, Macklin was just toweling himself off when he heard the knock at the door.

The bath Mrs. Nevers had prepared—a big metal tub filled with scalding hot water and a soap so strong it left his skin tingling—had felt wonderful. Leaning back and letting himself sink into the steaming depths had been to recapture life itself and to feel the aches of his day's ride fade away, along with the stink of horse and sweat. He'd damned near fallen asleep in that tub and had finally hauled himself out only because he was on the verge of dropping off. Besides, the water was turning cold and was by now as gray and dingy as dead dishwater. Had all of that crud been caked on him?

So he was out of the tub and drying himself when he heard the knock. Padding to the locked door, he called out, "Yes?"

"It's Sarah Nevers, Mr. Macklin. I have your dinner for you."

"Oh . . . ah . . . leave it on the floor outside, would you?" He was naked and not exactly anxious to climb back into his discarded, trail-stiffened clothing for the sake of modesty. And reminded now of prevailing nudity taboos, he found himself actually feeling embarrassed, though he wasn't sure why.

"Just wrap yourself up and let me in, Mr. Macklin," Sarah replied. "It's okay."

He fumbled with the towel but got it at last tucked around his waist. Would she be shocked at seeing his bare chest? His hand touched the enigmatic black disk embedded in his flesh just above his breastbone. She'd seen that already, at least. And she'd *said* it was okay. . . .

Clutching at the towel, he opened the door.

Sarah swept in, cool and businesslike, neither looking at him nor looking away. She carried a tray with a plate of roast beef and potatoes, a glass of milk, and a jar of some yellowish substance. A red and white striped garment of some sort was folded over her arm. She set the tray on a small table by the window, put the garment over the back of a chair, walked back to the door to close and lock it, then turned to face him, her hands primly clasped in front of her.

"I got to thinking, Mr. Macklin, that it would be best if we got that salve onto you right after your bath . . . and also that we've got to do something about those trail-filthy clothes of yours." She pointed. "I want you to get on that bed and lie down, facedown, and no nonsense!"

"But—"

"It's okay, Mr. Macklin. I won't tell if you won't."

He did as he was told, and a moment later, he felt her tugging at the tuck in the towel and she pulled it away. A cool breeze was coming through the open window, and he shivered a bit at its touch.

She started with his shoulders and back, rubbing the ointment on and in with small, tight, circular motions of her hands. The salve, whatever it was, felt a bit greasy . . . but as she kept rubbing, it began feeling warm, then quite hot. It smelled vaguely of turpentine.

He could feel his muscles loosening up even further. "That," he said, his voice muffled by the pillow he was facedown on, "feels wonderful."

"Hush. Just lay still and let me work."

Her hands worked their way lower, massaging his lower back and sides. "Your, ah, sister came by earlier today."

"Mmfn." Then, startled, he raised his head. "Sister?"

"Yes. Doris Macklin? Do you remember having a sister?"

"No. No, I don't." He almost rolled over so he could look Sarah in the eye but thought better of it. "Sister?"

"She's *quite* pretty." Sarah's voice sounded tight. "Dark hair. Lovely eyes. What you men call 'full figured.' She *said* she was your sister. She wanted to see you."

Macklin shook his head. "I really can't remember. Doris?" What was it about that name? He thought he could almost remember. . . .

He closed his eyes, and for just an instant, he saw again the woman in his dream. Dark hair. Slender, but with lovely, full breasts. And eyes that burned their way into his soul. Doris . . . Macklin? That wasn't right, but he didn't know *how* it wasn't right.

Sarah's hands were working on his buttocks now, moving more gently. "You've got a nasty sore back here," she told him. "This might sting a bit."

It did, but it felt good, too.

"What did . . . did this woman say anything about me?"

"Not much. She said she'd come back to see you tonight."

"And?"

"She hasn't been by yet. If she comes any later, I'll have to tell her to come back tomorrow." She pressed a little harder, eliciting a small gasp of pain. "I'm very strict about the rules concerning lady guests visiting my male boarders. This is a respectable house, Mr. Macklin, and I can't afford to let my reputation suffer."

Macklin decided not to point out that her reputation could scarcely benefit if anyone found out she was in his room, rubbing salve into his naked rear end.

"Come on," she told him. "Spread your legs apart. You don't have anything down there I've not seen before, believe me. Wider. That's it."

He felt her hand slipping between his legs, spreading the ointment and the warmth. He felt himself becoming aroused—he could hardly help it, considering what she was doing—and began concentrating simply on not moving. Her hand brushed lightly against his erection and he gasped.

"Sorry," she said. "Anyway, I'm not entirely sure she's really your sister."

"Mmpf?"

"No. There was something about her I didn't quite trust . . . something that told me she wasn't being entirely truthful." She began working on his upper legs, concentrating on the insides of his thighs, where the long ride had rubbed him red and chafed.

"Anyway, as I said, if she shows up later, I'll tell her to come back tomorrow at around one. If you would rather have me tell her you don't wish to see her, I will be most happy to do so.

"There! Now, I'm going to go out of the room and wash up. While I'm gone, you get up and put on that nightshirt I left for you on the chair. It was my husband's. You're a lot bigger . . . you're a lot taller than he was, but it should fit you well enough and keep you comfortable for the night. I'll launder your clothes, and they should be dry for you to wear tomorrow morning. And you can have your dinner and then turn in." She paused, listening. "Mr. Macklin? Mr. Macklin?"

But Macklin, exhausted by the day's ride, was already sound asleep.

◇ **2** ◇

THE WOMAN WHO WAS NOW CALLING HERSELF "DORIS" paused a moment to make certain her clothing was properly draped and arranged. The cultures of primitive worlds like this one frequently placed an exaggerated importance on bodily decoration and other ranks of status, place, or position within the community, and it was imperative that she blend in successfully, without calling attention to herself.

She stood for a moment in the evening moon-shadow of a building, watching the front of Sarah Nevers's boarding-house across the street, just as she had for some hours that morning. It was growing late, but there were still plenty of lights on throughout the structure. Ma'khleen . . . no, she reminded herself. *Macklin* ought to have returned by now from whatever mysterious wanderings he'd been engaged in. He was in there, and she was going to find him.

Doris had spent much of the day . . . shopping. *Clothes* shopping. It was appalling how much time and expense the members of this culture applied to adorning themselves, but she needed to look the part if she was going to get any-where with people like Sarah Nevers. Clothing, she'd found, was the authoritative badge of caste, rank, and po-sition in this place. While cowboys in from the range on a drinking spree could be a nuisance, most of them, she'd found, treated women with an exaggerated sense of respect, honor, and delicacy . . . so long as they thought you a *proper* woman, a real lady. Give them any reason to think otherwise, however, and they were all over you.

She'd learned that her first day in town. She and Macklin had been on their way to Earth with costumes matching acceptable dress in this part of the planet, but neither of them had bothered with frills like hats while in space. Worse, Doris had refused to wear the long, straight skirt with the fashionable bustle or the clumsy leather shoes with the heavy heels while they were aboard; those things could be dangerous in zero-gravity, where a long skirt could snag on controls or billow up over your head while you were trying to move about. When she'd landed alone in the Ar-izona desert that night, she'd been rather unfashionably clad in a black thermalskin and ship shoes.

She'd been able to see the lights of the town from her

landing site up in the hills, so it hadn't taken her long to reach civilization. Some drunken cowboys in the street had seen her, however, as she walked into town, and they'd been after her in a braying, whooping, cat-calling pack. She'd been able to lose them easily enough, but the chase had shaken her. Her Companion, its voice a gentle whisper at the back of her mind, had pointed out that it was probably her attire—or her lack of it—that had stimulated the cowboys.

The dress she'd worn that night had come off the clothesline behind a house on the edge of town. The shoes, lace-frilled hat, shawl, and jacket she'd purchased the next day, along with a new skirt. She'd left the stolen dress on the same clothesline the following night; these people, with a technology barely capable of steam engines and electricity, had a culture that to Doris's eyes hovered on the ragged edge of abject poverty. She would *not* steal from the natives if she could help it.

She'd spent this afternoon trying on and buying even more clothing. If she was going to be stuck on this benighted world for very long, she was going to need to stay presentable. She wasn't sure how long her supply of gold coins was going to last her, though. Jobs for women—the other thing she'd been checking into that afternoon—were in awfully short supply.

First things first. She had to find Macklin. Squaring her shoulders, she crossed the street, climbed the steps onto the boardinghouse's front porch, and tugged the bellpull.

Sarah Nevers opened the door, wiping her hands on an apron. "Yes? Oh, it's you."

"Good evening, Mrs. Nevers," Doris said. "I've come to see Mr. Macklin. Is he in? I told you I'd be back later."

Doris watched Sarah's face, which betrayed several conflicting emotions. It was an extremely pretty face, Doris thought. Ma'khleen always had had a way with attractive women, and it was clear he'd had his way here. She couldn't detect any sign of a sexual relationship behind those clear, wide, blue eyes, but it was obvious that this woman was suspicious, jealous, and more than a little in love. Doris was going to have to handle her very carefully.

"Well, there's later and then there's later," Sarah said. "It's well past nine P.M.!"

"Oh, I won't take more than a few minutes. I just need—"

"Please! This is a *respectable* house! I do *not* permit female visitors with my guests after the hour of eight!"

Doris sighed. "Mrs. Nevers, I'm sorry but I really must insist. I am Mr. Macklin's sister. I learned from Dr. Shea that he was injured, that he'd suffered some sort of memory loss. I *must* see him!"

"And I must insist . . . Miss Macklin, is it? I must insist, Miss Macklin, that no female visitors are allowed here this late at evening under *any* circumstances."

"Can you just tell me if he's in? Could you give him a message, tell him I'm here! I know he'll want to see me!"

Sarah gave her a sour look. Plainly, she was on the verge of losing her temper. "Miss Macklin. I do *not* know if he is in. I do *not* keep tabs on my male guests. And even if he *is* in, he is probably in bed and asleep by now, because Mr. Macklin seems a very upright and respectable gentleman, not given to late-night carousing or to . . . to *dalliances* with soiled doves! Good night!"

Query, Doris thought, accessing her Companion's database. *What is the term for local law enforcement officers?*

There are several, the voice of her Companion whispered in her mind. *Sheriff, marshal, constable . . .*

Sarah was closing the door. Doris stepped forward, blocking it with her foot. "I'll go to the sheriff!" she said.

"You can't stop me from seeing my brother!"

"You just do that," Sarah said, fire in her eyes. "You just do that, and give Johnny Behan my best when you do! I'll give *him* a piece of my mind, too!" She hesitated a moment, then seemed to think of something. "Just tell me one thing."

"Yes?"

"If you're Mr. Macklin's sister . . . what's his Christian name?"

His Christian name? Doris felt a flutter of panic. What if Macklin had already made something up? What if this was a test, away to catch her out? "I . . . don't see that I have to discuss that with you!"

"It's a simple and proper question. What is his first name?"

Quickly, Doris accessed the database again, looking for a list of common first names in this culture. "Algernon," she said, picking one at random.

"Thank you," Sarah said sweetly. "Now, kindly get your foot out of my door, or I'll send for the sheriff and have *you* arrested for solicitation!"

Doris stood staring at the closed door for several puzzled moments. *Query,* she thought. *What does the term "soiled dove" mean? I'm not sure, but I have the feeling that I've just been insulted.*

Unknown, the Companion's voice replied. *That expression is not in my files.*

Query. Why would anyone arrest me for "solicitation"? In any case, I was not attempting to sell or advertise a product.

She could sense her Companion working on the problem. *The word "dove" can be applied commonly to any of a number of species of avians native to this continent. "Soiled," clearly, is "dirty," a word which can also be used in this culture to refer to scandalous, immoral, or improper behavior, especially of a salacious or sexual nature.*

The word "solicitation" commonly refers to entreaty or request but in this sense may refer to the selling of sexual services. There is a smaller chance that the word refers to an offer of legal services, such as those provided by a solicitor, or lawyer.

I submit, with a probability of seventy-two percent, that Sarah Nevers believes you to be someone who sells sexual favors. There is a lesser probability, on the order of eighteen percent, that she believes you to be someone who sells legal services instead.

Why, Doris asked, bewildered, *would anyone want to sell a sexual experience?*

This culture places extraordinary importance on what is perceived as proper moral behavior was the reply. *Where free and natural sexual behavior is discouraged or prohibited, other outlets will develop. This culture has a bewildering array of terms for women who sell sex to men. Prostitutes, hookers, joy girls, whores, ladies of the night—*

But not "soiled doves"?

Our knowledge of this civilization is still incomplete, her Companion whispered. *There are gaps both in our understanding of the culture and in our apprehension of the language. Expressions appear and evolve with bewildering rapidity, and often are quite localized in their occurrence. It is possible—*

Halt, she thought. She was tired and didn't want to go into a long discussion of linguistic or cultural analysis with her Companion. Clearly, though, she was going to have to study everything she could find on this culture in her Companion's files.

Her survival, and Macklin's, depended on it.

TEN

◆ **1** ◆

*P*AINSPINNER HAD SPENT LONGER THAN IT HAD EXPECTED WAIT-*ing in the shadows outside the doctor's house. There'd been several humans present, and the Hunter had not been sure which was the one it sought. There were four, all together, and when Painspinner peered in through a convenient window, they seemed to be simply sitting around a table, each studying a handful of small, pasteboard rectangles with printed symbols on them. A ritual of some sort was under way, one in which the men discarded and retrieved rectangles and occasionally moved small stacks of metal disks and crumpled paper back and forth on the table top between them.*

The ritual meant nothing to the Hunter, though it imagined it might learn more about it if it studied the Hank Attwater memories.

Human rituals—was it part of some primitive religion?—were of no interest to the Hunter. It only wanted the other humans to leave so that it could get access to Doc Shea.

Part of the ritual involved consuming large amounts of amber fluid, sometimes from open-topped glass containers, sometimes from bottles. The ceremony grew progressively louder until, at last, three of the humans rose unsteadily, bid Doc Shea good night, and staggered out the door into what was now almost total darkness. This planet's sole natural satellite was rising in the east, nearly full-phase and very bright, but the light only served to make the darkness down here among these squalid habitations all the darker.

That was good. The Hunter preferred the darkness as a mask. It didn't want to unduly startle its prey.

Painspinner went to the front door of the house, eased it open, and stepped inside.

"Eh? Who're you?" Shea demanded as the Hunter entered the parlor, where the doctor was still sitting at the table, drinking from a bottle.

The human did not appear to be functioning with full efficiency. Painspinner could taste the sharp tang of chemicals—alcohol, in particular—exuding from the human's breath and body and from the bottle in its hand.

"I need to know if a stranger has come to this town recently," Painspinner said. "It . . . he was possibly wounded. Had an injury of some sort."

"Wha . . . stranger? No, no strangers." The human tried to rise, then sat back again, heavily. He appeared about to fall out of his chair. "Who are you, anyway?"

"Hank Attwater. I am a friend of the Clantons."

"Clantons, huh? Well, jus' steer clear of the Earps!"

"You must know something about a man who came to you with an injury recently. It would have been three days ago."

Shea appeared to try to concentrate. "Uh? Oh, sure. Th' queer guy. Couldn't remember his own name. Dressed funny . . . and he wouldn't take off his shirt. I remember that. Feller was as skittish 'bout showin' his tits as a spring bride."

*All three of Painspinner's hearts quickened in response.
"Where is he? Where can I find this person?"*

*The doctor peered up at the image of Hank Attwater.
"Damnedest thing. You're the second person today to go
askin' 'bout that guy. His sister was here, too, just today."*

*"Sister?" The word apparently indicated a bloodline re-
lationship. "What was the name?"*

*"Uh . . . Mac, something. Maclean? No. Macklin. That
was it. They was both named Macklin."*

"And where is this Macklin now?"

"I imagine the same place I told his sister. . . ."

*Frustrated, Painspinner allowed the gah-projection to
slip, then to fade. It extended itself, stretching up to his full
height on its hind legs, its flat head brushing the ceiling as
it glared down at the human.*

*The human stood before the Kra'agh, blinking up at it
stupidly. Then the eyes rolled back in their sockets, and the
being swayed, then toppled over backward, landing flat on
its back with a crash. The half-empty bottle clunked and
rolled across the floorboards, dribbling amber fluid.*

*Painspinner paused, staring at the human. Was it . . .
dead? No, the Hunter's sharp ears could detect its single
heartbeat, hear its ragged and somewhat liquid-clogged
breathing. The creature was alive. Was it shamming death?
Or genuinely unconscious?*

*Gently, the Hunter reached down and touched the still
form, experimentally rocking its head back and forth. There
was no response. Was it possible that when faced with extreme danger, these creatures went to sleep? It hardly
seemed credible. Painspinner had encountered many
strange life-forms throughout this part of the Galaxy but
never one that behaved in quite so blatant a nonsurvival
way.*

It would have to probe for Shea's memories directly.

He brought out the patternmaker, positioned it above and between the unconscious human's eyes, and punched it through bone and into the soft cerebral tissue beyond. Painspinner hissed a foul imprecation; the creature's brain was barely functioning. The strangest aspect of that was the fact that the creature appeared to have damaged its own neural system by deliberately exposing itself to poison.

Astonishing. These creatures deserved extinction; they were too stupid to be allowed to live.

It kept working, probing deeper, peeling its way through layer upon layer. There were thoughts to be patterned and rich beds of memories, but most were jumbled, confused, almost incoherent. It had treated a human that had called itself Macklin, three days ago. And . . . it had passed the information on to others. Macklin was carrying a great deal of money, and there was some speculation about how that money might be stolen by two other humans of Shea's acquaintance and divided up among them.

These creatures preyed upon one another, then. It had already guessed that this was so, from the memories contained in Hank Attwater's mind, but Painspinner had scarcely been able to credit the idea. No Hunter would do such a thing. Barbarians!

He traced the memories, one linked to another in a complex web. Another had been here yesterday, asking about Macklin. A woman who called herself Macklin's sister.

That, Painspinner reasoned, must be the second Monitor, searching for the first. Excellent! Find one, and the Hunters would find both.

But where was either of them staying? This swarming heap of a town contained thousands of the creatures. Locating any two would be almost impossible.

But the Hunters would find them, if they had to track

*them by scent alone. The sooner those two troublesome
creatures were killed, their thoughts patterned, their very
souls and essences devoured and assimilated, the better.*

◈ **2** ◈

THAT NIGHT, SARAH DREAMED.

She dreamed first of Curtis, as she often did, dreamed of
him coming close, reaching out, touching her cheek, her
chin, then lightly between her breasts.

Then, when she looked up from what he was doing to
stare into his brown eyes, it wasn't Curtis at all . . . but the
stranger, Macklin, pale blue eyes looking into hers with an
intensity that was at once savage, terrifying, and comfortable. He was nude, and it frightened her that she wanted
him this much. The ladies of the Purity League would never
understand. . . .

She placed her hands on his chest, feeling the grizzled
hair there, but when she looked at the strange, black disk
set into his chest, she saw that it was a mirror . . . only
instead of her own features, she saw those of the woman
she'd met today, watching, somehow disapproving.

"Curtis," she said. He took her in his arms, but it wasn't
Curtis, it was Macklin. . . .

"What's your name?" she asked him. He had to have a
first name. It wasn't right to be this, this intimate with a
man, and not even know his Christian name.

She looked up into his face . . .

. . . but his face was withering as she watched, the eyes
rotting, the skin crinkling, then crumbling into dust and
blowing away, leaving nothing but desert-bleached bone, a
grinning skull's death-mask, leering down at her through
empty eye sockets.

She screamed. . . .

❖ 3 ❖

MACKLIN DREAMED.

He saw again the blue-glowing city, the ringed giant planet in a green sky, the red sun. Home. He missed home with a trembling flood of longing that shook him. And Dorree. He missed her . . . needed her. . . .

Where was she?

"Ma'khleen?"

He turned at the name, but it wasn't Dorree who'd called. It was Sarah . . . Sarah Nevers, and she was reaching toward him with a question in her eyes.

"Where's Dorree?" he asked.

"She is looking for you," Sarah replied, but the voice was the whispered voice of his Companion. Where was she? The last time he'd seen her . . .

He saw again the moon, bathing the ship's small cabin in silver-white radiance. They were being pursued, hunted down by the Enemy. The base was gone, obliterated. There was no place left to run . . . except . . . just perhaps . . . the blue, cloud-wreathed world hanging in a black velvet sky just ahead.

"Hang on!" His hands danced across the touchscreen controls. "We might be able to lose them!"

Dorree was strapped into the other seat, at the navigation con. "Range seven-five-one-one, closing!"

Stars wheeled past the cockpit, which plunged into an eerie, instrument-lit darkness as the moon fell astern. Ahead, Earth hung against a star-glittered sky, a blue-and-white marble, a gemstone, impossibly fragile and alone. . . .

"Ma'khleen," Dorree said. "If the Monitor base is gone, if they have a fleet moving toward Earth . . . !

"The primitives won't have a chance," he replied. "But maybe we can—"

Explosions hammered at them . . . a first, and, seconds later, a second, as air screamed into hard vacuum.

They fell toward a fast-growing expanse of white and blue and brown. He was trying . . . something. He couldn't remember. Yes! He was trying to set down close to a certain place on the planet. They'd been on their way to a rendezvous with Associative agents on the planet, at a particular meeting place, when the Enemy had attacked.

Perhaps he could still bring them down close enough that they could find help.

Where was it? He couldn't remember the name of the place.

And he couldn't control the ship's fall, not entirely, at any rate. The vessel was breaking up as it tumbled wildly into the planet's upper atmosphere. He could feel the buffeting now as the outer hull began to heat.

They were falling . . . falling . . .

"Eject!" Macklin shouted. "Eject! Eject!"

"Ma'khleen!" she shrieked. . . .

The escape capsules sealed around him, and he felt the emergency gravs pulse, hurling him into a whirling sky. Did Dorree get out, too? Did she . . . ?

He felt that they *must be close behind, perhaps even following them down. They* were *relentless. They* never *allowed their prey to escape. They would track the two of them down, whatever it took, and destroy them.*

Alone now, he fell toward the alien planet.

He screamed. . . .

◆ **4** ◆

MACKLIN AWOKE WITH AN ICY START TO THE SILVER BRILliance of a nearly full moon, his head still fuzzy with strange dreams. It was still dark, but the moon, huge and settling toward the west, blotted the stars from the sky and edged the ramshackle buildings of Tombstone with silver ice.

He was standing, he found, without knowing how he'd gotten there, next to the wide-open window in his bedroom, hands gripping the wood of the window ledge, leaning far out into the night. If he'd leaned just a little farther forward, he might easily have tumbled over the sill and dropped to the street, a good twenty feet below.

He couldn't remember ever having been a sleepwalker. But then, he didn't remember much at all, so he supposed almost anything was possible.

Frightened, now, he stared up into the moon. There was something . . . something he had to remember about the moon. About . . . some*one*.

No. The harder he strained to capture the thought, the more it slithered out and away from him, vanishing into confusion.

He stared up at the moon for a long time, trying to remember. When he dropped his eyes to the town of Tombstone, a chill not of the cool October breeze pricked at the back of his neck.

*Someone . . . some*thing *is out there. Waiting.*

He could feel it.

Somewhere in the town, a dog was barking, a mournful, lonely, desperate sound. Tombstone was never completely quiet. Even now, in the wee hours, he could hear shouts and drunken laughter, hear the tinkle of a piano, hear the raucous, far-off commotion of a brawl with broken glass and rowdy laughter. Several thousand people lived and played and worked and dreamed out there. And Macklin couldn't shake the edgy, spine-prickling conviction that they were all, in some sense he couldn't begin to understand, depending on *him*.

For what?

He thought of the mysterious woman, the one Sarah said claimed to be his sister. She would be out there, somewhere . . . and Macklin knew that he had to find her. He didn't know who she might be, but he was certain that she held the key to his past, to who he was, to what he was supposed to be doing here in this place where he felt so hellishly out of place.

But that wasn't what was bothering him the most right now. In his dream, he recalled, there were . . . *things* chasing him. Nightmare specters, phantoms he could never quite see but that he knew were hunting him down relentlessly, seeking his death, or worse.

He thought they were out there as well. Searching. Waiting. Perhaps they already knew where he was and were waiting only for the proper moment to strike.

He shook his head. This was crazy. He had no reason to think there was anyone out there trying to get him. It was just dreams . . . the ghosts of dreams. He shook his head, trying to clear it. There was no danger. No lurkers in the shadows. No invisible pursuers. . . .

The dog's bark became more frantic, then rose in a sharp, sudden squeal . . . and fell silent. Another dog, farther off, began barking, and then two more joined in, a shrill, yapping chorus.

ELEVEN

❖ 1 ❖

ELEANOR SMYTHE'S BOARDINGHOUSE FOR LADIES ON SEVENTH Street was one of the more recent business ventures in Tombstone, a respectable boarding establishment catering only to women. Almost with the first influx of miners at the beginning of Tombstone's silver boom, women had begun arriving in the town, but the first of them, for the most part, had been dance hall and saloon girls and practitioners of the oldest profession—soiled doves, for the most part, who could never have presumed to positions in *decent* society.

It wasn't very long, though, before miners arrived from the East bringing their wives . . . and close behind them came the men who made their own livings off the miners rather than from the earth directly—saloon keepers, haberdashers, saddle makers, druggists, coopers, drummers, and wrights. With this second wave of immigration came wives, sisters, and sweethearts, decent women who would bring the trappings of culture and civilization to Tombstone's shabby and disreputable streets. A few, even, were something strange—professional women seeking careers and opportunities of their own. Several of the writers at the *Epitaph* were women, a career choice for the fairer sex unheard of back East.

Decent ladies needed decent lodgings . . . places to stay of unimpeachable character to preserve their lodgers' genteel reputations.

"Doris Macklin" had been happy to find the place. She had enough on her mind just now without having to fend off the clumsy advances of drunken cowboys or town lechers who assumed that a woman traveling alone *must* be a woman of low moral character. She remembered too well her first encounter with the denizens of this place three nights ago. She would *not* leave herself open to such misinterpretation again.

It was early in the morning when she descended the front steps of Mrs. Smythe's, checking to see that her shawl was draped properly and tugging down the hems of her puffed sleeves. She was every inch the fashionable traveler from someplace back East; if the tote bag slung over her right elbow was a bit heavier than similar bags carried by other women, she gave no sign.

She turned west on Toughnut, making her way toward Sarah Nevers's boardinghouse with a grim and no-nonsense determination. She was still furious at having been blocked the evening before by the woman's cultural hang-ups. Well, she was going to see Macklin today if she had to shoot Sarah Nevers and walk in over her fallen body.

Several blocks along Toughnut Street, she slowed down. There was a crowd ahead and a great deal of commotion. Coming closer, she found that the crowd was gathered at the mouth of an alley—men, mostly, but a few women and a number of kids. Doris stopped, trying to peer over the shoulders of the people huddled around the alley's mouth and failing. "What is it?" she asked a man in a bowler just in front of her. "What's happened?" She had a sudden flash, a kind of urgent presentiment. *Was someone hurt in that alleyway? Or killed . . . ?*

Was it Macklin?

"Nothin' here for you to see, ma'am," the man said, looking down at her and tipping the hat. He turned away, shaking his head. "Nasty business. . . ."

"Has someone been hurt?"

Before the man could answer, a tall, grave man emerged from the alley. He stood at least six-two, a giant compared to most of the folks in the town. He was richly dressed in a white shirt, string tie, and black frock coat, with a flat-crowned hat and a luxuriant, thick mustache that completely hid his mouth.

His eyes were . . . cold. Cold and hard. "That's all, people," the man said in a commanding voice. "Nothing to see here. Go on about your business!"

The crowd was starting to disperse. She walked over to the big man and looked up at him. "Sir? What's happened here?"

"I wouldn't go in there, miss," the man said. "It's not a good sight for a delicate woman."

"I am *not* delicate, thank you. Who are you?"

The man's eyes widened slightly. "Earp, ma'am. Virgil Earp. I'm the town marshal. And you are . . . ?"

"Doris Macklin. And I'm looking for someone . . . my brother. Algernon Macklin."

She was certain that she saw a flicker of recognition behind those cold eyes, but then a shutter slammed shut. Virgil Earp's expression would have done credit to any poker player who'd ever lived.

"I haven't been able to find him," she went on. "I was afraid, well . . . I was afraid he might be in there."

She started to enter the alley again, forcing ahead against the slowly dissolving crowd, but Virgil stopped her. "It's not a man in there, if that's what you're worried about, miss. But it's still not a fit sight. Looks like some sick individual was going around town last night gutting dogs. That's all.''

"Dogs?"

"As if we didn't have enough to worry about in this town!'' Virgil shook his head. "I've never seen the like. Looks like they used a Bowie knife or something similar. But it's *not* your brother, I assure you.''

"I . . . see. Thank you, Marshal.''

"Don't mention it.'' He touched the flat brim of his hat. "Ma'am.''

She wanted to go in and look but didn't wish to call undue attention to herself. Doris wondered, though, if the death of several dogs in Tombstone last night meant what she was very much afraid it meant. Kra'agh Hunters? Here? She found herself looking nervously to the left and the right, studying the faces of the people around her on the street and sidewalks. Hunter camouflage projection wasn't perfect, by any means, and the beings probably wouldn't risk exposing themselves to public view in broad daylight. But still . . .

Hunters, here. This planet was defenseless, its technology so primitive, its worldview so laughably self-centered, its governments so jealously divided and squabbling. If the Hunters decided to make Earth their next target, the planet's defenders would have virtually no chance at all against them.

She needed to get off this planet, reach the nearest Monitor communications station, and warn the Associative. If they acted fast enough, before the Hunters decided to move . . .

But first she had to find Macklin, and that meant going around, past, over, or *through* Sarah Nevers to reach him.

✦ 2 ✦

MACKLIN HAD LEFT THE NEVERS BOARDINGHOUSE EARLY, stepping out into the bright, fresh light of a new day with the terrors of the night still tugging at his thoughts. He never had been able to get back to sleep in the predawn hours that morning. The shadows of his dreams had clung to him, and the heart-pounding fear he'd felt waking to find himself by the window, staring up at an unforgiving moon, had made further sleep impossible.

Without any clothes but the nightshirt of Mrs. Nevers that he'd found draped on his chair, though, he'd not been able to do much but lie there and think, until about 6:30 by the wall clock, when Sarah Nevers had tapped at his door and slipped in, handing him jeans, shirt, socks, and underwear, all laundered, hung-dry, and neatly folded.

"Did my sister come by last night?" he'd asked her.

She'd nodded primly.

"And did you tell her to come back today?"

"I'm afraid I did not, Mr. Macklin. I confess I was somewhat irritated with her manner of address."

"I've got to talk to her," he'd said, deciding to go find her. He needed to see Earp or Holliday in any case and let them know about the failure out at the Clanton ranch yesterday. Maybe he could find this mystery woman as well.

"You can take some time for breakfast first, can't you? Got a fresh pot of strong coffee on, and plenty of flapjacks and syrup."

"Thank you . . . but no. I've got to find her."

"Is she really your sister, Mr. Macklin?" She'd seemed worried . . . or disappointed.

He spread his hands. "I honestly don't know. I don't remember . . . anything."

"You remembered your name."

"Yes . . ."

"Tell me something? If you wouldn't think me too forward."

"If I can."

"What's your first name, Mr. Macklin? You never told me."

"My . . . first name?" He thought a moment. He wasn't sure he *had* a first name, but that would seem awfully strange to Sarah. Everyone he'd met here so far had two names, first and last, and it must seem strange that he remembered the one and not the other.

Well . . . he was known as "Johnny" to the Earps and Doc Holliday. That would do. "Johnny . . . John," he told her. "John Macklin."

Surprisingly, she grinned. "You're sure?"

"Yes . . ."

"It wouldn't be something like *Algernon,* now, would it?"

"I certainly don't think so."

"Thank you . . . John."

"So . . . I'm going out, and try to find my sister. If she comes here, will you have her wait for me? Please? It's really important."

"It'll be my pleasure, John."

Stepping out onto Toughnut Street, he started making his way toward the center of town. He was still sore, he found, but the soreness was not nearly so bad as his outraged muscles had been promising him the night before. He still felt raw and chafed up around the insides of his thighs and around the bottom of his buttocks, but even that was not as bad as it had been when he'd finally set foot again on solid ground, yesterday afternoon, there at the O.K. Corral.

Macklin had decided, though, that he didn't ever want to *see* a horse again, much less ride one.

The new boots hurt his feet, and he wondered if that was also Sam Peabody's idea of a joke . . . sell the tenderfoot boots too small for him. He decided, though, to tough it out and see if he could break them in. He also needed to see about a hat. After spending some time studying the assorted headgear of other men on the city streets, he found another haberdashery—Adolph Cohen's Clothing Store— and ducked inside.

The sun was well up by the time he stepped out again, wearing a new gray Stetson on his head, and a vest over his white shirt. He had to admit that he didn't feel nearly so conspicuous now as he had before. It had taken him a while to realize the fact, but everyone in Tombstone wore headgear of some sort, with no exceptions. He'd been the only one going about bare-headed.

No wonder people had stared.

Properly dressed now, he headed toward the Oriental Saloon on Allen. He might as well get the bad business of the day over with. He wondered how the Earps and Holliday would react to his failure to bring back any useful information about the Clantons.

As near as he could tell, the Oriental never closed . . . but the morning was usually its slow time, a time when the chairs could be put up and the floors swept and the spittoons emptied. Not this morning. There was a fair-sized crowd of people inside, standing about in small knots next to the bar, talking with one another in low, urgent voices. Something had just happened in the town, something that had the people worried.

Macklin checked the back table where he'd met Holliday and the Earps two days before. Sure enough, Holliday and Wyatt were there again, together with another man who looked so much like Wyatt that Macklin decided it must be yet another of the town's Earps. Virgil was nowhere to be seen.

"Morning," Macklin said, approaching the table. "What's happened?"

"You don't know?" Holliday asked.

"No. Should I?" He looked at the unintroduced Earp. "Hi. My name's—"

"Johnny Waco," the man said quietly. "Or Macklin. I know."

"This here's Morgan Earp," Doc Holliday said. "Virgil and Wyatt's brother. He deals faro here at the Oriental sometimes, and he rides shotgun for Wells Fargo. He also gets deputized from time t'time, when there's trouble. Like now."

"You mind telling us where you were last night, Waco?" Wyatt said. His voice was low, even, and very dangerous. Macklin suddenly had the feeling that a wrong move on his part could release something inside the man opposite him, something like a tightly coiled steel spring.

"I was at Mrs. Nevers's boardinghouse," he replied.

"All night? Say . . . after midnight or so?"

"That's right."

"Can anybody else vouch for that?" Morgan asked.

"Mrs. Nevers. She put me to bed. . . ." He could tell by the expressions on the other men's faces that he'd just said the wrong thing.

"Oh, it's like *that,* is it?" Doc Holliday said.

"Look, just what is this?" Macklin demanded. He looked at Wyatt. "I rode out to the Clanton place yesterday, like you asked me to. I'm afraid I couldn't find very much out. I talked with someone named Billy Claiborne, and someone else named Phineas. Phineas Clanton. Learned a little about the people in the gang, but—"

"I don't care about any of that right now, Waco," Wyatt said. "Have you seen Doc Shea lately?"

"Milo Shea? The guy who fixed me up when I first came into town. That was . . . what? Three days ago."

"You ain't seen him since?" Doc asked.

"No. Why?"

"Someone," Wyatt said, "killed Doc Shea last night. Put a bullet hole in his head big enough to stick your finger in." He held up his own forefinger, as illustration. Then he tapped himself on the forehead, squarely between and above his eyes. "Right there."

"Three of his buddies were over there playing cards last night," Morgan added. "They left about midnight and said Doc Shea was fine then. So someone came in after midnight and plugged him."

"Why are you telling me this?" Macklin's eyes widened. "Wait. You don't think *I* shot him, do you?"

"Doc here was telling us," Wyatt said, "how Shea sicced a couple of guys on you, the night you came into town. Tried to rob you. That could be motive enough."

"Doc Shea was a greedy, larcenous, thieving, drunken old coot," Doc said, "but walking into a man's home and blowing a hole in his skull is still murder, plain and simple. And right now, you're our number one suspect."

Macklin blinked. "Why?"

"You're a stranger in town. And you had a reason."

"Is that a crime?"

"Not by itself," Doc said. "But this memory loss thing you claim to have is damned convenient. No way to check up on you, who you really are, where you come from."

"You *call* yourself Macklin," Wyatt added, "but you handle a gun like a big-name shootist. I still think you look like Johnny Waco, and that's a man capable of almost anything, if he thought he'd been wronged."

"I never claimed to be Waco," Macklin said. "That was *your* idea!"

Wyatt held out his hand, palm up. "Let me have your gun."

Macklin frowned, but he surrendered the weapon, drawing it carefully between thumb and forefinger, so the men facing him, all of them visibly tense and very, very still, wouldn't get the wrong idea.

Wyatt cracked the cylinder open and looked at the bullets . . . five of them, in six chambers, the empty chamber under the hammer. He held the weapon to his nose and sniffed. Then he looked at Morgan and shook his head. "Hasn't been fired. Not lately, anyhow." He placed the pistol on the table and studied Macklin, an icy scrutiny.

"I haven't killed anybody," Macklin said, stubborn. "Look, I last saw Mrs. Nevers at . . . I'm not sure what time it was. But it was before midnight. There were lots of people still up at her place. I could hear laughter and talking and so on downstairs. I imagine she'll be able to tell you what time she saw me last, and she'll tell you that I was in my room. And I don't think I could have slipped downstairs and out the door without anyone seeing me."

He'd been about to point out that Sarah had taken his clothes to wash them. It seemed to be the perfect defense. If people in this town had been looking at him strangely when he hadn't been wearing a hat, they would have looked at him a hell of a lot more strangely if he'd gone out in the town streets naked . . . not exactly the proper attire in which to commit a murder.

But he remembered Sarah's obvious consternation last night when he'd first asked her to help him with the salve. The way she'd been unable to even say certain words. There were fragments of—not memories, really, but *impressions*—fragments that suggested that being seen nude or partly undressed by others was not normal for this culture, that sex was a secret and shameful thing, that people tended to be very concerned about their reputations . . . which had something to do with who they had sex with.

Sarah, he guessed, wouldn't want others to know that she'd been alone in a room with a naked man. The thought, when he reasoned it out, seemed bizarre, even nonsensical, and he couldn't put his finger on where the impressions were coming from. Memory? Something he'd been told? By whom?

Dream fragments . . . shreds of memories: a blue-glowing city beneath a vast, ringed planet and a ruby-hued sun. A dark-haired woman in his arms, naked and beautiful. A voice, whispering in his mind, "Let go. Let go, and let your body remember. If you stop to think, you are already dead."

Whatever the source, he decided to keep quiet about the situation last night and let Sarah Nevers do her own explaining. For her reputation's sake.

He just hoped this problem didn't come down to a choice between her reputation and his life.

"Well, I see you boys found Macklin," a new voice said.

Macklin turned and saw Virgil Earp standing behind him, hands on his hips.

"Hello, Marshal," Macklin said.

"Hello yourself. I was out looking for you this morning."

"I gather you men think I killed Doc Shea." He shook his head. "I didn't do it."

"Hmm. Don't s'pose you're responsible for the slaughter of all those dogs, either."

"Dogs? What dogs?"

He sighed. "Never mind. We do still have rule by law around here, and that means a man's innocent until proven guilty. But we're going to be keeping our eyes on you, mister.''

Macklin turned to Wyatt. ''Can I have my gun back?''

''I think we'll just keep this for a bit, Macklin,'' Wyatt said. ''There's a law in Tombstone about carrying weapons, you'll recall. You're supposed to check 'em as soon as you come in, pick 'em up on your way out. We cut some slack for most folks, but until this gets cleared up, I think we'll hang on to it.''

''Fair enough,'' Macklin said. He unbuckled the belt and empty holster and laid it on the table. ''Can I go?''

''Go on,'' Virgil said. ''But . . . we'll be watching you. By the way . . . I ran into your sister just now.''

''You did? Where is she? I've been trying to find her.''

''On Toughnut Street. Not far from Mrs. Nevers's place, in fact.''

''Would you gentlemen excuse me, then? I need to find her.''

Wyatt dismissed him with a careless movement of his hand. He walked out of the Oriental, pushing through the bat-wing doors and into the late-morning heat.

⋄ 3 ⋄

DORIS STILL INTENDED TO PAY A VISIT TO MRS. NEVERS, BUT she had another chore to attend to first. Turning onto Fourth Street, she walked up across Allen to G. F. Spangenberg's Gun Shop, which she'd noticed the day before.

Inside the dimly lit shop, a small man with spectacles looked up from behind a glass display case. The case was filled with pistols, and more were hanging on pegs on the wall behind. One entire wall of the place was taken up by a rack holding dozens of rifles and shotguns, while boxes of ammunition were piled high in the back.

It looked, Doris thought, like a military arsenal.

"Yes, ma'am? What can we do for you today?" the proprietor said.

"I need a weapon," Doris told him. In fact, she had a weapon—the Corps-issue pulser she was carrying in her handbag. She'd decided, however, that she needed something that *looked* like a weapon, at least to these people.

Her experience with the drunken cowboys the other night had raised the question: Suppose they'd managed to corner her in a dead-end alley somewhere? She could have threatened them with the pulser, but since these people had never seen such a device, they most likely would have laughed and kept on coming. She might have had to kill them . . . and she would have had to have killed them all, so that survivors wouldn't be spreading wild tales about a woman with a magical device that burned holes in people. That could be entirely too destructive to the local culture.

If, however, she'd been able to brandish one of the chemical-propellant slug-throwers these people knew were weapons, she would have been able to scare them off.

"Well, you've come to the right place!" the shop owner crowed. "Looking for something in a lady's model, for personal defense, I should think. How about this little beauty right here . . . ?"

The pistol he laid on the counter was tiny, small enough to be hidden in the palm of a big man's hand. It had a cylinder with four chambers, tiny ones. The shopkeeper said it was chambered for .22 caliber long . . . which she gathered was a reference to the thickness of the bullet, expressed in hundredths of an inch. When she saw one of the cartridges that fit the weapon, she laughed out loud.

"Something like that would just make an attacker mad," she said. "What about a gun like *that?*"

"That" was a Colt .45 Peacemaker, a beautifully designed six-shot hand weapon that decidedly looked as though it meant business. There were a number of different designs in the shop. A plain, blued-metal version with a wooden handle had a price tag of seventeen dollars. Another one, with a gleaming silver body covered with engravings, ivory handles, and an embossed leather holster, went for a hundred dollars.

It was the man's turn to laugh. "A .45? Good heavens, no! No *lady* would be able to handle such a monster!" He made it sound as though the recoil would shatter the bones of any woman's delicate hand . . . and told her that cocking the weapon before each shot was beyond any woman's strength. "They don't call it a 'thumb-buster' for nothing!"

Instead, he showed her an over-under derringer, another tiny weapon with two barrels. You fired one, rotated the barrels manually, and fired the other.

She argued. She couldn't tell him that her Monitor Corps training had taught her to competently handle weapons ranging from palm-pulsers smaller than that derringer up to shoulder-launched Hunter-killers and particle cannons. Nor could she tell him that her training downloads included experience with primitive weapons, everything from sharp sticks to backpack nukes. He let her handle the .45 and was surprised when she snicked the heavy, curved hammer back with the second joint of her thumb, but seemed completely unable to grasp the idea that *any* woman could possibly handle it without breaking her arm, shooting her own foot, or smashing her face with the muzzle when the recoil brought the weapon up and back.

At last they argued to a compromise. He agreed to sell her what he called a "pocket revolver," a .32 caliber pocket Smith and Wesson only about twice as long as the derringer, with a spur trigger—a stub with no trigger guard. Gentlemen, he told her, carried them as a backup weapon, easily concealed but still deadly. This particular model, he said proudly, was identical to the one carried by Wild Bill Hickok.

"And who is he?" she asked.

The man looked shocked. "Why, he was one of the greatest gunfighters ever, ma'am!"

"Was?"

"Oh, yes, ma'am. Shot and killed . . . oh, five years back, I reckon. Up in Deadwood, South Dakota, it was. Gunned down from behind when he was playin' cards!"

"Well, it didn't do him much good, then, did it?"

She purchased the pistol and a box of .32 ammunition, refusing the man's offer to wrap it up. "Just remember, ma'am," he warned her. "There's a gun law in this town. You're s'posed t'check your gun at most any place of business—a hotel, a saloon, whatever. Now, I don't figure anyone'll bother a respectable lady like you about carrying for your personal safety, but I wouldn't flash it around, if I was you."

She loaded the weapon in the store, placing rounds into four of the five chambers and leaving the fifth empty and under the hammer, as a safety. Her dress had one deep pocket which would carry the weapon, easily accessible. "Thank you," she told the man. "I *do* know how to use this."

TWELVE

❖ 1 ❖

SARAH NEVERS HAD BEEN UPSTAIRS TIDYING UP SEVERAL OF her boarders' rooms, making their beds and straightening up. Some men, she thought, needed a woman around just to keep them from getting lost in their own garbage.

Mr. Macklin, she noticed—*John*—lived very lightly, picking up after himself and even straightening up the bed.

She noticed the window was closed and opened it to air the place out. *Funny,* she thought. *He seems like the sort who'd like the out-of-doors.* Then she remembered his experience with riding and chuckled . . . before remembering something else and blushing deeply. Had she *really* done what she'd remembered doing for him last night?

And . . . what must he think of her? He hadn't seemed either upset or, well, *lustful* this morning. Maybe it was okay.

Just so long as no one else ever found out!

She was coming down the steps when she heard a peal of woman's laughter coming from the front parlor. Puzzled, she made her way to the room, then stopped in shock. It was that woman, Doris Macklin, so-called, and she was reading Dr. Benjamin Rush's book.

"Miss Macklin!"

The woman looked up, and laughed again out loud. "Mrs. Nevers! This is hysterical!"

"What are—"

"Listen!" She started reading. " 'Onanism produces seminal weakness, impotence, dysury, tabes dorsalis,' whatever *that* is, 'pulmonary consumption, dyspepsia, dimness of sight, vertigo, epilepsy, hypochondriasis, loss of memory, manalgia, fatuity, and death!' " She looked up and laughed again.

"Miss *Macklin!*" Sarah said, shocked and blushing. Her face felt hot. "If you *please!*" If any of her boarders had heard . . .

"Is 'onanism' what I think it is?" She held up a hand, fingers in a circle, forefinger touching thumb, then rapidly moved her hand back and forth, her eyebrows rising to make the crude gesture a question.

This time, Sarah was speechless. She clapped both hands to her mouth, horrified.

"I'm *so* sorry!" Doris Macklin tossed Rush's book carelessly onto a tabletop. "I just picked it up and started reading at random when I came across that passage. Is there *anything* that man doesn't blame on the practice?" She laughed again, as something else struck her funny. "Maybe *that's* what Mr. Macklin's problem is! Loss of memory!"

"Miss Macklin," Sarah said, recovering, at least in part. "It isn't right to make fun of . . . of *that*. It's a well-known fact that the insane asylums are crowded with men, and women, too, who have succumbed to . . . to *that!* Nor will I tolerate your making fun of that poor man. And . . . and you shouldn't be reading such things out loud! Someone might hear! And . . . and . . ." She was so angry, she could sputter for only a moment. "And what are you doing here? How did you get in here, anyway?"

"Please forgive me," Doris said, becoming more serious now. "I was just about to ring the bell when a gentleman came out the front door and graciously let me in. I thought I'd wait for you here, until you came down."

Sarah picked up the book and carefully replaced it on the bookshelf. "And your business?"

"Why, to see Mr. Macklin, of course."

"Mr. *Algernon* Macklin?"

"Yes."

"I'm terribly sorry to disappoint you, Miss Macklin, but there is no one here by that name."

"Mrs. Nevers. I am in *no* mood to play games!"

"And neither am I. I asked Mr. Macklin this morning what his name was. It is not Algernon. Since I would like to give you the benefit of the doubt and assume that you are an honest woman, I can *only* assume that the Mr. Macklin staying here is not your brother, but a different Mr. Macklin entirely!"

The look in the other woman's eye looked dark enough to strike someone dead, Sarah was delighted to see. She looked like she was doing a slow count in her head and growing more furious with each passing second.

Well, good! Maybe she would drop dead from the apoplexy.

"Mrs. Nevers . . ."

"*Miss* Macklin! You will kindly leave these premises and never return. You and your kind are not welcome here. I run a decent, respectable establishment, and I will *not* have my reputation sullied by the likes of you!"

Doris took a step forward, one hand sliding toward the pocket of her dress . . . and then she seemed to change her mind about something, and stopped. "Mrs. Nevers. Is Macklin here now? I want the truth!"

"I always tell the truth! He is not. He went out early. I don't know where." She drew herself up straighter. "The business of my boarders is no business of mine. And I don't care what they do outside these walls. But I *do* run—"

"A respectable establishment," Doris said, interrupting. "Okay, okay." She turned to leave.

"Miss Macklin. I do *not* want to see you here again. Or anywhere around here."

"No promises, dear," Doris said. And then she was gone.

◆ **2** ◆

DORIS DIDN'T *THINK* SHE WOULD HAVE SHOT SARAH NEVERS, though the thought was damned tempting. *Damn* the woman and her straight-laced, sexually frustrated, libido-inhibited, immature and ignorant culture!

During her wanderings about town in the last couple of days, she'd been picking up a fair amount of gossip and background detail. She'd learned that the Earps pretty much ran this town; in fact, there was a nasty stand-off just now between the Earps, who ran the town, and Sheriff Behan, who ran the county. If anyone in Tombstone knew about Macklin and where else he might be found besides the Nevers boardinghouse, it would be the Earps ... Virgil, especially. She was certain she'd seen recognition in his eyes when she mentioned Macklin's name that morning.

She could also try Sheriff Behan. He had connections with the Clanton gang, which, by all accounts, pretty much controlled everything happening outside the town limits.

And if she couldn't find satisfaction there, then by the Twelve Worlds and the Oath of Gharanoth, she would march back to Nevers's place and hold that woman at gunpoint until Macklin showed up!

The Earps, she'd heard, liked to hang out at the Oriental Saloon. Maybe she could find one of them there and see what he knew.

Still seething, she started back toward Tombstone's business district.

◆ **3** ◆

"HEY!" BILLY CLAIBORNE SAID. "THERE HE IS! THAT'S THE guy!"

Ike Clanton turned, looking in the direction Claiborne had pointed. He saw a young, clean-shaven man just passing Hafford's Corner Saloon, on the opposite side of the broad thoroughfare.

"What . . . him? He don't look tough."

"Looks like a damned greenhorn," Billy Clanton put in.

"Well, that's the guy who was out at the ranch yesterday, askin' all them questions. You said you wanted me to point him out. There he is."

Ike Clanton tipped the brim of his hat back and studied the other man, walking now along the opposite side of the street with just a trace of a limp. It looked like his boots were hurting him.

"What do you figure the Earps want with the likes of him?" Frank McLaury asked.

"Damifino," Ike said. "But I think we'd better find out."

"And . . . lookee there!" Billy Clanton said, gleeful. "The son of a bitch ain't even carrying!"

"So, what's the plan, boss?" Tom McLaury asked.

Ike smiled. He liked it when they called him *boss*. "We'll go give him an invite to come have a talk with us out at the ranch. Tom, you and Frank go get our horses ready." They'd left their horses at the O.K. Corral that morning when they'd ridden into town. "And see if you can get an extra horse. We'll go get our new *friend* and bring him along.''

❖ **4** ❖

MACKLIN HAD BEEN WALKING ALL OVER TOWN LOOKING FOR the mysterious woman who called herself his sister. He had just turned north onto Fourth Street when he became aware of a presence at his back. "You just keep walkin' there, mister," a voice said, low and as grim as death. "And don't you try no funny stuff, either!"

"Yeah. You just keep your hands where we can see 'em, mister!" a second voice said.

Macklin felt the chill of their voices. He couldn't see them, but he had no doubt whatsoever that they were armed. "What do you want?"

"Shaddup," the first voice said. "Keep on walkin'."

How many were there? He was pretty sure he could take one, maybe even two in hand-to-hand, but there might be more, and he couldn't make a move unless he knew exactly where they were. Out of the corner of his eye, he caught movement in the street. Billy Claiborne was flanking the group, twenty feet away.

So that made at least *three,* and one of them positioned to shoot him down if he tried to make a break for it.

It looked like he had no choice but to go along with them.

They continued along Fourth Street, passing Spangenberg's Gun Shop. Macklin felt a tug of despair; all of the Earps were back at the Oriental on Allen and Fifth. There would be no help for him from that quarter.

Where the hell were these people taking him?

❖ **5** ❖

DORIS HAD FINALLY SEEN MACKLIN.

She'd been coming down Allen Street, on her way to the

Oriental, when she saw Macklin straight ahead of her, walking toward her on the boardwalk and then turning right onto Fourth. She broke into a smile and started forward . . . and then she saw the other men.

There were three of them, and they looked like rough characters. One, a short man with a coat folded over his arm, stepped up behind Macklin and seemed to be talking to him. The other two stood farther back, and as they moved, Doris noticed they had their hands on the butts of pistols riding in their holsters. There was a brief conversation, and then they started moving again. Doris caught a brief glimpse of the glint of a pistol partly concealed by the frock coat folded over the short man's arm, the muzzle pointed squarely at Macklin's back.

For a moment she stood there, paralyzed. Should she follow? Or go for help? The three men who'd captured Macklin appeared ready for trouble, were trying to look in every direction at once. She didn't think she would be able to get close enough to hold them at gunpoint, not without risking Macklin's life, or hers.

No, if she went for help, she wouldn't know where those men were taking him. After looking for Macklin for this long, she wasn't about to lose him now.

✦ 6 ✦

HIS CAPTORS HUSTLED MACKLIN ALONG AT A BRISK PACE, urging him to move with steel-hard prods in the back from what could only be the muzzle of a gun. Turning west onto Fremont, they passed the Papago Cash Store and came to a building with FLY'S ROOMS TO LET on a sign outside. Beyond the Fly building was a vacant lot.

"This way," the voice at Macklin's back said, and he felt the jab of something hard in his kidney, nudging him into the lot past the Fly boardinghouse. Behind the first building was a second, with huge, colorful and ornate lettering on the sign—C. S. FLY, PHOTOGRAPHY GALLERY.

Macklin recognized the area as part of the O. K. Corral, though the main entrance was on Allen Street. Two men were in the corral, holding the reins of six horses. They appeared to be waiting for the grim little parade as it turned off Fremont and entered the lot.

Macklin's eyes shifted left and right, looking for opportunity. A large stable and barn backed the corral, which ran partway around behind the Fly buildings. Fences and walls everywhere; there was no escape in that direction. His captors had him in a box.

"Look, what do you boys want with me?" he asked, trying to keep his voice reasonable and easy. He could sense the nervousness in the men around him. Nervous men and guns; it was not an attractive combination.

"Shaddup, Waco. We're goin' for a little ride."

As they reached the corral gate, Macklin was able to turn and see his captors for the first time. The man with the icy voice was short and angry looking, with light-colored, curly hair and mustache and the kind of beard that was known as an "Imperial," covering just his chin and waxed to a delicate point. He held a Colt .45 in his right hand, partly covered by a frock coat that he'd draped carelessly over his right arm. His eyes had a mean-looking squint, and his mouth seemed set in a perpetual scowl.

From the way he carried himself, swaggering, confident, in control, Macklin guessed that this was Ike Clanton. The younger man standing beside him was almost certainly his brother, Billy Clanton. Billy Claiborne, of course, he'd already met.

The two men with the horses looked as hard and as ruthless as Ike Clanton. One was young—probably still in his teens—and clean-shaven, with long, lank, black hair falling over his forehead, but his eyes were the eyes of a killer. The other man was older, like Ike sporting an Imperial, but his hair was dark, his face more open, and he had eyes that saw everything. Macklin immediately tagged him in his own mind as the smart one of the group . . . the one to watch out for. While Ike was clearly dangerous, he also seemed erratic. This man looked like he knew *exactly* what he was going to do and like he was always calculating the angles.

Dangerous men, all of them. Macklin wondered if he was going to come through this interview alive.

"Got Waco's nag right here," the shaven-faced youngster said with a sneer. "The stable hand knew which one was his and brought him out."

"Where are we going?" Macklin demanded.

"We're going to have a little talk, mister," Ike Clanton said. "Frisk him, Billy!"

Macklin thought he meant Billy Claiborne, but it was the other man with Ike who stepped forward and ran his hands around Macklin's waistband, checked under his vest, and felt the tops of his boots. Macklin decided his guess was right. This was the other Billy in the gang, Billy Clanton.

"I want to know just what the hell you're doing with the Earps," Ike said while Billy frisked him, "and what you thought you'd find out at the ranch yesterday."

"He's clean, Ike."

"Okay. C'mon." Ike gestured with the pistol. "Mount up!"

"Ike Clanton . . ."

The voice, cold as death, called to Ike from the shadows of the barn on the far side of the corral. There was something about that voice, Macklin thought, something that grated on the nerves

"What the—" Clanton stopped, squinting at the figure

masked in darkness. "Oh, it's you, Hank! You blamed near
startled the liver out of me! What you doing in there, anyway?"

"Bring Macklin here. . . ."

" 'Macklin'?" Billy Claiborne said. "Shoot, his name's
Johnny Waco!"

"His name is Macklin," the voice from the shadows
said, "and he is an enemy. Bring him here."

"Hank, what the hell's gotten into you?" Clanton said,
but there was a power for command behind the voice that
compelled obedience. He was already opening the gate and
prodding Macklin inside. The youngster grabbed Macklin
by one elbow, guiding him.

Macklin knew he couldn't let them take him in there.

He wasn't sure what it was, but there was something
about that icy-death voice from the shadows of the barn
that filled him with a deep and trembling terror. He couldn't
let them take him into the barn. He *had* to get away.

His knees felt like water. He was able to use that, sagging
a bit, starting to drop to the ground.

Billy Clanton turned then, stooping to catch Macklin as
he fell, leaning forward, and at that moment, Macklin
shifted all his weight to his left leg and lashed out with his
right, sweeping the legs out from under Billy Clanton and
helping him along with a twist and a snap of his elbow.

Billy Clanton went flying forward, colliding with the corral fence in a flailing tangle of arms and legs. Macklin kept
turning, bringing his right hand around and up, jamming
rigid fingers into Ike Clanton's throat.

Ike gasped and staggered back. Macklin stepped forward
and past the gunman, slamming his elbow into the side of
Clanton's head, catching his gun hand at the same time and
bending it out and back, until nerveless fingers let the Colt
fall.

"God damn you son of a bitch!" Clanton swore.

Macklin was reaching for the gun, his fingers inches away, when Billy Claiborne stepped up behind him and swung the muzzle of his own pistol hard, slamming it into the side of Macklin's skull.

Pain exploded in his head; darkness shot through with flickering lights closed in around him, and he crumpled unconscious into the dust.

◆ **7** ◆

DORIS HAD FOLLOWED MACKLIN AND HIS CAPTORS AND WAS watching from between the two Fly buildings. She saw Macklin's desperate break for freedom, saw one of his captors bring the barrel of a pistol down on his head, saw him being dragged unceremoniously through the gate and into the corral.

She had her newly bought pistol out now but knew she couldn't use it. Not here, not now. It was loaded with four rounds, and there were five abductors. Worse, handguns of all kinds, with their short barrels, were shockingly inaccurate as weapons, and she estimated the range to be at least ten *kij* . . . almost fifty feet. She would have to move closer to be sure of hitting anything, and the cowboys would see her coming.

The pulser wouldn't be much better. She could probably kill all of them, but she risked hitting Macklin, and others in the street would see the dazzling flash of light. She bit off a bitter Gtai curse.

No, damn it, she needed help.

She waited only long enough to see that the men were dragging Macklin into the barn and not, as she'd at first feared, putting him onto one of the horses to take him elsewhere. As soon as they were out of sight, she dropped the pistol back into the pocket of her skirt, then turned and hurried back into the heart of Tombstone.

Perhaps she could find Virgil Earp, or the local sheriff . . . what was his name? Behan, that was it. Johnny Behan. *He* would be able to help her. . . .

⋄ 8 ⋄

"WE'LL START WITH THE EASY QUESTIONS," IKE CLANTON said. "What's your name?"

Macklin blinked, trying to force his eyes open, and to keep them open. Something warm and sticky was trickling down the right side of his head, and he couldn't keep it out of his eye.

He wasn't sure how long he'd been unconscious. All he knew was that after the blackness had closed in on him, he'd started to surface through waves of terrible pain wracking his arms. Looking up, he saw now why. They'd hauled him up against a ladder leading up to the barn's loft, tying his wrists together above his head to one of the rungs. His feet were also tied to the ladder's lowest rung, leaving him stretched him out tight; the pain up his back and stabbing into his shoulders felt like a hot knife.

His clothes were soaking wet, and an empty wooden bucket lay on the floor nearby. They must have doused him with water to bring him around.

"Y'hear me, shorthorn?" Clanton demanded. "What's your name!"

"What the hell good does his name do us?" the man with the dark Imperial said in a tired, exasperated voice.

"Shaddup, Frank!" Ike Clanton said. *"I'm* handlin' this!"

"His name," the cold voice said, "is Macklin. That is the name he used when he arrived in this town."

"And how do you know that, Hank?" Ike said. "Look, I don't need . . . your . . ."

Clanton's voice trailed off. There was something about Hank Attwater, about his voice, that could turn a strong man's will to water.

Macklin was staring at the one they called Hank. The man looked ordinary enough. He was tall, a bit on the thin side, with a long face and a drooping mustache, his cheeks and chin rough with several days' growth of beard. His clothing looked pretty ordinary, too—well-worn jeans, boots, a faded red shirt, a vest like Macklin's, a red kerchief, and a broad-brimmed hat. Ordinary . . . and yet . . .

"I know this man," Attwater said. How could a mere voice carry such cold menace? "His name is Macklin."

"How you know that, Hank?" Billy Clanton asked.

"I *know*." And there was no arguing with that.

"He called hisself 'Johnny Waco' at the ranch yesterday," Claiborne said.

"You're sure he's the same guy?" the clean-shaven kid asked.

"I'm sure, Tom."

Macklin was still trying to piece together the fragments of what he was hearing. Tom and Frank. Tom and Frank McLaury? Had to be, if they were running with Ike and Billy Clanton, and Billy Claiborne. And he'd heard the name "Hank Attwater" mentioned by Finn, yesterday, another member of the Cowboy gang.

There was something different about Attwater, something that made Macklin's skin crawl. He wished he could put his finger on just what it was. It wasn't much more than a feeling, though sometimes, when he moved, Hank just seemed . . . wrong somehow. It was as though Macklin was watching a three-dimensional picture of someone, a picture that moved and talked and acted like a real person but sometimes didn't quite match the background. Once, Macklin saw him turn for a moment, and it was as though his entire body had turned, rotating on an invisible turntable.

An illusion, in other words. An illusion that was almost, but not quite, perfect.

Why did that concept fill Macklin with such dread . . . and such a determination to break free? He struggled against the ropes binding his wrists and found he could do nothing but chafe the skin.

"So tell me, Macklin," Ike said. "I hear you was talkin' with the Earps yesterday, over at the Oriental. They friends of yours?"

Macklin said nothing.

"Answer me when I'm talkin' to you, you son of a bitch!"

Suddenly, Ike swung his fist, a hard-driven roundhouse that landed squarely on Macklin's gut. The blow was so sudden, so unexpected, that Macklin hadn't had time to brace against it. He gave a loud *oof* and tried to double over, but the ropes kept him tightly stretched out.

Ike hit him in the stomach again . . . and then again. The pain was intolerable; Macklin felt like he was about to be sick.

He decided that if he was, he'd try to catch Ike in the explosion.

"Did the Earp boys hire you?" Frank McLaury said. "That's really what we want to know. Did you throw in with them?"

"Yeah," Macklin said. "They're real good pals of mine, and if you don't let me down, they're going to come in here and take you people apart."

There was little point to trying to hold out against the interrogation, Macklin thought. His spy mission to the Clanton ranch had been a flat failure, and the Earps didn't seem that interested in what he had to say anymore in any case. If he admitted that he was working with the Earps, maybe they'd let him go. Or maybe he could negotiate somehow, maybe convince them he was ready to help them against the Earps.

Clanton hit him again, and he groaned. No . . . no . . . he was getting fuzzy in the head. No way would the Clantons let him walk out of here alive after this.

Besides, there was Attwater. Macklin realized he was far more afraid of Attwater than he was of all the rest of them put together.

"Screw this, Ike," Billy Clanton said. "Let's just shoot him and get the hell out."

"That's right, Ike," Tom McLaury said. "We ain't gonna learn nothing from this bastard."

"No!" Ike said. "This guy was bein' used by the Earps to spy on us. I think he knows what they're plannin'!"

An evil light flickered behind Ike Clanton's squinting eyes. Reaching down, he plucked a cowboy's work knife from the scabbard on his belt. Reaching up, he grabbed Macklin's jaw and lifted his head, letting him look at the blade as he turned it in the shaft of light falling through the open barn door.

"See this, Macklin? I can make it easy for you or real, real hard. I want to know everything the Earps are planning. I want to know if they're figurin' on moving against me and the boys. I want to know everything, hear me? Otherwise . . ." For emphasis, he tapped the point of the blade against Macklin's chest. Even through the cloth of his shirt, the metal blade hitting the round disk riding above Macklin's breastbone made a sharp clicking sound. "What the hell . . . ?"

"Ike Clanton . . ." Hank Attwater moved closer, appearing to *glide* over the floor of the barn, more than walking.

Ike whirled about. "Fer Chrissakes, *now* what?"

"Allow me to interrogate Macklin. I can learn everything he knows, and in less time than it will take you."

"What?"

"Leave me alone with the prisoner."

"Not on your life!" Ike glared at Hank. "This here's my prisoner, and I'm gonna find out what he knows!"

"You are presumptuous," Attwater replied.

Somehow, he seemed to be larger now than he'd been a moment ago, the voice deeper. Macklin renewed his struggles against the rope, but to no avail.

"Ike," Frank said. "I think you should do what he says."

"But . . . but . . ." Ike spluttered, trembling at the edge of sheer rage.

"C'*mon,* Ike," Billy said, taking his brother's arm. "Let's clear out, okay?" He looked at Attwater in a way that suggested he was as scared of the man as Macklin was.

Hank Attwater reached out. In his hand, he held something gleaming silver and gold. It looked like a very slender railway spike, the pointed end as sharp as the tip of any knife. "I promise you, Ike Clanton, that you will have the information you want. He can*not* lie to me."

"Well . . ." Ike's fury seemed to evaporate. He, obviously, was frightened, too. "Just so we find out," he said. "C'mon, boys. . . ."

The Clantons started to leave, abandoning him to Attwater.

THIRTEEN

◆ **1** ◆

THE GUNSHOT CRACKED IMPOSSIBLY LOUD IN THE ECHOING confines of the barn. Clanton jumped and whirled, dropping the knife, and several of the men with him reached for their own guns.

"Just hold it right there, boys," a woman's voice said from the doorway. "Put your hands up where I can see 'em! Move!"

Ike Clanton was practically shaking with pent-up tension and anger. Who the hell was that? He couldn't see very well in the barn's dim interior, nothing much more than a slender figure standing in the door, silhouetted against the light outside. A woman! She was holding a pistol, and gunsmoke hung thick in the doorway, drifting slowly in the sunlight.

"Who the hell are you?" Frank demanded.

"Never mind. That man you have there is a friend of mine. You men get the hell out of here, out that back door, over there. Don't look back, and I just might let you live!"

"You *might* let us . . ." Ike's eyes opened wide, and he brandished the knife in his hand. "You bitch! I'll cut your heart out!"

The pistol in the woman's hand swung to point squarely at Clanton's face. "You'll find that kind of hard to manage," the woman said, "with the gray jelly you call a brain splattered all over that back wall behind you, there. Want to try me?"

"You have no right to interfere here! This ain't none of your business!"

"I'm making it my business," the woman said. Every man in the barn heard the chilling *snick* as she thumbed the pistol's hammer back. "I *won't* tell you again!"

Ike muttered something foul under his breath, but Frank laid a hand on his shoulder. "C'mon, Ike. This isn't the place or the time." Reluctantly, Ike started moving toward the barn's back door. Frank, Tom, and both Billys turned to follow.

Hank Attwater stood rooted to the spot, an unreadable expression on his face. Suddenly, he swung about, bellowed something incomprehensible . . . and lunged for the woman in the doorway. . . .

❖ 2 ❖

DORIS SAW THE COWBOY TURN AND JUMP TOWARD HER. HE was fifteen feet away as she whipped the .32 away from the one called "Ike" and aimed it squarely at the man in the red shirt. He was ten feet away when she pulled the trigger.

Her second shot crashed out, the stab of orange flame from the muzzle startlingly bright in the barn's dim light, the smoke a sudden cloud of blue-white haze swirling in the dusty air. She hit him . . . she *knew* she'd hit him. The cowboy skidded to a clumsy stop five feet away but didn't appear to be otherwise hurt. She squeezed the trigger again, aiming for his center of mass, and he seemed to fold a bit, to take a staggering step backward. It was almost as if . . . as if he *shimmered* for a brief moment. . . .

"Hank!" one of the other men shouted. "Hank! Did she getcha?"

Astonishingly, Hank did not fall. He turned and moved toward the others, unsteadily wavering toward the barn's back door. There was something odd about his movements, Doris thought, as she squinted through the hanging cloud of smoke, something not quite right. *Damn* the light. It was hard to see.

"We'll get you, bitch!" Ike screamed at her. "We'll hunt you down and *get* you for this!"

One of the others tried to put an arm around Hank, but the wounded cowboy straightened up. *"Don't touch me!"*

"Let's *go,* Ike!" Frank said. Doris kept her pistol aimed at them as they shouldered open the door and backed out through the opening.

And then she was alone in the barn with the trussed-up Macklin.

Hurriedly, she cracked open the revolver's cylinder, which now held only a single round and three empty casings. She emptied the spent brass on the floor, then thumbed in four more cartridges snatched from the handful loose in her pocket. The cowboys might be back at any moment, and she was badly outnumbered and outgunned. The one called Ike had dropped a knife on the floor in the confusion. Stooping, she scooped it up, cut through the rope binding Macklin's ankles to the ladder, then reached high and cut the rope on his wrists.

Macklin collapsed to the floor like a sack of potatoes. "Who . . . are you?" Macklin asked through bloodied lips.

Doris felt a pang of hurt and fear slash through her. Doc Shea had said he'd lost his memory. If he didn't even remember *her* . . .

"Never mind that now," she told him, struggling to keep her voice crisp and businesslike. "We've got to get you out of here. Those . . . people might be back any minute now, and I don't want to be here when they come! Think you can walk?"

Macklin looked like he was in pretty bad shape. There was a nasty gash on the right side of his head where one of the cowboys had clubbed him, and it looked as though they'd worked him over with their fists pretty well both before they'd tied him up and after. With her help, he pulled himself up into a sitting position. "Think . . . so," he murmured. "Can . . . can you help me up?"

It took all her strength to get him on his feet, and he had to use the ladder to help pull himself up, but somehow they managed. He took a tottering step or two toward the barn door. She stepped in close, put her arm around his back, and let him lean on her. Together, they began making their way toward the sunlight.

"Hank . . . Attwater," Macklin said, the name slurred. "Dangerous . . ."

"I shot him," Doris said, wondering. "I shot him *twice.* I know I didn't miss! What the hell *is* he?"

But she was pretty sure that she knew the answer to that question already.

⋄ 3 ⋄

OUT BEHIND THE BARN, THE SIX COWBOYS TOOK STOCK OF their situation. All but Hank had their guns out now, and they were looking back at the barn with mingled fury and fear.

"I say we should rush her!" Ike said. "There ain't but one of her, and there's six of us!"

"You want to go in first, Ike?" Frank said. "She might have the door covered from in there."

"We could just start shooting through the barn's walls," Billy Clanton pointed out.

"They's probably gone already," Tom McLaury said.

"We need to get Hank to a doctor," Billy Claiborne pointed out. "That bitch shot him."

"I am . . . not seriously hurt," Hank said. He was sitting on a bale of straw against the back wall of the stable, deep in the shade.

"We should at least take a look," Frank said. "Where'd the whore nail you?"

"Never mind," Hank said. "Stay . . . away. It is . . ." He hesitated, as though searching for the right phrase. "Just a scratch."

"I'm gonna go back in there . . ." Ike said, waggling his revolver in the air. But he didn't move. He didn't like the idea of being the first one through that door one bit, and he was hoping one of the others would go in first.

"There's people comin', Ike," Frank pointed out. "C'mon, you guys. Put the hardware away. We've got company!"

Even in a wild town like Tombstone, gunshots brought out the curious and the morbid. A small crowd of townspeople, men, mostly, but a scattering of kids, were coming down Fremont Street in several noisy packs, some spilling through the vacant lot, the corral, and entering the barn, and others coming around behind Fly's place, approaching the gunmen hiding at the building's rear.

In the lead was John Clum, the town's mayor and the editor of the *Tombstone Epitaph*. He was the head of the Citizens' Law and Order League and a solid pro-Earp man. "Clanton!" he shouted, when he saw Ike. "What in tarnation's going on here?"

"We should arrest 'em for disturbin' the peace!" another

voice called out. Ike looked and saw Doc Holliday in the crowd.

"We was just in there," Billy Clanton said, excited, "and this woman—"

"Nothing going on here," Ike said, nudging his brother hard in the ribs with an elbow, and stepping out in front of him. "Nothing at all!"

"What was all the shootin' we heard?" Clum demanded.

"Wasn't us, Mayor," Ike said, truthfully enough. He spread his hands. "We heard some gunshots and came 'round back here to check 'em out. Didn't find nothing. You boys see anything around front?"

"Ike, you yellow-bellied liar," Holliday snarled.

"And you're a damned son of a bitch, Holliday. . . ."

Clum put a hand on Holliday's arm as the man started to reach for his gun. "Enough, Doc. Let it go."

"I'll see you later, Clanton," Holliday said, shaking a finger at Ike. The crowd began breaking up, disappointed that there was nothing to see.

"Ike? What the deuce is goin' on around here?"

Ike turned to face Sheriff Behan, just coming out of the barn. "This crazy girl came runnin' into my office a few minutes ago. Told me a wild story about some guy bein' kidnapped, and that I should get right over here. From her description, it sounded like you boys were involved."

"Yeah? What'd you tell her, Sheriff?" Frank demanded.

"To mind her own business, of course. She left, mad as a skinned rattler. Then I heard shots and figured I'd better see what the story was."

"That woman is crazy, Sheriff!" Ike said. "She like t've killed us. She shot poor Hank over there. . . ."

"Hank Attwater?" Behan looked past Ike. "Where is he?"

"Why right—" Ike turned to point. The hay bale against

the wall was empty. There was no sign of Hank.

"Must've lit out when the crowd showed up," Billy Claiborne said. "Anybody see him go?"

None of them had.

"He was shot, y'say?"

"He wouldn't let us see the wound," Frank said. "But it looked to me like he was hit, maybe pretty bad."

"I *want* that bitch," Ike said. "Who the hell was she?"

"Friend of Macklin's, she claimed," Tom said. "That tells us something. We find Macklin, we should find her."

"I wouldn't mind gettin' hold of her," Billy Clanton said.

"She was a real looker, and no mistake!" Tom agreed.

"Not after I get done with her," Billy said, sneering. "I'd like to get her alone out in the range someplace. I'd like t'stake her out, cut all that pretty, store-bought finery off her body, an'—"

"You stop that kind of talk, Billy," Sheriff Behan warned. "I don't want t'hear it."

"You just mind your sheriffin', Sheriff," Ike said. "We'll take care of that bitch real good an' proper. *And* her boyfriend. Let's go, boys."

As they started to leave, Frank McLaury stopped and looked around. "Wish I knew where Hank had got to," he said. "Wish I knew if he was all right!"

As they left the lot behind the barn, none of them noticed the droplets of milky blue liquid seeping into the dust in several spots and in the hay where Hank had been sitting.

Blue droplets the color of Hunter blood. . . .

◆ **4** ◆

DORIS MADE IT BACK TO SARAH NEVERS'S BOARDINGHOUSE with Macklin leaning against her. They got a few off-looks in the street, but by the time they approached the Nevers house, a man who introduced himself as Tom McGreevy, a long-term boarder there, came out to help. One on either side of the injured man, the two of them supported Macklin up the steps and through the door. Sarah was there, holding a dish towel.

"What happened?" she exclaimed.

"The Clanton boys were playing a little rough," Doris told her.

Sarah glared and started to say something to her, but Doris brushed past, still helping Macklin walk. "Can't stay to chat, dear. I want to get my brother upstairs and into bed, fast! Which room is it?

"Top of the stairs, to your right, third door." She sounded resigned.

"Thank you!" Doris said with a musical cant.

"Should . . . should I fetch a doctor?"

Doris and the others already had him halfway up the stairs. "Not necessary, Mrs. Nevers. I'll have him fixed up in no time."

If she only knew. . . .

McGreevy helped ease Macklin onto the bed. "Sure we shouldn't get a doctor, ma'am?" he said.

"He's just a little bruised, is all," Doris said. "One of the Clantons whacked him over the head with his gun, then worked him over a little. Help me with his boots."

"He might have a concussion, ma'am," McGreevy said, tugging off one of the mule-ear boots by the loops at the top that gave them their name, then the other. "That's a right nasty cut he has on his head."

"I've had some training," she replied. "I'll see that he's all right."

The moment McGreevy was out the door, Doris closed and locked it behind him, then opened her handbag and pulled out the medwand from her escape pod's survival kit.

She passed the wand over Macklin's entire body from head to toe, watching the lights flicker in its translucent depths, listening to the whisper of her Companion as it recited the wand's findings in her mind.

Cuts . . . bruises . . . contusions . . . and a slight concussion. No internal damage, thank the Old Ones, no ruptured organs or internal bleeding. A cracked rib on the right side. Strained muscles in the shoulders and back. Nothing crippling.

First things first, however. With a mental command to her Companion, the medwand glowed bright blue and gave a faint hum. She held it above the cut on Macklin's head, letting it stimulate and program the microscopic nanomeds in Macklin's blood. After a few minutes, she moved the wand to Macklin's right side and held it there to program the knitting of his rib.

When she glanced back at his face, his eyes were open and clear, and he was staring at her, recognition etched in his face. "You . . ."

Her heart gave a leap. "You remember me?"

His forehead creased with the puzzled frown she knew so well. "I'm . . . sorry. Not really. But I think I've seen you before . . . in a dream. That sounds crazy, I know."

Somehow, she managed to conceal her disappointment, to keep her voice light. "Not at all."

"But . . . you *know* me? You know who I am? What I'm doing here?"

His helplessness, his vulnerability was so complete it hurt, bringing tears momentarily to her eyes. "Yes, Ma'khleen. I know you *very* well!"

" 'Ma'khleen'? " He tasted the name. "They call me 'Macklin' here."

"I know. I've been hunting for you a long time, you know that? For the past four days, it seems, every place I go, you've been there but already gone! You're a hard man to pin down, 'Mr. Macklin.' ''

"I . . . I thought I was going crazy! I didn't know who I was! I just knew . . . just knew I didn't belong here!''

"What *do* you remember?"

"I . . . I remember being in the desert."

"Nothing before that?"

He shook his head, then winced with the effort. "No. Except for the dreams."

"What do you remember of them?"

"I remember . . . a city, with blue light everywhere. People, lots of people and . . . and people who didn't look like me. Like *us*. The sky . . . the sky was very different. Beautiful, spectacularly beautiful, but very different. Different stars. A different sun. I guess this isn't making much sense. It's kind of hard to explain."

"You're doing fine. That's Shanidar you're remembering. That's *home.*''

"Home?"

"We're not from Earth, you know. Either of us. We're . . . visitors here. Observers."

"That's . . . kind of hard to take in. I don't remember . . .'' He rubbed his eyes. "This, this Shanidar. Where is it?"

She sighed. "Right now, friend Macklin, home is so far away that a beam of light would take almost ten thousand Earth years to get there."

"Is that far?"

"That is very far, believe me. Do you remember anything else from your dreams?"

"I remember seeing you. . . .'' He closed his eyes. "We were . . . we were making love." His eyes opened again, and he looked worried, as if he might have said the wrong thing. "There's something in me telling me I shouldn't say things like that. There's a part of me that feels it's okay. I . . . I'm sorry. . . .''

"Go on. You're doing fine. We were lovers on Shanidar.'' The words hurt as she said them. *And damn it, when he remembers, we will be again!*

She was thinking furiously. Macklin's AI must be intact and still trying to guide him, but the mere fact that he had near-total amnesia suggested that either the AI or the connections with Macklin's cerebral cortex were damaged.

"And I remember a . . . a ship of some kind. And the moon, very bright, very close. There was an attack. Some . . . some terrible danger. And I remember falling. . . .''

"It sounds like you remember quite a lot. Or else your Companion is feeding you log playbacks while you sleep. How are you feeling now?''

She could see him taking mental stock. "Better.'' He blinked, surprised. "A *lot* better! My head's stopped hurting. So has my side. How . . . ?''

"You have some extremely tiny machines inside you, machines smaller than your blood cells.'' She gestured with the medwand. "Through this, my Companion can program them to heal specific injuries . . . patch torn blood vessels and muscles, dry up edema to reduce swelling, knit bones, accelerate healing in cuts, that sort of thing.''

"What the hell is this 'Companion' you keep mentioning?''

She returned the medwand to her handbag, then reached over and unbuttoned his shirt, tugging it open to expose his chest. She brushed the black disk on his breastbone lightly with her fingers.

"A Class Three implant,'' she told him. "A computer and communications nexus with a resident artificial intelligence and nanolinkages grown inside your brain, especially throughout the cerebral cortex, where your memories are housed, and the cerebellum, where certain reflexes and muscular training can be coordinated. The computer includes an extremely complete database on Earth cultures, technologies, and languages, to help us blend in during our mission here.'' She frowned at his blank expression. ''Are you following any of this?''

''A word here and there,'' he told her. '' 'Mission'?''

''Don't worry. It'll all be clear very soon. We just have to let our Companions link directly.''

Bending over, she untied her high, stiff, black leather shoes and kicked them off. Then, gracefully, watching him with a playful, sidelong smile, she rose from the side of the bed and began unbuttoning her blouse. Macklin's eyes stayed locked on her as she discarded the blouse, stepped out of her skirt with its ridiculous and uncomfortable bustle positioned over her bottom, and began attacking the various items of clothing she'd worn underneath. A long shift. A corset. Other arcane and mysterious items for which she couldn't even remember the name without perusing her Companion's database.

Standing before him now in the ship suit she'd worn beneath the Earth clothing, a black smartgarment that hugged each curve as tightly as a second skin, she reached up and dragged her thumbnail down the center of her body, from throat to crotch. As she did so, the skinsuit split open, curling back, peeling away from her sides and legs, folding upon itself and then dropping away in a small, neat package the size of her thumb, leaving her gloriously, comfortably naked.

''I am *so* glad to be out of those damned, stinking rags!'' she said, stretching her arms high and breathing deeply. ''You be glad you're a man and don't have to wear all of that stuff!''

She walked over and climbed into the bed, sitting cross-legged, facing him.

His eyes widened as he stared at her torso. Set into the pale skin between and beneath her full, round breasts was another smooth, glassy, black disk, identical to his own. "You know," he said, "I was starting to go crazy for a while there." He touched his Companion. "I didn't know what this was. I didn't know if there was anyone else in the whole world who had one. I just knew it wasn't . . . wasn't a part of me."

"Normally it's not," she told him. "Most people on Shanidar get along with Class One or maybe Class Two implants. Enough for communication and downloading the news. Entertainment. Maybe learning a new language or getting to experience the latest *fel*. We get Class Threes because we're in the Monitor Corps. We need the extra AI, and we need the big on-board database."

"You know, I don't have the faintest idea what you're talking about." He cocked his head to the side in the manner she loved so much, studying her face. "What's your name?"

She started to tell him, but he held up his hand. "Wait! Is it . . . Dorree?"

"That's my Gtai name. Like yours is Ma'khleen. Here, you'd better call me 'Doris.' "

"Doris." He sounded like he was trying it on for size. "Doris. I like that."

"Let's see now," she said. She reached over and pressed her fingertip against the black disk in his chest. As she leaned over him, she felt his eyes watching the hang of her breasts, a warm caress. Deliberately, with a mischievous smile, she let the tips brush across the taut skin of his belly, just above the waistband of his jeans, a promise for later.

Then a feeder filament sprouted from his Companion,

weaving in the air above his chest like an angry black snake. Macklin started, eyes bulging, and nearly leaped out of the bed.

"It's okay! It's okay!" she told him, laying a gentling hand on his chest. "I'm sorry! Poor darling, I should have warned you!"

Guided by her Companion's silent call, the filament stretched itself through the air and seemed to merge its head with Doris's Companion, sinking in and becoming one with it. Other filaments snaked through the air, some from her implant, some from Macklin's, crisscrossing one another to complete the link between the two AIs.

Data flowed freely between the two. Doris could hear her own Companion AI's whispers . . . and the whisper of Macklin's Companion as well, describing what had happened to it, the damage it had suffered, in a lightning flicker of hard data.

The computer AIs, of course, spoke with one another in a language and at a speed far beyond human comprehension, but Doris heard the translation from her Companion.

The cranial nanoconnections between Ma'khleen's AI and his left cerebral hemisphere have been badly damaged or severed, her Companion whispered. *The connections with his right brain are damaged but, for the most part, remain intact. Ma'khleen's AI has been trying to reestablish communication with his conscious mind but with only minimal and extremely intermittent success. Thus far, most contact has been limited to feelings, intuitions, and when Ma'khleen is asleep, dreams. He retains some of the special skills implanted before the mission—in particular, his expertise with the weapons common to this culture. However, he has lost access both to his native memories and to the cultural patterns stored in his AI's files. He has been having a great deal of trouble understanding the local sexual mores, for example, though his Companion has managed to guide him, through feelings of embarrassment and intuition, to keep him from making serious cultural blunders.*

"He appears to have settled on the English language implant for this region, though he still retains limited understanding of Gtai and a few other languages. His coordination is—"

Yes, but can he be healed? Doris's thought was a silent, anguished scream. *Has his mind been permanently damaged?*

Unknown was the less than reassuring reply. *His Companion retains its self-repair facilities, but the damage—especially to Ma'khleen's left cerebral cortex—is severe and probably beyond the scope of the nanomeds now implanted in his bloodstream. His AI reports that it requires significant quantities—on the order of a tenth to two-tenths' microgram—of several elements not yet known to this civilization's science.* The AI gave the element's Gtai names, words referring to atomic weights that would have translated as lutetium and europeum. *It also requires approximately a microgram of tellurium, an element known to this world but not easily available.*

If we get these elements to him, he can be healed? The question trembled with desperate hope.

Almost certainly. Either pure traces of these elements could be ingested by Ma'khleen or unrefined samples could be absorbed by his Companion and refined by its materials processor. Finding these elements, however, will be difficult in this primitive culture.

"Jia neh!" Doris replied aloud, a Gtai curse, a dismissal of trivialities. She added, in thought, *When we reestablish contact with the other Monitors, we'll be able to signal for help. He'll be fine if we can get him home.*

I must point out, her Companion replied, *that we are cut off from all contact with other Monitors, both in space and on this planet. It is likely that the Monitor base on this planet's moon has been destroyed by the Kra'agh. There must be ships still within this system, and we may even be able to signal them . . . but the indications are that the Kra'agh have blockaded this planet. We can expect no help from off-world.*

A Kra'agh blockade . . . and, almost certainly, at least one Hunter on the planet, searching for the two of them.

Not an inviting prospect.

Not an inviting prospect at *all*. . . .

FOURTEEN

❖ 1 ❖

"WELL, DOC?" MACKLIN ASKED, STUDYING THE FROWN NES-
tled over Doris's lovely face. "What's the diagnosis?"

Doris leaned back then, as the links connecting her AI
with his silently snapped, the severed filaments whipping
back into the implants' black, translucent depths. She
looked so grave, so serious. He wondered if she was going
to put her clothes on again, now that she'd done what she
had to with the AIs. He hoped not. He liked looking at her
this way, liked watching her. He was feeling warm and
comfortable and *safe* in a way he hadn't felt at all since his
earliest clear memories . . . stumbling alone and lost
through the desert somewhere north of Tombstone.

He felt accepted. Known. Peaceful. *At home.* And it was
all due to this beautiful woman sitting next to his legs at
the foot of the bed.

And . . . she'd said they'd been lovers, once? His heart
beat a little faster at the thought. He wanted her . . . wanted
her very badly. . . .

"The diagnosis?" she said. She'd appeared to be listening to something, or someone, a voice Macklin couldn't

hear. "Nothing that can't be fixed, if we can get you back to someplace civilized."

Macklin was still having some trouble coming to grips with the idea that he was from another planet. He looked about the room, at the chintz curtains, the flowered wallpaper. "This isn't civilization?"

She sighed, laying a hand on his knee. He liked the touch. "Macklin, these people still believe in *bleeding* people, of all things, as a cure for almost anything you could imagine. They're one step removed from witchcraft, black magic, and healing ceremonies! I was just reading a book downstairs that recommended bloodletting and *leeches* for—" She stopped herself, watching his puzzlement. "Leeches. Do you know what those are?"

"A kind of . . . of worm. A parasite that sucks blood, frequently used in medical treatment in this culture." His brows came together. "How do I know things like that? The other day, I knew words like *pommel* and *saddle* and *horse.*" He shook his head. "I felt like I'd never seen any of those things, yet I knew them. But I didn't know I needed to wear a hat out in the desert. . . ."

"Your AI," Doris told him, "contains a database, a kind of memory of millions of facts, things about language, culture, and just getting along with people on this planet. There's an awful lot to know. Too much to learn without AI assistance." She pointed at his head. "You took some damage up there when your lifepod crashed. Some connections with your AI were severed. Others damaged. You can't communicate directly with your Companion anymore. It has to rely on intuition and feeling to get thoughts through."

"I don't understand."

"Humans essentially have two brains. The cerebrum, the big, thinking and remembering part, is divided into two halves, the left and right hemispheres. Follow?''

He nodded.

"Okay. It's almost like we do have two brains. Most of the cognitive processes, numbers, language skills, are all centered on the left side. The right side handles things like intuition, feeling, emotion. That's not an absolute breakdown, of course, and the processes in women's brains tend to be more evenly distributed than in men's.'' She smiled. "That's why we tend to rely a bit more on emotions and feelings than you men do.''

"Except that I've been feeling like I've been living on nothing *but* feelings and guesses and intuitions lately,'' he told her. "I guess this explains why.''

"Partly. And you've also been feeling pretty lost, I imagine, just not knowing who you were, where you were. . . .''

"Will I get my memories back?''

"Yes. . . .'' She didn't sound entirely sure about that, and her hesitation chilled Macklin's soul.

"What's the matter? Is there a problem?''

"The problem,'' she told him, "is that we're both stranded on this primitive dirtball of a planet. Our ship was destroyed, and we have no immediate way to get off this rock and back home.''

He sighed. "And home, I take it . . . Shanidar, you said?'' She nodded. "Shanidar is where I have to go to get myself fixed up?''

"Shanidar, or any of the other Associative worlds. Even one of our starships would have the medical facilities to fix you right up.''

"Associative?''

"Um . . . that's a kind of loosely knit collective of civilizations that have banded together for mutual protection and to protect emergent species, like ours. Like Earth. The Monitor Corps is a kind of guardianship over young cultures. We're Monitors . . . you and I, working for the Associative.''

''I'm not sure I understand,'' he told her. ''Are we . . . human?''

She laughed. ''Oh, yes! As human as anyone on this planet. Our ancestors came from here.''

''Our . . . ancestors?''

''There are more different races among the stars than anyone could possible imagine,'' she told him, ''and each one is different from every other. The chances that a species evolving on one world would look *anything* like the natives of another, well, they're so small they're not worth thinking about.

''Obviously, the Monitors need to be able to watch over worlds, especially primitive ones, like Earth, that can't be considered yet for membership in the Associative, and they need to have operatives who can live on those worlds without calling attention to themselves. What usually happens is they secretly pick up a number of natives, usually people who were in terrible danger, for one reason or another, and isolated, out of the mainstream of their civilization. They'd take them to another, uninhabited world to start a colony. Those people are carefully trained, given the advantages of advanced civilization. Within a few hundred years, you have people who can return to the homeworld and serve as the Associative's eyes and ears without being noticed by the locals.''

''So . . . our ancestors came from Earth. They were kidnapped?''

''Ours were from a place called Roanoke, to be exact,'' she told him. ''A colony of English settlers was planted there almost three hundred Earth years ago, in 1587 by the local calendar. But the colony was dying, threatened by disease, by hostile natives, by war with an enemy nation,

Spain. They were in the process of trying to move their colony anyway, to a neighboring island called Croatoan, when the Gtai ships arrived." She shrugged. "It wasn't really a mass kidnapping. The colony was on the verge of extinction. Our ancestors were happy enough to get away from there. So far as the rest of the world was concerned, though, those hundreds of people just . . . vanished.

"For the past two centuries now, our people have been watching Earth for the Associative. We have . . . we *had* a base on Earth's moon, and we have agents scattered about the planet in various places, in hidden outposts, as observers. We were on our way to become observers here, you and I, when . . . when we were attacked."

"Attacked? By who?"

She sighed. "I'm . . . not sure. There are a number of species who don't adhere to the Associative Charter. Or who oppose Associative policies on emergent worlds."

Macklin had the impression that Doris wasn't telling him all she knew. She sounded worried . . . maybe even a little scared. He wondered what she was hiding from him. He shook his head.

"Are you okay?" she asked.

"This . . . this is all a little hard to take in."

"Having trouble believing it?"

"Not really. There's just so much. It . . . it kind of takes getting used to."

"We're going to have to leave here, you know."

"Leave? And go where?"

"Out of Tombstone, first of all. Maybe up into the hills outside of town. I have an emergency communicator from the lifepod. If I can establish contact with one of our ships, we may be able to call one in for a pickup."

"But . . . why can't we do that here?" He found he didn't want to leave Sarah Nevers's place. It had become like home these past few days, a place of refuge. Of safety.

"Well, first off, we wouldn't want a Gtai ship setting down at high noon in the middle of Fremont Street, would we? It would attract attention . . . and do some serious damage to this culture. People on Earth, you see, still think theirs is the only inhabited world in the universe. It'll be a real shock for them when they learn differently, unless they're carefully prepared first.

"Besides . . ." She hesitated, and Macklin sensed again the worry in her. "We're not safe here. Or we won't be for long. I want to get out of this place as quickly as we can."

He levered himself up on his elbow. "When. Now?"

She considered the question. "We have some time, I think. . . ."

"How long?" He smiled at her. "I'd kind of like to get to know my traveling companion first, before we head off over the desert."

Her answering smile was radiant. Warming. Gently, leaning forward, she laid her hand on his chest and pushed him back down on the bed. "For one thing, you need rest, and time for the nanomeds to finish your healing. We won't get far if I have to carry you. I think I'd like us to be on the move tomorrow."

"Then there's still tonight," he told her.

"Oh, yes. There's still tonight."

Still smiling, she unbuckled his belt, and began tugging off his pants.

❖ 2 ❖

IN THE HALLWAY OUTSIDE, SARAH STOOPED OVER, PRESSING her eye close to the door's keyhole. The bed in the room beyond was off to the right and hard to see, but she could just make out *that* woman, her back to the door, sitting on the bed. She'd just pulled Macklin's jeans off and tossed them on the floor, and now . . . and now . . .

Sarah stifled a gasp, pressing one fist against her mouth. The way Doris's head was moving . . . Disgusting! She'd *heard* about that sort of thing . . . but so far as she knew, only whores ever used their mouths to . . . to . . .

Well, she thought bitterly, *what did you expect?*

"Mrs. Nevers?"

It was Harry Fulbright coming up the stairs. Quickly, she reached down and fiddled briefly with the hem of her skirt before straightening up again. "Why, yes, Mr. Fulbright?"

"Anything wrong, Mrs. Nevers?"

"Why, nothing," she said airily. "Nothing at all. Good afternoon, Mr. Fulbright."

She kept her composure until she reached her room.

She cried for a long time after that.

◆ 3 ◆

IT WAS MIDAFTERNOON WHEN IKE CLANTON WALKED INTO Hafford's Corner Saloon, striding up to the bar and demanding a bottle of McBryan's. He was still shaken by the encounter with that woman in the barn behind the O.K. Corral and figured a few shots of the good stuff would steady his nerves. He paid for the bottle and was on the way to a table in the back when he was stopped by a familiar voice at his back.

"There he is," Doc Holliday said in an easy drawl, loud enough to be heard by everyone in the saloon. "The boy who let a *woman* get the drop on him!"

Clanton set the bottle on the table, then turned. Holliday was standing near the saloon's door, hands at his sides, the right hand an inch away from the grip of his holstered revolver.

"Shaddup, Holliday."

"You gonna make me, Ike?" Holliday said with an oily sneer. "I'm not sure you're as tough as everybody used t'think."

"Who the hell told you I got pushed around by a girl?"

"Oh, the word's been gettin' around. Tom McLaury was talkin' about it, over in the Alhambra Saloon."

"God *damn* it!" Ike exploded. Damn McLaury and his big mouth!

Holliday laughed. "I figure if a little slip of a girl can push you around, you're not such a big man after all. More of a pathetic little windbag, if you ask me."

"Back off, Holliday," Clanton said. He kept his voice low and dangerous.

"Or what?" Holliday chuckled again. The chuckle turned to a rasping cough, but the man quickly recovered. "You gonna have your girlfriend beat me up? That must've really stuck in your craw, havin' a filly get the drop on you, and a young, pretty one at that! Ha! Wish I'd been there to see it!"

Ike drew himself up taller, making himself as imposing as he could. His right hand dropped slowly to the butt of his Colt, the fingers curling around the grip but not pulling it clear of leather. "I'm warnin' you, Holliday. I don't take that crap from anybody."

Holliday's eyes flicked down, then up to Ike's face. "Yeah? What you gonna do about it, son? You gonna draw on me? You want to have it out, right here, right now? 'Cause you've been goin' around this town, bad-mouthing me and bad-mouthing my friends, and I figure it's about time for you to put up or shut up!"

"You filthy pig. . . ."

"And you are a no-account, yellow-bellied mongrel bag of wind who ain't never gonna amount to nothin'. You're as full of hot air as a bull at green corn time, Clanton, and

I think you don't have the guts to go for that gun right here, right now!''

"If'n I was to plug you right now, Holliday, every man in this town would cheer me! They'd give me a medal!''

"Yeah? Let's see.'' Holiday's right hand was on his gun now. "Go ahead! Let's have it out, right now!''

Ike Clanton swallowed hard, his breath coming in short, panting gasps. He'd been thinking for a long time how good it would be to shoot Holliday down like a dog, but he hadn't figured on it being face-to-face, like this. When he had a score to settle, he preferred to do it the safe and sure way . . . from the back.

And then Ike saw something else, something that made his blood turn to ice.

Virgil Earp was in the bar. Damn, when had he come in? Ike hadn't noticed. Virgil was seated by the lunch counter, though. He was watching the tableau between Ike and Holliday . . . and right now, his right hand was hidden inside his coat.

A setup. A damned setup! Holiday was goading him on, trying to get him to pull a gun . . . just so Virgil Earp could shoot him down, shoot him, or haul him off to jail.

No. Ike was too smart for that. Slowly, he let his breath out . . . and slowly, he moved his hand away from his revolver.

"No, Holliday,'' he said. "You sons-of-bitches won't get me like that!''

"I knew you were a yellow, lily-livered coward, Clanton!'' He coughed again, then added with a wheeze, "You don't have the guts for a stand-up fight!''

"You want a fight, Holliday, you'll get it!'' He nodded toward Earp. "But not with your *friends* ready to plug me in the back!''

Grabbing the bottle of whiskey, gathering what remained

of his dignity about him, Clanton stormed toward the door.

Holliday stepped into his path. ''You runnin', Clanton? You're a coward!''

''It's you and the Earps who'll be runnin' after today!'' Ike snapped back. ''Just wait and see!'' Furious, he brushed past Holiday, banged through the bat-wing doors, and stepped out into the afternoon heat.

He heard Holliday's cackle at his back, a grating, consumptive sound that only fed the black, ice-cold hatred already filling his heart, mind, and soul.

✦ 4 ✦

ITS INJURIES HAD NOT BEEN SEVERE, BUT THEY HURT. PAINspinner had never known such exquisite pain, even when sampled from the minds and souls of the still-living beings it patterned and devoured. Feelings experienced at secondhand were always remote, a bit fuzzy, made dull by distance. There was nothing dull at all about the sharp fire lancing through its body when the human female shot it.

Her first round had penetrated Painspinner's upper jaw and passed cleanly through its head. Fortunately, its anatomy was considerably different from that of humans and many other bilaterally symmetrical beings throughout the galaxy; the Kra'agh brain was safely tucked away beneath a massive bone shell in the hump on its back. The second round had buried itself in its body, close to the base of its neck.

After slipping away from the Clantons, Painspinner had found an out-of-the-way, out-of-the-sunlight hiding place beneath the front porch of a nearby house. There, it examined its wounds, using a small laser to cauterize the wounds in its head and stop the bleeding.

The other wound, with the bullet still deep inside, would require sterner measures.

It was angry at Macklin's escape, angrier still at the sudden and dramatic rescue staged by the human female. It had been reasonably certain that Macklin was one of the shipwrecked Monitors; now it was certain that the female was the other one. It should have had *them, had them both, and they'd escaped.*

Finding them now, in this warren of human habitations, would not be easy. It might be possible to pick up their scent . . . or a bloodtrail, if Macklin was bleeding from his injuries.

Working swiftly, it thrust one black slasher claw into the wound at the base of its neck, probing deep, finding the deep-buried bullet and working it free. The pain . . . the pain was a searing fire. Painspinner's shriek startled dogs to wild yapping in every direction and convinced several residents in the area that a mountain lion had wandered down from the Dragoon Mountains to scavenge through garbage at the edge of town. Pain was an important part of Kra'agh culture, a proof of life, an offering to an indifferent cosmos.

Sealing the wound at last, Painspinner lay back, panting. It would need some time to recuperate, to regain its strength. After that . . . perhaps it could find the place where Macklin was hiding. Perhaps not.

Either way, tonight it would return to Deathstalker, in the hills outside of the town.

In the human Ike Clanton, Painspinner had sensed . . . not a kindred spirit, exactly, but a comprehensible one. A mind saturated with a greed and a blind lust for power that the Kra'agh could use, to exploit for their own purposes.

It would need to talk to Ike Clanton tonight, to see if some sort of arrangement could be made. . . .

And then the two Monitor fugitives could be tracked down and killed.

❖ 5 ❖

IT WAS GROWING DARK WHEN DORIS CLIMBED OUT OF BED AND padded across the bare wooden floor to the window. Tombstone, it seemed, lived two lives. By day, it was a rough place and no mistake, but there were plenty of respectable citizens about, making a living and going on about their lives. At night, though, most of the respectable types vanished indoors, leaving the streets to the wild and rowdy elements, to celebrating cowboys, to gamblers and prostitutes, to people looking for trouble, or finding it.

From here, she could hear shouts and laughter floating up from Tombstone's red-light district over on Sixth Street and from Whiskey Row on Allen.

She watched, listening, and shivered.

Doris looked back at Macklin, sprawled on his back, sound asleep. Briefly, she considered waking him so they could go find some dinner, then decided against it. The Nevers woman hadn't bothered them, but there was a fair chance that once they emerged from this room, they'd be asked, politely but firmly, to leave. Certainly she wouldn't be allowed to stay . . . and now that she'd found Macklin, Doris was damned if she'd let the two of them be separated ever again. Better to skip dinner and get as much sleep as they possibly could. Tomorrow was going to be an exhausting day.

She'd not told Macklin the whole truth that afternoon, and she felt guilty about that. She knew the identity of the ships that had intercepted them shortly after they'd lifted off from the Monitor base on the moon. There was no mistaking the black, menacing bat-winged shapes of Kra'agh Slasherclaw fighters. There'd been reports for some time of a Kra'agh fleet in this sector, though Associative scouts hadn't yet been able to pinpoint its location.

If the Kra'agh were interested in this planet, they might well have advance scouts here already, Hunters slipped in past the Monitor watchstations and satellites to report on whether this emergent civilization could put up any kind of coherent defense.

She already knew what those Hunters must have reported. The humans of Earth had only recently begun to harness electricity. No nuclear power, no space capability, not even aircraft. No radio. No weapons more powerful than explosive artillery shells or primitive, hand-cranked machine guns. A world of dozens of nation-states, warring governments, colonies, petty kingdoms, empires, republics, tribes, and monarchies.

Yes, the Kra'agh would do well here, a world ripe for the plucking.

And that man with the Clantons . . . Hank Attwater. She couldn't be positive, but she would be willing to bet that he'd been a Hunter, using their *gah*-projection technology.

If so . . . was he hunting the two of them?

She shivered again and turned away from the window. If there were Hunters here, they were in terrible danger. She wondered if they should instead have fled Tombstone that afternoon.

But . . . no. The Hunters might not yet know they were here . . . or found this house if they did. To flee precipitously might attract unwanted attention.

And Macklin *had* needed sleep and time for the nanomeds to work on him. His abused body would have given out if they'd tried to walk or ride more than a few miles. They were safe enough until tomorrow . . . she hoped.

She wondered if she should stay awake all night, keeping guard, then decided against it. Her Companion could keep watch for her, with senses sharper than hers. And she needed rest as well.

Should she have told him everything? Ma'khleen, the *old* Ma'khleen, would have wanted to know everything, the risks, the threats, the chances for survival. But this Macklin seemed so vulnerable, so lost. Doris thought it better to break things to him slowly, rather than overwhelming him with too much, too fast.

She covered Macklin with a thin, wool blanket, then crawled beneath it herself.

But she couldn't get to sleep again for a long time.

⋄ 6 ⋄

IKE CLANTON WASN'T ABOUT TO GO TO SLEEP. HE AND TOM McLaury had checked into the Grand Hotel, figuring on spending the night in Tombstone, rather than trekking all the way back out to the ranch with Claiborne, Billy Clanton, and Frank. But right now, at just past 10 P.M., he was restless and wanted some action. A plan was forming in his head, and he needed to work things out.

His confrontation with Holliday had crystallized things. The Earps had to be run out of this town, run out or killed or discredited so badly they left with their tails between their legs like the damned yellow dogs they were.

He also felt like he needed to reassert himself, to prove to anyone who would listen that he hadn't really been forced to back down from a fight with Holliday that afternoon. He'd heard from Johnny Behan that the sheriff was going to be playing poker with Wyatt and Virgil tonight, and that Holliday might be there as well.

And that suited Ike just fine. He thought he and Tom might just go over to the Oriental and sit in on that game. They'd checked their guns at the hotel, just so the Earps didn't try to sucker the two Clantons into a draw. He was pretty sure none of them would shoot an unarmed man; he intended to use that against them.

The problem was, he still wasn't quite sure how. At least, though, he could prove to them and to the whole damned town that Ike Clanton wasn't a coward, that he wasn't afraid of Holliday or Virgil or the whole damned Earp clan.

They were walking down Allen Street on the way to the Oriental when a familiar, chill voice called from a side street.

"Ike Clanton!"

"Wha—? Oh, it's you, Hank! Jesus, where you been? You had us all worried about you! You okay?"

"I am well." Hank Attwater moved, and something else moved at his side. Ike squinted into the shadows.

"Who's that with you?" Ike asked nervously.

"A friend," Hank replied. "Max Carter."

"Max Carter?" Ike scowled. "I heard your place burned down the other day!"

"It did. I escaped."

"That was . . . lucky."

"We have a proposal for you," Hank said.

"Yeah?"

"We have found the place where Macklin is staying," Hank said, his voice cold and silky. "We believe the woman is with him."

"The devil you say!"

"We are going to kill both of them. We need others, however, to make certain the locals do not interfere."

"Well, shoot," Tom put in, "if by 'locals' you mean the sheriff, Marshal Earp, and his deputies, they're all over at the Oriental right now playin' cards. We're gonna be joinin' 'em soon."

"That is . . . satisfactory."

Ike scratched the back of his head. Damn but Hank was

talking and acting funny lately. "So . . . what's this proposal you mentioned?"

"My colleague and I have decided that the Earps must be eliminated. With them gone, you and Sheriff Behan will be indisputably in control of this town."

"That, friend, has been the idea all along," Ike said. "But eliminatin' the Earps ain't as easy as the sayin' of it."

"I believe we can be of assistance. If you will keep the local law enforcement officials away from us while we take care of our business with Macklin and the woman, we will be able to help you trap the Earps and kill them without endangering yourselves."

Hank was getting some damned strange notions, but just now Ike didn't care. His biggest worry in the whole problem of how to take care of the Earps lay in how he could go about it without getting himself killed or arrested in the process. Even Johnny Behan wouldn't be able to stand by and do nothing if he was caught shooting the Earps in the back.

If Hank had an idea, though, especially one that kept Ike out of the Earps' line of fire, that was just fine with him. Let Hank take the fall, if someone had to. Ike Clanton would be sitting pretty when the smoke cleared.

"Just one thing," Ike said, as he considered Hank's offer.

"Yes?"

"The woman. I don't want you to kill her. I want you to bring her out to the ranch, where I can deal with her m'self. I got a score to settle with that bitch."

"Do you to intend to kill her yourself?" Hank sounded as calm as though he were discussing the weather.

"Eventually. Maybe not right away, y'know what I

mean? But that's the idea. I just want to be lookin' in her eyes when it happens, understand?''

"Perfectly." The voice might have been the voice of Death himself. "Capturing the woman, rather than killing her, will make our own plans more complex, however. Let us say that we will capture her if possible . . . but that we will kill her rather than allow her to escape. She *must* die.''

"Okay, okay, sure," Ike said. The way Hank was talking was starting to make him nervous. "We'll keep the Earps out of your hair, don't you worry! You take care of Macklin, and bring the girl out to the ranch, and then you help take down the Earps. Deal!''

But there was no answer. The shadowy figures of Hank and Max had faded back into darkness before Ike had even realized they were gone.

"C'mon," Ike told Billy.

"What the hell's gotten into Hank lately?'' Tom wanted to know.

"Damfino. I think that bitch really shook him." Ike didn't like it at all. It had been as though Hank was giving him orders, rather than the other way around. He didn't like that at all.

But Hank, clearly, had an idea for killing the Earps.

And Ike was willing to put up with almost anything if *that* could be made to happen.

FIFTEEN

❖ 1 ❖

"SO WHAT'S THE GAME?" IKE ASKED WITH AN EASY SMILE, pulling up a chair.

The players looked up at Ike with expressions ranging from surprise to cold indifference. Wyatt and Virgil Earp were sitting together with their backs toward the wall. Johnny Behan was opposite them, with Morgan Earp and Doc Holliday to either side.

"Ike, what the deuce do you think you're doin' here?" Behan said, dropping his cards, facedown, on the table.

"Just thought we'd see if we could join you fellas in a friendly game," Tom McLaury said, grinning. "Anything wrong with that?"

Wyatt continued to study his hand. "We're kind of particular about who we play with," he said.

"I don't know, Wyatt," Morgan said, with something that might have been a smile. He nodded toward Behan. "We're playing this guy, aren't we?"

"What kinda talk is that, Morgan?" Behan wanted to know.

Virgil leaned back and gave an easy gesture. "Why not? Drag yourselves some chairs and have a seat." He looked at Wyatt and winked. "Their money's as good as anyone's, I reckon."

Holliday snickered. "I know why you're here, Ike. You just want to pretend like you didn't skedaddle this afternoon." He laughed, then, but the laugh turned into a prolonged coughing fit.

"Nasty cough you got there, Holliday," Ike said, sneering.

"You're a damned yellow coward," Holliday managed to say at last, pressing a handkerchief to his mouth. There were flecks of bright red on it when he tucked it away.

Ike went cold at the insult. "I'd take that back, Holliday, if I was you."

"You gonna make me?"

Ike's fists were clenched, but Wyatt's right hand, Ike saw, was off the table, at his side. He made himself relax. He smiled and carefully opened his vest, showing that he wasn't wearing a gunbelt. "Easy there, Earp," he said. "I'm not armed."

"Aw, Christ," Holliday said. "Let 'em sit in." He dropped his cards on the table. "I got nothin' anyway."

"So . . . what's the game?" Ike asked again, dragging up a chair.

"Stud poker," Morgan told him. "Virge? Your deal?"

"Well, deal us in!" Tom said, laughing. "The night's still young!"

◆ **2** ◆

DEATHSTALKER AND PAINSPINNER STOOD IN THE SHADOWS *across the street from the house. Both had carefully quartered the area earlier, picking up the mingled smells of countless humans who'd walked these streets. Both agreed that Macklin's smell was strong here, and Painspinner was certain that he could detect the woman's smell here as well.*

Almost without doubt, both Monitors were in that building.

It was late, and most of the lights in the house were extinguished, which suggested that the inhabitants had entered their dormant phase. That was one of the most astonishing things about humans. While Kra'agh rested periodically, in an altered state of consciousness called hio vaghn, *the idea of becoming unconscious for a large percentage of each day seemed ludicrous, a frighteningly countersurvival trait as strange as the idea of becoming unconscious when faced with extreme danger.*

These humans presented scarcely any real challenge at all.

The Kra'agh had evolved on a world where survival meant running down, trapping, outthinking, or outfighting prey larger, faster, tougher, and often more ferocious than the Kra'agh themselves. Without prey that struggled as they fed, triggering their digestive processes, Kra'agh tended to lose interest in food, even in living; while they could go for long periods without eating anything at all, they eventually starved to death if they didn't have living, interesting food.

Initial reports on this planet had suggested a source of food animals that would keep the Kra'agh Worldfleet interested and fed for eight-to-the-fourth grand cycles, at least. But Painspinner was beginning to wonder if the conquest of this world would be worth the eating. Hank Attwater had put up a spectacular struggle, true . . . but Doc Shea had been so lethargic and poisons-sodden that Painspinner hadn't had any appetite for him at all.

It wondered how the Monitors would be in the chase, in the pin, in the eating. The female, certainly, had shown spirit and might pose a challenge; Painspinner wasn't sure yet whether they would spare her for Ike Clanton's amusement or not.

"Tcha graad," Deathstalker rumbled softly. "Our prey waits for us."

Silently, they made their way to the front door. It was locked—a primitive tooth-and-gap mechanism within the door-opening apparatus held a simple bolt shut. It took no more than a few seconds for Deathstalker to reach into the narrow aperture with its feeding hands and manipulate the mechanism until the bolt snapped open. The door swung open, and the two Kra'agh stepped inside.

◇ **3** ◇

SARAH NEVERS HADN'T BEEN ABLE TO SLEEP. SHE WAS SITTING up in bed now, eyes wide open, fuming slowly at the intolerable position in which she'd been placed.

She should have gone up and knocked on the door at 8 P.M., demanding that the woman leave. She should have ordered her out as soon as she'd taken Macklin upstairs. No, she should have forbidden the hussy to even set foot inside the house. That was what she should have done.

But she'd been worried about Macklin, like a fool . . . and after letting the two of them go up there, she hadn't been able to bring herself to confront them. She cursed herself for being weak, for being sentimental, for being such an *idiot* as to fall for a man like Macklin. . . .

And now it was just past midnight—she could just make out the face of the big clock in the corner by the pale light falling through her window—and there wasn't a damned thing she could do. Best now would be to wait until morning. Then she could confront them and throw them both out on their ears.

The trouble was, every one of her lodgers would know. Her reputation would be ruined. She wondered . . . was it possible? Marshal Earp or Sheriff Behan might even arrest her, on charges of keeping a "disorderly house," as the law phrased it.

That slut. That *hussy*. . . .

She heard the door downstairs opening.

Now what? It was possible that that woman was slipping out. If so, Sarah intended to give her a piece of her mind. Slipping out of bed, she pulled a light robe on over her shift and started for her bedroom door.

She paused, her hand on the knob. She could hear other sounds now . . . a stealthy *creak-creak-creak* of someone walking downstairs, past the front parlor, someone heavy from the way those floorboards were chirping.

The hair prickled at the back of Sarah's neck. It wasn't *that* woman. It was someone, maybe two someones, entering her house. A sharper creak told her they'd begun mounting the stairs.

Quickly, she lit the kerosene lamp on her bedside table, then went to her closet and pulled out her husband's old 12-gauge, a massive double-barreled affair, and a box of double-ought shells. Working the side lever, she broke it open and dropped two shells into the breech. Snapping the weapon shut, she hauled the large, curved hammers back until they clicked, first one, then the other. The creaking footsteps drew closer. . . .

◆ **4** ◆

WARNING!

Doris came wide awake as her Companion's voice whispered in her head. "What?"

I am detecting the emissions of two gah-*projection units and the sounds of footsteps. Range twelve* merim *and closing, from the northeast*. . . .

The hallway! Doris rolled over, punching Macklin hard.

"Ma'khleen!" she whispered fiercely. "Quick! Wake up! *Macklin!*"

"Huh? Whazzit . . . ?"

She threw the blanket back and leaped out of bed. "Get up!" Where was her handbag? "Quickly! *Now!*"

◆ 5 ◆

WITH THE BUTT OF THE SHOTGUN TUCKED UP UNDER HER ARM, Sarah took a deep breath and moved toward the door.

It wasn't the first time Sarah had had to defend her place. Once, she'd broken up a small riot between some drunken cowboys practically on her front step. And another time, a down-on-his-luck miner had tried to jimmy open a window, and she'd been waiting for him inside with this same shotgun. He'd surrendered peaceably enough, once he'd found himself staring down the weapon's two big bores.

None of that made this time any easier, though. Trying to keep her knees from shaking, she pushed the bedroom door open and stepped out into the hallway. By the wavering, torchlike yellow light of the lantern at her back, she could see two shadowy shapes just reaching the landing at the top of the stairs.

"Hold it, you two!" she shouted, bringing the shotgun up to her shoulder. "Another step and you're dead!"

"We're here for Macklin," one of the shapes said with a voice that chilled like ice on the spine. "Where is he?"

"I said stop where you are! Get your hands up!"

And then the shape was moving . . . moving impossibly quickly, lunging for her as fast as a striking snake.

Sarah stumbled back a step, finger clamping down on the shotgun's triggers. Both barrels went off. She'd not meant to fire both, but the double blast thundered in the hallway like the crack of the Apocalypse. Already off-balance, she was slammed by the recoil and landed on her rear end, hard.

Her attacker shrieked, a bay like a wounded mountain lion. . . .

Sarah looked up and screamed. He . . . it . . . an impossible, horrible, nightmare *it* stood before her, its flat, scaled head whipping back atop a snakelike neck, a horror of a misshapen body below, weirdly articulated legs and black claws. . . .

She tried to scramble back, scrabbling at the bare wood floor with hooked fingers. She screamed again, a sound ripped from her deepest soul, tearing at her throat.

✦ 6 ✦

DEATHSTALKER SCREAMED AGAIN, DELIRIOUS WITH PAIN. The primitive weapon had done it no serious harm, but dozens of small, round pellets had been driven deep into its hide, and its gah-*projector had been damaged, knocking it off-line.*

It reached for the human female, but Painspinner called to it from behind. "The prey! It is here!"

Whirling then, Deathstalker joined its companion at the other end of the passageway. Yes, it could smell the human, Macklin, here. "Take the prey!"

Painspinner threw itself against the flimsy wooden door. . . .

✦ 7 ✦

DORIS HAD JUST SNATCHED HER PULSER FROM THE DEPTHS OF the handbag when the bedroom door splintered inward. A human—the one the Clantons had called Hank—came through, and she was still trying to thumb the pulser's power switch and there wasn't time, there wasn't time . . . and then thunder roared as Macklin, standing knee-bent beside the bed, squeezed the trigger of her .32 pocket pistol, pulled from her dress pocket.

Hank Attwater gave an inhuman, demonic shriek. Or rather, something behind or within Hank shrieked; the man's face was unperturbed, the mouth closed, but the image seemed to waver a bit, as though viewed through moving water.

Doris had the pulser aimed now, gripped in both hands, and the thin, high whine of the charge indicator told her it was ready to fire. At the same instant, Macklin dragged the hammer of the pocket pistol back and fired again, and blue-white blood splattered the door frame behind the wavering image of Hank Attwater. Doris pressed her thumb down hard on the pulser's discharge key. A dazzling bolt of energy seared the air, like lightning, with a harsh crackle and the stink of ozone and burned wood.

Hank Attwater was gone, and in his place was an indescribable horror of leathery black scales and claws and teeth.

The pulse beam had only grazed the screaming creature. Most of the energy had been absorbed by the wall and door frame, and flames were rippling up the side of the door beneath a boiling cloud of smoke. Doris aimed again, willing the recharge to hurry . . . but the creature had ducked back and out of sight.

"Macklin!" Doris yelled, keeping the pulser aimed at the blazing, shattered door. "The window!"

Macklin backed away from the door, keeping the Smith & Wesson aimed at the opening. Then he reached the window, threw it open, and leaned out, looking into the night. Turning, he snatched the sheet off the bed, tore it down the middle, and knotted a makeshift rope. Tying one corner to the bedpost, he tossed the other end out the window. Next, he scooped up clothing, his and Doris's both, and tossed a double armful out into the night.

"Let's go!" he shouted. The flames filled the doorway

now and the hall beyond, feeding greedily on floral-print wallpaper. "We'll still have a drop at the bottom!"

"You go first! I'll cover us!"

Grabbing his boots and Doris's shoes, which he tossed out after the clothing, Macklin swung his bare legs over the windowsill, then lowered himself down the sheet. Doris stood there for a moment longer, then turned, slipped through the window, and holding the pulser in one hand, let herself down the sheet with the other.

The sheet reached only halfway to the ground, and when she came to the end, she let go. Macklin caught her as she let go and dropped the last ten feet.

Smoke was billowing out of the upstairs window now, and they could hear shrill yells of "Help!" and "Fire!" coming from inside.

Macklin was struggling into his jeans.

"Never mind that," Doris told him. "We've got to get out of here! They'll be after us any moment!"

"Who? What were those things?"

"Never mind!" She scooped up the last of her clothing. "Run!"

A blue-violet thread of energy snapped down at them from the open window, striking the ground with a crack and a brilliant flash and a stink of ozone. Doris and Macklin ran, keeping close to the house until they could break away and duck through an alley. In a few moments more, they reached a shed at the corner, where they could catch their breath, finish pulling on clothes and boots, and take stock.

"We should go back!" Macklin told her. "Those people—"

"We can't, Macklin!" she said. "The Kra'agh are probably on our trail at this moment! We've got to *move!*"

"But—"

"You hear that bell? That's the local fire brigade. They'll

take care of the fire . . . and the people. We need to get out of here *now!*''

She heard the crunch of heavy feet running outside and motioned to Macklin to keep quiet. When the sound had faded into the distance, she signaled, and the two of them slipped back out into the night. Behind them, dozens of people were spilling out into the street, screaming, shouting, barking orders, crying.

She thought she knew a place where they could hide. . . .

◇ **8** ◇

''HEY, SHERIFF!'' NED COURTNEY CALLED, DUCKING INTO THE saloon. ''they's trouble over at the Nevers's place!''

''What kind of trouble?'' Behan demanded, looking up from his cards.

''Dunno, Sheriff. But there's a hell of a lot of shoutin' and hollerin'!''

''Oh. Fer the love of—''

''I'll go,'' Virgil said, pushing back from the table. ''Need to stretch my legs anyhow.''

''Aw, shoot,'' Ike said. ''Probably ain't nothin'. Finish the game.''

''I'm folding. Bad hand.''

''Lemmee know what's goin' on, Marshal,'' Behan called.

''Johnny, you ought t'go, not the marshal.''

''What's the matter, Ike?'' Wyatt said, suspicious. ''You don't want Virgil out of your sight?''

''Uh, no. It's not that at all. . . .''

''Then play your damned hand.''

''Thanks for your concern, Ike,'' Virgil told him, ''but I'll be fine!'' Chuckling, Virgil walked out into the night.

Oh, God, he thought as he neared the Nevers boarding-house a few minutes later. *Another fire!* In June, a fire, beginning at the Arcade Cigar Store and Saloon, had swept down Allen Street, reducing sixty-five businesses and most of one whole block to ashes. There'd been quite a to-do about it, too, with most of the citizens blaming the town's two law enforcement branches and their ongoing feud as the reason the fire had gotten out of hand. Not that that made all that much sense; politics rarely did. But fear of a major fire was never far from any town- or city-dweller's mind, especially when most of the buildings were constructed of wood and canvas, and lit by gas or lanterns.

Fortunately, this fire had been caught early enough and was already out. The firehouse was on Toughnut, only three blocks down the street, and the Tombstone Citizens' Volunteer Fire Brigade had arrived in moments with their hand-operated pumpers. A huge crowd of people was milling about in front of the house, though, most in robes and nightgowns, as smoke continued to rise from several of the fire-blackened upper windows of the place.

One woman was sobbing hysterically, surrounded by a number of well-meaning townspeople and lodgers. As Virgil approached, he recognized Sarah Nevers, the boarding-house owner.

"What happened here?" he asked.

"Damfino, Marshal," one man in a seedy-looking bathrobe said. His face was smoke-grimed, and Virgil thought he must have been helping to put out the blaze. "I heard screaming, then gunshots. By the time I got up, the whole upstairs of the place was full of smoke."

"You're a lodger here?"

"Harry Fulbright," the man said. "That's right. Mrs. Nevers, here, kept talking about seein' something. Don't rightly know what."

"Well, I heard somethin' in there," another man said. "Sounded like a cougar caught in a trap!"

"Mrs. Nevers? Mrs. Nevers? Are you all right?"

But the woman continued to sob, shaking her head, trying to point, unable to communicate coherently at all. He wondered if she'd been drinking or if the fire had unhinged her somehow.

"Did everybody get out okay?" Virgil asked Fulbright.

"Well, we ain't seen that stranger, Macklin," Fulbright replied. "He was in the end room, over at that side of the house. But the fire weren't that bad, actually. Mostly just smoke. Didn't take long at all to—"

"How'd the fire start, anyway?"

"Hell, I was asleep! How should I know? Like I say, I heard shots. . . ."

Virgil entered the house and climbed the stairs. The fire and smoke damage was considerable, but the bucket brigade had doused the fire before the building's structural integrity was compromised. Most of the damage appeared to be from the smoke. The damage seemed worst at the end of the hall, where Fulbright said that Macklin had been staying. Virgil poked around the hallway and the room, noting the splintered door, the bullet hole next to the door frame, and the torn sheet, tied to a bedpost and still dangling out the window.

So Macklin had gotten out that way. But what the hell had happened here?

At first, Virgil thought the room's occupant had tried to smash his way out, but from the wreckage, it looked more like someone outside had tried to break *in*. People said they'd heard gunshots. Macklin—if that's who it was— might've discharged a revolver at an intruder. That would explain the bullet in the door frame, and black powder firearms could easily set things like curtains ablaze if the shooter wasn't careful.

Somehow, though, the pieces of the puzzle just weren't adding up.

He paused in the smashed-open doorway. Funny. It was hard to pick up under the smell of smoke and char, but there was also a faint but unmistakable sweet-sour smell, like decaying meat.

Like he'd smelled the other day, out at the Carter ranch.

That place had burned, too.

At the other end of the hallway, he found a shotgun lying on the floor in the doorway to what was probably Mrs. Nevers's bedroom. In the breech were two empty shells. The weapon had been fired and recently. He lay the weapon on the bed.

With no answers that made any sense at all, Virgil went back outside and tried to talk to Sarah Nevers again.

"It was . . . big . . ." she was telling the others. Her eyes were glassy, unfocused. "And black. All black. With . . . with teeth. Horrible teeth . . ."

"Mrs. Nevers?"

"Horrible teeth . . ."

Fulbright looked at him. "She's been goin' on this way, Marshal."

"I think she saw a mountain lion," an elderly man said.

"What, inside the house? You gotta be crazy, Sullivan!"

"All I know is it sure *sounded* like a mountain lion! And when I came outta my room, somethin' was goin' down the stairs, and it wasn't a man!"

"Was it a mountain lion?" Virgil asked.

"Just saw a . . . a shape. Didn't look like much of anything."

"Does Mrs. Nevers lock the boardinghouse up at night?"

"Oh, she's religious about it, Marshal," Fulbright said. "Almost makes a ceremony of it, y'might say. Always wants us t'know she won't open up after hours.''

"What do you think she might have seen?" Virgil asked.

"I think she had some kinda nightmare," another man said.

"I wonder if we should get her to a doc."

"I can take her over to my tent," the man said.

Virgil gave him a second look. It was Doc Clarke, one of Tombstone's small circle of doctors . . . a circle smaller now, Virgil remembered with a frown, with Doc Shea's still unexplained death. "Hell, Doc. Almost didn't recognize you with the smoke smudge on your face." He must have been in there, helping to fight the fire. "She going to be okay?"

"She's plainly hysterical," Clarke said. "I'd not thought Mrs. Nevers given to vapors, and so far as I know, she's not a drinking woman. I'll give her something to calm her nerves. Maybe we can get some sense out of her in the morning."

"Okay, Doc. You do that. You need help getting her over there?"

"I'll help," Fulbright offered, taking Sarah by the arm. She allowed herself to be led, still murmuring softly about "horrible teeth" and "big . . . it was big. . . .''

Virgil watched Clarke, helped by a half-dozen other townspeople, guide Sarah off down the street. His frown deepened. First the Carter ranch burns to the ground, and now this. And Doc Shea's murder. He wondered if Macklin fit into this puzzle somehow. Macklin had seen Shea his first night in town and had reason enough to go after the poor son-of-a-bitch. Macklin had been staying here at the Nevers boardinghouse . . . and from the look of things he'd been engaged in some gunplay in his room, might even have been responsible for the fire.

As far as he knew, Macklin hadn't had anything to do with the Carter ranch burning down.

But then again, there was no reason to think he didn't. Where *was* Macklin on Saturday night or early Sunday? Had anyone seen him? Sarah Nevers, maybe . . . but she wouldn't be answering many questions for a while.

Where had Macklin gotten a gun? Virgil had relieved him of his weapon just that morning. He'd have to check with Spangenberg and some of the other gun store owners in town and see if Macklin had picked himself up a new piece.

He was going to have to ask that young man some more questions.

But . . . later. There was nothing more to be done here. He turned away and headed back for the card game.

❖ 9 ❖

THE KRA'AGH HAD BOTH BEEN WOUNDED, PAINSPINNER worse than Deathstalker. They'd searched briefly for the fugitive prey but decided to retreat instead to their hiding place in the town, the barn where Painspinner had encountered Macklin and the female earlier in the day. They needed to effect repairs to their gah-projection gear, they needed to treat their wounds and burns . . . and they needed to decide what they were going to do next.

"These humans are proving more resourceful, and more dangerous, than expected," Deathstalker said. Painspinner extracted another small metal sphere from its bleeding hide, and Deathstalker keened softly with the pain. "Chna! Life!"

"Pain is life," Painspinner replied, continuing to work. Its own pain, two new bullet wounds and a savage burn where the human's pulser weapon had grazed its side, had left it feeling light-brained and a little euphoric.

"*We should warn the Fleet,*" Deathstalker said.

"*We must kill the Monitors first. They may have fled the town. They may even have means for communicating with other Associative vessels in the system.*"

"*It will do them no good. Our fighters have blockaded this world. A* ganth *could not slip through our web.*"

"*You have more confidence in our Fleet's abilities than do I.*"

"*We face a serious problem now,*" Deathstalker said, as Painspinner claw-hooked another ball from its skin. "*The Monitors are warned. They know we are here and that the hunt has begun. If we follow their scent into the hills, they will have set an ambush for us.*"

"*True. Rather than walk into a trap of their preparation, we should find some way to get them to come to us.*"

"*To step into our trap instead.*"

"*Exactly.*" Painspinner carefully searched Deathstalker's scarred and oozing hide for any more of the pernicious lead balls and found none. "*We must proceed with great care, as though we stalk a wounded full-grown* arregh'n. *The humans appear defenseless and weak, but we have been surprised twice now. We must not underestimate them again.*" It held up one of the small lead balls, slimy with Deathstalker's blood. "*Even such primitive weapons as these can still kill. We are not invulnerable. Our best trapping remains the creation of a safe haven here. This town is comparatively remote. Control it and we will have an excellent base of operations.*"

"*You still seek an alliance with the Clanton-creatures,*" Deathstalker said. It had never been completely convinced that working with food that way would produce results.

"*The Clanton-creatures are the most aggressive humans I have tasted yet,*" Painspinner replied. "*In a surprising number of ways, they are like us.*"

Deathstalker made a rude noise. "The prey is not the Hunter. The food is not the eater."

"I have tasted the Clanton-creatures in Hank Attwater's pattern. They are like us, especially in their regard for lesser creatures. They are survivors. They are chra'chna." The phrase literally meant *"life-living"* but had no easy translation. It embraced the single-purposed, supremely ruthless struggle of life to overcome all obstacles.

"We will use the Clanton-creatures to our purposes," Painspinner continued. *"We will help them eliminate the Earp-creatures and their allies. In exchange, we will gain control, directly or indirectly, of this entire region ... what they call 'Cochise County.' This will provide us with our necessary base of operations and a steady supply of food. It will also give us the means to hunt down the Monitors, no matter where they are hiding."*

"There is something else we can do," Deathstalker pointed out. *"If we find the right bait, we can lure the Monitors to us."*

"What is the right bait?"

"These humans care for one another in ways I do not entirely understand. Max Carter felt strange emotions for its mate and offspring and even for a young quadruped of a different species, a colt. We can use this."

"The Monitors are from one of the Associative's colony worlds, almost certainly. They would have no emotional attachments to humans native to this planet."

"Possibly. Or possibly not. I was attacked by a female tonight who might have been defending itself. Or ... it might have been defending Macklin. It didn't attack until I mentioned Macklin's name."

"You have its scent?"

"I do."

Painspinner's feeder hand closed in agreement. "Then perhaps we can use it, as a backup to the main plan."

"That was my idea. Now . . . let me attend your wounds."

Painspinner's pain was . . . exquisite.

SIXTEEN

✦ 1 ✦

THE WESTSIDE MINE WAS LOCATED ON A HILL RIGHT OUTSIDE of Tombstone proper, practically looking down into the town's streets, its workings dominating the western skyline. Beyond rose the three-peaked ridge of the Tombstone Hills.

Though it was still being worked, the surface was pretty much abandoned after dark. Doris had noted some private guards walking the property, but they were easy enough to stay clear of, since they rarely strayed from well-worn, well-established paths.

The place Doris had in mind wasn't close to the Westside workings in any case. Farther up the hillside, just behind the main shaft with its big cable drum for the mine elevator, was a tangle of house-sized boulders and scattered piles of mine tailings dumped there over the past several years. Erosion had carved away some man-deep gullies, and it was possible to find a place to hide among the rocks and sagebrush that gave you a good view of the slope leading back to the edge of town below. They could even see Sarah Nevers's boardinghouse from here, see that the fire was out, that the crowd outside had dispersed. If anyone came up this hill after them, they'd be able to see that, too.

She'd found the site the night of the crash. Her lifepod had come down less than a mile from here, and she'd spent a long time on this hilltop, gathering her strength and planning her next move, before her first abortive attempt to enter the town.

The moon was high and westering, flooding the landscape with silver. She noticed that Macklin was staring at it and wondered what he was thinking. "You okay?"

"I think so." He watched the moon a moment more. "Where's home?" he asked.

"Home?"

"Shanidar. Can we see it from here?"

She sighed. "Shanidar's sun is too dim and way too far away for us to see it. And this time of year, Earth's sun is between us and home. We wouldn't be able to see it anyway."

"I've been thinking all along that the night sky looks all wrong," he said quietly. "It's so . . . so empty. So lonely."

"I feel that myself, sometimes." The truth was, she'd felt it nearly all the time since the crash. Were they ever going to be able to get off this rock? Her Companion was maintaining a constant radio watch, in case an Associative ship came near enough to hail.

But given the sheer, endless depth of space and the fact that Kra'agh Slasherclaws must be swarming about this planet now, the possibility of contacting friendly vessels seemed remote indeed.

"Doris? What were those things?"

She'd been dreading the question but certain it would come. She was worried about how Macklin might take the knowing and how he might carry it afterward. His conscious mind and memories, apparently, had retained a fair amount of the special cover information downloaded by his

Companion for the mission; he knew words like "horse" and "saddle" without ever having been exposed to them.

But by the same token, he'd lost chunks of his native memories. It wasn't all gone, certainly, but it was true that he was a lot more fluent right now in English than in the Gtai they'd both grown up with. He probably only had the fuzziest notion of stars and planets and interstellar gulfs, of AI computers, radio, or starships. It was as though an enormous part of Ma'khleen's life, of who he was and what he'd experienced, had been locked away in his subconscious, the better to make room for the much smaller Macklin of 1881 Arizona, a Macklin who didn't remember the Associative . . . or the Kra'agh.

That sort of information could be harmful to the primitives of this world, if dropped on them without proper preparation. The same held true for Macklin. Could she tell him without risking complete rejection of what she had to say . . . or far worse, insanity?

"I've had the feeling," he told her, "that you've been holding back on me. Treating me like a child. If all these things you say are true . . . about other planets and other civilizations, if I'm really a part of all of that, maybe you should stop treating me like a kid and tell me all of it."

"It's not that I'm treating you like a child . . ." she began.

"No? Then tell me what those . . . those things were back at the boardinghouse. Some of the nonhuman people you were talking about earlier?"

She took a deep breath. "They were Kra'agh." She pronounced the name with a guttural accent, a snarl or a harsh cough more than a spoken word.

"What's that?"

"Not that. They. They call themselves 'Hunters.' They're a very old civilization. Starfarers . . . but they have rather a different way of looking at the universe, at other races, than we do. Where we see potential friends, trading partners, even possible enemies in wartime, they see only . . . resources. Food. Slaves. *Things* to be used.

"We actually don't know a lot about them. Our contact has been rather limited, as you might imagine, though they seem to know a lot about us. We do know they move in on an inhabited planet and spend the next few thousand years stripping the world down to bare rock, taking everything of value to them, destroying all that is not. The native population becomes food, if the biochemistry of the conquered species is right . . . or slave labor to help in the dismantling of their own world, and sometimes both. Either way, the natives are extinct, the entire population simply wiped away, by the time they abandon that world and seek another.

"They're predators, Macklin. Worse. *Vandals,* they might be called in English. Utterly rapacious. Utterly vicious and ruthless." She shivered. "They've destroyed thousands of other newly arisen civilizations across this part of the galaxy over the past few million years."

"So if they're here . . ."

"We think Earth may be their next stop. It was a Kra'agh fighter that destroyed our vessel five local days ago, while we were en route from the Moon to Earth. At the same time they attacked us, they hit our base on the Moon." She touched her chest, her fingers resting over the Companion implant there, hidden now beneath her blouse. "I've been unable to pick up any signals from our ships or from the base. I'm afraid they've all been destroyed, which leaves us very much on our own.

"And if the Kra'agh are on the move that openly, it can only mean that their worldfleet is nearby, possibly already within striking distance. The two Kra'agh we saw tonight . . . they may be scouts for the main force, or they could be Hunters detailed to find and kill any Associative Monitors they can find on the planet.''

"Monitors. Like us.''

"Like us . . . though right now our job is to survive long enough to report what we know, rather than simply observing what's going on here.''

Macklin gave a half smile. "All the time I was trying to come to grips with who I was, with what I was . . . I felt like there was something, something important, that I was supposed to do. I guess that's it, huh?'' He shook his head. "But those kraug things . . . they looked human at first. I thought you said these other people, the other races out there among the stars, I mean, didn't look like humans.''

"Believe me, neither do the Kra'agh. But, well, they have ways of imitating human appearance. They . . . they *pattern* humans they capture. Never mind how. But they can use that pattern as a disguise. That's also how they learn about us. Our language. Our thoughts, even.''

Macklin shuddered. "Those things in Sarah's house. They were . . . nightmares on legs. . . .''

"As good a description of the Kra'agh as I've ever heard.'' She considered the rest that she had to tell him. "This isn't over, you know.''

"Well, we have to figure out how to talk to your people. *Our* people.'' He corrected himself.

"We have to survive. That's the first rule. And it's not going to be easy.''

"These Hunters . . .''

"The Kra'agh Hunters are . . . persistent. You have no idea *how* persistent. Once they're on your trail, the only thing that stops them from coming after you is their death, or yours. They have a sense of smell much better than ours and eyes that see into the infrared. They can actually see your footprints on a cold surface after you've walked there, see them as long as an hour after you're gone. They can drop down on four legs and gallop across open ground for hours upon hours without getting tired. And they have devices, their *gah*-projectors, that allow them to create a holographic image, a kind of three-dimensional picture of creatures or things they've patterned. It hides them, makes you see something else entirely. A rock. An animal. Another person. Or even nothing at all.''

"Is that why you were so careful checking this hilltop out?'' he asked her, smiling. ''The way you were wandering around with that gun of yours out, I thought you were hunting for our dinner.''

"Partly. Mostly, I guess.'' She touched her chest again. ''My Companion can sense them when they're close, within twenty or thirty feet or so. I was making sure that none of these boulders was a Kra'agh waiting in ambush.''

"So wherever we go, those things will be on our trail.''

"Almost certainly.''

"Not a real fun idea.''

"If we can make contact with an Associative ship, we might be able to set up a rendezvous,'' she told him. ''A pickup. And failing that, there are other Monitors here on this planet.''

"Oh?''

"The nearest is in a city in this same territory, a place called Tucson. We were on our way to relieve him when we were shot down. He'll have equipment we can use, weapons, and a communication system with more range and power than my Companion.''

"So . . . that's it?'' Macklin asked her. ''We just up and leave? Right now?''

"That's the idea.''

He shook his head. ''I've got to go back,'' he told her.

"Not for long, but . . . well, I've got to go back."

"What? Why?"

"Well, for one thing, I had a supply of gold coins in that pouch around my neck." He patted his chest. "I guess I left it in the boardinghouse. All I have on me is a few dollars in my pockets."

"Macklin, it's not worth it, believe me. No amount of gold would be worth it. If we can get to Tucson, our contact there will provide us with more money. *Nothing* is worth going back and letting the Kra'agh pick up your trail."

"Well, there's something else," he said, stubborn. "It's not just the gold."

"What, then?" Doris was beginning to feel exasperated. Couldn't he *see*?

"It's Sarah," he said. "Sarah Nevers. If these Hunters are as determined, as thorough as you claim, don't you understand? If they're going to track us, what's the one place they could pick up our trail where they knew it was fresh?"

"The boardinghouse, of course."

"The boardinghouse. If *I* were them, the first thing I'd do is go right back there and wait, just in case we came back. Looking for that gold, maybe?"

Doris looked at Macklin with a new respect. Even with most of his memories lost or suppressed, even working at a fraction of his old efficiency, he was sharp, quick on the uptake and working at putting himself in the other person's place.

"I can't just leave her. If the Hunters go back to her place and find her still there . . ."

"Why would she? After the fire, everybody in that place must've gone somewhere else."

"Not Sarah," Macklin told her. "Not unless the house burned clear to the ground, and it didn't. The place means too much to her. It has . . .'' He stopped and gave a self-conscious smile. ''It has too many memories for her to be able to just walk away. It was special to her . . . and her husband.''

''She's dead, then.''

''Sarah helped me, Doris. A lot. She took me in, she fixed me up that first evening, when I couldn't even walk. She cared enough, took enough of an interest in me, that she helped me get my feet under me at a time when I didn't even know which way was up. I can't just run away and leave her to face those horrors.''

''But what can you do about it? You said yourself she wouldn't leave. It may be too late already.''

''Maybe. But I've got to try.'' He looked thoughtful for a moment. ''Tell me something, Doris. Can those things be killed?''

''The Kra'agh. Yes, of course.''

''I put two good, clean shots into that one in the doorway. Didn't look like I'd even slowed it down.''

''They're *hard* to kill,'' she told him, ''but it can be done. First of all, it looked to me like you were aiming at the head. That's no good.''

''It isn't?''

''Kra'agh don't keep their brains in their heads. They have a kind of a hump between their shoulders. Their brain is there, kind of riding on their backbone, and protected by bone this thick.'' She held up her thumb and forefinger to demonstrate. ''You can't really see it or get at it when it's standing up on two legs, like those were tonight, but if you could get a shot when it was down on all fours—they do that when they're traveling—or if you could shoot it from behind.'' She sighed. ''I wish we had a Colt .45. That little .32 I got is a bit underpowered for big game.''

''Will it do the trick?''

"It ought to. . . ." She didn't sound convinced.

"What about that thing you were using tonight?" He groped for a word, searching his faulty memory. "Pulser?"

"That's right. It'll kill them again, *if* you can get a shot from behind or the side, and even if you hit them in the front, it'll make them take notice. I was rushed tonight and missed my shot, but I still think I burned him pretty good. The big problem with a pulser is that it takes a while to charge for each shot, three seconds or so. That's a *long* time in combat. On the upside, a pulser is accurate out to a longer range than a handgun. We might be able to pick one off at a hundred yards or so."

"What I'm wondering," Macklin said quietly, "is if we shouldn't try to solve this a different way than running."

"You mean, we stand and fight?"

He nodded. "Look, if we just head for Tucson, those things will be following us. You said it yourself. They never give up. They'll find our trail and they'll come after us. We won't know when or from what direction, but they'll find us eventually . . . and probably long before we reach your friend in Tucson.

"But . . . what if I left you here with the pulser. We set you up at the head of this gully maybe, with a good clear shot down the hill. I go back down into town. Find Sarah, if I can, and warn her. And if I find the Hunters, I get them to chase me."

"Back up here," Doris said.

"Right into your line of fire. If you can kill them, we can go on to Tucson or wherever and not worry about these things following us."

"That may be one of the bravest things I've ever heard, Macklin," she said. "It's also got to be one of the *stupidest.*"

His face fell. For a brief moment, he looked like a disappointed little boy. "You don't think it'll work?"

She looked away. "I don't know. If they're waiting for you down there, you'd be dead before you knew they were there. If they chase you, well, they're awfully fast. They can drop down onto all fours and run as fast as a horse can gallop. They could run you down long before you brought them into range."

"I don't see that how we have much choice. Do you?"

"No, we have a choice. I could go. You could stay."

He shook his head. "That pulser is a mystery to me," he told her. "Maybe I was able to use it once, but right now I wouldn't even be able to turn it on. It would make a lot more sense for me to go down there with the .32, and for you to wait here with the gun that has the best chance of killing them as far away as possible."

Doris closed her eyes, leaning back against the cool, hard roughness of a boulder. She didn't want to admit it, didn't want to agree . . . but Macklin's plan was a good one. They had very little chance out in the desert alone with the Hunters in pursuit, especially on foot. But if they could kill the Hunters, *if* . . .

Yes, they might have a chance. Everything rode on that one small, magical, promise-filled word, *if*. . . .

"Okay," she said at last. "You're right. We don't have much else in the way of choices." She opened her eyes and looked at him. He was leaning back against his own boulder, staring up into the empty night sky. "But you'll be careful? You won't take any chances?"

He smiled at her. "Absolutely."

He took the .32 and reloaded it, tucking it then into the waistband of his jeans. He also took a handful of shells from Doris's handbag, tucking them into his pockets. "That'll do me," he said. "I'll try to pick up something bigger, if I can."

"Remember! Don't get too close! The Kra'agh have much higher metabolisms than we do. They're strong, and they can move *very* fast. Faster than you can possibly imagine. And they can disguise themselves as things other than people. A large rock or a piece of furniture, maybe. Anything man-sized, or bigger, up to maybe the size of a horse. But you should be able to smell them if they're close."

He rose to his feet and nodded. "I've smelled them. You don't forget it." He looked down at the town for a moment. The moon was nearing the western horizon, and the sky was growing lighter. The sun would be coming up in another hour or so. "I'd better go."

"Be careful."

"I will. I'll be back before you know it!"

She stood and stepped closer, reaching for him. He took her in his arms, and they kissed for a long time. "You come back, John Macklin."

"For another kiss like that one? You bet!"

Doris watched his back as he made his way down the hill, walking toward the town. She was remembering all over again why she loved this man. Even with his memory all but gone, his courage, his sense of personal responsibility, his honorable character remained. It was, she thought, what separated him from thugs like Clanton.

"Come back to me, Ma'khleen," she said softly.

◈ **2** ◈

DOC CLARKE HAD TAKEN HER TO A COT IN HIS CANVAS-walled office, handed her a blanket, and told her to try to get some sleep, but Sarah knew she wasn't going to sleep, not tonight, maybe not ever again. Each time she closed her eyes, she saw that demonic horror before her again, huge and black and bristling, utterly indescribable, utterly unlike anything she'd ever seen in her life.

Fulbright had tried to tell her that a mountain lion had somehow gotten into the house. She knew mountain lions. That thing was like no animal that had ever walked God's good earth. Doc Clarke kept trying to tell her it was a dream, a nightmare, but she knew better. Nightmares were dreams coming up from deep in your soul about things that scared you or worried you, sure. She'd had nightmares about Curtis's death ever since he'd been shot down in the streets of Tombstone.

What she'd seen had been no animal and no figment of her imagination. Sarah Nevers was not a particularly religious woman and hadn't been to church since her wedding day, but she believed in God and she'd wondered, sometimes, about stories she'd heard about Satan and his legions. The only thing that made any sense at all was that she'd seen a demon straight from hell. That awful smell—it might be brimstone. The way those golden eyes had stared at her, measuring her . . . they could have been the eyes of a demon coming for her soul.

Dr. Rush, she knew, had nothing about this in his book. There were things, she knew now, in this world—and out of it as well—that even Dr. Benjamin Rush had never heard of. Maybe . . . maybe she was going mad. No! She knew what she'd seen. It had been *real!*

She wanted to go home. She wanted to find her mother's Bible, which she knew was in the big bookshelf in the parlor, and she wanted to go back up to her room and lock herself in. It was going to be hard to go back to the place where she'd seen . . . it, but she figured it was like getting thrown from a horse. The sooner you went back and faced your fears, the sooner you got over them.

And she wasn't about to let even a devil straight out of hell chase her out of her and Curtis's home. . . .

The doctor had given her something to drink that had

left her feeling a bit light-headed, but as soon as he'd left her on the cot and gone outside, she rose again and quietly slipped out of the tent he used as an office. She saw him standing there in the darkness smoking a cigarette, but she was able to slip away in the other direction without being noticed.

Now she was at the front step of her house, and her heart was hammering away beneath her breast. Suppose it was still in there? And . . . though her memory was a bit ragged right now about what she'd actually seen, she was pretty sure there'd been two intruders. Two demons, coming in disguised as men? Why were they after her?

No, it had demanded to know where Macklin was. They'd come for Macklin. . . .

Inside the front door, her house was dark and as silent as death. The smell of smoke still lingered here. Her lodgers . . . her lodgers must have all left, maybe been taken in by other boardinghouses or gone to a hotel. There wasn't a sound except for the hollow *tick-tick-tick* of the grandfather clock and the creak of floorboards beneath her slippered feet.

She remembered the creakings, as if beneath a very heavy tread, when the intruders had come up the stairs. *Those* stairs.

She went to the front parlor, where the grandfather clock, newly arrived from Illinois, was still ticking patiently away. The room was dark, save for the faintest light falling through the windows from a predawn sky and setting moon, but she found her mother's Bible by touch alone. Tucking it under her arm, gathering her shift about her, she started up that long, empty, and forbidding stairway, heading for her room.

The smell of smoke was much stronger at the top of the stairs. She walked the hallway; all of the doors were open, all of her lodgers gone. She felt an almost exhausting rush of relief as she inspected the damage and found that it wasn't nearly as bad as it could have been. The worst seemed to be the smashed-in door to Macklin's room. That would have to be replaced, of course, and the whole upstairs needed wallpapering, but the fire hadn't done much damage at all. Puddles of water still stood on the hallway floor, where the volunteer firemen had doused the blaze.

She walked down the hallway then and entered her room.

The smell, that smell, was much stronger here, strong enough to override the smoke, strong enough to prick the hairs up at the nape of her neck, and set her heart pounding even harder. She clutched the Bible to her chest like a talisman. *There's nothing here,* she told herself. *Whatever it was, it's gone now.*

Her shotgun was lying on her bed. Some shells were still scattered on the floor. Setting the Bible aside, she picked up the gun, broke it open, and reloaded. One way or another, if those night horrors showed up again, she would be ready, a Bible in one hand, a shotgun in the other. Whatever those things were, they *could* be hurt. She'd heard the pain in its shriek when she'd shot it.

She was reaching for the Bible once more when she sensed something move at her back. . . .

SEVENTEEN

❖ **1** ❖

IKE CLANTON WAS MAD. . . .

"The ball will *open* today!" he screamed, reeling in the middle of the street outside of the Oriental. He shook his fist. "You Earps . . . and Holliday! You must *fight* . . . !"

Wyatt stepped out onto the plank walkway in front of the saloon, thumbs tucked into his waistband above his gun belt. "Go home, Clanton," he said, with only the faintest sketch of a smile. "Get the hell out of here."

Morgan, Virgil, and Doc Holliday joined Wyatt at the door, and Ike was suddenly feeling very much alone. Tom McLaury had left the game sometime in the hours after midnight, returning to the Grand Hotel, he said, to get some sleep.

Clanton had the feeling the bastards were running him off . . . that they'd used him, taken his money, and now were shooing him off like a pesky kid, an annoyance to be summarily dismissed. In a flash of bravado, he made an obscene gesture, then turned and stalked off down the street, his path wavering a little under the influence of whiskey, exhaustion, and blind fury.

The card game had gone on all night. He'd been doing

pretty well, too . . . until about the time Virgil came back
from the call that had summoned him away from the table.
After that, Ike had started losing, and losing heavily. By
the time the game finally broke up at eight o'clock on Tues-
day morning, he'd lost about three hundred dollars.

It wasn't the money. It was the principle of the damned
thing. Every time he tried to square off against the Earps—
especially against Wyatt—he came out second-best, and he
was getting sick of it.

Those high-and-mighty Earps. That low-down cheat and
liar, Doc Holliday. They made a man want to puke. He and
his boys were going to run the bastards clear out of Tombstone. In fact, that running was long overdue.

Three hundred dollars! They were using a marked deck!
They *had* to be! Ike hadn't had luck that bad at cards in as
long as he could remember!

His guns. Where the hell were his guns . . . his Colt, and
the '73 Winchester he'd brought into town yesterday? He
stopped a moment, standing in the middle of the dusty
street, thinking. Yeah. He'd checked them both at the
Grand Hotel, where he was supposed to stay last night.
He'd get the boys together. Tom was at the hotel, but he
could telegraph the ranch and get some more of the boys
out here.

He'd go get his guns, and then he'd *show* those damned
Earps a thing or two!

◆ **2** ◆

MACKLIN STEPPED UP ONTO THE FAMILIAR FRONT PORCH OF
the boardinghouse, taut, his every sense alert. The door was
unlocked and he pushed it open, the floorboards creaking
as he stepped inside.

"Anybody home?"

The place felt empty. A smoky taste still hung in the air, and he thought he could detect a sharper, sweeter smell as well . . . the well-remembered stink he'd noticed in the barn yesterday, when the Clantons and that Hank Attwater *thing* had strung him up . . . and again, during the attack last night.

Kra'agh. At least, that was what Doris had called those things.

Macklin was not honestly sure he believed everything Doris had told him. Not that he thought she was lying . . . but so much of that stuff just didn't seem *real.* He'd seen that monstrous shape—a glimpse against the wavering light of the fire—but lately, some of his dreams had had more clarity, more reality than that fear-frozen moment in the night.

And as for that story about his being from another planet . . .

It was a hell of a lot to digest, and Macklin needed time for the digesting. Avoiding the puddles of water in the hallway, he started up the steps, Doris's .32-caliber pocket pistol in his hand.

"Sarah? Are you here?"

The bedrooms at the top of the stairs were all empty. Smoke still stained the ceiling above the smashed-in ruin that had been his door. At the other end of the hallway, Sarah's door stood open.

"Sarah?"

Pistol in hand, he walked down to Sarah's room and cautiously stepped inside. A Bible lay on the floor next to a shotgun. The bed had been pulled out from the wall and turned on its side. A chair lay splintered beneath the closed window, next to an overturned nightstand. What the hell? It looked like there'd been a struggle.

Tucking the pistol into his belt, he picked up the shotgun

and broke open the breech. It was loaded. Empty shells on
the floor, however, showed where Sarah had shot at something during the night attack.

Had her room been torn apart then? Where was she?

Something flickered across the floor just at the edge of
Macklin's vision. Ducking his head, he peered beneath the
bed frame and saw a large, brown insect unlike any he'd
seen before scuttle into a crack in the wall.

A cockroach? Sarah, he knew well, ran a *very* clean
house. He'd not seen any roaches or any other vermin during his week's stay. There was something . . . unnatural
about it, too, about the way it moved. He shrugged off the
sudden chill tickling his spine and the deeper, unvoiced
urgency he could feel hammering somewhere behind his
eyes. It was just a bug. . . .

Sarah wasn't here. Where had she gone?

There was no sign of the Kra'agh, either. If they were
watching the house, hoping for another chance at Macklin,
they hadn't shown themselves yet.

Thoughtful, he picked up the shotgun and scooped up
some loose shells he found lying on the floor as well. Cradling the shotgun, he started back down the hall.

✦ 3 ✦

IKE HAD HIS GUNS NOW, AND DAMN IT, HE WAS GOING TO USE
them. Tombstone's gun laws said you couldn't carry in the
street unless you were just coming into town or just leaving,
but that was a law only occasionally enforced. Hell, everybody Ike knew always carried at least a pocket revolver
tucked into a coat pocket or the back of their jeans, even
when they weren't wearing leather.

And who was going to stop him? Not Johnny Behan. The
county sheriff knew which pot his beans were in. The
Earps? Ha! The Earps were dead! All of them!

He was making his way down Fremont Street, swaggering, waving his Winchester. "The Earps die today!" he shouted. "Wyatt Earp, especially! They're dead men!"

What he needed, he decided, was to find an alley or side street where he could wait, someplace not far from the marshal's office. The Earps would be along soon, and he could wait until they passed by, then step out into the street behind them and open fire.

It was almost eleven in the morning now, on a chilly and overcast day. It had taken him longer to get to the hotel and check out his guns than he'd thought . . . thanks to a few stops at a few saloons along the way.

He found a likely looking side street and took a position, leaning against the side of the building, looking out onto Fremont Street. Yeah, the Earps would be along this way any minute, he figured.

A pair of nicely dressed, prissied-up women walked past the alley, giving Ike dark and worried looks.

"Howdy, ladies!" he said, grinning widely and touching the brim of his hat. "Y'know, I come t'town special today just to kill the Earps!"

The women gasped, gathered their shawls tighter about them, and hurried off. Ike laughed, cradling the Winchester in one arm.

And then he sensed a movement at his back. "So you're killing Earps today, huh? Will *I* do?"

Ike whirled, eyes wide. Virgil Earp was standing a few feet behind him, silent and as deadly as a coiled rattler, his Colt pistol in his hand. Ike tried to bring the Winchester up, fumbling with it . . .

. . . and then Virgil had stepped inside the reach of the rifle's muzzle, grabbing the barrel with his left hand as he swung his pistol with the right, whipping it around in a fast, flat circle and cracking Ike across the side of the head with it.

Pain exploded behind Ike's eyes. He let go of the Winchester and sat down, hard, on the wooden walkway beside the street. For a dangerous moment, the street, the earth itself spun and wobbled beneath him, and there was a terrible ringing in his ears. He tried to get up and failed.

Virgil Earp stood over him, shaking his head with disgust. "Clanton, you are *pathetic*!" Holstering his own pistol, he drew Ike's Colt from his holster, then held it and the Winchester in one hand, and reached down and grabbed Ike's arm with the other. "Come on, boy! We're going to go see a justice!"

It was, for Clanton, the ultimate humiliation, being dragged through the streets of Tombstone in front of everybody in the city like a common thief. Without another word, Virgil hauled him into the courthouse and slammed him down into a straight-backed chair. Morgan was in the courtroom, arms crossed, looking dangerous.

"I hear you've been talking pretty big, Clanton," Morgan said. "Care to put your money where your fat mouth is?"

"This has gone far enough!" Ike replied, flushing. "It's time we had this out, once and for all! You Earps are cowards and oughta be run out of town!"

"You damned son of a bitch!" Morgan shouted. Snatching Ike's pistol from Virgil's hand, he spun around and shoved the butt of the gun in Ike's face. "You want to fight? Huh? Let's see your hand, Clanton! Let's see whatcha got! Right here! Right now! *Are you going to take the damned gun?*"

The ringing in his ears had become a dull roar, pounding with the beat of his heart. He looked at the Colt stupidly. They outnumbered him two to one. Damn, they *wanted* him to take the gun and try to shoot them down. He would be dead before he even finished the thought. . . .

But he reached for the weapon anyway, as Virgil's and Morgan's hands dropped to their own holstered guns. . . .

The arrival of the justice at that moment probably stopped a bloody gun battle right there inside the courtroom. The judge didn't say anything about the display of weapons but took his place behind a bench and called the hearing to order. . . .

◇ **4** ◇

WYATT EARP WAS THINKING ABOUT MACKLIN AS HE WALKED toward the courthouse. Virgil had told him a bit that morning about the fire out at Sarah Nevers's place and his curiosity about whether the stranger who'd lost his memory might have any connection with that, with the death of Doc Shea, with the deaths and fire out at the Carter spread, with so many of the strange things happening in town this past week. Everybody in Tombstone was on edge, it seemed. People had been reporting the damnedest things . . . dogs butchered like hogs. Mountain lions shrieking inside the town. Gunplay.

Macklin couldn't be connected with all of that stuff, sure, but the more Wyatt thought about him, the more suspicious a character he seemed to be.

A man stepped out in front of Wyatt, hand on the butt of his pistol. It was Tom McLaury. "We've taken about all we're gonna take from the likes of you, Earp!"

"You don't have the balls for a fight, McLaury," Earp said with a cold sneer.

"If you want to make a fight, I'll fight you anywhere!"

Wyatt nodded. So be it. "All right. Make a fight right here!"

He watched McLaury's eyes widen, saw the flash of fear.

It was as Wyatt had thought. The man was all bluff and bluster.

Wyatt drew his Peacemaker. When Tom made no move for his own gun, Wyatt brought his left hand up and slapped McLaury across the face. "Is that what you want?"

McLaury, shocked, brought his hand up to his face. In that instant, Wyatt knew the man had no stomach for a gunfight. He was as big a bullying coward as Ike. Wyatt snapped his pistol up and cracked the barrel across Tom's head.

Tom McLaury dropped to the ground, stunned, blood on his face. A woman standing nearby screamed.

◆ **5** ◆

IKE WAS JUST COMING OUT OF THE COURTHOUSE WHEN HE SAW Wyatt Earp a few yards away, standing above Tom, who was sprawled on the ground. "What the hell is goin' on?" Ike demanded.

"I suggest, Clanton," Wyatt said with a level, quiet voice promising instant death, "that you take your friend here and ride out of town. Now! Before this gets really ugly."

Tom groaned, and Ike dropped to his knee, helping his friend up. "What'd you do to him?"

"A sore head," Wyatt said with a maddening, philosophical calm, "is better than being *dead!*"

And right then, at that moment, something broke inside of Ike.

He'd been *that* close to grabbing his gun out of Morgan Earp's hand, back there in the courtroom . . . that close, and he knew that if he'd grabbed it, Virgil and Morgan both would have gunned him down, right there where he sat. If the judge hadn't walked into the courtroom at that moment, that, Ike knew, was exactly what would have happened.

The judge had fined Ike twenty-five dollars for breaking Tombstone's gun laws, the final insult added to the last injury. Then he'd come outside, only to find that Wyatt Earp had just buffaloed his friend, pistol-whipping him and knocking him into the dust.

It was almost more than a man could stand. . . .

◆ 6 ◆

"SHOCK, MR. MACKLIN," DOC CLARKE SAID. THEY WERE standing inside his tent-clinic, where Macklin had finally tracked him down. It had taken him a while to find Harry Fulbright and find out where Sarah had been taken last night. "It can do weird things to you. Make you crazy in the head, even."

"So what made her start seeing things?"

"It's really hard to say, Mr. Macklin. It might have been an unusually vivid dream, a nightmare. Or the shock of waking up and finding her home on fire could have triggered some latent, hallucinatory—"

"Uh-uh." Macklin rubbed the side of his head. "Sarah Nevers is one of the steadiest people I know," he said.

"Oh, I agree," Clarke said. "Sensible, levelheaded even, for a woman. A bit unconventional, of course, insisting on staying out here and opening her own business after her husband died. . . ."

"Where did she go when she left here?"

"I really can't say. I gave her a small glass of brandy, to settle her nerves and help her sleep." He pointed at a cot. "I told her she could lay there until she felt better. But when I turned again, she was gone."

"And you didn't go after her?"

"Mr. Macklin, she seemed sound enough. A bit confused, perhaps, and upset, all of which was quite natural. If she felt like going back to her house, that was her business."

Except she didn't go back, Macklin thought. Or if she did . . .

A horrible fear was growing in his mind. If the Kra'agh had come back to the house to set a trap for Doris and Macklin, perhaps Sarah had been the one to spring it.

"Thanks, Doc."

"Let me know if you find her," Clarke said. "I want to know she's all right."

"So do I, Doc." He hurried from the tent and back into the blistering heat of the midday sun.

❖ 7 ❖

"WE'RE GONNA FIX THOSE EARPS," IKE SAID. "TODAY! RIGHT now! Are you boys with me?"

Tom McLaury and Jake Thurston were standing on the boardwalk in front of the Grand Hotel, Tom still nursing a nasty, swollen bump on his head where Earp had buffaloed him earlier. Hank Attwater stood in the alley next to the hotel, a shadow among shadows, keeping out of the harsh noon sun.

"I dunno, Ike," Tom said, exploring the bump on his head delicately with his fingertips. "Four of us, four of them . . . and they're just waiting for us to make a move. I think they *want* us to move, so they can gun us all down!"

"You sayin' the four of us can't take them?" Jake asked. He spat a dark stream of tobacco juice into the dust of the street.

"What, you crazy? The Earps, they're good. Holliday, too."

"We need an advantage," Ike said. "In numbers. I'm headin' over to the Western Union right now. I'll send a telegraph out t'the ranch. We'll have reinforcements in here before you know it!"

"Gaining a numerical advantage is a good idea," Hank

said. "But I suggest another strategy as well."

Ike squinted at the gunman standing in the shadows. "What you goin' on about, Hank? You been talkin' strange-like ever since yesterday."

"Can the Earps be lured to a particular place?" Hank went on, ignoring Ike's question. "Can they be forced to fight at a place of our choosing?"

"I dunno. That could be tricky."

"Whatcha got in mind, Hank?" Tom asked.

"That corral, outside the barn where you were questioning Macklin yesterday," Hank went on. "Could you get the Earps to meet you there?"

"The O.K.," Ike said. "Mebee. What do you mean 'you,' though. Ain't you in this with us, Hank?"

"The barn has an upper area . . . a loft. With an opening overlooking the vacant lot behind the corral. I will be *there*. . . ."

Ike's eyes widened. "Oh . . . I get it. Sure! An old-fashioned bushwackin'!"

"If you get the Earps to confront you there," Hank continued, "I can bring them under fire from the barn."

"And while they're runnin' around and yellin' and dyin'," Ike added, "we can open up and finish 'em off! Slick!"

Tom grinned. "I like the way you think, Hank. Never knew you had it in ya!"

"I have . . . much in me of which you are unaware," Hank replied.

"Jake," Ike said. "You're good with a rifle. You get up there, too, with Hank. The two of you can take the Earps and Holliday down with two shots apiece. Ha! Might not even leave anything for the rest of us!"

"I work better alone," Hank said.

"And I'm still the God-damned boss of this outfit, Hank

Attwater,'' Ike exploded, ''and don't you be forgettin' it! Me and the rest of the boys'll be out there in front of the Earps' guns, gettin' them into position! Two shooters can put the Earps down in half the time as one, so *I* say we have two shooters! You hear me, boy?''

''I . . . hear.''

''Good. Jake, go get your Winchester and pick up one for Hank.'' There were rifles at the O.K. Corral, with the horses. ''Tom, you come with me while I send that telegram. We'll want all the boys in here we can get!''

''You don't want too many, Ike. It'll scare the damned Earps off!''

''Yeah!'' Jake grinned. ''Wouldn't want them scared off from their own funeral!''

''Nah. We'll do it so they have to fight or be branded as cowards forever. And we're gonna want all the boys in here we can get, because when the Earps are dead, we're gonna do us some *celebratin'*!'' He laughed, a flat, nasty cackle. ''Ha! After today, ol' Tombstone ain't never gonna be the same!''

◆ 8 ◆

MACKLIN STOOD IN THE COOL, HAY-SMELLING MUSTINESS OF the barn behind the O.K. Corral. Shafts of sunlight, made knife-edged and hard by the dust hovering in the air, sliced past rafters and high-piled bales from the loft window and from between the ill-fitting boards of walls. A large roach— or something like a roach—skittered away and vanished beneath a bale of hay. Macklin walked slowly across the floor, searching the shadows, Sarah's shotgun probing ahead of him, both hammers cocked and ready.

Nothing here, either.

He could taste just a whiff of death-sweetness in the air, the smell he now associated with the Kra'agh. But . . . had one of the creatures been here recently? Or was that faint, lingering odor something left here from yesterday? There was no way to tell.

He'd given up and was walking again toward the door when something flashed at the edge of his vision. Turning, he saw something shining in a shaft of light next to the hay bales. He stooped and uttered a soft-muttered curse.

A locket . . . *her* locket, the gold chain broken where it had been pulled from her neck. Nearby, almost lost in a spill of hay from a partly torn bale, was a handkerchief-sized scrap of muslin stained dark red.

His heart was beating harder as he pocketed the locket, the one she'd shown him a few days ago, with her husband's portrait. Sarah *had* been here and not willingly. The blood on the torn shred of cloth was still sticky-wet.

Panic jittered at the back of Macklin's thoughts. They had her, that much was certain. But . . . were they keeping her alive, using her as bait? Or had they patterned her, the way Doris had told him, killing Sarah but somehow keeping her image as a disguise?

When he saw Sarah again, would it be her . . . or a Kra'agh, luring him in close for the kill?

He shuddered.

He had to find where the Kra'agh were hiding out. All he had to go on was the fact that the Kra'agh appeared to be working with the Clanton gang for some reason . . . maybe for no better reason than that one of the gang had been caught and patterned early on by one of those monsters.

The Clantons would know where "Hank Attwater" was, but he couldn't take that gang on by himself. He knew some men who could, though. The Earps would help him.

By the Twelve Worlds, he'd go find the Earps and *make* them help. . . .

EIGHTEEN

✦ 1 ✦

IN THE HILLS WEST OF TOMBSTONE, DORIS HAD PICKED UP A Monitor ship.

She'd had a channel open all morning, her AI listening with electronic ears to the static cascading from an empty sky. She'd caught several snatches of tightly coded gibberish—almost certainly signals from Kra'agh blockaders—but at just past local noon, her AI played for her a snatch of a static-garbled transmission in Gtai . . . something about confirmation that Monitor Station Eight-three had been destroyed.

Hurriedly, she opened her blouse and the skin garment beneath, exposing her implant. A thought produced a slender, almost hair-fine tendril growing from the disk's black translucence. Attaching the free end to a boulder, she backed away, letting the tendril grow as she moved, creating an antenna almost five *kij* long.

"Monitor ship!" she called. "Monitor ship! This is Observer *Taled* One-three-three! Do you read?"

Static . . . worse than before. She stepped to her left, shifting the angle of the antenna. "Monitor ship! Do you read?"

This . . . onitor Scout Chardemiad, *calling . . . observer,* a faint and hiss-broken voice whispered in the back of her mind, speaking Gtai. *Your . . . garbled. Say again. . . .*

"Chardemiad!" she called, letting her AI capture her words and fling them into the crystal blue of the sky. "*Chardemiad,* this is Observer *Taled* One-three-three! Come in! This is an emergency!"

There was a long pause . . . long enough to make Doris wonder how far out the scoutship was. With a time lag like that . . .

Observer Taled. *Dorree! Is that you?*

The voice in her mind, clearer now, was one she recognized.

"Lomac! Yes, it's me! Ma'khleen and I are marooned on the planet. A Kra'agh slasherclaw hit us, and we had to eject. We require emergency pickup!"

Again that maddening, gut-wrenching delay. *Okay, Dorree,* Lomac's voice said at last. *This isn't going to be easy, though. The Kra'agh have thrown a picket screen of light ships around Earth, and there are a couple of* Bloodhunt-*class battlecruisers in orbit over the moon. We'll have to come in very fast, and stealth-cloaked. Can you send a beacon?*

"Yes. . . ."

It will take at least forty olit *to reach you . . . assuming we can slip through that blockade. Can you be ready to send a signal when we tell you to?*

"Lomac, there's a problem. Ma'khleen isn't here right now. He's gone . . . gone to attend to something. I don't know when he'll be back!"

Dorree, we're only going to get one chance here. We can't wait, or those battlecruisers are going to sniff us out! It's got to be now . . . or never!

Doris caught her lower lip between her teeth. Lomac must be here checking on the sudden loss of communications from the Monitor watchstation on the Moon. Word that the Kra'agh were arriving in Earth's system in strength *had* to be relayed to the Associative. The needs of the mission always came first. . . .

"You'd better not try, Lomac," she said. "We can't jeopardize your mission."

That won't be a problem. Lodarrenon is here. She'll get our report back. I'm coming in to pick you two up! Be ready in . . . thirty-nine point three olit.

A little more than two Earth hours. Would Macklin be back by then?

Damn it, he would be back if she had to go down and drag him up to this hilltop herself.

"We'll be ready, Lomac. Thank you! And . . . the Ancients hold you."

They're going to have to this time, Dorree. See you soon!

The connection was broken, and Doris listened once more to the hiss of an empty sky.

◆ 2 ◆

WYATT, VIRGIL, AND MORGAN EARP WERE STANDING TOgether on the covered boardwalk just in front of Hafford's Saloon, on the corner of Allen and Fourth. The four horsemen riding into town meant trouble . . . and no mistake.

Virgil leaned against the hitching rail, hands folded, as Billy Clanton, Frank McLaury, Billy Claiborne, and Wes Fuller all rode at a slow walk down Allen Street. Billy Clanton and Frank both wore overalls, which made them look more like farmhands than cowboys; Virgil was willing to bet almost anything that those four had been called in by their friends and told to hurry.

All four turned hard, cold stares at the Earps as they walked their horses past, heading down the street toward the O.K. Corral.

Virgil pulled out his pocket watch and glanced at it. It was just past 1:30.

"Should we go disarm 'em, Virge?" Morgan asked quietly. Virgil could hear the tension, the eagerness in his youngest brother's voice as he pocketed the watch. "They're all packing."

"They just got into town, Morg," Wyatt said, puffing on the cigar he'd just purchased inside Hafford's. "Let's give 'em rope enough for them to knot their own nooses."

"Uh-oh," Morgan said, nodding at two men approaching the riders from the west. "That's real trouble brewing."

They watched silently as Ike Clanton and Tom McLaury stopped the four in the street. There was a furious, fast-paced discussion going on, though the Earps couldn't catch the words. Every once in a while, one of the cowboys would turn and shoot a cold, angry look at the watching Earps up the street.

"What do you think, Virge?" Morgan asked. "Is it going to be a fight?"

"Wish I knew," Virgil replied. " 'Scuse me. I'll be back in a minute."

Strolling slowly, unhurriedly, Virgil walked down the line of buildings to the Wells Fargo office, several doors up from Hafford's. He exchanged a few words with Marshal Williams, the agent, then accepted a Greener 10-gauge double-barreled shotgun from the rack on the wall behind the counter. He checked to see if it was loaded, then strolled back out to the street.

Several men were waiting to see him.

"Virgil," Mayor John Clum said, sounding anxious. The

handful of men behind him included several prominent town businessmen, all armed. "We heard the Clantons are talking about having it out with you boys. The Safety Committee's with you, one hundred percent. We figure all of us can march up there and surround the lot of 'em. They can't take us *all* on. You just tell us what you want us to do."

Virgil looked at the men, the nervous faces, the white knuckles gripping rifles and shotguns. "You men just stay out of the way," he told them softly. "It's *us* that crowd wants, Mayor. This is between them and us."

He rejoined his brothers in front of Hafford's.

Wyatt looked at the shotgun. "So it's going to be a fight?" He sounded eager.

"I don't know yet. Let's see what they decide to do. We'll let *them* make the first move."

"We should *take* those bastards," Morgan said.

All six of the cowboys were coming back up the street now, all of them on foot, leading the four horses by the reins. The Earps watched and waited . . . but the Cowboys walked past Hafford's Corner, turning onto Fourth, throwing the Earps some more dark looks but not doing anything provocative or illegal. They crossed the street, tied the horses to the hitching rail outside of Spangenberg's Gun Shop, and went inside.

Doc Holliday, wearing a long overcoat that flapped as he walked, came up and joined the waiting Earps. He was carrying his trademark silver-knobbed cane. "Heard there could be trouble. It's all over town how they've been bad-mouthing you boys. Where are the sons-of-bitches?"

Virgil nodded toward the gun shop. "Over there. Stocking up, maybe."

"What's it gonna be, gents?" Holliday asked. "A fight?"

"I just wish they'd make up their minds and get on with it," Morgan said.

"Take it easy, Morg," Virgil said, a shadow of a smile lost behind his luxuriant gray mustache. Morgan could be such a hot-head sometimes. The trait was going to get him into real trouble someday, if he didn't learn to rein back.

"They can fight or they can run," Wyatt said. "Doesn't make much difference, either way. We're going to *finish* this today, one way or the other."

◇ 3 ◇

"WE'RE GOING TO FINISH THIS TODAY," IKE TOLD BILLY CLAIborne, "one way or the other!"

The six of them were crowded into Spangenberg's Gun Shop. Tom was picking up a Colt he'd left here yesterday for cleaning, and all of them were picking up some extra .32 and .45 caliber bullets.

"So what's the plan?" Billy asked.

Ike darted a glance at Spangenberg, who was talking to his brother. "We've gotta get the Earps to face us over at the O.K. Corral," he said, voice low. "Hank and Jake are already there, up in the loft."

Billy grinned. "I get it. The Earps come after us, they walk into an ambush." He glance at Ike's belt. "You're not wearing your gun."

"The bastards arrested me this morning for carrying," Ike said. "Besides, that idiot Behan might be on our side, but I don't want to give him any excuses later, when the Earps are dead. I'll say they came at me when I was unarmed."

"Lettin' us do the dirty work, huh?"

Ike winked, then turned, lifting his vest so that Billy could see the butt of a .32 caliber pocket revolver tucked into his waistband at the small of his back. "Hey, I wouldn't leave you boys in the lurch. *You* know that.''

There was a loud clump from the front of the shop, and a shape blotted out the sunlight falling through the open door. Ike and Billy turned, startled . . . but it was only one of the Clanton horses, stepping up on the sidewalk and poking its long nose into the shop. Both men laughed at the sight.

◆ 4 ◆

MACKLIN STILL COULDN'T FIND THE EARPS.

He'd left the barn and cut across to Allen Street, hoping to catch them back at the Oriental Saloon, but they weren't there. ''None of the Earps've been in since early this morning,'' the bartender said gravely. He looked pointedly at the shotgun tucked under Macklin's arm. ''You figurin' on joinin' the fight, son? Or you want to park that piece of yours here?''

''Fight? What fight?''

''Talk is, there's gonna be blood today, between the Earps and the Clantons and McLaurys.'' He went on to tell about how Virgil had dragged Ike Clanton in just a short while before on a charge of carrying firearms and disturbing the peace, and how Wyatt had had a run-in with Tom McLaury in the street shortly after.

The way Clanton had been mouthing off all morning, there was going to be a fight.

Macklin patted the barrels of the shotgun. ''Thanks just the same. I'll hang on to it, if you don't mind,'' Macklin said. ''I have to find the Earps.''

''Last I heard, they was all over at the courthouse. You might try there.''

''Thanks.''

They weren't at the courthouse, either, though a fussy-looking clerk with ink-stained fingers told Macklin all

about the confrontation with Ike Clanton an hour before . . .
and how Clanton had bragged about how he was going to
settle things with the Earps once and for all. "Wyatt said
something about heading back to the town marshal's office," the clerk told him. "He might be there. . . ."

But he wasn't at his office either, though a man with a
badge who must have been Sheriff Behan told Macklin that
Wyatt had been there earlier, had left, in fact, only a few
minutes ago. He might try back at the courthouse.

By this time, Macklin was seething with worried impa-
tience. Tombstone was *not* that large a town . . . but finding
its three most prominent citizens was becoming an endless
round of dead ends, shrugs, and finger-pointing frustration.

"Thanks." He hurried out onto the street.

⋄ 5 ⋄

"Hey!" BILLY CLANTON SHOUTED. "WHAT THE HELL ARE YOU
doin' with my horse?"

Ike turned to see what the commotion was about. Wyatt
Earp was standing at the door to the gun shop, roughly
tugging at the bridle to back the horse out of the shop, off
the plank sidewalk, and into the street.

"That's a misdemeanor, Clanton," Wyatt said. "Horses
aren't allowed on city sidewalks. You want to go talk to
the judge about it? Ike here'll vouch that he's in today."

The horse backed clear of the doorway, and Ike stormed
out, fists clenched. "Get your hands off that horse, Earp!"

"Maybe you want to see the judge again, too, Clanton?
That's fine with me!"

Ike felt the pounding of his blood in his ears and behind
his eyes. A cowboy's most treasured, most precious, most
personal possession was his horse; that was why horse
thieves were often hung without a trial in these parts . . . or
if the thief was lucky, he got off with a good hard thrashing

with a cane or a whip. Seeing Earp's hands on the animal's bridle like that very nearly sent him over the edge.

"Easy, Ike," Tom said, laying a hand on Ike's arm. "He *wants* you to go for him."

"What's it going to be, Clanton?" Wyatt said, showing his teeth. "You want to show me what you have? Or are you all mouth and hot air?"

Billy Clanton snatched the reins away from Earp and started tying them to the hitching rail. "You got no *right* to ride us like this, Earp!"

"The law says I got all the right I need, Clanton. I want you people out of town. Now." Turning on his heel, he strode away, the sight of his broad back a deliberate, contemptuous snub.

Ike took a step forward, his fury a burning fire deep in his belly and hot in his eyes. His hand dropped to his thigh, reaching for the .45 that he remembered, too late, wasn't there.

"This ain't the place, Ike," Tom said softly, leaning close. Ike was suddenly aware of the two other Earps, and that bastard Doc Holliday as well, all of them in front of Hafford's down the street, watching closely. If any of the Clantons or McLaurys went for a gun . . .

Damn it, Earp was deliberately trying to provoke them into a fight!

"You was sayin' something about bushwacking those buzzards?" Billy Clanton said, grim.

"At the O.K. Corral," Ike said, cold. "Hank and Jake oughta be in position by now. Let's *do* it!"

"Yeah," Frank McLaury aid. "Time to settle some old scores."

"Fer Pa," Billy Clanton added. Yeah, there was no proof that the Earps had been behind the ambush of Old Man

Clanton two months back, but Ike wasn't interested in proof just now, or even justice.

He wanted blood.

They untied the horses and slowly started walking the animals back down the street, moving now toward the O.K. Corral, a block down Allen. The Earps and Holliday watched them coldly as they passed, but made no further move.

It was 2:10.

"You think they'll follow us, Ike?" Tom McLaury asked a few minutes later as they approached the corral.

"We'll make sure they do," Ike replied. As they walked past Thompson's Saddle Shop, next to the O.K. Corral's entrance, Ike spotted a man in a cheap cloth suit watching them from across the street. He knew the man somewhat . . . a mining engineer named R. J. Coleman. The man had the reputation for being a busybody and a gossip. Perfect. "Hey!" he shouted. "Coleman!"

"W-what?"

"Get your tail over here!"

Coleman scuttled closer, removing his bowler. He looked terrified, and that gave Ike a feeling of real power and importance. "Listen here. You know the Earps?"

"Why . . . yessir. Yes, I do!"

"Okay. They're standin' up there in front of Hafford's Corner Saloon. I want you to give 'em a message from us. Tell 'em that the Clantons and the McLaurys are waiting for them back behind the O.K. Corral."

Coleman's eyes widened. He glanced at the others, already in the vacant lot in front of the corral. "You tell the Earps," Ike went on, "that if they don't come here to fight it out, then they're all cowards, and we'll come gunning for them one at a time and shoot them down in the street like dogs! You got that?"

"Yes, sir!" His voice rose to a squeak.

"You tell 'em they ain't got a choice!" Frank McLaury added, calling after him as he raced away down the street.

"That'll fetch 'em out, I reckon," Billy Clanton said, grinning.

Ike grinned back, but he was looking past his brother and up at the barn loft behind the corral. The wooden door on the window there had been swung wide, and he could just make out Hank Attwater's bulky shape in the shadows of the loft, a Winchester cradled in his arm. He waved, and the shadow nodded a grave response.

Yeah, this was going to be *great*!

⋄ 6 ⋄

VIRGIL LISTENED AS COLEMAN BLURTED OUT THE MESSAGE, the words coming in a confused tumble as the breathless man described the meeting. "And . . . and then he said that if you didn't, they'd come after y'all one at a time and shoot you down in the street!"

"Anything else?" Virgil asked.

"Just . . . just that you didn't have no choice."

"Well, boys," Wyatt said softly. "Seems to me the man's right."

"So . . . what's it going to be, Virge?" Morgan asked. "We gonna arrest 'em? Or give them the fight they want?"

Virgil had been considering just that question for a long several moments. He knew Clanton, and the man was mostly bluff. The question was whether he'd backed himself into such a tight corner with his big-shot bragging that he couldn't back down in front of his brother or the McLaurys.

He made up his mind. Gesturing to Holliday, he handed him the Wells Fargo shotgun and took the cane in exchange. Holliday tucked the weapon away, out of sight beneath his overcoat.

If it was to be a fight, it wouldn't be the Earps who started it. "Let's go, boys."

Together, they stepped out into the street and started walking toward the corral.

It was 2:23.

❖ 7 ❖

IT COULD TASTE THE APPROACHING BLOOD OF THE PREY....

Painspinner watched the humans in the vacant lot before its shooting position. The Earps, when they arrived, would come through there . . . giving Painspinner a perfect, clear shot. It had thoroughly studied the workings of the weapon it now held in its feeder arms. The tubular magazine under the barrel held fifteen rounds and was replenished through a side slot in the breech. Cranking the lever after each shot ejected a spent casing and brought another round into position in the firing block. An almost laughably primitive and simple mechanical device, but undeniably deadly. It would serve well.

Assisting the Clantons against their enemies would put the two Kra'agh in the perfect position to direct the politics of this settlement. Control of the larger area—the "county," as the humans called it—through the county sheriff and the Clantons would allow them to establish an ideal base of operations from which to conduct further reconnaissance ahead of the arrival of the Worldfleet.

Helping to kill the Earps would also give the two Hunters a free claw in running down the two Monitors. With the Clantons in charge—and doing whatever Deathstalker and Painspinner commanded—there was no place the Associative observers could hide for long.

It still wondered, somewhat idly, whether it would allow

the food-beast Clanton to continue to think that it was in charge, or if it would be easier to devour the human and pattern him . . . using his image when necessary. It hardly mattered. Soon, all of the food-beasts of this world would be so much meat for the eating.

Bloodtaste! It sensed the rising excitement of the humans below. The prey was approaching at last.

⋄ 8 ⋄

MACKLIN REACHED HAFFORD'S CENTER SALOON IN TIME TO find a considerable crowd gathered in the street—twenty or thirty people, many of them carrying weapons.

A flighty-looking man in a suit and bowler hat was talking rapidly with several of the men nearby. "Yessir, that's *just* what I told 'em! They have to go face the Clantons or be branded as cowards!"

"What's going on?" Macklin asked a man at the fringes of the crowd.

"Looks like a showdown," the man replied around a wad of chewing tobacco. He spat a thin stream into the dust. " 'Afore too long, we're gonna know who the real power in this town is, the Earps or the Cowboy gang."

"Where?"

"Down't th' corral. Way I heerd it—"

But Macklin was already gone, breaking into a jog as he ran toward the O.K. Corral.

If the Earps were squaring off against the Clantons, chances were that Attwater was there somewhere, and he . . . or *it* . . . would know where Sarah was being held.

If she wasn't dead already.

"Mr. Macklin!"

The cry brought him up short and he stopped dead in the street. It was Jimmy, the stable hand who'd sold him the

horse and tack and had given him his first lessons in riding.
"Can't talk now, Jimmy."

"You goin' t'join in the fight?"

"What do you know about a fight?"

"It's gonna happen at the corral any second now!"
Jimmy looked terrified rather than excited. He pointed
wildly. "They're gonna be *killed!* They're gonna be *murdered!*"

"Whoa, slow down, son. Who's going to be killed?"

"The Earps, if they show up! The Clantons've got two
men hiding in the loft with rifles! If the Earps show, they'll
get cut down for sure!"

"How do you—"

"I was there, mucking out the stalls, when those two
came in, carrying Winchesters, both of 'em! They was
laughing and joking . . . well, one of 'em was. The other
looked cold enough to freeze your heart with a glance! They
went inside the feed barn. Then a few minutes later,
the Clanton brothers and the McLaury brothers and a coupla others showed up, and they was kind of taking up positions in the lot, waiting, like! I heard 'em telling some
guy to give a message to the Earps, that the Earps had to
fight or die. I figure it's a trap, see?"

"It sure sounds like it."

"I slipped out quiet like, so they wouldn't see me, then
ran like bejeezus. Thought I could find Marshal Earp and
warn him!"

"They've already left for the corral. But maybe there's
still time."

"You gonna try to warn the Earps?"

"If I can. Or else . . ."

He broke into a run.

"What can I do?" Jimmy called after him.

"Stay clear of the corral!" he called back. "Maybe find

the sheriff, tell him what's happening!'' He kept running.

Ducking down Allen Street, he approached the O.K. Corral from its main entrance. From here, he could see the back of Fly's studio, up on Fremont, and the big loading dock that butted up against the barn. He doubted he could warn the Earps . . . at least not without touching off the ambush that was being laid.

But if Attwater was in the barn, maybe Macklin could catch the thing while it was distracted, make it tell him where Sarah was.

Damn it, he'd find a way to make that nightmare thing talk!

❖ 9 ❖

It was 2:28.

The Earps and Doc Holliday walked four abreast down Fremont Street, striding past the Capitol Saloon. The proprietor of the Papago Cash Store called out from his storefront and waved, and Virgil gave him a calm nod and touched his hat in reply.

A few paces farther on, Sheriff Behan emerged from a barbershop, shaving cream still globbed in white patches to his quivering chin. ''What are you men thinking of doin'?'' Behan demanded, his piggish eyes narrowed to slits. ''What the sam hill's goin' on?''

''*Those* people are in violation of the town's gun laws,'' Virgil told him calmly. ''I intend to disarm them.''

''What, the Clantons? They ain't even armed! I saw 'em pass by this way not ten minutes ago, and I disarmed them then!''

Virgil gave Behan a cold and contemptuous stare for an answer. Behan's mouth worked soundlessly for a moment. Then he held up his hands, shook his head, and backed away. ''Ain't none of my affair, then.''

"That's right, Sheriff," Wyatt said. "It's not." They continued their march.

❖ 10 ❖

BREATHLESS, MACKLIN ARRIVED AT THE BACK OF THE CORRAL, just in time to see the three Earps and Doc Holliday coming past Fly's boardinghouse on Fremont and swinging in toward the lot. If he cried out, if he shouted a warning, the gunmen in the barn loft would certainly open fire. If he kept moving, he might have a precious few more seconds. . . .

Reaching the door in the back of the barn, Macklin tugged the rope handle and pulled it open, stepping at once into deep gloom pierced by dusty shafts of light. Hay and dust sifted down from the loft overhead, and he heard the ominous creak of something heavy taking a step.

He ran for the ladder leading up to the loft.

❖ 11 ❖

JAKE HAD BEEN GROWING MORE AND MORE NERVOUS DURING the past half hour. Damn it, there was something just not right about Hank. Hell, he'd known Hank for the better part of five years. The two had gone drinking and whoring together, played cards together, rustled cattle in Mexico together, and gotten in and out of more than their fair share of scrapes together . . . enough so that he thought he knew the guy.

The man crouched in the shadows next to him was *not* Hank Attwater!

Jake couldn't put his finger on it. Partly, mostly even, it was the way he talked . . . slow and measured like, as though he was having to choose every word carefully. And there was that God-awful smell, like dead bodies too long in the sun. Shoot, *no* one smelled like that, unless he'd been dead three or four days.

And Hank was always cracking jokes ... but this guy was cold as a corpse.

Outside, the Earps had just arrived. Doc Holliday was hanging back, standing in the street with a shotgun, positioning himself where he could block any reinforcements coming to help the Cowboys. The Earps were standing in a line, Morgan, Virgil, and Wyatt, left to right. Morgan and Wyatt both had their guns out; Virgil was holding a cane.

Now was the time. Jake's heart was hammering as he raised his rifle to his shoulder ... but he made the mistake of glancing at Hank first.

Something was terribly wrong. It wasn't Hank ... or if it was ...

It was almost as though Hank was turning transparent as the sunlight from outside hit him, but there was a darker shape, a nameless horror of a shape inside. And the rifle ... Hank wasn't holding it in his hands. The rifle appeared to be floating in front of his face, but there were black things like slender black branches holding it there.

For a nightmare second or two, Jake didn't respond, couldn't respond as his numb brain tried to make sense of what he was seeing.

"What the blue hell ... !" he cried, his voice a hoarse, terror-whipped whisper.

Hank turned to look at him, and the transparency flickered. For a moment, Jake saw Hank looking perfectly normal, the rifle in his hands, something like a dark smile lightly touching his normally grinning features. Then there was something else behind Hank, a darker, horrific something with golden eyes as deadly as any rattler's.

Jake stumbled back, the rifle clattering to the floor. His eyes bugged out in terror as he made helpless, gobbling noises.

The thing hissed its reply. ...

❖ 12 ❖

NOW! NOW! IKE CLANTON WAS NEARLY FRANTIC. IT WAS ALL
he could do not to turn around and stare up at the loft
behind him. *Damn it, why don't they shoot?*

The six men waiting in the lot wavered, suddenly un-
certain. The plan had seemed so right a moment ago, but
now the moment was past.

"You sons of bitches have been looking for a fight!"
Morgan Earp snapped. "Now you can have it!"

"Don't shoot!" Billy Clanton blurted out. "I don't want
to fight!"

"I ain't got nothin'," Tom McLaury said, spreading his
hands from his side. He was standing next to his horse,
however, a rifle tucked into a saddle holster.

"Throw up your hands!" Wyatt called, gesturing with
his pistol.

The Earps stood in a line opposite them, just a few feet
away, with Holliday backing them up in the street. They
were perfectly positioned.

God damn it, why didn't Hank and Jake shoot?

❖ 13 ❖

MACKLIN WAS HALFWAY UP THE LADDER WHEN HE HEARD
that deadly, unearthly hiss. He scrambled up onto the floor
of the loft, bringing his shotgun to the ready.

The . . . thing was there, crouched over a human body.
For a moment, the image blurred, a stomach-twisting blend
of human features with a shape utterly alien . . . a bulky
body out of nightmare, large and powerful hind legs,
smaller forelegs that might double as arms but with razor-
tipped black claws . . . a snake's head on a boneless neck
and enormous, hooded, golden eyes.

Eyes that were now staring at him with an icy glitter.

Macklin had time only to register the fact that the body on the loft floor was not Sarah's but another gunman, dead or fainted, he couldn't tell which. He brought the shotgun to his shoulder. . . .

But the eldritch horror was already moving with a speed that left the senses numb, paralyzed, and unable to respond. A muscular, scaled arm swept out, descending, and the shotgun was ripped from his grasp and hurled across the loft.

And then the claws were descending toward Macklin's face. . . .

✦ 14 ✦

VIRGIL HELD UP HIS CANE. "I'VE COME TO ARREST YOU! YOU men must give up your guns!"

Billy Claiborne and Wes Fuller, both standing toward the edge of the lot, looked at each other and then, suddenly, broke and ran, racing toward the back stoop behind Fly's studio.

Ike and Billy Clanton, Frank and Tom McLaury, remained. Tom was holding the bridle of his horse and looked like he was trying to decide whether to mount up and ride out, or stick it out.

The unendurable, bow-taut agony of the second dragged on, as both Morgan and Doc cocked their weapons, the harsh snicks loud in the sudden silence . . . and then both Billy Clanton and Frank McLaury dropped their hands to their holsters and dragged out their guns.

For a bewildered instant, Virgil thought that he'd been misunderstood. "Hold!" he shouted, thinking they thought he'd told them to go for their guns. "I don't mean that!"

Gunfire thundered . . . and the battle so long deferred commenced at last.

It was 2:32.

NINETEEN

Trying to understand what happened at the O.K. Corral gunfight is like writing obituaries on soap bubbles.

There are as many stories as there are participants. . . . The only facts we can be sure of are that when the acrid smoke cleared, three men were dead, three were wounded and a legend had been created that would live forever.

—Leon Claire Metz,
The Shooters

❖ 1 ❖

BILLY CLANTON, FRANK MCLAURY, AND WYATT EARP FIRED nearly simultaneously. Wyatt felt the snap of a bullet through the hang of his frock coat, but both of the cowboys missed. Wyatt had already singled Frank out as the most dangerous of the targets facing him and fired, doubling him up with a round smack above his belt buckle.

Morgan fired an instant later, hitting Billy Clanton in the chest and knocking him back against the house on the west side of the lot. Virgil, cane still in hand, seemed paralyzed by the sudden eruption of noise and violence.

Ike, standing only a few feet away, lunged forward, grabbing at Wyatt's coat. Thinking the man was trying to knock him down, Wyatt raised his pistol to hit him in the face. "Don't shoot me!" Ike cried, his face suddenly crumpling with fear. "I ain't armed! Don't shoot me!"

"Fight or get out!" Wyatt snapped back, pushing Ike back. Ike released Wyatt's coat, then scrambled past him, almost crashing into Virgil, then running wildly for the street. Doc, who was still keeping his shotgun under his overcoat, had a nickle-plated revolver in his hand, and he loosed two shots at the running Ike Clanton, missing both times.

Both Tom and Frank were tugging at their horses' bridles now, trying to use the animals for cover in the battle that was now becoming general. . . .

◆ **2** ◆

AS THE ALIEN HORROR LUNGED TOWARD HIM, MACKLIN TUM-bled backward, falling to the floor. The sudden thunder of gunfire outside seemed to make the monster hesitate, as though it were torn between two courses of action.

Thinking that Macklin was disarmed, it turned then, rais-ing the rifle it held in the branchlike twisting of arms sur-rounding its hideous head.

In the same instant, lying flat on his back, Macklin dragged Doris's pistol out of his waistband, gripped it between both hands and fired once . . . twice . . . a third time . . . just as the monster fired the rifle out through the loft window.

The thing shrieked, a grating, unholy sound as it twisted away from the window, the rifle flying through the air and across the loft. The alien Hunter lurched toward Macklin once again, eyes glittering with pain, a black slasher claw whipping out toward the downed man. . . .

◆ **3** ◆

MORGAN FIRED TWICE AT FRANK, MISSING BOTH TIMES AS THE Cowboy ducked behind his plunging, struggling horse. Wy-att was still looking for a clear field of fire . . . but both

Tom and Frank were sheltered by their mounts, and Billy was down, slumped against the side of the house, a pistol still in his hand.

A sharper, harsher crack echoed through the lot, followed by several more muffled blasts . . . shots fired from somewhere back toward the corral, possibly from the barn, possibly from the stoop behind Fly's Gallery. Wyatt couldn't see an attacker back there—it might have been Billy Claiborne, or it could have been some other Cowboy supporter. Wyatt fired a shot toward the stoop to make the unknown gunman keep his head down, then turned his full attention back to the threats closer at hand.

◆ **4** ◆

MACKLIN WAS ALREADY RISING TO HIS FEET THOUGH AND stepping forward, into the oppressive stink and horror of the thing, inside the savage, glittering sweep of the thing's claw, jamming the revolver up hard against its horror of a body and triggering the fourth and final round in its cylinder.

The explosion staggered the monster, and it vented a shrill, escaping-steam hiss, twisting away. One of its heavy, clawed forelimbs caught Macklin across the side of the head, slamming him to the floor again in a haze of blood and pain. . . .

◆ **5** ◆

TOM MCLAURY HAD MANAGED TO DRAW A PISTOL CONCEALED in his waistband and fire it across his horse's back at Morgan, but he missed. Doc fired once at the wounded Frank, who was also using his horse for cover, circling the animal about, looking for a clear shot at the Earps.

Virgil, giving up his attempt to make the Cowboys surrender, finally dropped the cane—almost reluctantly—and drew his pistol instead. Doc Holliday holstered his pistol and dragged the shotgun out from beneath his coat.

Morgan fired again at Billy, hitting him in the hand. Tom shot a second time at Morgan, who stumbled back a step into the street, clutching his right shoulder. . . .

◆ **6** ◆

*P*AIN!

Sweet, savage pain flooded Painspinner's very core, as the gunfire outside faded beneath the roaring thunder deep within its own ears, within its brain. Milky, pale blue-white blood cascaded from the wounds in its body, a flow it knew it could never staunch.

It stood for a moment, trembling. The human Monitor lay on its back, twisted, bright red blood coating its face like a mask. It looked dead . . . but the Hunter neither knew nor cared.

It was too lost in the sheer ecstasy of pain suffusing its very soul. . . .

Deathstalker. It had to find . . . Deathstalker, find the other Hunter before it bled to death.

Its enjoyment of pain, in others or in itself, demanded a compensating survival mechanism, a means induced by a million years of natural selection to keep it alive and functioning even when gravely injured. That instinct now drove it to find its own kind and the safety of blood-kinship.

It stumbled toward the ladder, leaking blue-white blood. . . .

◆ **7** ◆

MORGAN COLLAPSED IN THE STREET AND STRUGGLED TO GET up. "Stay down, Morg!" Wyatt called out. He fired into Billy, who shrieked, *"You're murdering me!"*

Frank kept circling his horse, trying to get a clear shot

at Virgil, who stood in the center of the fight, his drawn pistol still unfired. Billy Clanton, slumped against the side of the house, had shifted his pistol from his shattered right hand to his left and now shot at Virgil but missed. Frank fired and hit Virgil in the right calf, sending the man lurching back into the street. He fell but then struggled to his feet again.

Wyatt, frustrated by the lack of a clear shot, sent a round snapping into the withers of Tom's horse. The animal screamed and bolted, dragging Tom along for a few steps and pulling him into the open. The instant he was in the open, Doc Holliday pivoted, his shotgun held at waist level, and squeezed both triggers. The double *ba-boom* of the 10-gauge weapon caught Tom McLaury at point-blank range, savaging him from throat to knee and slamming him back up the street.

Virgil and Frank exchanged missed shots, the Cowboy trying to steady his lunging horse and firing beneath its neck. Billy Clanton fired as well, the bullet slapping into the wall of the Fly boardinghouse above Virgil's head. Virgil returned the shot, then fired again, hitting the already badly wounded Billy in the side. Damn it, why wouldn't the man go *down*?

Frank, the only Cowboy still on his feet, released his horse and darted toward Holliday, who'd just dropped his empty shotgun. Frank, his left hand clutching at the wound in his belly, fired once with his right and missed. "I think I have you this time!" he snarled, sighting down his pistol for another shot.

"I don't believe you have," Doc replied, bringing up his revolver from beneath his coat.

Wyatt and Morgan both fired at Frank in the same second that Doc and Frank shot at each other, catching Frank in a body-tearing crossfire. Firing from flat on his stomach in the street, Morgan sent his bullet smashing through Frank's brain, killing him instantly. Doc Holliday gasped and sagged as Frank's bullet grazed him high in the hip.

Billy Clanton, hit by at least four bullets, in the chest and left side, his right arm and right hand, sat hunched over, back against the wall, sobbing as he tried desperately to reload his gun. Bullets spilled into the dust from nerveless fingers. Rising, he staggered around the corner of the house and into Fremont Street, weaving, bleeding, then collapsing in the dust.

"Give me more bullets. . . ." he whimpered. "I need more bullets. . . ."

Camillus Fly, the photographer who'd witnessed the entire battle from his studio, emerged now as Virgil and Wyatt gathered around the badly wounded Morgan.

Billy Clanton was still trying to reload when Fly gently pried the pistol from his bloody fingers, and the gunman sagged back onto the street, whimpering with pain and fear. The entire chaotic fight, from start to finish, had lasted just twenty-three seconds. Thirty-two shots had been fired.

Wyatt, Virgil, and Doc Holliday had just pulled Morgan to his feet when Sheriff Behan hurried up. "You Earps are under arrest!" he called. "You're under arrest for murder!"

The Earps stared at him coldly, then turned and walked slowly away, supporting Morgan between them, Virgil limping heavily on his wounded leg.

In the lot behind them, Frank McLaury lay dead. Both Tom McLaury and Billy Clanton were dead before the hour was out. Billy Claiborne and Ike Clanton would be dragged from hiding later, begging to be locked up in Behan's jail for their own protection. Of all who participated in the shoot-out, only Wyatt Earp and Ike Clanton emerged unscathed.

The gunfight at the O.K. Corral was over. In the hills

west of town, however, another struggle had yet to be completed.

✦ 8 ✦

IN THE LOFT, MACKLIN SLOWLY SWAM BACK INTO LIGHT AND pain-seared awareness. He tried sitting up and nearly fell over as his head exploded in pain. Gingerly touching himself with his fingers, he found a deep furrow across the left side of his scalp and down his forehead and left cheek. The alien Hunter's claw had opened the skin nearly to the bone, and the wound was bleeding freely.

It was, he decided shakily, a damned lucky wound. There'd been so much blood that the monster must have decided he was dead.

He heard a shivering whimper from nearby. The man who'd been up here with the Hunter was curled into a tight, fetal ball, arms around his knees. He was trembling and moaning, jaw slack, eyes glazed, staring at some horror Macklin could not see.

No . . . staring at the horror Macklin had seen earlier, a sight that must have seared itself into this man's brain.

Macklin tried speaking to him, but the man couldn't hear . . . or couldn't respond. There was nothing Macklin could do for him.

Outside, the battle was over. Macklin could see a crowd of curious onlookers gathering. He could see three bodies lying on the ground . . . all of them Clanton Cowboys. The Earps had either survived or already been taken away.

Macklin no longer needed the Earps, however. A sticky, blue-white liquid was splattered on the rough, hay-strewn floor of the loft—Hunter blood. The thing had left a clear trail across the floor to the ladder . . . and down.

He needed a better weapon than Doris's pocket pistol, though. Returning to the mind-blasted man on the floor,

Macklin stooped and unbuckled the man's gun belt, strapping it on himself. Next, he picked up the man's Winchester and a cardboard box of blunt-tipped .44-40 shells, lying nearby. He studied the rifle a moment, making sure he understood its operation and checking to see that it was loaded.

He was feeling woozy and dizzy, and he nearly fell climbing back down the ladder, but somehow he steadied himself, then followed the blood trail—already disappearing into the hay strewn about the barn's floor—to the back door and out.

More and more people were gathering, but all on the north side of the barn, in the vacant lot off Fremont Street. Macklin stepped out onto Allen Street and turned right, tracking the blood trail. It wasn't much more than wet patches in the dust, but they led unerringly toward the west. He raised his eyes to the Tombstone Hills. And the silver mine workings atop the ridge just outside of town.

The wounded alien was headed *that* way . . . toward Doris.

Or did that mean the other creature was out in those hills as well . . . possibly with Sarah?

He turned at the sound of a heavy, nervous whicker at his back; a chestnut horse was pawing the ground, a saddle on its back and its reins trailing in the dust. It looked like it might have been startled by the gunfire.

"Easy boy," Macklin said, taking a step toward the animal. It shied, eye rolling wildly in its head, lips pulled back to bare its teeth. Macklin scooped up the reins and tugged the animal gently toward him. "Steady . . . it's okay."

He wasn't excited by the prospect of trying to ride again . . . especially on an animal as skittish as this one, but as weak as he was right now, he knew he wouldn't get very

far on foot. Clutching the reins, he approached the horse—
from the left side—put one foot in the stirrup, and hauled
himself up into the saddle. The weight on its back seemed
to steady the animal somewhat, though it sidestepped a bit
and tossed its head, rattling its snaffle bit.

Macklin reeled and almost fell, dizzy, but he managed
to recover himself. His face and scalp still felt sticky beneath a searing, hot pain, but he didn't seem to be bleeding
badly now. Maybe the wound was clotting up. With the
rifle propped across the saddle in front of him, Macklin
tugged on the reins and gave the horse a nudge with his
heels. Obediently, it started walking, still nervous but seem-
ing happier for having a man on its back.

Following the wet spots on the ground, Macklin slowly
rode west out of town.

✧ 9 ✧

*IN THE HILLS OVERLOOKING THE HUMAN NEST, DEATHSTALKER
sensed Painspinner's pain as a dull, aching throb . . .
sensed, too, the bitterness of its companion's failure. Rising, it walked to the edge of a boulder outcropping, staring
down into the town.*

*There. Deathstalker could just make out the moving blob
of heat that marked Painspinner as it toiled up the eastern
face of the ridge. It was moving fast . . . but not nearly fast
enough. Painspinner must have been badly injured to have
been slowed that much, and several times it stopped, as
though trying to recover some of its fast dwindling strength.*

*Searching back along Painspinner's trail, Deathstalker
spotted the heat flare of one of this world's riding beasts,
a human astride its back. It was moving more slowly than
Painspinner . . . but relentlessly, unstopping.*

Excellent. . . .

Deathstalker could sense enough of Painspinner's pain

to know that the other Hunter was dying, but before it bled to death, it would lead the human into Deathstalker's trap. Deathstalker was reasonably sure that the mounted human was one of the Associative Monitors, was sure, too, that the other Monitor must be close by.

It heard a whimper and felt a shudder of horror and pain. Turning, it looked down at its captive, the food that called itself Sarah Nevers. It appeared to be regaining consciousness.

After forcing it to climb this hill, Deathstalker had struck the side of its head to incapacitate it, then used strips of fabric ripped from its artificial body covering to tie its legs and hands; normally, the Hunter would simply have sliced the tendons at the backs of the creature's legs to keep it from running away, but Deathstalker's own injuries, suffered in the attack on the house the night before, had made carrying so heavy a bundle difficult.

Besides, Deathstalker preferred to keep the food relatively intact and mobile for the time being; severe damage might reduce its bargaining value if the Monitors didn't obediently step into the trap.

The human's eyes snapped open, saw Deathstalker standing over her, and uttered a shrill, piercing ululation. Deathstalker pressed the flat of a slasherclaw across the gaping orifice, which seemed to produce the desired result. ''Remain silent,'' it said, using Max Carter's voice, speaking English. ''I will provide the appropriate stimulation when you must scream. Do you understand?''

The human jerked its head up and down, a gesture that Deathstalker assumed meant ''yes.'' Removing the claw from the food's face, it turned again to study the panorama below. Painspinner had stopped again, halfway up the ridge to the primitive human mining complex. It was much weaker now.

Reaching into its harness, Deathstalker extracted a cold, steel-gray slickness that twisted in its mouth-hand like something alive, elongating and warming at its touch.

It shouldn't be much longer. . . .

◇ 10 ◇

MACKLIN HAD BEEN FOLLOWING THE HUNTER'S TRAIL FOR ALmost an hour now, leaving the town and winding up the slope of the rocky, barren ridge beyond. To his left, he could hear the sounds of the miners at the Westside Mine at work, shouts and calls, the creak of the big winch, the rattling clatter of ore carts and the clink and chunk of tools and rock. Doris was over there somewhere, but he didn't dare leave the fast-vanishing trail to find her. He had to find the Hunter and get some answers out of it, or else let it lead him to its camp.

Was Sarah still alive? He wanted to believe so. He owed the woman so much and felt responsible for bringing this curse upon her. If he hadn't shown up on the front porch of her boardinghouse . . .

He'd done this to her, and he needed to make amends.

But it was more than that. If everything Doris said was true, then this entire civilization, the Earth itself, was in danger.

His conscious memories encompassed such a brief instant of time . . . six short days since he'd awakened in the desert to the sound of hoofbeats and wagon wheels. Throughout that time, he'd been the outsider, the passive observer of events he neither understood nor could participate in, even as those events were sweeping him along in a tumble of confusion and frustration.

Even so, these were his people, by adoption if not by birth. His ancestors had lived on this world, before the coming of the Gtai.

He couldn't stand by, an observer only, and see this world devoured by the Kra'agh. There was pathetically little he could do about it, he knew . . . but he also knew that at least one of this world's enemies was badly wounded and waiting for him somewhere just up ahead.

He would meet the responsibilities demanded of him by his adoptive world one threat at a time.

His horse snorted sharply, then shied back, head jerking up as it tried to turn away. Macklin tugged the reins gently, trying to control the animal. Clearly, it didn't want to proceed any farther. "What's the matter, boy?" he asked. "Smell something you don't like?"

He could smell it, too, the unpleasantly sick-sweet smell of rotting flesh. The enemy was here . . . somewhere close by.

Sliding off the horse, Macklin tied the reins to the sun-bleached twist of a dead branch and, carrying the rifle like a talisman, advanced slowly on foot. The wet patches he'd been following had been harder and harder to see for the past half hour, as the desert-dry dust drank the alien blood, but now he could see fresh patches up ahead, along the base of a sandstone outcropping at the top of the ridge as big as a house. The trail appeared to follow the base of the outcropping around to the left.

What was it Doris had said? These things could make themselves look like anything—patterned humans, animals, even boulders . . . or nothing at all. The hairs at the nape of Macklin's neck prickled unpleasantly. The thing could be invisible . . . or the next person he saw could be the Kra'agh Hunter in disguise.

They also were cunning, relentless, patient . . . and if that blue bolt that had stabbed at the two of them during their escape from Sarah's boardinghouse last night was any indication, they were armed with weapons that made the Winchester he was holding look pretty lame in comparison.

He decided not to follow the obvious trail but to try working his way up the ridge to the right and circle around instead. He wanted to see what was behind that outcropping before he made too obvious a target of himself.

"Macklin!"

The cry snapped his attention back to the left; Doris was there, standing on top of the ridge, dark against the sky. She'd removed her dress and was wearing her black skintights, the front opened to reveal her implant.

But . . . was it Doris? Or the Hunter?

"Macklin, we've got to hurry!" She was starting toward him down the bare-rock slope, thirty yards away. He raised his rifle . . . but didn't shoot. Damn it, how to tell reality from Kra'agh illusion? There was no question he could ask her, no password he could demand; if a Hunter had taken her while he was down in Tombstone, it would have learned all that she had known. . . .

"Doris!" he yelled, his voice echoing off the rocks. "Get down!"

Blue light flickered, almost invisible in the brightness of the afternoon. Doris dropped and rolled, tumbling down the bare rock shelf as the bolt struck an outcropping behind her and shattered it with an ear-ringing crack. The shot had come from . . . *there!*

Pivoting, the rifle still at his shoulder, Macklin aimed at a man-sized boulder at the base of the large outcropping, just to the right of the place where the blood trail was clearly visible. Something screamed . . . a shrill, harsh-rasped shriek of pain and fury. The boulder shimmered, the illusion wavering. He could see the Hunter within the rock's outline, writhing. . . .

He worked the lever on the Winchester, aimed, and fired again. From the left, Doris took aim with her pulser, and the beast shrieked again as its invisible energies brushed it.

"The hump!" Doris screamed. She was lying flat on her stomach, her pulser clutched in one hand as she tried for a clear shot. "Shoot at the hump!"

The Hunter had turned away from him to face Doris . . . the greater threat with her beam weapon. Macklin could see the thing's body clearly, a hunched-over shape both shaggy and scaled, the short but powerfully muscled hind legs, the longer but more slender clawed forelegs, the nightmarish head with its branchlike arms. He could see now the black and thick-furred hump on the back just above the forelegs, behind the place where that monstrous body narrowed to a sinuous neck.

He fired, aiming for the hump. He cocked, aimed, and fired again . . . and once again. . . .

The Kra'agh shuddered through the length of its body with each impact, slammed back against the outcropping, and finally collapsed in an untidy heap, legs still twitching in death-spasm tremors. Blue-white blood pooled around the thing, soaking into the greedy sand.

Doris was trying to get up, but couldn't. He ran to her. "Doris! Are you okay?"

She held her left leg. "A piece of rock hit me, I think," she said. "When the beam exploded that boulder. Doesn't matter. Macklin, I've made contact! They're on the way!" Her eyes widened, and she reached up to touch the side of his face. "You're hurt!"

"It's nothing. What are you saying? Who's on the way?"

"I managed to make contact with an Associative scout ship," she said, her eyes bright as they searched his face. "They're slipping in through the Kra'agh blockade right now. I've got my implant sending out a beacon. They'll be

here in another ten olit or so . . . maybe thirty minutes!
Macklin, we're going home!''

Macklin's heart gave a sharp, hard thud beneath his
breastbone. "Doris, I . . . I can't!''

"What do you mean? You idiot, this is a *rescue!''*

"Sarah,'' he said. "She's been taken by those things.
She may still be alive.'' The signs of struggle in the barn
at the O.K. Corral suggested she'd still been alive then. If
they'd kept her alive that long . . .

But he didn't have time to explain his reasoning.

"Macklin. When that scout touches down in a few
minutes, it's not going to be able to wait for us. It comes
in, takes us aboard, and then it's *gone,* before the Hunter
slasherclaws can home on it. They won't be able to come
back for a second try!''

"I know. But there's another Hunter out there, and I
can't leave Sarah in its hands.''

She nodded, reluctantly. "I'll come with you. . . .'' She
tried to get up, favoring her leg. Macklin saw blood on the
rock when she moved.

"You can't even walk!''

"I'll manage,'' she said through gritted teeth.

"No!'' He looked up into the blue sky, searching, then
looked at her. "No. You've got to get back to . . . to where
we came from. Tell them what's happening here. I've got
to find that other Hunter and kill it, if I can.''

He could see her wrestling with her own emotions. Finally, she nodded. He could see tears glistening on her
lashes.

"Then . . . here. Take this.'' She handed him her pulser.

He took the weapon, hefting it. It was oddly shaped and
uncomfortably balanced, not really designed for a human
hand at all. He grimaced, then handed it back. "Thanks,
but you keep it. You might need it if I miss the Hunter out

there. And I don't even know how to turn it on.''

"You just don't remember . . . yet.''

"I don't know why, but whatever you people loaded into me before the mission about the weapons and technology here, that stuck with me.'' He patted the Winchester. "I'd better stick to the things I understand.'' He started to rise.

She lay one slim hand on his arm, holding him. "One thing. Just now, in the fight. I saw you aim your rifle at me. You obviously thought I might be a Kra'agh.''

He nodded.

"You saved my life, you know. You saved *both* of us by shouting that warning. How did you know it was me?''

He smiled. "I didn't. At least, I wasn't sure. . . .''

"Then why . . . ?''

"I figured if you were the Kra'agh and I shouted, you would just keep coming, trying to get closer. And I wasn't going to let you get any closer unless I *knew.*''

"That, Ma'khleen, was very good thinking,'' she told him. "Sounds like you still have the instincts of an Associative Monitor.''

"I'll take that as a compliment.''

"It is. It's also advice. Trust your instincts. Your implant's connections have been damaged, but the AI is still trying to leak information to you through your right brain. Through emotions. Through feelings and intuition. *Listen* to it.''

"I'll try.'' He looked away, searching the top of the ridge further toward the north. "I'm *trying* to. It's how I know the other Hunter is out there . . . very close. *That* way.''

She shivered. "I know. I feel it, too. I think it was using the one you killed to lure us close.'' She reached out and touched him lightly. "I don't want to leave you.''

"And I want to go with you. I hate this . . . this not remembering who I am. What I am. But, damn it . . . do you

see? I have to try to rescue Sarah. I won't be able to live
with myself if I just . . . *leave*. Knowing what would happen
to her. I'll try to make it back in time.''

"You keep surprising me, Ma'khleen," she told him.
"You keep showing me new reasons why . . . I love you."

They kissed.

He was the one who broke the embrace at last. "I'm
going," he said. "Have them wait as long as possible. I'll
be back if I can.''

"If . . . if you don't get back in time, remember there's
a Monitor Observer in Tucson. Ask around for 'Apache
Slim.' When you find him, tell him *'Taled* One-three-
three.' ''

"Taled One-three-three," he repeated.

"He'll know you're a Monitor, then, and help you. And
I swear I'll be back to find you, as soon as it's possible."

"I'll be waiting."

"G-good luck, Macklin."

"Have them wait as long as they can," he told her, grinning with a confidence he could not feel. "I'll be back.
Believe me, I *don't* want to stay here!"

He hurried away, leaving her there on the rock, before
he could change his mind.

TWENTY

Under no circumstances should Kra'agh scouts, warriors, or directors be approached alone or without substantial military support. Though little is known of their psychology, they do not seem to be slowed by pain or fatigue, they are utterly single-minded in the pursuit of their goals, and their poorly understood ability to project illusory images gives them a decided advantage in one-on-one combat encounters. . . .

Extreme care should be exercised when attempting to approach any Kra'agh operative.

—Contact: A Listing of Known Intelligences Within
the Associative Sphere of Operations
AI Download 828726

◆ 1 ◆

MACKLIN WAS TRYING TO LISTEN TO HIS INSTINCTS, BUT HE still wasn't sure how he was going to find the other Hunter. The west flank of the hills overlooking Tombstone was a desolate tangle of boulders, sheer-sided gullies, and rock-bound arroyos, a labyrinth through which a man could wander for days before finding his way out. An army of Kra'agh could be hidden here, and he would never find them until they wanted him to.

But he couldn't shake the feeling of nearby danger, of hostile eyes watching him. He found himself trying to think about the problem tactically . . . and from the enemy's point

of view. South along the ridge lay the Westside Mine workings. The Hunters would have avoided them; if the surviv-
ing Kra'agh was on this hill, it had to be toward the north.
He'd crossed the ridgeline to approach along the western
slope; he hoped the Hunter would be focused on the eastern
approaches, toward the town.

He had to hurry, though. He desperately wanted to be
back in time to catch that rescue ship, once it appeared. It
was a little strange—the realization that only out among
the stars would he ever be able to recapture his knowledge
of who and what he was.

He found himself thinking about the people he'd met
during this past week, which was all of his life that he could
remember. Earth's inhabitants, if these people were anything to go by, were a fractious, hard-to-figure lot. The
Earps and the Clanton-McLaurys . . . two sides of the same
double eagle. Both claiming to be in the *right,* both claiming to be on the side of law and order. The Earps, possibly,
had the better claim to that position, but it obviously wasn't
as simple as good against evil, civilization against anarchy.
The Earps, and Doc Holliday, had their own faults and
failings. Macklin thought about the three bodies he'd seen
lying on the ground in front of the O.K. Corral.

In a way, the fight between the Earps and the Clanton-
McLaurys was a clash between alien cultures. The Clantons
represented a way of life that was already passing—the
freedom of the open range. They were Southerners, most
of them . . . and democrats, most of them. They were cowboys, and they resented the encroachment of Eastern civilization, of law and order and government, of men
presuming to tell them what to do. The Earps, for their part,
represented civilization. Towns. Growth. Order. Business.
They were Northerners and republicans, with a whole different way of looking at the world.

A war of cultures as mutually alien as human and Kra'agh. No doubt the winners of the gunfight at the O.K. Corral would write the histories by which men would judge it.

He wished he'd been able to see what had happened.

Did the Kra'agh think of themselves as being in the right? Did good or evil, right or wrong, always depend on who wrote the histories once the shooting had stopped?

Macklin didn't think so. It might be hard to sort the good from the bad with the likes of the Earps and the Clantons . . . but then there were people like Sarah Nevers, folks who might have faults and might have failings but who were indisputably *good* people.

People worth knowing. People worth saving. People who—

He heard the scream, a piercing shriek from just ahead and higher up on the ridge. It was hard to tell direction among these echoing rock faces, but he thought it had come from *that* way. . . .

It was Sarah, he was sure of it. Gripping the Winchester tightly, bending low to stay concealed behind the rocks, he sprinted ahead, climbing the slope, his breath coming in tight, painful gasps beneath the dazzling Arizonan sun.

At the top of the ridge, he dropped into a shallow arroyo winding north. On hands and knees, he crawled its length. Sarah's scream came again, louder this time, longer . . . a liquid shriek of pain and fear. He tried not to let the sound hurry him faster; the Kra'agh wanted him to come, wanted to draw him into the open. His only hope was to spot the monster before it spotted him.

He reached the end of the arroyo, dropping for cover behind a large, flat rock. Beyond, the ridge crest opened into a broad, flat bowl, rock-ringed and exposed. In the center of the bowl was Sarah Nevers.

Macklin bit off a hard curse. Sarah was alive; he could see her moving, twisting fitfully. She was also tied hand and foot, and even from twenty yards away he could see a vivid splash of scarlet on her belly and on the rock beneath her. It was all he could do not to leap up and go to her.

Instead, he studied the ring of boulders encircling the bowl. The Kra'agh was out there, somewhere, waiting for him. But where? Hell, the Hunter might even *be* one of those rocks!

Macklin was vividly aware through every sense, aware of the sharp impact of orange rock beneath blue sky . . . of the taste of hot air . . . a lingering scent of decay . . . of the feel of hot, sandy rock beneath his chest and arms. He heard Sarah sob . . . and caught the faintest rasp of something metal-hard dragging against stone. . . .

Moving slowly, his eyes anchored on the far rim of the bowl, Macklin picked up a flat stone the size of his hand and skimmed it, hard, sending it flying off to the left. For a second or two, there was silence, and then the stone struck rock with a bright clatter.

Something moved on the far side of the bowl, just beyond where Sarah lay bleeding. It moved fast, a boulder dissolving into a dark gray blur, moving left.

Macklin brought his rifle up and fired. The Winchester's bark was followed instantly by the shrill ping of the round skipping off rock. The shape, half glimpsed and incredibly fast, was gone.

But where? He couldn't see anything alive along that rock-strewn rim now . . . and it didn't look as though the position of any of the boulders had changed.

"Macklin!" Sarah screamed, twisting around and trying to sit up. "Macklin! Get away! It's a trap!"

"Macklin!" Sarah's voice again . . . but this time from the left. "Macklin! It's a trap!"

The thing was mocking her. Or him. Or both of them.
"Mack . . . lin!"

He fired, aiming at the second voice, then shifting left
and firing again, shifting right and firing a third time,
throwing rounds blindly, hoping to hit *something*. The ech-
oes of the shots, the shriek of the ricochets, hung in the
bright, startled air for a long second.

Something—a flicker of movement—made him look further to the left in time to see a hulking, shaggy shape
against the skyline. He raised his rifle and squeezed off
another shot, cocked the lever, and fired again.

There was nothing there. Had he even seen anything at
all?

Macklin was beginning to realize that he was outclassed.
The Kra'agh he'd killed minutes ago had been deadly . . .
but badly hurt, possibly not even able to move. This one
was extraordinarily mobile. If it was as silent as it was fast,
Macklin knew he would have absolutely no warning as it
attacked, that it could strike from any direction, and he
would never see it coming.

He searched the skyline, aware that the creature was trying to work around the west side of the bowl in order to
get behind him . . . or to come at him from the flank.

Either that, or it had been trying to draw his fire, trying
to pinpoint his position.

The thought was as cold a shock as ice water in the face.
Ducking behind the rock, he rolled to the right, then started
crawling for deeper cover down a shallow embankment,
among a giant's spill of chaotically tumble-down boulders.

Before he'd crawled five feet, a sharp, fried-bacon sizzle
hissed in his ear, his nose caught the sharp tang of ozone,
and the boulder he'd been hiding behind exploded with a
shrill crack that left this ears ringing. He lay flat, head
down, as hot fragments pattered across his back and

bounced in front of his face . . . and then he was crawling again, faster, scrambling for better cover.

He chanced another glance into the rock-bottomed bowl. Sarah was still there, slumped over on the bare rock with her hands behind her back. He couldn't tell if she was conscious or not. She wasn't moving now.

Hiss . . . *crack*! The Hunter's beam exploded with a sun-bright flash engulfing the rock next to his face, stinging him with hurtling fragments. He yelped and tumbled backward, rolling and sliding down a short slope before colliding with a boulder. The impact brought stars to his already throbbing head. He blinked at the swimming, purple shadow suddenly clouding his vision. Flash-dazzled, he rubbed his eyes. His left hand came away wet with blood; either his scalp wound had opened again, or he'd been cut anew.

His rifle! Where was his rifle? He felt about, groping through the slow-lifting haze of his partial blindness. The Winchester had flown from his grasp when he'd fallen. He'd heard its clatter when it hit the rock, somewhere to the right. Where was it?

His vision cleared . . . but he still couldn't see the rifle. He did see a hollow among the boulders, though, just a few feet away . . . a partial cave beneath an overhang, a hollow in the rock wall perhaps three or four feet deep, just big enough to tuck himself away in, out of sight.

He'd lost all hope now of making it back to Doris in time for rescue. Maybe, though, he could at least delay the Kra'agh, keep it from hindering Doris's pickup. If he could kill the thing, he might yet save Sarah.

The trouble was killing it. He would have to lure it close enough to get at least one clear shot . . . and that would have to be into the hump on its back where Doris said it kept its brains.

Reaching up to his face, he dragged his hand across his stinging forehead, dragging away a palmful of scarlet blood. He wiped his hand on the rock at his feet. He crawled on another couple of yards and repeated the gesture, marking the rock with his own blood. He moved on again, well past the hollow he'd noticed, laying down a third bloodmark, before doubling back on his trail.

Then he scrambled for the hollow, backing into the low-ceilinged embrace of cool sandstone, back pressed to the rock, facing out. If the Kra'agh was coming for him, it would have to come at him *this* way, from the front. He drew the .45 Colt he'd taken from the gunman in the barn and cocked it. Then he held his breath, waiting . . . listening with his entire being.

There! A slithering, scales-on-rock sound out of sight to his left, a low rasping hiss, moving closer.

He tensed. He would have only an instant in which to act. He *knew* how fast these things could move. . . .

But when a tall shape moved into his field of view, Macklin was transfixed by surprise. It wasn't the beast . . . but a human, a man wearing overalls, a *farmer*.

Macklin hesitated for only a moment. . . .

The farmer turned suddenly, staring straight into the rock niche in which Macklin was hiding. The image of the farmer rippled and faded, replaced by a nightmare horror of scales and black fur, of golden eyes and hasp jaw, of black, branching arms clutching a gray-silver shape that moved and twisted in the thing's grasp like something alive. . . .

He couldn't see its back, couldn't see the vulnerable hump. Bringing the Colt high, he squeezed the trigger, aiming for that bloated, misshapen body.

The gunshot echoed, impossibly loud in the confined space, and the Kra'agh shrieked in response. Dragging the hammer back, Macklin cocked and fired again . . . but the

Hunter was still coming toward him, a glitter that might have been triumph flickering behind cold, reptilian eyes of gold and black.

And then a new thunder sounded, not a shot . . . but a rumbling, pounding roar that filled the sky. Startled, the Hunter turned to Macklin's left, looking up.

Its hump was exposed as it stood at the very edge of a sharp drop-off.

He cocked . . . and fired . . . cocked and fired again. Blue-white smoke obscured his vision, and he scrambled forward. Had it fallen off the cliff? Or moved? He couldn't see it.

He reached the edge of the cliff and peered over. Ten feet below was an empty expanse of sand and sandstone. The Kra'agh was gone . . . but its blue-white blood was splattered on the rock at Macklin's feet.

He turned, looking up, eyes widening as he saw the thunder descending from a clear sky.

The rescue ship. It looked like it was cast from purest gold, a flattened sphere made complex by bumps and vents and odd protuberances, and the way it floated in the air had the spine-tingling aura of something magical. Featherlight, it settled down behind the boulder-broken horizon of the ridge crest to the south, in the direction of the mine . . . and the place where he'd left Doris.

He wondered if he still had time to reach the ship . . . and Doris. It was landing perhaps a half mile away, not far at all . . . a few minutes if he ran. . . .

But there was still Sarah.

And the beast. There was a lot of blood on the rock, but he didn't see its body. He wanted to be certain it was dead before he left.

Hurrying now, he picked his way across the boulder-strewn ridgetop. Sarah was still in the center of the bowl.

Sitting up now, staring toward the south.

"Macklin?" She sounded dazed and very weak. He scooped her up in his arms and carried her away. If the Kra'agh was still out there, he didn't want the bait to trap him in the end after all.

In the shelter of a large boulder, he set her down gently, then freed her wrists and ankles. The lower half of her shift had been torn away, and much of what was left was blood-stained and wet. He tore some more of the fabric, though, and used it to try to stop the bleeding from a pair of deep gashes on her stomach and thigh. The cuts weren't deep, he found to his considerable relief. They'd been meant to inflict pain, to make her scream on cue, not to kill.

She clung to him. "Macklin! What . . . what *was* it?"

He wasn't sure what to tell her or what she would be able to understand. He remembered the madness-glazed eyes of the man in the barn and wondered if her mind could survive the horrors she'd endured.

"Do you mean what attacked you?" he asked gently. "Or what you just saw in the sky?"

"I *know* what attacked me," she said. "It was a demon. A demon from the deepest pits of hell!" She started crying. "Oh, Macklin . . . !"

"Easy . . . easy . . ." He stroked her hair lightly as she cried. He thought that if she could put a name to the horror she'd seen, she would probably be all right. Madness came from what was *not* known, what could not be fit into an understandable reality.

"Tell me I'm not going crazy!" she cried.

He sighed. "There are . . . things in this universe," he told her, "things in this world that are simply beyond human comprehension. They're a lot bigger and more powerful than we are, in their science, in their wisdom . . . and sometimes in their evil. You've had the very bad luck to run into one. But it's over now. And it can't hurt you anymore."

"It's gone?"

His eyes were on the rocks around them as he spoke. "It's gone." The way he saw it, though, the Kra'agh was either dead, or it had been so badly hurt that it had fled. If it was still after him, it would have reappeared by now.

He hoped he was telling her the truth.

He hoped he was telling *himself* the truth.

"The best thing you can do," he told her, "is try to forget. You're not crazy. You really did see it. I saw it, too. But you mustn't let it gnaw at your mind, or it's going to fill your dreams and your thoughts and you'll never be free of it."

Fresh thunder sounded in the south. He looked up, and the golden ship rose into view once more . . . the rescue ship, bound once more for the sky. *Good-bye, Doris,* he thought. *Thanks . . . for everything!* As the ship suddenly dwindled to a speck, he added, *I'll see you in Tucson!*

Swift as thought, a trio of black hawk shapes flashed out of the northwest, ugly, bad-dream shapes swooping low above the ridge, then arcing high, following the escaping scout. Thunder boomed with their passage.

Kra'agh ships, chasing the rescue vessel.

He desperately hoped that Doris would be safe. . . .

"Was that an angel?" Sarah asked.

"What?"

"The golden thing in the sky. Was it an angel, here to fight the demon?"

"I think it must have been."

She shivered.

"You okay?"

"Just . . . cold."

He scooped her up in his arms. There was a blanket, he

remembered, tied to the saddle of the horse. He would get her warm first, then take her back into town. "C'mon," he told her. "Let's get you back to Tombstone. We'll have Doc Clarke look at those cuts."

"Macklin?"

"Yeah?"

"We can't tell him. We can't tell *anyone*. They'd never believe us. We'll tell them I was grabbed by Indians. That you saved my life." She snuggled her head closer against his shoulder. "You did, you know. Thank you."

"Nothing to thank me for, Sarah. You just remember what I told you."

If she was reasoning things out like that, he thought, her mind was going to be okay. She was tough . . . and a survivor.

She would survive.

Macklin wondered, though, if he was as much of a survivor as she was. The encounter with the Hunters had left him shaken, and the second beast might still be out there somewhere.

And Macklin was all alone on a strange and hostile world, with no past, no memory, no true feeling for who and what he really was . . . and the person who had the key to his identity was lost to him now, somewhere among the stars.

He hoped he would see Doris again.

He would have to go to Tucson . . . and after that, he would just have to see where the trail led him. Somehow, he would find out who he was.

With Sarah in his arms, he started back down the ridge in the warm light of the fading afternoon.

EPILOGUE

NA-A-CHA, *DIYI* OF THE N'DE, WAS COMING DOWN FROM THE mountains northwest of the white eyes community called Tombstone when he met the *ga he*.

He knew the *ga he* well; though he'd never seen one, even in a vision, he believed they'd spoken to him on several of his spirit quests in the past. Every Chiricahua Apache knew the mountain spirits, who were impersonated by the Crown Dancers—elaborately garbed men who danced at healing rites, protection ceremonies, and the *na ih es,* the girls' puberty rite. The dancers themselves had no power, but the one who led them in the ceremony, who fashioned their distinctive, black buckskin masks with the brightly painted upright structures, like branching antlers of split oak, and created the painted designs on their bodies, had to be a powerful shaman. Na-a-cha had dreamed of being such a shaman, but his Power had never given him the ceremony.

Now, though, he was standing in front of a living *ga he*—not a Crown Dancer, not an unseen spirit, but a living, flesh-and-blood Mountain Spirit. Its body was somewhat like Bear—but with long forearms and shorter hind legs, and covered with a leathery hide that showed a faint scaling, rather than in fur. The claws were the claws of Puma, the hump was the hump of Buffalo, the head was the head of Snake . . . well, more or less. Snake never had teeth or multiple tongues or writhing *things* upon its face like that. So much was utterly unlike anything Na-a-cha had ever seen, even in a vision, that he could not grasp it all; he would look, he would see, but when he blinked or looked away, the memory of what he'd seen was not there. In fact, Na-a-cha had always pictured the Mountain Spirits as people more or less like himself—powerful, yes, but still *men* . . . not as composites of *hoddentin schlawn* animal spirits.

But sprouting from that impossible head were branching arms like the horns of a Crown Dancer, and that was how Na-a-cha knew he faced one of the holy *ga he.* These horns were living, twisting, grasping, suppler than his own arms and hands, to say nothing of painted oak slats.

The *ga he* appeared to be hurt. It was moving slowly and oozed something like blue-white blood from several vicious wounds in its massive body. But when it saw Na-a-cha, it stopped, turned, and moved toward him with a hiss like Snake, horns outstretched against the sky.

Na-a-cha reached into his buckskin pouch and withdrew a clump of hoddentin, which he tossed at the advancing spirit. *"Ga he, bi hoddentin ashi!"* he called softly, chanting. *"Gun-ju-le, ga he hoddentin schlawn, inzayu, ijanal."*

"Mountain Spirit, you hoddentin I offer. Be good to me, holy Mountain Spirit, do not let me die. . . ."

Deathstalker did not know what to make of the human.

Every time it had confronted food-humans so far, they had screamed in terror, collapsed in an imitation of death, or attacked it with passionate fury. The screaming it understood. The death imitations it did not. The attacks it

A sky-wagon awaited it on the desert plain nearby, a door open and inviting.

It was said that a shaman who'd received the Lightning Ceremony was sometimes taken into the sky by the Mountain Spirits, to be shown the world as it appeared from the heavenly realms. That, apparently, was not to be. This time, at least. It didn't matter. Na-a-cha had been given his ceremony.

He was a Lightning Shaman now, most powerful, most revered of the N'de.

The wagon, angular and jagged, as black as obsidian, rose into the blue, early morning sky with a shriek of Wind and Puma. In the sky, the moon was narrowing now on its way to *Tzontzose,* the crescent moon, and Na-a-cha offered it hoddentin as well, as ceremony required.

And then he blessed the *ga he* wagon. . . .

Aboard the Slasherclaw ship, rising skyward, the Hunter could not control its shaking. It knew it would have to return to this world, and quickly. At least one of the Associative Monitors, the one that had wounded it so badly, was still loose on the planet and would have to be captured or killed. The Hunt would continue until the prey was taken. That was the Way. . . .

But for the first time in its life, Deathstalker, Hunter of the Kra'agh, was genuinely, deeply afraid. . . .

understood ... but was worried about. Food *had hunted and killed Painspinner, a reversal of the ancient roles, an astonishing slasherclaw attack gutting the ancient rationality of* Chahh kkit, *the Blood Law.*

The humans might well pose more of a threat than had been anticipated.

The human before it now neither screamed, feigned death, nor attacked. It tossed a yellow powder on the ground before the Hunter, chanting words in an unknown tongue.

Deathstalker drew closer, intending to devour the food, reaching out with its senses to taste the prey's mind-terror and pain.

What it tasted instead was ... unexpected.

Ga he, bi hoddentin ashi! Gun-ju-le, ga he, inzayu, ijanal.

The words were still without meaning. The thoughts, though ... while intelligible, were strange, almost bewildering. Trust. Wonder. A deep and all-encompassing, fierce-burning joy. Gratitude. . . .

Some of these thoughts were just barely comprehensible. Others were as alien as the words the creature spoke. It threw another handful of yellow powder, then spilled pinches of the same powder on its own head, shoulders, chest, and tongue.

Deathstalker reached out with its feeder hands, drawing closer. The sensations were far stronger now. Intense joy. An almost childlike awe. Appreciation. An intense burst of creativity ... something about the song that it would make, the ceremony it had been shown. . . .

No. Deathstalker would not devour this creature ... not with so many disturbing unknowns.

Na-a-cha spread his arms to embrace the Mountain Spirit as brother, but the being turned, moving swiftly with a soft-gliding gait that belied its great weight.